Scenes of Clerical Life

George Eliot

W F HOWES LTD

This large print edition published in 2013 by
W F Howes Ltd
Unit 4, Rearsby Business Park, Gaddesby Lane,
Rearsby, Leicester LE7 4YH

1 3 5 7 9 10 8 6 4 2

First published in the United Kingdom in 1857
by *Blackwood's Edinburgh Magazine*

A CIP catalogue record for this book is available
from the British Library

ISBN 978 1 47122 801 8

Typeset by Palimpsest Book Production Limited,
Falkirk, Stirlingshire
Printed and bound in Great Britain
by MPG Books Ltd, Bodmin, Cornwall

MIX
Paper from
responsible sources
FSC
www.fsc.org   FSC® C018575

THE SAD FORTUNES
OF THE
REVEREND AMOS BARTON

CHAPTER 1

Shepperton Church was a very different-looking building five-and-twenty years ago. To be sure, its substantial stone tower looks at you through its intelligent eye, the clock, with the friendly expression of former days; but in everything else what changes! Now there is a wide span of slated roof flanking the old steeple; the windows are tall and symmetrical; the outer doors are resplendent with oak-graining, the inner doors reverentially noiseless with a garment of red baize; and the walls, you are convinced, no lichen will ever again effect a settlement on – they are smooth and innutrient as the summit of the Rev. Amos Barton's head, after ten years of baldness and supererogatory soap. Pass through the baize doors and you will see the nave filled with well-shaped benches, understood to be free seats; while in certain eligible corners, less directly under the fire of the clergyman's eye, there are pews reserved for the Shepperton gentility. Ample galleries are supported on iron pillars, and in one of them stands the crowning glory, the very clasp or aigrette of Shepperton church-adornment – namely, an organ, not very much out of repair, on which a collector of small rents, differentiated by the force of circumstances into an organist, will accompany the alacrity of your departure after the blessing, by a sacred minuet or an easy 'Gloria.'

Immense improvement! says the well-regulated mind, which unintermittingly rejoices in the New Police, the Tithe Commutation Act, the penny-post, and all guarantees of human advancement, and has no moments when conservative-reforming intellect takes a nap, while imagination does a little Toryism by the sly, revelling in regret that dear, old, brown, crumbling, picturesque inefficiency is every-where giving place to spick-and-span new-painted, new-varnished efficiency, which will yield endless diagrams, plans, elevations, and sections, but alas! no picture. Mine, I fear, is not a well-regulated mind: it has an occasional tenderness for old abuses; it lingers with a certain fondness over the days of nasal clerks and top-booted parsons, and has a sigh for the departed shades of vulgar errors. So it is not surprising that I recall with a fond sadness Shepperton Church as it was in the old days, with its outer coat of rough stucco, its red-tiled roof, its heterogeneous windows patched with desultory bits of painted glass, and its little flight of steps with their wooden rail running up the outer wall, and leading to the school-children's gallery.

Then inside, what dear old quaintnesses! which I began to look at with delight, even when I was so crude a member of the congregation, that my

4

nurse found it necessary to provide for the reinforcement of my devotional patience by smuggling bread-and-butter into the sacred edifice. There was the chancel, guarded by two little cherubim looking uncomfortably squeezed between arch and wall, and adorned with the escutcheons of the Oldinport family, which showed me inexhaustible possibilities of meaning in their blood-red hands, their death's-heads and cross-bones, their leopards' paws, and Maltese crosses. There were inscriptions on the panels of the singing-gallery, telling of benefactions to the poor of Shepperton, with an involuted elegance of capitals and final flourishes, which my alphabetic erudition traced with ever-new delight. No benches in those days; but huge roomy pews, round which devout church-goers sat during 'lessons,' trying to look anywhere else than into each other's eyes. No low partitions allowing you, with a dreary absence of contrast and mystery, to see everything at all moments; but tall dark panels, under whose shadow I sank with a sense of retirement through the Litany, only to feel with more intensity my burst into the conspicuousness of public life when I was made to stand up on the seat during the psalms or the singing.

And the singing was no mechanical affair of official routine; it had a drama. As the moment of psalmody approached, by some process to me as mysterious and untraceable as the opening of the flowers or the breaking-out of the stars, a slate

5

appeared in front of the gallery, advertising in bold characters the psalm about to be sung, lest the sonorous announcement of the clerk should still leave the bucolic mind in doubt on that head. Then followed the migration of the clerk to the gallery, where, in company with a bassoon, two key-bugles, a carpenter understood to have an amazing power of singing 'counter,' and two lesser musical stars, he formed the complement of a choir regarded in Shepperton as one of distinguished attraction, occasionally known to draw hearers from the next parish. The innovation of hymn-books was as yet undreamed of; even the New Version was regarded with a sort of melancholy tolerance, as part of the common degeneracy in a time when prices had dwindled, and a cotton gown was no longer stout enough to last a lifetime; for the lyrical taste of the best heads in Shepperton had been formed on Sternhold and Hopkins. But the greatest triumphs of the Shepperton choir were reserved for the Sundays when the slate announced an ANTHEM, with a dignified abstinence from particularization, both words and music lying far beyond the reach of the most ambitious amateur in the congregation: – an anthem in which the key-bugles always ran away at a great pace, while the bassoon every now and then boomed a flying shot after them.

As for the clergyman, Mr Gilfil, an excellent old gentleman, who smoked very long pipes and preached very short sermons, I must not speak of him, or I might be tempted to tell the story of his life, which had its little romance, as most lives have between the ages of teetotum and tobacco. And at present I am concerned with quite another sort of clergyman – the Rev. Amos Barton, who did not come to Shepperton until long after Mr Gilfil had departed this life – until after an interval in which Evangelicalism and the Catholic Question had begun to agitate the rustic mind with controversial debates. A Popish blacksmith had produced a strong Protestant reaction by declaring that, as soon as the Emancipation Bill was passed, he should do a great stroke of business in gridirons; and the disinclination of the Shepperton parishioners generally to dim the unique glory of St Lawrence, rendered the Church and Constitution an affair of their business and bosoms. A zealous Evangelical preacher had made the old sounding-board vibrate with quite a different sort of elocution from Mr Gilfil's; the hymn-book had almost superseded the Old and New Versions; and the great square pews were crowded with new faces from distant corners of the parish – perhaps from Dissenting chapels.

You are not imagining, I hope, that Amos Barton was the incumbent of Shepperton. He was no such thing. Those were days when a man could hold three small livings, starve a curate a-piece on two of them, and live badly himself on the third. It was so with the Vicar of Shepperton; a vicar given to bricks and mortar, and thereby running into

7

debt far away in a northern county – who executed his vicarial functions towards Shepperton by pocketing the sum of thirty-five pounds ten per annum, the net surplus remaining to him from the proceeds of that living, after the disbursement of eighty pounds as the annual stipend of his curate. And now, pray, can you solve me the following problem? Given a man with a wife and six children: let him be obliged always to exhibit himself when outside his own door in a suit of black broadcloth, such as will not undermine the foundations of the Establishment by a paltry plebeian glossiness or an unseemly whiteness at the edges; in a snowy cravat, which is a serious investment of labour in the hemming, starching, and ironing departments; and in a hat which shows no symptom of taking to the hideous doctrine of expediency, and shaping itself according to circumstances; let him have a parish large enough to create an external necessity for abundant shoe-leather, and an internal necessity for abundant beef and mutton, as well as poor enough to require frequent priestly consolation in the shape of shillings and sixpences; and, lastly, let him be compelled, by his own pride and other people's, to dress his wife and children with gentility from bonnet-strings to shoe-strings. By what process of division can the sum of eighty pounds per annum be made to yield a quotient which will cover that man's weekly expenses? This was the problem presented by the position of the

Rev. Amos Barton, as curate of Shepperton, rather more than twenty years ago.

What was thought of this problem, and of the man who had to work it out, by some of the well-to-do inhabitants of Shepperton, two years or more after Mr Barton's arrival among them, you shall hear, if you will accompany me to Cross Farm, and to the fireside of Mrs Patten, a childless old lady, who had got rich chiefly by the negative process of spending nothing. Mrs Patten's passive accumulation of wealth, through all sorts of 'bad times,' on the farm of which she had been sole tenant since her husband's death, her epigrammatic neighbour, Mrs Hackit, sarcastically accounted for by supposing that 'sixpences grew on the bents of Cross Farm;' while Mr Hackit, expressing his views more literally, reminded his wife that 'money breeds money.' Mr and Mrs Hackit, from the neighbouring farm, are Mrs Patten's guests this evening; so is Mr Pilgrim, the doctor from the nearest market-town, who, though occasionally affecting aristocratic airs, and giving late dinners with enigmatic side-dishes and poisonous port, is never so comfortable as when he is relaxing his professional legs in one of those excellent farmhouses where the mice are sleek and the mistress sickly. And he is at this moment in clover.

For the flickering of Mrs Patten's bright fire is reflected in her bright copper tea-kettle, the home-made muffins glisten with an inviting

9

succulence, and Mrs Patten's niece, a single lady of fifty, who has refused the most ineligible offers out of devotion to her aged aunt, is pouring the rich cream into the fragrant tea with a discreet liberality.

Reader! *did* you ever taste such a cup of tea as Miss Gibbs is this moment handing to Mr Pilgrim? Do you know the dulcet strength, the animating blandness of tea sufficiently blended with real farmhouse cream? No – most likely you are a miserable town-bred reader, who think of cream as a thinnish white fluid, delivered in infinitesimal pennyworths down area steps; or perhaps, from a presentiment of calves' brains, you refrain from any lacteal addition, and rasp your tongue with unmitigated bohea. You have a vague idea of a milch cow as probably a white-plaster animal standing in a butterman's window, and you know nothing of the sweet history of genuine cream, such as Miss Gibbs's: how it was this morning in the udders of the large sleek beasts, as they stood lowing a patient entreaty under the milking-shed; how it fell with a pleasant rhythm into Betty's pail, sending a delicious incense into the cool air; how it was carried into that temple of moist cleanliness, the dairy, where it quietly separated itself from the meaner elements of milk, and lay in mellowed whiteness, ready for the skimming-dish which transferred it to Miss Gibbs's glass cream-jug. If I am right in my conjecture, you are unacquainted with the highest possibilities of tea; and Mr

Pilgrim, who is holding that cup in his hand, has an idea beyond you.

Mrs Hackit declines cream; she has so long abstained from it with an eye to the weekly butter-money, that abstinence, wedded to habit, has begotten aversion. She is a thin woman with a chronic liver-complaint, which would have secured her Mr Pilgrim's entire regard and unreserved good word, even if he had not been in awe of her tongue, which was as sharp as his own lancet. She has brought her knitting – no frivolous fancy knitting, but a substantial woollen stocking; the click-click of her knitting-needles is the running accompaniment to all her conversation, and in her utmost enjoyment of spoiling a friend's self-satisfaction, she was never known to spoil a stocking.

Mrs Patten does not admire this excessive click-clicking activity. Quiescence in an easy-chair, under the sense of compound interest perpetually accumulating, has long seemed an ample function to her, and she does her malevolence gently. She is a pretty little old woman of eighty, with a close cap and tiny flat white curls round her face, as natty and unsoiled and invariable as the waxen image of a little old lady under a glass-case; once a lady's-maid, and married for her beauty. She used to adore her husband, and now she adores her money, cherishing a quiet blood-relation's hatred for her niece, Janet Gibbs, who, she knows, expects a large legacy, and whom she is determined to disappoint. Her money shall all go in a lump to a distant relation of her husband's, and Janet shall be saved the trouble of pretending to cry, by finding that she is left with a miserable pittance.

Mrs Patten has more respect for her neighbour Mr Hackit than for most people. Mr Hackit is a shrewd substantial man, whose advice about crops is always worth listening to, and who is too well off to want to borrow money.

And now that we are snug and warm with this little tea-party, while it is freezing with February bitterness outside, we will listen to what they are talking about.

'So,' said Mr Pilgrim, with his mouth only half empty of muffin, 'you had a row in Shepperton church last Sunday. I was at Jem Hood's, the bassoon- man's, this morning, attending his wife, and he swears he'll be revenged on the parson – a confounded, methodistical, meddlesome chap, who must be putting his finger in every pie. What was it all about?'

'O, a passill o' nonsense,' said Mr Hackit, sticking one thumb between the buttons of his capacious waistcoat, and retaining a pinch of snuff with the other – for he was but moderately given to 'the cups that cheer but not inebriate,' and had already finished his tea; 'they began to sing the wedding psalm for a new-married couple, as pretty a psalm an' as pretty a tune as any's in the prayer-book. It's been sung for every new-married couple since

I was a boy. And what can be better?' Here Mr Hackit stretched out his left arm, threw back his head, and broke into melody—

"'O what a happy thing it is,
    And joyful for to see,
Brethren to dwell together in
    Friendship and unity.'

But Mr Barton is all for th' hymns, and a sort o' music as I can't join in at all.'

'And so,' said Mr Pilgrim, recalling Mr Hackit from lyrical reminiscences to narrative, 'he called out Silence! did he? when he got into the pulpit; and gave a hymn out himself to some meeting-house tune?'

'Yes,' said Mrs Hackit, stooping towards the candle to pick up a stitch, 'and turned as red as a turkey-cock. I often say, when he preaches about meekness, he gives himself a slap in the face. He's like me – he's got a temper of his own.'

'Rather a low-bred fellow, I think, Barton,' said Mr Pilgrim, who hated the Reverend Amos for two reasons – because he had called in a new doctor, recently settled in Shepperton; and because, being himself a dabbler in drugs, he had the credit of having cured a patient of Mr Pilgrim's. 'They say his father was a Dissenting shoemaker; and he's half a Dissenter himself. Why, doesn't he preach extempore in that cottage up here, of a Sunday evening?'

13

'Tchaw!' – this was Mr Hackit's favourite inter-jection – 'that preaching without book's no good, only when a man has a gift, and has the Bible at his fingers' ends. It was all very well for Parry – he'd a gift; and in my youth I've heard the Ranters out o' doors in Yorkshire go on for an hour or two on end, without ever sticking fast a minute. There was one clever chap, I remember, as used to say, 'You're like the wood-pigeon; it says do, do, do all day, and never sets about any work itself.' That's bringing it home to people. But our parson's no gift at all that way; he can preach as good a sermon as need be heard when he writes it down. But when he tries to preach wi'out book, he rambles about, and doesn't stick to's text; and every now and then he flounders about like a sheep as has cast itself, and can't get on'ts legs again. You wouldn't like that, Mrs Patten, if you was to go to church now?'

'Eh, dear,' said Mrs Patten, falling back in her chair, and lifting up her little withered hands, 'what 'ud Mr Gilfil say, if he was worthy to know the changes as have come about i' the church these last ten years? I don't understand these new sort o' doctrines. When Mr Barton comes to see me, he talks about nothing but my sins and my need o' marcy. Now, Mr Hackit, I've never been a sinner. From the fust beginning, when I went into service, I al'ys did my duty by my emplyers. I was a good wife as any's in the county – never aggravated my husband. The cheese-factor used to say my cheese

14

was al'ys to be depended on. I've known women, as their cheeses swelled a shame to be seen, when their husbands had counted on the cheese-money to make up their rent; and yet they'd three gowns to my one. If I'm not to be saved, I know a many as are in a bad way. But it's well for me as I can't go to church any longer, for if th' old singers are to be done away with, there'll be nothing left as it was in Mr Patten's time; and what's more, I hear you've settled to pull the church down and build it up new?'

Now the fact was that the Rev. Amos Barton, on his last visit to Mrs Patten, had urged her to enlarge her promised subscription of twenty pounds, representing to her that she was only a steward of her riches, and that she could not spend them more for the glory of God than by giving a heavy subscription towards the rebuilding of Shepperton church – a practical precept which was not likely to smooth the way to her accept-ance of his theological doctrine. Mr Hackit, who had more doctrinal enlightenment than Mrs Patten, had been a little shocked by the heathenism of her speech, and was glad of the new turn given to the subject by this question, addressed to him as churchwarden and an authority in all parochial matters.

'Ah,' he answered, 'the parson's boddered us into it at last, and we're to begin pulling down this spring. But we haven't got money enough yet. I was for waiting till we'd made up the sum, and, for my part, I think the congregation's fell off o' late; though Mr Barton says that's because there's been no room for the people when they've come. You see, the congregation got so large in Parry's time, the people stood in th' aisles; but there's never any crowd now, as I can see.'

'Well,' said Mrs Hackit, whose good-nature began to act now that it was a little in contradiction with the dominant tone of the conversation, '*I* like Mr Barton. I think he's a good sort o' man, for all he's not overburthen'd i' th' upper story; and his wife's as nice a lady-like woman as I'd wish to see. How nice she keeps her children! and little enough money to do't with; and a delicate creatur' – six children, and another a-coming. I don't know how they make both ends meet, I'm sure, now her aunt has left 'em. But I sent 'em a cheese and a sack o' potatoes last week; that's something towards filling the little mouths.'

'Ah!' said Mr Hackit, 'and my wife makes Mr Barton a good stiff glass o' brandy-and-water, when he comes in to supper after his cottage preaching. The parson likes it; it puts a bit o' colour into's face, and makes him look a deal handsomer.'

This allusion to brandy-and-water suggested to Miss Gibbs the introduction of the liquor decanters, now that the tea was cleared away; for in bucolic society five-and-twenty years ago, the human animal of the male sex was understood to be perpetually athirst, and 'something to drink' was

16

as necessary a 'condition of thought' as Time and Space.

'Now, that cottage preaching,' said Mr Pilgrim, mixing himself a strong glass of "cold without," 'I was talking about it to our Parson Ely the other day, and he doesn't approve of it at all. He said it did as much harm as good to give a too familiar aspect to religious teaching. That was what Ely said – it does as much harm as good to give a too familiar aspect to religious teaching.'

Mr Pilgrim generally spoke with an intermittent kind of splutter; indeed, one of his patients had observed that it was a pity such a clever man had a ''pediment' in his speech. But when he came to what he conceived the pith of his argument or the point of his joke, he mouthed out his words with slow emphasis; as a hen, when advertising her accouchement, passes at irregular intervals from pianissimo semi-quavers to fortissimo crotchets. He thought this speech of Mr Ely's particularly metaphysical and profound, and the more decisive of the question because it was a generality which represented no particulars to his mind.

'Well, I don't know about that,' said Mrs Hackit, who had always the courage of her opinion, 'but I know, some of our labourers and stockingers as used never to come to church, come to the cottage, and that's better than never hearing anything good from week's end to week's end. And there's that Track Society as Mr Barton has begun – I've seen more o' the poor people with going tracking, than all the time I've lived in the parish before. And there'd need be something done among 'em; for the drinking at them Benefit Clubs is shameful. There's hardly a steady man or steady woman either, but what's a dissenter.'

During this speech of Mrs Hackit's, Mr Pilgrim had emitted a succession of little snorts, something like the treble grunts of a guinea-pig, which were always with him the sign of suppressed disapproval. But he never contradicted Mrs Hackit – a woman whose 'pot luck' was always to be relied on, and who on her side had unlimited reliance on bleeding, blistering, and draughts.

Mrs Patten, however, felt equal disapprobation, and had no reasons for suppressing it.

'Well,' she remarked, 'I've heared of no good from interfering with one's neighbours, poor or rich. And I hate the sight o' women going about trapesing from house to house in all weathers, wet or dry, and coming in with their petticoats dagged and their shoes all over mud. Janet wanted to join in the tracking, but I told her I'd have nobody tracking out o' my house; when I'm gone, she may do as she likes. I never dagged my petticoats in *my* life, and I've no opinion o' that sort o' religion.

'No,' said Mr Hackit, who was fond of soothing the acerbities of the feminine mind with a jocose compliment, 'you held your petticoats so high, to show your tight ankles: it isn't everybody as likes to show her ankles.'

This joke met with general acceptance, even from the snubbed Janet, whose ankles were only tight in the sense of looking extremely squeezed by her boots. But Janet seemed always to identify herself with her aunt's personality, holding her own under protest.

Under cover of the general laughter, the gentlemen replenished their glasses, Mr Pilgrim attempting to give his the character of a stirrup-cup by observing that he 'must be going.' Miss Gibbs seized this opportunity of telling Mrs Hackit that she suspected Betty, the dairymaid, of frying the best bacon for the shepherd, when he sat up with her to 'help brew;' whereupon Mrs Hackit replied, that she had always thought Betty false; and Mrs Patten said, there was no bacon stolen when *she* was able to manage. Mr Hackit, who often complained that he 'never saw the like to women with their maids – he never had any trouble with his men,' avoided listening to this discussion, by raising the question of vetches with Mr Pilgrim. The stream of conversation had thus diverged; and no more was said about the Rev. Amos Barton, who is the main object of interest to us just now. So we may leave Cross Farm without waiting till Mrs Hackit, resolutely donning her clogs and wrappings, renders it incumbent on Mr Pilgrim also to fulfil his frequent threat of going.

CHAPTER 2

It was happy for the Rev. Amos Barton that he did not, like us, overhear the conversation recorded in the last chapter. Indeed, what mortal is there of us, who would find his satisfaction enhanced by an opportunity of comparing the picture he presents to himself of his own doings, with the picture they make on the mental retina of his neighbours? We are poor plants buoyed up by the air-vessels of our own conceit: alas for us, if we get a few pinches that empty us of that windy self-subsistence! The very capacity for good would go out of us. For, tell the most impassioned orator, suddenly, that his wig is awry, or his shirt-lap hanging out, and that he is tickling people by the oddity of his person, instead of thrilling them by the energy of his periods, and you would infallibly dry up the spring of his eloquence. That is a deep and wide saying, that no miracle can be wrought without faith – without the worker's faith in himself, as well as the recipient's faith in him. And the greater part of the worker's faith in himself is made up of the faith that others believe in him.

Let me be persuaded that my neighbour Jenkins considers me a blockhead, and I shall never shine in conversation with him any more. Let me discover that the lovely Phœbe thinks my squint intolerable, and I shall never be able to fix her blandly with my disengaged eye again.

Thank heaven, then, that a little illusion is left to us, to enable us to be useful and agreeable – that we don't know exactly what our friends think of us – that the world is not made of looking-glass, to show us just the figure we are making, and just what is going on behind our backs! By the help of dear friendly illusion, we are able to dream that we are charming – and our faces wear a becoming air of self-possession; we are able to dream that other men admire our talents – and our benignity is undisturbed; we are able to dream that we are doing much good – and we do a little.

Thus it was with Amos Barton on that very Thursday evening, when he was the subject of the conversation at Cross Farm. He had been dining at Mr Farquhar's, the secondary squire of the parish, and, stimulated by unwonted gravies and port wine, had been delivering his opinion on affairs parochial and otherwise with considerable animation. And he was now returning home in the moonlight – a little chill, it is true, for he had just now no greatcoat compatible with clerical dignity, and a fur boa round one's neck, with a waterproof cape over one's shoulders, doesn't frighten away the cold from one's legs; but entirely unsuspicious, not only of Mr Hackit's estimate of his oratorical powers, but also of the critical remarks passed on him by the Miss Farquhars as soon as the drawing-room door had closed behind him. Miss Julia had observed that she *never* heard any one sniff so frightfully as Mr Barton did – she had a great mind to offer him her pocket-handkerchief; and Miss Arabella wondered why he always said he was going *for* to do a thing. He, excellent man! was meditating fresh pastoral exertions on the morrow; he would set on foot his lending library, in which he had introduced some books that would be a pretty sharp blow to the Dissenters – one especially, purporting to be written by a working man who, out of pure zeal for the welfare of his class, took the trouble to warn them in this way against those hypocritical thieves, the Dissenting preachers. The Rev. Amos Barton profoundly believed in the existence of that working man, and had thoughts of writing to him. Dissent, he considered, would have its head bruised in Shepperton, for did he not attack it in two ways? He preached Low-Church doctrine – as evangelical as anything to be heard in the Independent Chapel; and he made a High-Church assertion of ecclesiastical powers and functions. Clearly, the Dissenters would feel that 'the parson' was too many for them. Nothing like a man who combines shrewdness with energy. The wisdom of the serpent, Mr Barton considered, was one of his strong points.

Look at him as he winds through the little churchyard! The silver light that falls aslant on church and tomb, enables you to see his slim black figure, made all the slimmer by tight pantaloons, as it flits past the pale gravestones. He walks with a quick step, and is now rapping with sharp decision at the vicarage door. It is opened without delay by the nurse, cook, and housemaid, all at once – that is to say, by the robust maid-of-all-work, Nanny; and as Mr Barton hangs up his hat in the passage, you see that a narrow face of no particular complexion – even the small-pox that has attacked it seems to have been of a mongrel, indefinite kind – with features of no particular shape, and an eye of no particular expression, is surmounted by a slope of baldness gently rising from brow to crown. You judge him, rightly, to be about forty. The house is quiet, for it is half-past ten, and the children have long been gone to bed. He opens the sitting-room door, but instead of seeing his wife, as he expected, stitching with the nimblest of fingers by the light of one candle, he finds her dispensing with the light of a candle altogether. She is softly pacing up and down by the red firelight, holding in her arms little Walter, the year-old baby, who looks over her shoulder with large wide-open eyes, while the patient mother pats his back with her soft hand, and glances with a sigh at the heap of large and small stockings lying unmended on the table.

She was a lovely woman – Mrs Amos Barton; a

large, fair, gentle Madonna, with thick, close chestnut curls beside her well-rounded cheeks, and with large, tender, short-sighted eyes. The flowing lines of her tall figure made the limpest dress look graceful, and her old frayed black silk seemed to repose on her bust and limbs with a placid elegance and sense of distinction, in strong contrast with the uneasy sense of being no fit, that seemed to express itself in the rustling of Mrs Farquhar's *gros de Naples*. The caps she wore would have been pronounced, when off her head, utterly heavy and hideous – for in those days even fashionable caps were large and floppy; but surmounting her long arched neck, and mingling their borders of cheap lace and ribbon with her chestnut curls, they seemed miracles of successful millinery. Among strangers she was shy and tremulous as a girl of fifteen; she blushed crimson if any one appealed to her opinion; yet that tall, graceful, substantial presence was so imposing in its mildness, that men spoke to her with an agreeable sensation of timidity.

Soothing, unspeakable charm of gentle womanhood! which supersedes all acquisitions, all accomplishments. You would never have asked, at any period of Mrs Amos Barton's life, if she sketched or played the piano. You would even perhaps have been rather scandalized if she had descended from the serene dignity of *being* to the assiduous unrest of *doing*. Happy the man, you would have thought, whose eye will rest on her in the pauses of his fireside reading – whose hot

24

aching forehead will be soothed by the contact of her cool soft hand – who will recover himself from dejection at his mistakes and failures in the loving light of her unreproaching eyes! You would not, perhaps, have anticipated that this bliss would fall to the share of precisely such a man as Amos Barton, whom you have already surmised not to have the refined sensibilities for which you might have imagined Mrs Barton's qualities to be destined by pre-established harmony. But I, for one, do not grudge Amos Barton this sweet wife. I have all my life had a sympathy for mongrel ungainly dogs, who are nobody's pets; and I would rather surprise one of them by a pat and a pleasant morsel, than meet the condescending advances of the loveliest Skye-terrier who has his cushion by my lady's chair. That, to be sure, is not the way of the world: if it happens to see a fellow of fine proportions and aristocratic mien, who makes no *faux pas*, and wins golden opinions from all sorts of men, it straightway picks out for him the loveliest of unmarried women, and says, *There* would be a proper match! Not at all, say I: let that successful, well-shapen, discreet and able gentleman put up with something less than the best in the matrimonial department; and let the sweet woman go to make sunshine and a soft pillow for the poor devil whose legs are not models, whose efforts are often blunders, and who in general gets more kicks than halfpence. She – the sweet woman – will like it as well; for her sublime capacity of loving will have all the more scope; and I venture to say, Mrs Barton's nature would never have grown half so angelic if she had married the man you would perhaps have had in your eye for her – a man with sufficient income and abundant personal éclat. Besides, Amos was an affectionate husband, and, in his way, valued his wife as his best treasure.

But now he has shut the door behind him, and said, 'Well, Milly!'

'Well, dear!' was the corresponding greeting, made eloquent by a smile.

'So that young rascal won't go to sleep! Can't you give him to Nanny?'

'Why, Nanny has been busy ironing this evening; but I think I'll take him to her now.' And Mrs Barton glided towards the kitchen, while her husband ran up-stairs to put on his maize-coloured dressing-gown, in which costume he was quietly filling his long pipe when his wife returned to the sitting-room. Maize is a colour that decidedly did *not* suit his complexion, and it is one that soon soils; why, then, did Mr Barton select it for domestic wear? Perhaps because he had a knack of hitting on the wrong thing in garb as well as in grammar.

Mrs Barton now lighted her candle, and seated herself before her heap of stockings. She had something disagreeable to tell her husband, but she would not enter on it at once.

'Have you had a nice evening, dear?'

'Yes, pretty well. Ely was there to dinner, but

went away rather early. Miss Arabella is setting her cap at him with a vengeance. But I don't think he's much smitten. I've a notion Ely's engaged to some one at a distance, and will astonish all the ladies who are languishing for him here, by bringing home his bride one of these days. Ely's a sly dog; he'll like that.'

'Did the Farquhars say anything about the singing last Sunday?'

'Yes; Farquhar said he thought it was time there was some improvement in the choir. But he was rather scandalized at my setting the tune of "Lydia." He says he's always hearing it as he passes the Independent meeting.' Here Mr Barton laughed – he had a way of laughing at criticisms that other people thought damaging – and thereby showed the remainder of a set of teeth which, like the remnants of the Old Guard, were few in number, and very much the worse for wear. 'But,' he continued, 'Mrs Farquhar talked the most about Mr Bridmain and the Countess. She has taken up all the gossip about them, and wanted to convert me to her opinion, but I told her pretty strongly what I thought.'

'Dear me! why will people take so much pains to find out evil about others? I have had a note from the Countess since you went, asking us to dine with them on Friday.'

Here Mrs Barton reached the note from the mantelpiece, and gave it to her husband. We will look over his shoulder while he reads it: –

27

'Sweetest Milly, – Bring your lovely face with your husband to dine with us on Friday at seven – do. If not, I will be sulky with you till Sunday, when I shall be obliged to see you, and shall long to kiss you that very moment. – Yours, according to your answer,

'Caroline Czerlaski.'

'Just like her, isn't it?' said Mrs Barton. 'I suppose we can go?'

'Yes; I have no engagement. The Clerical Meeting is to-morrow, you know.'

'And, dear, Woods the butcher called, to say he must have some money next week. He has a payment to make up.'

This announcement made Mr Barton thoughtful. He puffed more rapidly, and looked at the fire.

'I think I must ask Hackit to lend me twenty pounds, for it is nearly two months till Lady-day, and we can't give Woods our last shilling.'

'I hardly like you to ask Mr Hackit, dear – he and Mrs Hackit have been so very kind to us; they have sent us so many things lately.'

'Then I must ask Oldinport. I'm going to write to him to-morrow morning, for to tell him the arrangement I've been thinking of about having service in the workhouse while the church is being enlarged. If he agrees to attend service there once or twice, the other people will come. Net the large fish, and you're sure to have the small fry.'

'I wish we could do without borrowing money, and yet I don't see how we can. Poor Fred must have some new shoes; I couldn't let him go to Mrs Bond's yesterday because his toes were peeping out, dear child! and I can't let him walk anywhere except in the garden. He must have a pair before Sunday. Really, boots and shoes are the greatest trouble of my life. Everything else one can turn and turn about, and make old look like new; but there's no coaxing boots and shoes to look better than they are.'

Mrs Barton was playfully undervaluing her skill in metamorphosing boots and shoes. She had at that moment on her feet a pair of slippers which had long ago lived through the prunella phase of their existence, and were now running a respectable career as black silk slippers, having been neatly covered with that material by Mrs Barton's own neat fingers. Wonderful fingers those! they were never empty; for if she went to spend a few hours with a friendly parishioner, out came her thimble and a piece of calico or muslin, which, before she left, had become a mysterious little garment with all sorts of hemmed ins and outs. She was even trying to persuade her husband to leave off tight pantaloons, because if he would wear the ordinary gun-cases, she knew she could make them so well that no one would suspect the sex of the tailor.

But by this time Mr Barton has finished his pipe, the candle begins to burn low, and Mrs Barton goes to see if Nanny has succeeded in lulling Walter to sleep. Nanny is that moment putting him in the little cot by his mother's bedside; the head, with its thin wavelets of brown hair, indents the little pillow; and a tiny, waxen, dimpled fist hides the rosy lips, for baby is given to the infantine peccadillo of thumb-sucking.

So Nanny could now join in the short evening prayer, and all could go to bed.

Mrs Barton carried up-stairs the remainder of her heap of stockings, and laid them on a table close to her bedside, where also she placed a warm shawl, removing her candle, before she put it out, to a tin socket fixed at the head of her bed. Her body was very weary, but her heart was not heavy, in spite of Mr Woods the butcher, and the transitory nature of shoe-leather; for her heart so overflowed with love, she felt sure she was near a fountain of love that would care for husband and babes better than she could foresee; so she was soon asleep. But about half-past five o'clock in the morning, if there were any angels watching round her bed – and angels might be glad of such an office – they saw Mrs Barton rise up quietly, careful not to disturb the slumbering Amos, who was snoring the snore of the just, light her candle, prop herself upright with the pillows, throw the warm shawl round her shoulders, and renew her attack on the heap of undarned stockings. She darned away until she heard Nanny stirring, and then drowsiness came with the dawn; the candle was put out, and she sank into a doze. But at nine o'clock she was at the breakfast-table, busy cutting bread-and-butter for five hungry mouths, while Nanny, baby on one arm, in rosy cheeks, fat neck, and night-gown, brought in a jug of hot milk-and-water. Nearest her mother sits the nine-year-old Patty, the eldest child, whose sweet fair face is already rather grave sometimes, and who always wants to run up-stairs to save mamma's legs, which get so tired of an evening. Then there are four other blond heads – two boys and two girls, gradually decreasing in size down to Chubby, who is making a round O of her mouth to receive a bit of papa's 'baton.' Papa's attention was divided between petting Chubby, rebuking the noisy Fred, which he did with a somewhat excessive sharpness, and eating his own breakfast. He had not yet looked at Mamma, and did not know that her cheek was paler than usual. But Patty whispered, 'Mamma, have you the headache?'

Happily, coal was cheap in the neighbourhood of Shepperton, and Mr Hackit would any time let his horses draw a load for 'the parson' without charge; so there was a blazing fire in the sitting-room, and not without need, for the vicarage garden, as they looked out on it from the bow-window, was hard with black frost, and the sky had the white woolly look that portends snow.

Breakfast over, Mr Barton mounted to his study, and occupied himself in the first place with his letter to Mr Oldinport. It was very much the same sort of letter as most clergymen would have written under the same circumstances, except that instead of *per*ambulate, the Rev. Amos wrote *pre*ambulate, and instead of 'if haply,' 'if happily,' the contingency indicated being the reverse of happy. Mr Barton had not the gift of perfect accuracy in English orthography and syntax; which was unfortunate, as he was known not to be a Hebrew scholar, and not in the least suspected of being an accomplished Grecian. These lapses, in a man who had gone through the Eleusinian mysteries of a university education, surprised the young ladies of his parish extremely; especially the Miss Farquhars, whom he had once addressed in a letter as Dear Mads., apparently an abbreviation for Madams. The persons least surprised at the Rev. Amos's deficiencies were his clerical brethren, who had gone through the mysteries themselves.

At eleven o'clock, Mr Barton walked forth in cape and boa, with the sleet driving in his face, to read prayers at the workhouse, euphemistically called the 'College.' The College was a huge square stone building, standing on the best apology for an elevation of ground that could be seen for about ten miles round Shepperton. A flat ugly district this; depressing enough to look at, even on the brightest days. The roads are black with coal-dust, the brick houses dingy with smoke; and at that time – the time of handloom weavers – every other cottage had a loom at its window, where you might see a pale, sickly-looking man or woman pressing a narrow chest against a board, and doing a sort of tread-mill work with legs and arms. A troublesome district for a clergyman; at least to one who, like Amos Barton, understood the 'cure of souls' in something more than an official sense; for over and above the rustic stupidity furnished by the farm-labourers, the miners brought obstreperous animalism, and the weavers an acrid Radicalism and Dissent. Indeed, Mrs Hackit often observed that the colliers, who many of them earned better wages than Mr Barton, 'passed their time in doing nothing but swilling ale and smoking, like the beasts that perish' (speaking, we may presume, in a remotely analogical sense); and in some of the alehouse corners the drink was flavoured by a dingy kind of infidelity, something like rinsings of Tom Paine in ditch-water. A certain amount of religious excitement, created by the popular preaching of Mr Parry, Amos's predecessor, had nearly died out, and the religious life of Shepperton was falling back towards low-water mark. Here, you perceive, was a terrible stronghold of Satan; and you may well pity the Rev. Amos Barton, who had to stand single-handed and summon it to surrender. We read, indeed, that the walls of Jericho fell down before the sound of trumpets; but we nowhere hear that those trumpets were hoarse and feeble. Doubtless they were trumpets that gave forth clear ringing tones, and sent a mighty vibration through brick and mortar. But the oratory of the Rev. Amos resembled rather a

Belgian railway-horn, which shows praiseworthy intentions inadequately fulfilled. He often missed the right note both in public and private exhortation, and got a little angry in consequence. For though Amos thought himself strong, he did not *feel* himself strong. Nature had given him the opinion, but not the sensation. Without that opinion he would probably never have worn cambric bands, but would have been an excellent cabinetmaker and deacon of an Independent church, as his father was before him (he was not a shoemaker, as Mr Pilgrim had reported). He might then have sniffed long and loud in the corner of his pew in Gun Street Chapel; he might have indulged in halting rhetoric at prayer-meetings, and have spoken faulty English in private life; and these little infirmities would not have prevented him, honest faithful man that he was, from being a shining light in the Dissenting circle of Bridgeport. A tallow dip, of the long-eight description, is an excellent thing in the kitchen candlestick, and Betty's nose and eye are not sensitive to the difference between it and the finest wax; it is only when you stick it in the silver candlestick, and introduce it into the drawing-room, that it seems plebeian, dim, and ineffectual. Alas for the worthy man who, like that candle, gets himself into the wrong place! It is only the very largest souls who will be able to appreciate and pity him – who will discern and love sincerity of purpose amid all the bungling feebleness of achievement.

But now Amos Barton has made his way through the sleet as far as the College, has thrown off his hat, cape, and boa, and is reading, in the dreary stone-floored dining-room, a portion of the morning service to the inmates seated on the benches before him. Remember, the New Poor-law had not yet come into operation, and Mr Barton was not acting as paid chaplain of the Union, but as the pastor who had the cure of all souls in his parish, pauper as well as other. After the prayers he always addressed to them a short discourse on some subject suggested by the lesson for the day, striving if by this means some edifying matter might find its way into the pauper mind and conscience – perhaps a task as trying as you could well imagine to the faith and patience of any honest clergyman. For, on the very first bench, these were the faces on which his eye had to rest, watching whether there was any stirring under the stagnant surface.

Right in front of him – probably because he was stone-deaf, and it was deemed more edifying to hear nothing at a short distance than at a long one – sat 'Old Maxum,' as he was familiarly called, his real patronymic remaining a mystery to most persons. A fine philological sense discerns in this cognomen an indication that the pauper patriarch had once been considered pithy and sententious in his speech; but now the weight of ninety-five years lay heavy on his tongue as well as in his ears, and he sat before the clergyman with protruded chin, and munching mouth, and eyes that seemed to look at emptiness.

Next to him sat Poll Fodge – known to the magistracy of her country as Mary Higgins – a one-eyed woman, with a scarred and seamy face, the most notorious rebel in the workhouse, said to have once thrown her broth over the master's coat-tails, and who, in spite of nature's apparent safe-guards against that contingency, had contributed to the perpetuation of the Fodge characteristics in the person of a small boy, who was behaving naughtily on one of the back benches. Miss Fodge fixed her one sore eye on Mr Barton with a sort of hardy defiance.

Beyond this member of the softer sex, at the end of the bench, sat 'Silly Jim,' a young man afflicted with hydrocephalus, who rolled his head from side to side, and gazed at the point of his nose. These were the supporters of Old Maxum on his right.

On his left sat Mr Fitchett, a tall fellow, who had once been a footman in the Oldinport family, and in that giddy elevation had enunciated a contemptuous opinion of boiled beef, which had been traditionally handed down in Shepperton as the direct cause of his ultimate reduction to pauper commons. His calves were now shrunken, and his hair was grey without the aid of powder; but he still carried his chin as if he were conscious of a stiff cravat; he set his dilapidated hat on with a knowing inclination towards the left ear; and when he was on field-work, he carted and uncarted the manure with a sort of flunkey grace, the ghost of that jaunty demeanour with which he used to usher in my lady's morning visitors. The flunkey nature was nowhere completely subdued but in his stomach, and he still divided society into gentry, gentry's flunkeys, and the people who provided for them. A clergyman without a flunkey was an anomaly, belonging to neither of these classes. Mr Fitchett had an irrepressible tendency to drowsiness under spiritual instruction, and in the recurrent regularity with which he dozed off until he nodded and awaked himself, he looked not unlike a piece of mechanism, ingeniously contrived for measuring the length of Mr Barton's discourse.

Perfectly wide-awake, on the contrary, was his left-hand neighbour, Mrs Brick, one of those hard undying old women, to whom age seems to have given a network of wrinkles, as a coat of magic armour against the attacks of winters, warm or cold. The point on which Mrs Brick was still sensitive – the theme on which you might possibly excite her hope and fear – was snuff. It seemed to be an enbalming powder, helping her soul to do the office of salt.

And now, eke out an audience of which this front benchful was a sample, with a certain number of refractory children, over whom Mr Spratt, the master of the workhouse, exercised an irate surveillance, and I think you will admit that the university-taught clergyman, whose office it is to bring home the gospel to a handful of such souls, has a sufficiently hard task. For, to have any chance of success, short of miraculous intervention, he must bring his geographical, chronological, exegetical mind pretty nearly to the pauper point of view, or of no view; he must have some approximate conception of the mode in which the doctrines that have so much vitality in the plenum of his own brain will comport themselves *in vacuo* – that is to say, in a brain that is neither geographical, chronological, nor exegetical. It is a flexible imagination that can take such a leap as that, and an adroit tongue that can adapt its speech to so unfamiliar a position. The Rev. Amos Barton had neither that flexible imagination, nor that adroit tongue. He talked of Israel and its sins, of chosen vessels, of the Paschal lamb, of blood as a medium of reconciliation; and he strove in this way to convey religious truth within reach of the Fodge and Fitchett mind. This very morning, the first lesson was the twelfth chapter of Exodus, and Mr Barton's exposition turned on unleavened bread. Nothing in the world more suited to the simple understanding than instruction through familiar types and symbols! But there is always this danger attending it, that the interest or comprehension of your hearers may stop short precisely at the point where your spiritual interpretation begins. And Mr Barton this morning succeeded in carrying the pauper imagination to the dough-tub, but unfortunately was not able to carry it upwards from that well-known object to the unknown truths which it was intended to shadow forth.

Alas! a natural incapacity for teaching, finished by keeping 'terms' at Cambridge, where there are able mathematicians, and butter is sold by the yard, is not apparently the medium through which Christian doctrine will distil as welcome dew on withered souls.

And so, while the sleet outside was turning to unquestionable snow, and the stony dining-room looked darker and drearier, and Mr Fitchett was nodding his lowest, and Mr Spratt was boxing the boys' ears with a constant *rinforzando*, and he felt more keenly the approach of dinner-time, Mr Barton wound up his exhortation with something of the February chill at his heart as well as his feet. Mr Fitchett, thoroughly roused now the instruction was at an end, obsequiously and gracefully advanced to help Mr Barton in putting on his cape, while Mrs Brick rubbed her withered forefinger round and round her little shoe-shaped snuff-box, vainly seeking for the fraction of a pinch. I can't help thinking that if Mr Barton had shaken into that little box a small portion of Scotch high-dried, he might have produced something more like an amiable emotion in Mrs Brick's mind than anything she had felt under his morning's exposition of the unleavened bread. But our good Amos laboured under a deficiency of small tact as well as of small cash; and when he observed the action of the old woman's forefinger, he said, in his brusque way, 'So your snuff is all gone, eh?'

Mrs Brick's eyes twinkled with the visionary hope that the parson might be intending to replenish her box, at least mediately, through the present of a small copper.

'Ah, well! you'll soon be going where there is no more snuff. You'll be in need of mercy then. You must remember that you may have to seek for mercy and not find it, just as you're seeking for snuff.'

At the first sentence of this admonition, the twinkle subsided from Mrs Brick's eyes. The lid of her box went 'click!' and her heart was shut up at the same moment.

But now Mr Barton's attention was called for by Mr Spratt, who was dragging a small and unwilling boy from the rear. Mr Spratt was a small-featured, small-statured man, with a remarkable power of language, mitigated by hesitation, who piqued himself on expressing unexceptionable sentiments in unexceptionable language on all occasions.

'Mr Barton, sir – aw – aw – excuse my trespassing on your time – aw – to beg that you will administer a rebuke to this boy; he is – aw – aw – most inveterate in ill-behaviour during service-time.'

The inveterate culprit was a boy of seven, vainly contending against 'candles' at his nose by feeble sniffing. But no sooner had Mr Spratt uttered his impeachment, than Miss Fodge rushed forward and placed herself between Mr Barton and the accused.

'That's *my* child, Muster Barton,' she exclaimed, further manifesting her maternal instincts by applying her apron to her offspring's nose. 'He's al'ys a-findin' faut wi' him, an' a-poundin' him for nothin'. Let him goo an' eat his roost goose as is a-smellin' up in our noses while we're a-swallering them greasy broth, an' let my boy allooan.'

Mr Spratt's small eyes flashed, and he was in danger of uttering sentiments not unexceptionable before the clergyman; but Mr Barton, foreseeing that a prolongation of this episode would not be to edification, said 'Silence!' in his severest tones.

'Let me hear no abuse. Your boy is not likely to behave well, if you set him the example of being saucy.' Then stooping down to Master Fodge, and taking him by the shoulder, 'Do you like being beaten?'

'No-a.'

'Then what a silly boy you are to be naughty. If you were not naughty, you wouldn't be beaten. But if you are naughty, God will be angry, as well as Mr Spratt; and God can burn you for ever. That will be worse than being beaten.'

Master Fodge's countenance was neither affirmative nor negative of this proposition.

'But,' continued Mr Barton, 'if you will be a good boy, God will love you, and you will grow up to be a good man. Now, let me hear next Thursday that you have been a good boy.'

Master Fodge had no distinct vision of the benefit that would accrue to him from this change of courses. But Mr Barton, being aware that Miss Fodge had touched on a delicate subject in alluding to the roast goose, was determined to witness no more polemics between her and Mr Spratt, so, saying good morning to the latter, he hastily left the College.

The snow was falling in thicker and thicker flakes, and already the vicarage-garden was cloaked in white as he passed through the gate. Mrs Barton heard him open the door, and ran out of the sitting-room to meet him.

'I'm afraid your feet are very wet, dear. What a terrible morning! Let me take your hat. Your slippers are at the fire.'

Mr Barton was feeling a little cold and cross. It is difficult, when you have been doing disagreeable duties, without praise, on a snowy day, to attend to the very minor morals. So he showed no recognition of Milly's attentions, but sniffed and said, 'Fetch me my dressing-gown, will you?'

'It *is* down, dear. I thought you wouldn't go into the study, because you said you would letter and number the books for the Lending Library. Patty and I have been covering them, and they are all ready in the sitting-room.'

'O, I can't do those this morning,' said Mr Barton, as he took off his boots and put his feet into the slippers Milly had brought him; 'you must put them away into the parlour.'

The sitting-room was also the day-nursery and schoolroom; and while Mamma's back was turned,

42

Dickey, the second boy, had insisted on superseding Chubby in the guidance of a headless horse, of the red-wafered species, which she was drawing round the room, so that when Papa opened the door Chubby was giving tongue energetically.

'Milly, some of these children must go away. I want to be quiet.'

'Yes, dear. Hush, Chubby; go with Patty, and see what Nanny is getting for our dinner. Now, Fred and Sophy and Dickey, help me to carry these books into the parlour. There are three for Dickey. Carry them steadily.'

Papa meanwhile settled himself in his easy-chair, and took up a work on Episcopacy, which he had from the Clerical Book Society; thinking he would finish it and return it this afternoon, as he was going to the Clerical Meeting at Milby Vicarage, where the Book Society had its head-quarters.

The Clerical Meetings and Book Society, which had been founded some eight or ten months, had had a noticeable effect on the Rev. Amos Barton. When he first came to Shepperton, he was simply an evangelical clergyman, whose Christian experiences had commenced under the teaching of the Rev. Mr Johns, of Gun Street Chapel, and had been consolidated at Cambridge under the influence of Mr Simeon. John Newton and Thomas Scott were his doctrinal ideals; he would have taken in the *Christian Observer* and the *Record*, if he could have afforded it; his anecdotes were chiefly of the pious-jocose kind, current in

Dissenting circles; and he thought an Episcopalian Establishment unobjectionable.

But by this time the effect of the Tractarian agitation was beginning to be felt in backward provincial regions, and the Tractarian satire on the Low-Church party was beginning to tell even on those who disavowed or resisted Tractarian doctrines. The vibration of an intellectual movement was felt from the golden head to the miry toes of the Establishment; and so it came to pass that, in the district round Milby, the market-town close to Shepperton, the clergy had agreed to have a clerical meeting every month, wherein they would exercise their intellects by discussing theological and ecclesiastical questions, and cement their brotherly love by discussing a good dinner. A Book Society naturally suggested itself as an adjunct of this agreeable plan; and thus, you perceive, there was provision made for ample friction of the clerical mind.

Now, the Rev. Amos Barton was one of those men who have a decided will and opinion of their own; he held himself bolt upright, and had no self-distrust. He would march very determinedly along the road he thought best; but then it was wonderfully easy to convince him which *was* the best road. And so a very little unwonted reading and unwonted discussion made him see that an Episcopalian Establishment was much more than unobjectionable, and on many other points he began to feel that he held opinions a little too far-sighted and profound to be crudely and suddenly communicated to ordinary minds. He was like an onion that has been rubbed with spices; the strong original odour was blended with something new and foreign. The Low-Church onion still offended refined High-Church nostrils, and the new spice was unwelcome to the palate of the genuine onion-eater.

We will not accompany him to the Clerical Meeting to-day, because we shall probably want to go thither some day when he will be absent. And just now I am bent on introducing you to Mr Bridmain and the Countess Czerlaski, with whom Mr and Mrs Barton are invited to dine to-morrow.

CHAPTER 3

Outside, the moon is shedding its cold light on the cold snow, and the white-bearded fir-trees round Camp Villa are casting a blue shadow across the white ground, while the Rev. Amos Barton and his wife are audibly crushing the crisp snow beneath their feet, as, about seven o'clock on Friday evening, they approach the door of the above-named desirable country residence, containing dining, breakfast, and drawing rooms, &c., situated only half a mile from the market-town of Milby.

Inside, there is a bright fire in the drawing-room, casting a pleasant but uncertain light on the delicate silk dress of a lady who is reclining behind a screen in the corner of the sofa, and allowing you to discern that the hair of the gentleman who is seated in the arm-chair opposite, with a newspaper over his knees, is becoming decidedly grey. A little 'King Charles,' with a crimson ribbon round his neck, who has been lying curled up in the very middle of the hearth-rug, has just discovered that that zone is too hot for him, and is jumping on the sofa, evidently with the

46

intention of accommodating his person on the silk gown. On the table there are two wax-candles, which will be lighted as soon as the expected knock is heard at the door.

The knock is heard, the candles are lighted, and presently Mr and Mrs Barton are ushered in – Mr Barton erect and clerical, in a faultless tie and shining cranium; Mrs Barton graceful in a newly-turned black silk.

'Now this is charming of you,' said the Countess Czerlaski, advancing to meet them, and embracing Milly with careful elegance. 'I am really ashamed of my selfishness in asking my friends to come and see me in this frightful weather.' Then, giving her hand to Amos, 'And you, Mr Barton, whose time is so precious! But I am doing a good deed in drawing you away from your labours. I have a plot to prevent you from martyrizing yourself.'

While this greeting was going forward, Mr Bridmain, and Jet the spaniel, looked on with the air of actors who had no idea of by-play. Mr Bridmain, a stiff and rather thick-set man, gave his welcome with a laboured cordiality. It was astonishing how very little he resembled his beautiful sister.

For the Countess Czerlaski was undeniably beautiful. As she seated herself by Mrs Barton on the sofa, Milly's eyes, indeed, rested – must it be confessed? – chiefly on the details of the tasteful dress, the rich silk of a pinkish lilac hue (the Countess always wore delicate colours in an evening), the black lace pelerine, and the black lace veil falling at the back of the small closely-braided head. For Milly had one weakness – don't love her any the less for it, it was a pretty woman's weakness – she was fond of dress; and often when she was making up her own economical millinery, she had romantic visions how nice it would be to put on really handsome stylish things – to have very stiff balloon sleeves, for example, without which a woman's dress was nought in those days. You and I, too, reader, have our weakness, have we not? which makes us think foolish things now and then. Perhaps it may lie in an excessive admiration for small hands and feet, a tall lithe figure, large dark eyes, and dark silken braided hair. All these the Countess possessed, and she had, more-over, a delicately-formed nose, the least bit curved, and a clear brunette complexion. Her mouth, it must be admitted, receded too much from her nose and chin, and to a prophetic eye threatened 'nut-crackers' in advanced age. But by the light of fire and wax-candles that age seemed very far off indeed, and you would have said that the Countess was not more than thirty.

Look at the two women on the sofa together! The large, fair, mildeyed Milly is timid even in friendship: it is not easy to her to speak of the affection of which her heart is full. The lithe, dark, thin-lipped Countess is racking her small brain for caressing words and charming exaggerations.

'And how are all the cherubs at home?' said the

Countess, stooping to pick up Jet, and without waiting for an answer. 'I have been kept indoors by a cold ever since Sunday, or I should not have rested without seeing you. What have you done with those wretched singers, Mr Barton?'

'O, we have got a new choir together, which will go on very well with a little practice. I was quite determined that the old set of singers should be dismissed. I had given orders that they should not sing the wedding psalm, as they call it, again, to make a new-married couple look ridiculous, and they sang it in defiance of me. I could put them into the Ecclesiastical Court, if I chose for to do so, for lifting up their voices in church in opposition to the clergyman.'

'And a most wholesome discipline that would be,' said the Countess; 'indeed, you are too patient and forbearing, Mr Barton. For my part, *I* lose *my* temper when I see how far you are from being appreciated in that miserable Shepperton.'

If, as is probable, Mr Barton felt at a loss what to say in reply to the insinuated compliment, it was a relief to him that dinner was announced just then, and that he had to offer his arm to the Countess.

As Mr Bridmain was leading Mrs Barton to the dining-room, he observed, 'The weather is very severe.'

'Very, indeed,' said Milly.

Mr Bridmain studied conversation as an art. To ladies he spoke of the weather, and was accustomed to consider it under three points of view:

as a question of climate in general, comparing England with other countries in this respect; as a personal question, inquiring how it affected his lady interlocutor in particular; and as a question of probabilities, discussing whether there would be a change or a continuance of the present atmospheric conditions. To gentlemen he talked politics, and he read two daily papers expressly to qualify himself for this function. Mr Barton thought him a man of considerable political information, but not of lively parts.

'And so you are always to hold your Clerical Meetings at Mr Ely's?' said the Countess between her spoonfuls of soup. (The soup was a little over-spiced. Mrs Short, of Camp Villa, who was in the habit of letting her best apartments, gave only moderate wages to her cook.)

'Yes,' said Mr Barton, 'Milby is a central place, and there are many conveniences in having only one point of meeting.'

'Well,' continued the Countess, 'every one seems to agree in giving the precedence to Mr Ely. For my part I *cannot* admire him. His preaching is too cold for me. It has no fervour – no heart. I often say to my brother, it is a great comfort to me that Shepperton church is not too far off for us to go to; don't I, Edmund?'

'Yes,' answered Mr Bridmain, 'they show us into such a bad pew at Milby – just where there is a draught from that door. I caught a stiff neck the first time I went there.'

'O, it is the cold in the pulpit that affects me, not the cold in the pew. I was writing to my friend Lady Porter this morning, and telling her all about my feelings. She and I think alike on such matters. She is most anxious that when Sir William has an opportunity of giving away the living at their place, Dippley, they should have a thoroughly zealous clever man there. I have been describing a certain friend of mine to her, who, I think, would be just to her mind. And there is such a pretty rectory, Milly; shouldn't I like to see you the mistress of it?'

Milly smiled and blushed slightly. The Rev. Amos blushed very red, and gave a little embarrassed laugh – he could rarely keep his muscles within the limits of a smile.

At this moment John, the man-servant, approached Mrs Barton with a gravy-tureen, and also with a slight odour of the stable, which usually adhered to him throughout his in-door functions. John was rather nervous; and the Countess happening to speak to him at this inopportune moment, the tureen slipped and emptied itself on Mrs Barton's newly-turned black silk.

'O, horror! Tell Alice to come directly and rub Mrs Barton's dress,' said the Countess to the trembling John, carefully abstaining from approaching the gravy-sprinkled spot on the floor with her own lilac silk. But Mr Bridmain, who had a strictly private interest in silks, good-naturedly jumped up and applied his napkin at once to Mrs Barton's gown.

Milly felt a little inward anguish, but no ill-temper, and tried to make light of the matter for the sake of John as well as others. The Countess felt inwardly thankful that her own delicate silk had escaped, but threw out lavish interjections of distress and indignation.

'Dear saint that you are,' she said, when Milly laughed, and suggested that, as her silk was not very glossy to begin with, the dim patch would not be much seen; 'you don't mind about these things, I know. Just the same sort of thing happened to me at the Princess Wengstein's one day, on a pink satin. I was in an agony. But you are so indifferent to dress; and well you may be. It is you who make dress pretty, and not dress that makes you pretty.'

Alice, the buxom lady's-maid, wearing a much better dress than Mrs Barton's, now appeared to take Mr Bridmain's place in retrieving the mischief, and after a great amount of supplementary rubbing, composure was restored, and the business of dining was continued.

When John was recounting his accident to the cook in the kitchen, he observed, 'Mrs Barton's a hamable woman; I'd a deal sooner ha' throwed the gravy o'er the Countess's fine gownd. But laws! what tantrums she'd ha' been in arter the visitors was gone.'

'You'd a deal sooner not ha' throwed it down at all, *I* should think,' responded the unsympathetic cook, to whom John did *not* make love. 'Who d'you think's to mek gravy anuff, if you're to baste people's gownds wi' it?'

'Well,' suggested John, humbly, 'you should wet the bottom of the *duree* a bit, to hold it from slippin'.'

'Wet your granny!' returned the cook; a retort which she probably regarded in the light of a *reductio ad absurdum*, and which in fact reduced John to silence.

Later on in the evening, while John was removing the tea-things from the drawing-room, and brushing the crumbs from the table-cloth with an accompanying hiss, such as he was wont to encourage himself with in rubbing down Mr Bridmain's horse, the Rev. Amos Barton drew from his pocket a thin green-covered pamphlet, and, presenting it to the Countess, said,—

'You were pleased, I think, with my sermon on Christmas Day. It has been printed in *The Pulpit*, and I thought you might like a copy.'

'That indeed I shall. I shall quite value the opportunity of reading that sermon. There was such depth in it! – such argument! It was not a sermon to be heard only once. I am delighted that it should become generally known, as it will be, now it is printed in *The Pulpit*.'

'Yes,' said Milly innocently, 'I was so pleased with the editor's letter.' And she drew out her little pocket-book, where she carefully treasured the editorial autograph, while Mr Barton laughed and blushed, and said, 'Nonsense, Milly!'

'You see,' she said, giving the letter to the Countess, 'I am very proud of the praise my husband gets.'

The sermon in question, by the by, was an extremely argumentative one on the Incarnation; which, as it was preached to a congregation not one of whom had any doubt of that doctrine, and to whom the Socinians therein confuted were as unknown as the Arimaspians, was exceedingly well adapted to trouble and confuse the Sheppertonian mind.

'Ah,' said the Countess, returning the editor's letter, 'he may well say he will be glad of other sermons from the same source. But I would rather you should publish your sermons in an independent volume, Mr Barton; it would be so desirable to have them in that shape. For instance, I could send a copy to the Dean of Radborough. And there is Lord Blarney, whom I knew before he was chancellor. I was a special favourite of his, and you can't think what sweet things he used to say to me. I shall not resist the temptation to write to him one of these days *sans façon*, and tell him how he ought to dispose of the next vacant living in his gift.'

Whether Jet the spaniel, being a much more knowing dog than was suspected, wished to express his disapproval of the Countess's last speech, as not accordant with his ideas of wisdom and veracity, I cannot say; but at this moment he jumped off her lap, and turning his back upon her, placed one paw on the fender, and held the other up to warm, as if affecting to abstract himself from the current of conversation.

But now Mr Bridmain brought out the chess-board, and Mr Barton accepted his challenge to play a game, with immense satisfaction. The Rev. Amos was very fond of chess, as most people are who can continue through many years to create interesting vicissitudes in the game, by taking long-meditated moves with their knights, and subsequently discovering that they have thereby exposed their queen.

Chess is a silent game; and the Countess's chat with Milly is in quite an under-tone – probably relating to women's matters that it would be impertinent for us to listen to; so we will leave Camp Villa, and proceed to Milby Vicarage, where Mr Farquhar has sat out two other guests with whom he has been dining at Mr Ely's, and is now rather wearying that reverend gentleman by his protracted small-talk.

Mr Ely was a tall, dark-haired, distinguished-looking man of three-and-thirty. By the laity of Milby and its neighbourhood he was regarded as a man of quite remarkable powers and learning, who must make a considerable sensation in London pulpits and drawing-rooms on his occasional visits to the metropolis; and by his brother clergy he was regarded as a discreet and agreeable fellow. Mr Ely never got into a warm discussion; he suggested what might be thought, but rarely said what he thought himself; he never let either men or women see that he was laughing at them, and he never gave any one an opportunity of laughing at *him*. In one thing only he was injudicious. He parted his dark wavy hair down the middle; and as his head was rather flat than otherwise, that style of coiffure was not advantageous to him.

Mr Farquhar, though not a parishioner of Mr Ely's, was one of his warmest admirers, and thought he would make an unexceptionable son-in-law, in spite of his being of no particular 'family.' Mr Farquhar was susceptible on the point of 'blood,' – his own circulating fluid, which animated a short and somewhat flabby person, being, he considered, of very superior quality.

'By the by,' he said, with a certain pomposity counteracted by a lisp, 'what an ath Barton makth of himthelf, about that Bridmain and the Counteth, ath she callth herthelf. After you were gone the other evening, Mithith Farquhar wath telling him the general opinion about them in the neighbourhood, and he got quite red and angry. Bleth your thoul, he believth the whole thtory about her Polish huthband and hith wonderful ethcapeth; and ath for her – why, he thinkth her perfection, a woman of motht refined feelingth, and no end of thtuff.'

Mr Ely smiled. 'Some people would say our friend Barton was not the best judge of refinement. Perhaps the lady flatters him a little, and we men are susceptible. She goes to Shepperton church every Sunday – drawn there, let us suppose, by Mr Barton's eloquence.'

'Pshaw,' said Mr Farquhar: 'Now, to my mind, you have only to look at that woman to thee what she ith – throwing her eyth about when she comth into church, and drething in a way to attract attention. I should thay, she'th tired of her brother Bridmain, and looking out for another brother with a thtronger family likeneth. Mithith Farquhar ith very fond of Mithith Barton, and ith quite dithtrethed that she should athothiate with thuch a woman, tho she attacked him on the thubject purpothly. But I tell her it'th of no uthe, with a pig-headed fellow like him. Barton'th well-meaning enough, but *tho* contheited. I've left off giving him my advithe.'

Mr Ely smiled inwardly and said to himself, 'What a punishment!' But to Mr Farquhar he said, 'Barton might be more judicious, it must be confessed.' He was getting tired, and did not want to develop the subject.

'Why, nobody vithit-th them but the Bartonth,' continued Mr Farquhar, 'and why should thuch people come here, unleth they had particular reathonth for preferring a neighbourhood where they are not known? Pooh! it lookth bad on the very fathe of it. *You* called on them, now; how did you find them?'

'O! – Mr Bridmain strikes me as a common sort of man, who is making an effort to seem wise and well-bred. He comes down on one tremendously with political information, and seems knowing about the king of the French. The Countess is certainly a handsome woman, but she puts on the grand air a little too powerfully. Woodcock was immensely taken with her, and insisted on his wife's calling on her, and asking her to dinner; but I think Mrs Woodcock turned restive after the first visit, and wouldn't invite her again.'

'Ha, ha! Woodcock hath alwayth a thoft place in hith heart for a pretty fathe. It'th odd how he came to marry that plain woman, and no fortune either.'

'Mysteries of the tender passion,' said Mr Ely. 'I am not initiated yet, you know.'

Here Mr Farquhar's carriage was announced, and as we have not found his conversation particularly brilliant under the stimulus of Mr Ely's exceptional presence, we will not accompany him home to the less exciting atmosphere of domestic life.

Mr Ely threw himself with a sense of relief into his easiest chair, set his feet on the hobs, and in this attitude of bachelor enjoyment began to read Bishop Jebb's Memoirs.

CHAPTER 4

I am by no means sure that if the good people of Milby had known the truth about the Countess Czerlaski, they would not have been considerably disappointed to find that it was very far from being as bad as they imagined. Nice distinctions are troublesome. It is so much easier to say that a thing is black, than to discriminate the particular shade of brown, blue, or green, to which it really belongs. It is so much easier to make up your mind that your neighbour is good for nothing, than to enter into all the circumstances that would oblige you to modify that opinion.

Besides, think of all the virtuous declamation, all the penetrating observation, which had been built up entirely on the fundamental position that the Countess was a very objectionable person indeed, and which would be utterly overturned and nullified by the destruction of that premise. Mrs Phipps, the banker's wife, and Mrs Landor, the attorney's wife, had invested part of their reputation for acuteness in the supposition that Mr Bridmain was not the Countess's brother. Moreover, Miss Phipps was conscious that if the

Countess was not a disreputable person, she, Miss Phipps, had no compensating superiority in virtue to set against the other lady's manifest superiority in personal charms. Miss Phipps's stumpy figure and unsuccessful attire, instead of looking down from a mount of virtue with an auréole round its head, would then be seen on the same level and in the same light as the Countess Czerlaski's Diana-like form and well-chosen drapery. Miss Phipps, for her part, didn't like dressing for effect – she had always avoided that style of appearance which was calculated to create a sensation.

Then what amusing innuendoes of the Milby gentlemen over their wine would be entirely frustrated and reduced to nought, if you had told them that the Countess had really been guilty of no misdemeanours which need exclude her from strictly respectable society; that her husband had been the veritable Count Czerlaski, who had had wonderful escapes, as she said, and who, as she did *not* say, but as was said in certain circulars once folded by her fair hands, had subsequently given dancing lessons in the metropolis; that Mr Bridmain was neither more nor less than her half-brother, who, by unimpeached integrity and industry, had won a partnership in a silk manufactory, and thereby a moderate fortune, that enabled him to retire, as you see, to study politics, the weather, and the art of conversation, at his leisure. Mr Bridmain, in fact, quadragenarian bachelor as he was, felt extremely well pleased to receive his sister in her widowhood, and to shine in the reflected light of her beauty and title. Every man who is not a monster, a mathematician, or a mad philosopher, is the slave of some woman or other. Mr Bridmain had put his neck under the yoke of his handsome sister, and though his soul was a very little one – of the smallest description indeed – he would not have ventured to call it his own. He might be slightly recalcitrant now and then, as is the habit of long-eared pachyderms, under the thong of the fair Countess's tongue; but there seemed little probability that he would ever get his neck loose. Still, a bachelor's heart is an outlying fortress that some fair enemy may any day take either by storm or stratagem; and there was always the possibility that Mr Bridmain's first nuptials might occur before the Countess was quite sure of her second. As it was, however, he submitted to all his sister's caprices, never grumbled because her dress and her maid formed a considerable item beyond her own little income of sixty pounds per annum, and consented to lead with her a migratory life, as personages on the debatable ground between aristocracy and commonalty, instead of settling in some spot where his five hundred a-year might have won him the definite dignity of a parochial magnate.

The Countess had her views in choosing a quiet provincial place like Milby. After three years of widowhood, she had brought her feelings to contemplate giving a successor to her lamented

Czerlaski, whose fine whiskers, fine air, and romantic fortunes had won her heart ten years ago, when, as pretty Caroline Bridmain, in the full bloom of five-and-twenty, she was governess to Lady Porter's daughters, whom he initiated into the mysteries of the *pas de basque*, and the lancer's quadrilles. She had had seven years of sufficiently happy matrimony with Czerlaski, who had taken her to Paris and Germany, and introduced her there to many of his old friends with large titles and small fortunes. So that the fair Caroline had had considerable experience of life, and had gathered therefrom, not, indeed, any very ripe and comprehensive wisdom, but much external polish, and certain practical conclusions of a very decided kind. One of these conclusions was, that there were things more solid in life than fine whiskers and a title, and that, in accepting a second husband, she would regard these items as quite subordinate to a carriage and a settlement. Now she had ascertained, by tentative residences, that the kind of bite she was angling for was difficult to be met with at watering-places, which were already preoccupied with abundance of angling beauties, and were chiefly stocked with men whose whiskers might be dyed, and whose incomes were still more problematic; so she had determined on trying a neighbourhood where people were extremely well acquainted with each other's affairs, and where the women were mostly ill-dressed and ugly. Mr Bridmain's slow brain had adopted his sister's views, and it seemed to him that a woman so handsome and distinguished as the Countess must certainly make a match that might lift himself into the region of county celebrities, and give him at least a sort of cousinship to the quarter-sessions.

All this, which was the simple truth, would have seemed extremely flat to the gossips of Milby, who had made up their minds to something much more exciting. There was nothing here so very detestable. It is true, the Countess was a little vain, a little ambitious, a little selfish, a little shallow and frivolous, a little given to white lies. But who considers such slight blemishes, such moral pimples as these, disqualifications for entering into the most respectable society! Indeed, the severest ladies in Milby would have been perfectly aware that these characteristics would have created no wide distinction between the Countess Czerlaski and themselves; and since it was clear there *was* a wide distinction – why, it must lie in the possession of some vices from which they were undeniably free.

Hence it came to pass, that Milby respectability refused to recognize the Countess Czerlaski, in spite of her assiduous church-going, and the deep disgust she was known to have expressed at the extreme paucity of the congregations on Ash-Wednesdays. So she began to feel that she had miscalculated the advantages of a neighbourhood where people are well acquainted with each other's private affairs. Under these circumstances, you will imagine how welcome was the perfect credence and admiration she met with from Mr and Mrs Barton. She had been especially irritated by Mr Ely's behaviour to her; she felt sure that he was not in the least struck with her beauty, that he quizzed her conversation, and that he spoke of her with a sneer. A woman always knows where she is utterly powerless, and shuns a coldly satirical eye as she would shun a gorgon. And she was especially eager for clerical notice and friendship, not merely because that is quite the most respectable countenance to be obtained in society, but because she really cared about religious matters, and had an uneasy sense that she was not altogether safe in that quarter. She had serious intentions of becoming *quite* pious – without any reserves – when she had once got her carriage and settlement. Let us do this one sly trick, says Ulysses to Neoptolemus, and we will be perfectly honest ever after—

ἀλλ' ἡδὺ γάρ τοι κτῆμα τῆς νίκης λαξειν
τόλμα· δίκαιοι δ' αὖθις ἐκφανούμεθα.

The Countess did not quote Sophocles, but she said to herself, 'Only this little bit of pretence and vanity, and then I will be *quite* good, and make myself quite safe for another world.'

And as she had by no means such fine taste and insight in theological teaching as in costume, the Rev. Amos Barton seemed to her a man not only of learning – *that* is always understood with a clergyman – but of much power as a spiritual director. As for Milly, the Countess really loved her as well as the preoccupied state of her affections would allow. For you have already perceived that there was one being to whom the Countess was absorbingly devoted, and to whose desires she made everything else subservient – namely, Caroline Czerlaski, *née* Bridmain.

Thus there was really not much affectation in her sweet speeches and attentions to Mr and Mrs Barton. Still, their friendship by no means adequately represented the object she had in view when she came to Milby, and it had been for some time clear to her that she must suggest a new change of residence to her brother.

The thing we look forward to often comes to pass, but never precisely in the way we have imagined to ourselves. The Countess did actually leave Camp Villa before many months were past, but under circumstances which had not at all entered into her contemplation.

CHAPTER 5

The Rev. Amos Barton, whose sad fortunes I have undertaken to relate, was, you perceive, in no respect an ideal or exceptional character, and perhaps I am doing a bold thing to bespeak your sympathy on behalf of a man who was so very far from remarkable, – a man whose virtues were not heroic, and who had no undetected crime within his breast; who had not the slightest mystery hanging about him, but was palpably and unmistakably commonplace; who was not even in love, but had had that complaint favourably many years ago. 'An utterly uninteresting character!' I think I hear a lady reader exclaim – Mrs Farthingale, for example, who prefers the ideal in fiction; to whom tragedy means ermine tippets, adultery, and murder; and comedy, the adventures of some personage who is quite a 'character.'

But, my dear madam, it is so very large a majority of your fellow-countrymen that are of this insignificant stamp. At least eighty out of a hundred of your adult male fellow-Britons returned in the last census, are neither extraordinarily silly, nor extraordinarily wicked, nor extraordinarily wise; their eyes are neither deep and liquid with sentiment, nor sparkling with suppressed witticisms; they have probably had no hairbreadth escapes or thrilling adventures; their brains are certainly not pregnant with genius, and their passions have not manifested themselves at all after the fashion of a volcano. They are simply men of complexions more or less muddy, whose conversation is more or less bald and disjointed. Yet these commonplace people – many of them – bear a conscience, and have felt the sublime prompting to do the painful right; they have their unspoken sorrows, and their sacred joys; their hearts have perhaps gone out towards their first-born, and they have mourned over the irreclaimable dead. Nay, is there not a pathos in their very insignificance, – in our comparison of their dim and narrow existence with the glorious possibilities of that human nature which they share?

Depend upon it, you would gain unspeakably if you would learn with me to see some of the poetry and the pathos, the tragedy and the comedy, lying in the experience of a human soul that looks out through dull grey eyes, and that speaks in a voice of quite ordinary tones. In that case, I should have no fear of your not caring to know what farther befell the Rev. Amos Barton, or of your thinking the homely details I have to tell at all beneath your attention. As it is, you can, if you please, decline to pursue my story farther; and you will easily find reading more to your taste, since I learn from the newspapers that many remarkable novels, full of striking situations, thrilling incidents, and eloquent writing, have appeared only within the last season.

Meanwhile, readers who have begun to feel an interest in the Rev. Amos Barton and his wife, will be glad to learn that Mr Oldinport lent the twenty pounds. But twenty pounds are soon exhausted when twelve are due as back payment to the butcher, and when the possession of eight extra sovereigns in February weather is an irresistible temptation to order a new greatcoat. And though Mr Bridmain so far departed from the necessary economy entailed on him by the Countess's elegant toilette and expensive maid, as to choose a handsome black silk, stiff, as his experienced eye discerned, with the genuine strength of its own texture, and not with the factitious strength of gum, and present it to Mrs Barton, in retrieval of the accident that had occurred at his table, yet, dear me – as every husband has heard – what is the present of a gown, when you are deficiently furnished with the et-ceteras of apparel, and when, moreover, there are six children whose wear and tear of clothes is something incredible to the non-maternal mind?

Indeed, the equation of income and expenditure was offering new and constantly accumulating difficulties to Mr and Mrs Barton; for shortly after the birth of little Walter, Milly's aunt, who had lived with her ever since her marriage, had withdrawn herself, her furniture, and her yearly income, to the household of another niece; prompted to that step, very probably, by a slight 'tiff' with the Rev. Amos, which occurred while Milly was up-stairs, and proved one too many for the elderly lady's patience and magnanimity. Mr Barton's temper was a little warm, but, on the other hand, elderly maiden ladies are known to be susceptible; so we will not suppose that all the blame lay on his side – the less so, as he had every motive for humouring an inmate whose presence kept the wolf from the door. It was now nearly a year since Miss Jackson's departure, and, to a fine ear, the howl of the wolf was audibly approaching.

It was a sad thing, too, that when the last snow had melted, when the purple and yellow crocuses were coming up in the garden, and the old church was already half pulled down, Milly had an illness which made her lips look pale, and rendered it absolutely necessary that she should not exert herself for some time. Mr Brand, the Shepperton doctor so obnoxious to Mr Pilgrim, ordered her to drink port-wine, and it was quite necessary to have a charwoman very often, to assist Nanny in all the extra work that fell upon her.

Mrs Hackit, who hardly ever paid a visit to any one but her oldest and nearest neighbour, Mrs Patten, now took the unusual step of calling at the vicarage one morning; and the tears came into her unsentimental eyes as she saw Milly seated pale and feeble in the parlour, unable to persevere in sewing the pinafore that lay on the table beside her. Little Dickey, a boisterous boy of five, with large pink cheeks and sturdy legs, was having his turn to sit with Mamma, and was squatting quiet as a mouse at her knee, holding her soft white hand between his little red, black-nailed fists. He was a boy whom Mrs Hackit, in a severe mood, had pronounced 'stocky' (a word that etymologically, in all probability, conveys some allusion to an instrument of punishment for the refractory); but seeing him thus subdued into goodness, she smiled at him with her kindest smile, and, stooping down, suggested a kiss – a favour which Dickey resolutely declined.

'Now *do* you take nourishing things anuff?' was one of Mrs Hackit's first questions, and Milly endeavoured to make it appear that no woman was ever so much in danger of being over-fed and led into self-indulgent habits as herself. But Mrs Hackit gathered one fact from her replies, namely, that Mr Brand had ordered port-wine.

While this conversation was going forward, Dickey had been furtively stroking and kissing the soft white hand; so that at last, when a pause came, his mother said, smilingly, 'Why are you kissing my hand, Dickey?'

'It id to yovely,' answered Dickey, who, you observe, was decidedly backward in his pronunciation.

Mrs Hackit remembered this little scene in after

days, and thought with peculiar tenderness and pity of the 'stocky boy.'

The next day there came a hamper with Mrs Hackit's respects; and on being opened, it was found to contain half-a-dozen of port-wine and two couples of fowls. Mrs Farquhar, too, was very kind; insisted on Mrs Barton's rejecting all arrow-root but hers, which was genuine Indian, and carried away Sophy and Fred to stay with her a fortnight. These and other good-natured attentions made the trouble of Milly's illness more bearable; but they could not prevent it from swelling expenses, and Mr Barton began to have serious thoughts of representing his case to a certain charity for the relief of needy curates.

Altogether, as matters stood in Shepperton, the parishioners were more likely to have a strong sense that the clergyman needed their material aid, than that they needed his spiritual aid, – not the best state of things in this age and country, where faith in men solely on the ground of their spiritual gifts has considerably diminished, and especially unfavourable to the influence of the Rev. Amos, whose spiritual gifts would not have had a very commanding power even in an age of faith.

But, you ask, did not the Countess Czerlaski pay any attention to her friends all this time? To be sure she did. She was indefatigable in visiting her 'sweet Milly,' and sitting with her for hours together; and it may seem remarkable to you that she neither thought of taking away any of the

71

children, nor of providing for any of Milly's probable wants; but ladies of rank and of luxurious habits, you know, cannot be expected to surmise the details of poverty. She put a great deal of eau-de-Cologne on Mrs Barton's pocket-handkerchief, rearranged her pillow and footstool, kissed her cheeks, wrapped her in a soft warm shawl from her own shoulders, and amused her with stories of the life she had seen abroad. When Mr Barton joined them, she talked of Tractarianism, of her determination not to re-enter the vortex of fashionable life, and of her anxiety to see him in a sphere large enough for his talents. Milly thought her sprightliness and affectionate warmth quite charming, and was very fond of her; while the Rev. Amos had a vague consciousness that he had risen into aristocratic life, and only associated with his middle-class parishioners in a pastoral and parenthetic manner.

However, as the days brightened, Milly's cheeks and lips brightened too; and in a few weeks she was almost as active as ever, though watchful eyes might have seen that activity was not easy to her. Mrs Hackit's eyes were of that kind, and one day when Mr and Mrs Barton had been dining with her for the first time since Milly's illness, she observed to her husband – 'That poor thing's dreadful weak an' dilicate; she won't stan' havin' many more children.'

Mr Barton, meanwhile, had been indefatigable in his vocation. He had preached two extemporary sermons every Sunday at the work-house, where a room had been fitted up for divine service, pending the alterations in the church; and had walked the same evening to a cottage at one or other extremity of his parish to deliver another sermon, still more extemporary, in an atmosphere impregnated with spring-flowers and perspiration. After all these labours you will easily conceive that he was considerably exhausted by half-past nine o'clock in the evening, and that a supper at a friendly parishioner's, with a glass, or even two glasses, of brandy-and-water after it, was a welcome reinforcement. Mr Barton was not at all an ascetic: he thought the benefits of fasting were entirely confined to the Old Testament dispensation; he was fond of relaxing himself with a little gossip; indeed, Miss Bond, and other ladies of enthusiastic views, sometimes regretted that Mr Barton did not more uninterruptedly exhibit a superiority to the things of the flesh. Thin ladies, who take little exercise, and whose livers are not strong enough to bear stimulants, are so extremely critical about one's personal habits! And, after all, the Rev. Amos never came near the borders of a vice. His very faults were middling – he was not *very* ungrammatical. It was not in his nature to be superlative in anything; unless, indeed, he was superlatively middling, the quintessential extract of mediocrity. If there was any one point on which he showed an inclination to be excessive, it was confidence in his own shrewdness and ability in practical matters, so that he was very full of plans which were something like his moves in chess – admirably well calculated, supposing the state of the case were otherwise. For example, that notable plan of introducing anti-Dissenting books into his Lending Library did not in the least appear to have bruised the head of Dissent, though it had certainly made Dissent strongly inclined to bite the Rev. Amos's heel. Again, he vexed the souls of his church-wardens and influential parishioners by his fertile suggestiveness as to what it would be well for them to do in the matter of the church repairs, and other ecclesiastical secularities.

'I never see the like to parsons,' Mr Hackit said one day in conversation with his brother church-warden, Mr Bond; 'they're al'ys for meddlin' wi' business, an' they know no moor about it than my black filly.'

'Ah,' said Mr Bond, 'they're too high learnt to have much common-sense.'

'Well,' remarked Mr Hackit, in a modest and dubious tone, as if throwing out a hypothesis which might be considered bold, 'I should say that's a bad sort o' eddication as makes folks onreasonable.'

So that, you perceive, Mr Barton's popularity was in that precarious condition, in that toppling and contingent state, in which a very slight push from a malignant destiny would utterly upset it. That push was not long in being given, as you shall hear.

One fine May morning, when Amos was out on his parochial visits, and the sunlight was streaming through the bow-window of the sitting-room, where Milly was seated at her sewing, occasionally looking up to glance at the children playing in the garden, there came a loud rap at the door, which she at once recognized as the Countess's, and that well-dressed lady presently entered the sitting-room, with her veil drawn over her face. Milly was not at all surprised or sorry to see her; but when the Countess threw up her veil, and showed that her eyes were red and swollen, she was both surprised and sorry.

'What can be the matter, dear Caroline?'

Caroline threw down Jet, who gave a little yelp; then she threw her arms round Milly's neck, and began to sob; then she threw herself on the sofa, and begged for a glass of water; then she threw off her bonnet and shawl; and, by the time Milly's imagination had exhausted itself in conjuring up calamities, she said,—

'Dear, how shall I tell you? I am the most wretched woman. To be deceived by a brother to whom I have been so devoted – to see him degrading himself – giving himself utterly to the dogs!'

'What can it be?' said Milly, who began to picture to herself the sober Mr Bridmain taking to brandy and betting.

'He is going to be married – to marry my own maid, that deceitful Alice, to whom I have been the most indulgent mistress. Did you ever hear of anything so disgraceful? so mortifying? so disreputable?'

'And has he only just told you of it?' said Milly, who, having really heard of worse conduct, even in her innocent life, avoided a direct answer.

'Told me of it! he had not even the grace to do that. I went into the dining-room suddenly and found him kissing her – disgusting at his time of life, is it not? – and when I reproved her for allowing such liberties, she turned round saucily, and said she was engaged to be married to my brother, and she saw no shame in allowing him to kiss her. Edmund is a miserable coward, you know, and looked frightened; but when she asked him to say whether it was not so, he tried to summon up courage and say yes. I left the room in disgust, and this morning I have been questioning Edmund, and find that he is bent on marrying this woman, and that he has been putting off telling me – because he was ashamed of himself, I suppose. I couldn't possibly stay in the house after this, with my own maid turned mistress. And now, Milly, I am come to throw myself on your charity for a week or two. *Will* you take me in?'

'That we will,' said Milly, 'if you will only put up with our poor rooms and way of living. It will be delightful to have you!'

'It will soothe me to be with you and Mr Barton a little while. I feel quite unable to go among my other friends just at present. What those two wretched people will do I don't know – leave the neighbourhood at once, I hope. I entreated my brother to do so, before he disgraced himself.'

When Amos came home, he joined his cordial welcome and sympathy to Milly's. By-and-by the Countess's formidable boxes, which she had carefully packed before her indignation drove her away from Camp Villa, arrived at the vicarage, and were deposited in the spare bedroom, and in two closets, not spare, which Milly emptied for their reception. A week afterwards, the excellent apartments at Camp Villa, comprising dining and drawing rooms, three bedrooms and a dressing-room, were again to let, and Mr Bridmain's sudden departure, together with the Countess Czerlaski's installation as a visitor at Shepperton Vicarage, became a topic of general conversation in the neighbourhood. The keen-sighted virtue of Milby and Shepperton saw in all this a confirmation of its worst suspicions, and pitied the Rev. Amos Barton's gullibility.

But when week after week, and month after month, slipped by without witnessing the Countess's departure – when summer and harvest had fled, and still left her behind them occupying the spare bedroom and the closets, and also a large proportion of Mrs Barton's time and attention, new surmises of a very evil kind were added to the old rumours, and began to take the form of settled convictions in the minds even of Mr Barton's most friendly parishioners.

And now, here is an opportunity for an

accomplished writer to apostrophize calumny, to quote Virgil, and to show that he is acquainted with the most ingenious things which have been said on that subject in polite literature.

But what is opportunity to the man who can't use it? An unfecundated egg, which the waves of time wash away into nonentity. So, as my memory is ill-furnished, and my note-book still worse, I am unable to show myself either erudite or eloquent apropos of the calumny whereof the Rev. Amos Barton was the victim. I can only ask my reader, did you ever upset your ink-bottle, and watch, in helpless agony, the rapid spread of Stygian blackness over your fair manuscript or fairer table-cover? With a like inky swiftness did gossip now blacken the reputation of the Rev. Amos Barton, causing the unfriendly to scorn and even the friendly to stand aloof, at a time when difficulties of another kind were fast thickening around him.

CHAPTER 6

One November morning, at least six months after the Countess Czerlaski had taken up her residence at the vicarage, Mrs Hackit heard that her neighbour Mrs Patten had an attack of her old complaint, vaguely called 'the spasms.' Accordingly, about eleven o'clock, she put on her velvet bonnet and cloth cloak, with a long boa and a muff large enough to stow a prize baby in; for Mrs Hackit regulated her costume by the calendar, and brought out her furs on the first of November, whatever might be the temperature. She was not a woman weakly to accommodate herself to shilly-shally proceedings. If the season didn't know what it ought to do, Mrs Hackit did. In her best days, it was always sharp weather at 'Gunpowder Plot,' and she didn't like new fashions.

And this morning the weather was very rationally in accordance with her costume, for as she made her way through the fields to Cross Farm, the yellow leaves on the hedge-girt elms, which showed bright and golden against the low-hanging purple clouds, were being scattered across the grassy path by the coldest of November winds.

'Ah,' Mrs Hackit thought to herself, 'I dare say we shall have a sharp pinch this winter, and if we do, I shouldn't wonder if it takes the old lady off. They say a green Yule makes a fat churchyard; but so does a white Yule too, for that matter. When the stool's rotten enough, no matter who sits on't.'

However, on her arrival at Cross Farm, the prospect of Mrs Patten's decease was again thrown into the dim distance in her imagination, for Miss Janet Gibbs met her with the news that Mrs Patten was much better, and led her, without any preliminary announcement, to the old lady's bedroom. Janet had scarcely reached the end of her circumstantial narrative how the attack came on and what were her aunt's sensations – a narrative to which Mrs Patten, in her neatly-plaited night-cap, seemed to listen with a contemptuous resignation to her niece's historical inaccuracy, contenting herself with occasionally confounding Janet by a shake of the head – when the clatter of a horse's hoofs on the yard pavement announced the arrival of Mr Pilgrim, whose large, top-booted person presently made its appearance up-stairs. He found Mrs Patten going on so well that there was no need to look solemn. He might glide from condolence into gossip without offence, and the temptation of having Mrs Hackit's ear was irresistible.

'What a disgraceful business this is turning out of your parson's,' was the remark with which he made this agreeable transition, throwing himself back in the chair from which he had been leaning towards the patient.

'Eh, dear me!' said Mrs Hackit, 'disgraceful enough. I stuck to Mr Barton as long as I could, for his wife's sake; but I can't countenance such goings on. It's hateful to see that woman coming with 'em to service of a Sunday, and if Mr Hackit wasn't churchwarden and I didn't think it wrong to forsake one's own parish, I should go to Knebley church. There's a many parish'ners as do.'

'I used to think Barton was only a fool,' observed Mr Pilgrim, in a tone which implied that he was conscious of having been weakly charitable. 'I thought he was imposed upon and led away by those people when they first came. But that's impossible now.'

'O, it's as plain as the nose in your face,' said Mrs Hackit, unreflectingly, not perceiving the equivoque in her comparison, – 'comin' to Milby, like a sparrow perchin' on a bough, as I may say, with her brother, as she called him; and then, all on a sudden, the brother goes off wi' himself, and she throws herself on the Bartons. Though what could make her take up wi' a poor notomise of a parson, as hasn't got enough to keep wife and children, there's one above knows – I don't.'

'Mr Barton may have attractions we don't know of,' said Mr Pilgrim, who piqued himself on a talent for sarcasm. 'The Countess has no maid now, and they say Mr Barton is handy in assisting at her toilette – laces her boots, and so forth.'

81

'Tilette, be fiddled!' said Mrs Hackit, with indignant boldness of metaphor; 'an' there's that poor thing a-sewing her fingers to the bone for them children – an' another comin' on. What she must have to go through! It goes to my heart to turn my back on her. But she's i' the wrong to let herself be put upon a' that manner.'

'Ah! I was talking to Mrs Farquhar about that the other day. She said, "I think Mrs Barton a v-e-r-y w-e-a-k w-o-m-a-n."' (Mr Pilgrim gave this quotation with slow emphasis, as if he thought Mrs Farquhar had uttered a remarkable sentiment.) 'They find it impossible to invite her to their house while she has that equivocal person staying with her.'

'Well!' remarked Miss Gibbs, 'if I was a wife, nothing should induce me to bear what Mrs Barton does.'

'Yes, it's fine talking,' said Mrs Patten, from her pillow; 'old maids' husbands are al'ys well-managed. If you was a wife you'd be as foolish as your betters, belike.'

'All my wonder is,' observed Mrs Hackit, 'how the Bartons make both ends meet. You may depend on't *she's* got nothing to give 'em; for I understand as he's been havin' money from some clergy charity. They said at fust as she stuffed Mr Barton wi' notions about her writing to the Chancellor an' her fine friends, to give him a living. Howiver, I don't know what's true an' what's false. Mr Barton keeps away from our house now, for I gev him a bit o' my mind one day. Maybe he's ashamed of himself. He seems to me to look dreadful thin an' harassed of a Sunday.'

'O, he must be aware he's getting into bad odour everywhere. The clergy are quite disgusted with his folly. They say Carpe would be glad to get Barton out of the curacy if he could; but he can't do that without coming to Shepperton himself, as Barton's a licensed curate; and he wouldn't like that, I suppose.'

At this moment Mrs Patten showed signs of uneasiness, which recalled Mr Pilgrim to professional attentions; and Mrs Hackit, observing that it was Thursday, and she must see after the butter, said good-bye, promising to look in again soon, and bring her knitting.

This Thursday, by the by, is the first in the month – the day on which the Clerical Meeting is held at Milby Vicarage; and as the Rev. Amos Barton has reasons for not attending, he will very likely be a subject of conversation amongst his clerical brethren. Suppose we go there, and hear whether Mr Pilgrim has reported their opinion correctly.

There is not a numerous party to-day, for it is a season of sore throats and catarrhs; so that the exegetical and theological discussions, which are the preliminary of dining, have not been quite so spirited as usual; and although a question relative to the Epistle of Jude has not been quite cleared up, the striking of six by the church clock, and the simultaneous announcement of dinner, are sounds that no one feels to be importunate.

Pleasant (when one is not in the least bilious) to enter a comfortable dining-room, where the closely-drawn red curtains glow with the double light of fire and candle, where glass and silver are glittering on the pure damask, and a soup-tureen gives a hint of the fragrance that will presently rush out to inundate your hungry senses, and prepare them, by the delicate visitation of atoms, for the keen gusto of ampler contact! Especially if you have confidence in the dinner-giving capacity of your host – if you know that he is not a man who entertains grovelling views of eating and drinking as a mere satisfaction of hunger and thirst, and, dead to all the finer influences of the palate, expects his guest to be brilliant on ill-flavoured gravies and the cheapest Marsala. Mr Ely was particularly worthy of such confidence, and his virtues as an Amphitryon had probably contributed quite as much as the central situation of Milby to the selection of his house as a clerical rendezvous. He looks particularly graceful at the head of his table, and, indeed, on all occasions where he acts as president or moderator – a man who seems to listen well, and is an excellent amalgam of dissimilar ingredients.

At the other end of the table, as 'Vice,' sits Mr Fellowes, rector and magistrate, a man of imposing appearance, with a mellifluous voice and the readiest of tongues. Mr Fellowes once obtained a living by the persuasive charms of his conversation, and the fluency with which he interpreted the opinions of an obese and stammering baronet, so as to give that elderly gentleman a very pleasing perception of his own wisdom. Mr Fellowes is a very successful man, and has the highest character everywhere except in his own parish, where, doubtless because his parishioners happen to be quarrelsome people, he is always at fierce feud with a farmer or two, a colliery proprietor, a grocer who was once churchwarden, and a tailor who formerly officiated as clerk.

At Mr Ely's right hand you see a very small man with a sallow and somewhat puffy face, whose hair is brushed straight up, evidently with the intention of giving him a height somewhat less disproportionate to his sense of his own importance than the measure of five feet three accorded him by an oversight of nature. This is the Rev. Archibald Duke, a very dyspeptic and evangelical man, who takes the gloomiest view of mankind and their prospects, and thinks the immense sale of the 'Pickwick Papers,'recently completed, one of the strongest proofs of original sin. Unfortunately, though Mr Duke was not burdened with a family, his yearly expenditure was apt considerably to exceed his income; and the unpleasant circumstances resulting from this, together with heavy meat breakfasts, may probably have contributed to his desponding views of the world generally.

Next to him is seated Mr Furness, a tall young

man, with blond hair and whiskers, who was plucked at Cambridge entirely owing to his genius; at least, I know that he soon afterwards published a volume of poems, which were considered remarkably beautiful by many young ladies of his acquaintance. Mr Furness preached his own sermons, as any one of tolerable critical acumen might have certified by comparing them with his poems: in both, there was an exuberance of metaphor and simile entirely original, and not in the least borrowed from any resemblance in the things compared.

On Mr Furness's left you see Mr Pugh, another young curate, of much less marked characteristics. He had not published any poems; he had not even been plucked; he had neat black whiskers and a pale complexion; read prayers and a sermon twice every Sunday, and might be seen any day sallying forth on his parochial duties in a white tie, a well-brushed hat, a perfect suit of black, and well-polished boots – an equipment which he probably supposed hieroglyphically to represent the spirit of Christianity to the parishioners of Whittlecombe.

Mr Pugh's *vis-à-vis* is the Rev. Martin Cleves, a man about forty – middle-sized, broad-shouldered, with a negligently-tied cravat, large irregular features, and a large head, thickly covered with lanky brown hair. To a superficial glance, Mr Cleves is the plainest and least clerical-looking of the party; yet, strange to say, *there* is the true parish priest, the pastor beloved, consulted, relied on by his flock; a clergyman who is not associated with the undertaker, but thought of as the surest helper under a difficulty, as a monitor who is encouraging rather than severe. Mr Cleves has the wonderful art of preaching sermons which the wheelwright and the blacksmith can understand; not because he talks condescending twaddle, but because he can call a spade a spade, and knows how to disencumber ideas of their wordy frippery. Look at him more attentively, and you will see that his face is a very interesting one – that there is a great deal of humour and feeling playing in his grey eyes, and about the corners of his roughly cut mouth: – a man, you observe, who has most likely sprung from the harder-working section of the middle class, and has hereditary sympathies with the chequered life of the people. He gets together the working men in his parish on a Monday evening, and gives them a sort of conversational lecture on useful practical matters, telling them stories, or reading some select passages from an agreeable book, and commenting on them; and if you were to ask the first labourer or artisan in Tripplegate what sort of man the parson was, he would say, – 'a uncommon knowin', sensable, free-spoken gentleman; very kind an' good-natur'd too.' Yet for all this, he is perhaps the best Grecian of the party, if we except Mr Baird, the young man on his left.

Mr Baird has since gained considerable celebrity as an original writer and metropolitan lecturer, but at that time he used to preach in a little church something like a barn, to a congregation consisting of three rich farmers and their servants, about fifteen labourers, and the due proportion of women and children. The rich farmers understood him to be 'very high learnt;' but if you had interrogated them for a more precise description, they would have said that he was 'a thinnish-faced man, with a sort o' cast in his eye, like.'

Seven, altogether: a delightful number for a dinner-party, supposing the units to be delightful, but everything depends on that. During dinner Mr Fellowes took the lead in the conversation, which set strongly in the direction of mangel-wurzel and the rotation of crops; for Mr Fellowes and Mr Cleves cultivated their own glebes. Mr Ely, too, had some agricultural notions, and even the Rev. Archibald Duke was made alive to that class of mundane subjects by the possession of some potato-ground. The two young curates talked a little aside during these discussions, which had imperfect interest for their unbeneficed minds; and the transcendental and near-sighted Mr Baird seemed to listen somewhat abstractedly, knowing little more of potatoes and mangel-wurzel than that they were some form of the 'Conditioned.'

'What a hobby farming is with Lord Watling!' said Mr Fellowes, when the cloth was being drawn. 'I went over his farm at Tetterley with him last summer. It is really a model farm; first-rate dairy, grazing and wheat land, and such splendid farm-buildings! An expensive hobby, though. He sinks a good deal of money there, I fancy. He has a great whim for black cattle, and he sends that drunken old Scotch bailiff of his to Scotland every year, with hundreds in his pocket, to buy these beasts.'

'By the by,' said Mr Ely, 'do you know who is the man to whom Lord Watling has given the Bramhill living?'

'A man named Sargent. I knew him at Oxford. His brother is a lawyer, and was very useful to Lord Watling in that ugly Brounsell affair. That's why Sargent got the living.'

'Sargent,' said Mr Ely. 'I know him. Isn't he a showy talkative fellow; has written travels in Mesopotamia, or something of that sort?'

'That's the man.'

'He was at Witherington once, as Bagshawe's curate. He got into rather bad odour there, through some scandal about a flirtation, I think.'

'Talking of scandal,' returned Mr Fellowes, 'have you heard the last story about Barton? Nisbett was telling me the other day that he dines alone with the Countess at six, while Mrs Barton is in the kitchen acting as cook.'

'Rather an apocryphal authority, Nisbett,' said Mr Ely.

'Ah,' said Mr Cleves, with good-natured humour twinkling in his eyes, 'depend upon it, that is a corrupt version. The original text is, that they all dined together *with* six – meaning six children – and that Mrs Barton is an excellent cook.'

'I wish dining alone together may be the worst of that sad business,' said the Rev. Archibald Duke, in a tone implying that his wish was a strong figure of speech.

'Well,' said Mr Fellowes, filling his glass and looking jocose, 'Barton is certainly either the greatest gull in existence, or he has some cunning secret, – some philtre or other to make himself charming in the eyes of a fair lady. It isn't all of us that can make conquests when our ugliness is past its bloom.'

'The lady seemed to have made a conquest of him at the very outset,' said Mr Ely. 'I was immensely amused one night at Granby's, when he was telling us her story about her husband's adventures. He said, 'When she told me the tale, I felt I don't know how, – I felt it from the crown of my head to the sole of my feet."

Mr Ely gave these words dramatically, imitating the Rev. Amos's fervour and symbolic action, and every one laughed except Mr Duke, whose after-dinner view of things was not apt to be jovial. He said, –

'I think some of us ought to remonstrate with Mr Barton on the scandal he is causing. He is not only imperilling his own soul, but the souls of his flock.'

'Depend upon it,' said Mr Cleves, 'there is some simple explanation of the whole affair, if we only happened to know it. Barton has always impressed me as a right-minded man, who has the knack of doing himself injustice by his manner.'

'Now *I* never liked Barton,' said Mr Fellowes. 'He's not a gentleman. Why, he used to be on terms of intimacy with that canting Prior, who died a little while ago; – a fellow who soaked himself with spirits, and talked of the Gospel through an inflamed nose.'

'The Countess has given him more refined tastes, I dare say,' said Mr Ely.

'Well,' observed Mr Cleves, 'the poor fellow must have a hard pull to get along, with his small income and large family. Let us hope the Countess does something towards making the pot boil.'

'Not she,' said Mr Duke; 'there are greater signs of poverty about them than ever.'

'Well, come,' returned Mr Cleves, who could be caustic sometimes, and who was not at all fond of his reverend brother, Mr Duke, 'that's something in Barton's favour at all events. He might be poor *without* showing signs of poverty.'

Mr Duke turned rather yellow, which was his way of blushing, and Mr Ely came to his relief by observing,—

'They're making a very good piece of work of Shepperton Church. Dolby, the architect, who has it in hand, is a very clever fellow.'

'It's he who has been doing Coppleton Church,' said Mr Furness. 'They've got it in excellent order for the visitation.'

This mention of the visitation suggested the Bishop, and thus opened a wide duct, which entirely diverted the stream of animadversion from that small pipe – that capillary vessel, the Rev. Amos Barton.

The talk of the clergy about their Bishop belongs to the esoteric part of their profession; so we will at once quit the dining-room at Milby Vicarage, lest we should happen to overhear remarks unsuited to the lay understanding, and perhaps dangerous to our repose of mind.

CHAPTER 7

I dare say the long residence of the Countess Czerlaski at Shepperton Vicarage is very puzzling to you also, dear reader, as well as to Mr Barton's clerical brethren; the more so, as I hope you are not in the least inclined to put that very evil interpretation on it which evidently found acceptance with the sallow and dyspeptic Mr Duke, and with the florid and highly peptic Mr Fellowes. You have seen enough, I trust, of the Rev. Amos Barton, to be convinced that he was more apt to fall into a blunder than into a sin – more apt to be deceived than to incur a necessity for being deceitful: and if you have a keen eye for physiognomy, you will have detected that the Countess Czerlaski loved herself far too well to get entangled in an unprofitable vice.

How, then, you will say, could this fine lady choose to quarter herself on the establishment of a poor curate, where the carpets were probably falling into holes, where the attendance was limited to a maid of all work, and where six children were running loose from eight o'clock in the morning till eight o'clock in the evening? Surely you must be misrepresenting the facts.

Heaven forbid! For not having a fertile imagination, as you perceive, and being unable to invent thrilling incidents for your amusement, my only merit must lie in the faithfulness with which I represent to you the humble experience of an ordinary fellow-mortal. I wish to stir your sympathy with commonplace troubles – to win your tears for real sorrow: sorrow such as may live next door to you – such as walks neither in rags nor in velvet, but in very ordinary decent apparel.

Therefore, that you may dismiss your suspicions of my veracity, I will beg you to consider, that at the time the Countess Czerlaski left Camp Villa in dudgeon, she had only twenty pounds in her pocket, being about one-third of the income she possessed independently of her brother. You will then perceive that she was in the extremely inconvenient predicament of having quarrelled, not indeed with her bread and cheese, but certainly with her chicken and tart – a predicament all the more inconvenient to her, because the habit of idleness had quite unfitted her for earning those necessary superfluities, and because, with all her fascinations, she had not secured any enthusiastic friends whose houses were open to her, and who were dying to see her. Thus she had completely checkmated herself, unless she could resolve on one unpleasant move – namely, to humble herself to her brother, and recognize his wife. This seemed

94

quite impossible to her as long as she entertained the hope that he would make the first advances; and in this flattering hope she remained month after month at Shepperton Vicarage, gracefully overlooking the deficiencies of accommodation, and feeling that she was really behaving charmingly. 'Who, indeed,' she thought to herself, 'could do otherwise, with a lovely, gentle creature like Milly? I shall really be sorry to leave the poor thing.'

So, though she lay in bed till ten, and came down to a separate breakfast at eleven, she kindly consented to dine as early as five, when a hot joint was prepared, which coldly furnished forth the children's table the next day; she considerately prevented Milly from devoting herself too closely to the children, by insisting on reading, talking, and walking with her; and she even began to embroider a cap for the next baby, which must certainly be a girl, and be named Caroline.

After the first month or two of her residence at the Vicarage, the Rev. Amos Barton became aware – as, indeed, it was unavoidable that he should – of the strong disapprobation it drew upon him, and the change of feeling towards him which it was producing in his kindest parishioners. But, in the first place, he still believed in the Countess as a charming and influential woman, disposed to befriend him, and, in any case, he could hardly hint departure to a lady guest who had been kind to him and his, and who might any day spontaneously announce the termination of her visit; in the second place, he was conscious of his own innocence, and felt some contemptuous indignation towards people who were ready to imagine evil of him; and, lastly, he had, as I have already intimated, a strong will of his own, so that a certain obstinacy and defiance mingled itself with his other feelings on the subject.

The one unpleasant consequence which was not to be evaded or counteracted by any mere mental state, was the increasing drain on his slender purse for household expenses, to meet which the remittance he had received from the clerical charity threatened to be quite inadequate. Slander may be defeated by equanimity; but courageous thoughts will not pay your baker's bill, and fortitude is nowhere considered legal tender for beef. Month after month the financial aspect of the Rev. Amos's affairs became more and more serious to him, and month after month, too, wore away more and more of that armour of indignation and defiance with which he had at first defended himself from the harsh looks of faces that were once the friendliest.

But quite the heaviest pressure of the trouble fell on Milly – on gentle, uncomplaining Milly – whose delicate body was becoming daily less fit for all the many things that had to be done between rising up and lying down. At first, she thought the Countess's visit would not last long, and she was quite glad to incur extra exertion for the sake of making her friend comfortable. I can hardly bear to think of all the rough work she did with those lovely hands – all by the sly, without letting her husband know anything about it, and husbands are not clairvoyant: how she salted bacon, ironed shirts and cravats, put patches on patches, and re-darned darns. Then there was the task of mending and eking out baby linen in prospect, and the problem perpetually suggesting itself how she and Nanny *should* manage when there was another baby, as there would be before very many months were past.

When time glided on, and the Countess's visit did not end, Milly was not blind to any phase of their position. She knew of the slander; she was aware of the keeping aloof of old friends; but these she felt almost entirely on her husband's account. A loving woman's world lies within the four walls of her own home; and it is only through her husband that she is in any electric communication with the world beyond. Mrs Simpkins may have looked scornfully at her, but baby crows and holds out his little arms none the less blithely; Mrs Tomkins may have left off calling on her, but her husband comes home none the less to receive her care and caresses; it has been wet and gloomy out of doors to-day, but she has looked well after the shirt buttons, has cut out baby's pinafores, and half finished Willy's blouse.

So it was with Milly. She was only vexed that her husband should be vexed – only wounded because he was misconceived. But the difficulty about ways and means she felt in quite a different manner. Her rectitude was alarmed lest they should have to make tradesmen wait for their money; her motherly love dreaded the diminution of comforts for the children; and the sense of her own failing health gave exaggerated force to these fears.

Milly could no longer shut her eyes to the fact, that the Countess was inconsiderate, if she did not allow herself to entertain severer thoughts; and she began to feel that it would soon be a duty to tell her frankly that they really could not afford to have her visit farther prolonged. But a process was going forward in two other minds, which ultimately saved Milly from having to perform this painful task.

In the first place, the Countess was getting weary of Shepperton – weary of waiting for her brother's overtures which never came; so, one fine morning, she reflected that forgiveness was a Christian duty, that a sister should be placable, that Mr Bridmain must feel the need of her advice, to which he had been accustomed for three years, and that very likely 'that woman' didn't make the poor man happy. In this amiable frame of mind she wrote a very affectionate appeal, and addressed it to Mr Bridmain, through his banker.

Another mind that was being wrought up to a climax was Nanny's, the maid-of-all-work, who had a warm heart and a still warmer temper.

Nanny adored her mistress: she had been heard to say, that she was 'ready to kiss the ground as the missis trod on;' and Walter, she considered, was *her* baby, of whom she was as jealous as a lover. But she had from the first very slight admiration for the Countess Czerlaski. That lady, from Nanny's point of view, was a personage always 'drawed out i' fine clothes,' the chief result of whose existence was to cause additional bed-making, carrying of hot water, laying of table-cloths and cooking of dinners. It was a perpetually heightening 'aggravation' to Nanny that she and her mistress had to 'slave' more than ever, because there was this fine lady in the house.

'An' she pays nothin' for't neither,' observed Nanny to Mr Jacob Tomms, a young gentleman in the tailoring line, who occasionally – simply out of a taste for dialogue – looked into the vicarage kitchen of an evening. 'I know the master's shorter o' money than iver, an' it meks no end o' difference i' th' housekeepin' – her bein' here, besides bein' obliged to have a charwoman constant.'

'There's fine stories i' the village about her,' said Mr Tomms. 'They say as Muster Barton's great wi' her, or else she'd niver stop here.'

'Then they say a passill o' lies, an' you ought to be ashamed to goo an' tell 'em o'er again. Do *you* think as the master, as has got a wife like the missis, 'ud goo runnin' arter a stuck-up piece o' goods like that Countess, as isn't fit to black the

99

missis's shoes? I'm none so fond o' the master, but I know better on him nor that.'

'Well, I didn't b'lieve it,' said Mr Tomms, humbly.

'B'lieve it? you'd ha' been a ninny if yer did. An' she's a nasty, stingy thing, that Countess. She's niver giv me a sixpence or an old rag neither, sin' here she's been. A-lyin' a bed an' a-comin' down to breakfast when other folks wants their dinner!'

If such was the state of Nanny's mind as early as the end of August, when this dialogue with Mr Tomms occurred, you may imagine what it must have been by the beginning of November, and that at that time a very slight spark might any day cause the long smouldering anger to flame forth in open indignation.

That spark happened to fall the very morning that Mrs Hackit paid the visit to Mrs Patten, recorded in the last chapter. Nanny's dislike of the Countess extended to the innocent dog Jet, whom she 'couldn't a-bear to see made a fuss wi' like a Christian. An' the little ouzel must be washed, too, ivery Saturday, as if there wasn't children enoo to wash, wi'out washin' dogs.'

Now this particular morning it happened that Milly was quite too poorly to get up, and Mr Barton observed to Nanny, on going out, that he would call and tell Mr Brand to come. These circumstances were already enough to make Nanny anxious and susceptible. But the Countess, comfortably ignorant of them, came down as usual about eleven o'clock to her separate breakfast, which stood ready for her at that hour in the parlour; the kettle singing on the hob that she might make her own tea. There was a little jug of cream, taken according to custom from last night's milk, and specially saved for the Countess's breakfast. Jet always awaited his mistress at her bedroom door, and it was her habit to carry him down stairs.

'Now, my little Jet,' she said, putting him down gently on the hearth-rug, 'you shall have a nice, nice breakfast.'

Jet indicated that he thought that observation extremely pertinent and well-timed, by immediately raising himself on his hind-legs, and the Countess emptied the cream-jug into the saucer. Now there was usually a small jug of milk standing on the tray by the side of the cream, and destined for Jet's breakfast, but this morning Nanny, being 'moithered,' had forgotten that part of the arrangements, so that when the Countess had made her tea, she perceived there was no second jug, and rang the bell. Nanny appeared, looking very red and heated – the fact was, she had been 'doing up' the kitchen fire, and that is a sort of work which by no means conduces to blandness of temper.

'Nanny, you have forgotten Jet's milk; will you bring me some more cream, please?'

This was just a little too much for Nanny's forbearance.

'Yes, I dare say. Here am I wi' my hands full o' the children an' the dinner, and missis ill a-bed, and Mr Brand a-comin''; and I must run o'er the village to get more cream, 'cause you've giv it to that nasty little blackamoor.'

'Is Mrs Barton ill?'

'Ill – yes – I should think she *is* ill, an' much you care. She's likely to be ill, moithered as *she* is from mornin' to night, wi' folks as had better be elsewhere.'

'What do you mean by behaving in this way?'

'Mean? Why, I mean as the missis is a-slavin' her life out an' a-sittin' up o' nights, for folks as are better able to wait of *her*, i'stid o' lyin' abed an' doin' nothin' all the blessed day, but mek work.'

'Leave the room, and don't be insolent.'

'Insolent! I'd better be insolent than like what some folks is – a-livin' on other folks, an' bringin' a bad name on 'em into the bargain.'

Here Nanny flung out of the room, leaving the lady to digest this unexpected breakfast at her leisure.

The Countess was stunned for a few minutes, but when she began to recall Nanny's words, there was no possibility of avoiding very unpleasant conclusions from them, or of failing to see her position at the Vicarage in an entirely new light. The interpretation too of Nanny's allusion to a 'bad name' did not lie out of the reach of the Countess's imagination, and she saw the necessity of quitting Shepperton without delay. Still, she would like to wait for her brother's letter – no – she would ask Milly to forward it to her—still better, she would go at once to London, inquire her brother's address at his banker's, and go to see him without preliminary.

She went up to Milly's room, and, after kisses and inquiries, said —'I find, on consideration, dear Milly, from the letter I had yesterday, that I must bid you good-bye and go up to London at once. But you must not let me leave you ill, you naughty thing.'

'Oh no,' said Milly, who felt as if a load had been taken off her back, 'I shall be very well in an hour or two. Indeed, I'm much better now. You will want me to help you to pack. But you won't go for two or three days?'

'Yes, I must go to-morrow. But I shall not let you help me pack, so don't entertain any unreasonable projects, but lie still. Mr Brand is coming, Nanny says.'

The news was not an unpleasant surprise to Mr Barton when he came home, though he was able to express more regret at the idea of parting than Milly could summon to her lips. He retained more of his original feeling for the Countess than Milly did, for women never betray themselves to men as they do to each other; and the Rev. Amos had not a keen instinct for character. But he felt that he was being relieved from a difficulty, and in the way that was easiest for him. Neither he nor Milly suspected that it was Nanny who had cut the knot for them, for the Countess took care to give no sign on that subject. As for Nanny, she was perfectly aware of the relation between cause and effect in the affair, and secretly chuckled over her outburst of 'sauce,' as the best morning's work she had ever done.

So, on Friday morning, a fly was seen standing at the Vicarage gate, with the Countess's boxes packed upon it; and presently that lady herself was seen getting into the vehicle. After a last shake of the hand to Mr Barton, and last kisses to Milly and the children, the door was closed; and as the fly rolled off, the little party at the Vicarage gate caught a last glimpse of the handsome Countess leaning and waving kisses from the carriage window. Jet's little black phiz was also seen, and doubtless he had his thoughts and feelings on the occasion, but he kept them strictly within his own bosom.

The schoolmistress opposite witnessed this departure, and lost no time in telling it to the schoolmaster, who again communicated the news to the landlord of 'The Jolly Colliers,' at the close of the morning school-hours. Nanny poured the joyful tidings into the ear of Mr Farquhar's footman, who happened to call with a letter, and Mr Brand carried them to all the patients he visited that morning, after calling on Mrs Barton. So that before Sunday, it was very generally known in Shepperton parish, that the Countess Czerlaski had left the Vicarage.

The Countess had left, but alas! the bills she had contributed to swell still remained; so did the exiguity of the children's clothing, which also was partly an indirect consequence of her presence; and so, too, did the coolness and alienation in the parishioners, which could not at once vanish before the fact of her departure. The Rev. Amos was not exculpated – the past was not expunged. But, what was worse than all, Milly's health gave frequent cause for alarm, and the prospect of baby's birth was overshadowed by more than the usual fears. The birth came prematurely, about six weeks after the Countess's departure, but Mr Brand gave favourable reports to all inquirers on the following day, which was Saturday. On Sunday, after morning service, Mrs Hackit called at the Vicarage to inquire how Mrs Barton was, and was invited up-stairs to see her. Milly lay placid and lovely in her feebleness, and held out her hand to Mrs Hackit with a beaming smile. It was very pleasant to her to see her old friend unreserved and cordial once more. The seven months' baby was very tiny and very red, but 'handsome is that handsome does,' – he was pronounced to be 'doing well,' and Mrs Hackit went home gladdened at heart to think that the perilous hour was over.

CHAPTER 8

The following Wednesday, when Mr and Mrs Hackit were seated comfortably by their bright hearth, enjoying the long afternoon afforded by an early dinner, Rachel, the housemaid, came in and said,—

'If you please 'm, the shepherd says, have you heard as Mrs Barton's wuss, and not expected to live?'

Mrs Hackit turned pale, and hurried out to question the shepherd, who, she found, had heard the sad news at an alehouse in the village. Mr Hackit followed her out and said, 'Thee'dst better have the ponychaise, and go directly.'

'Yes,' said Mrs Hackit, too much overcome to utter any exclamations. 'Rachel, come an' help me on wi' my things.'

When her husband was wrapping her cloak round her feet in the pony-chaise, she said,—

'If I don't come home to-night, I shall send back the pony-chaise, and you'll know I'm wanted there.'

'Yes, yes.'

It was a bright frosty day, and by the time

Mrs Hackit arrived at the Vicarage, the sun was near its setting. There was a carriage and pair standing at the gate, which she recognized as Dr Madeley's, the physician from Rotherby. She entered at the kitchen door, that she might avoid knocking, and quietly question Nanny. No one was in the kitchen, but, passing on, she saw the sitting-room door open, and Nanny, with Walter in her arms, removing the knives and forks, which had been laid for dinner three hours ago.

'Master says he can't eat no dinner,' was Nanny's first word. 'He's never tasted nothin' sin' yesterday mornin', but a cup o' tea.'

'When was your missis took worse?'

'O' Monday night. They sent for Dr Madeley i' the middle o' the day yisterday, an' he's here again now.'

'Is the baby alive?'

'No, it died last night. The children's all at Mrs Bond's. She come and took 'em away last night, but the master says they must be fetched soon. He's up-stairs now, wi' Dr Madeley and Mr Brand.'

At this moment Mrs Hackit heard the sound of a heavy, slow foot, in the passage; and presently Amos Barton entered, with dry despairing eyes, haggard and unshaven. He expected to find the sitting-room as he left it, with nothing to meet his eyes but Milly's work-basket in the corner of the sofa, and the children's toys overturned in the bow-window. But when he saw Mrs Hackit come towards him with answering sorrow in her face, the pent-up fountain of tears was opened; he threw himself on the sofa, hid his face, and sobbed aloud.

'Bear up, Mr Barton,' Mrs Hackit ventured to say at last, 'bear up, for the sake o' them dear children.'

'The children,' said Amos, starting up. 'They must be sent for. Some one must fetch them. Milly will want to . . .'

He couldn't finish the sentence, but Mrs Hackit understood him, and said, 'I'll send the man with the pony-carriage for 'em.'

She went out to give the order, and encountered Dr Madeley and Mr Brand, who were just going.

Mr Brand said: 'I am very glad to see you are here, Mrs Hackit. No time must be lost in sending for the children. Mrs Barton wants to see them.'

'Do you quite give her up, then?'

'She can hardly live through the night. She begged us to tell her how long she had to live; and then asked for the children.'

The pony-carriage was sent; and Mrs Hackit, returning to Mr Barton, said she should like to go up-stairs now. He went up-stairs with her and opened the door. The chamber fronted the west; the sun was just setting, and the red light fell full upon the bed, where Milly lay with the hand of death visibly upon her. The feather-bed had been removed, and she lay low on a mattress with her head slightly raised by pillows. Her long fair neck seemed to be struggling with a painful effort; her features were pallid and pinched, and her eyes were closed. There was no one in the room but the nurse, and the mistress of the free school, who had come to give her help from the beginning of the change.

Amos and Mrs Hackit stood beside the bed, and Milly opened her eyes.

'My darling, Mrs Hackit is come to see you.'

Milly smiled and looked at her with that strange, far-off look which belongs to ebbing life.

'Are the children coming?' she said, painfully.

'Yes, they will be here directly.'

She closed her eyes again.

Presently the pony-carriage was heard; and Amos, motioning to Mrs Hackit to follow him, left the room. On their way down stairs, she suggested that the carriage should remain to take them away again afterwards, and Amos assented.

There they stood in the melancholy sitting-room – the five sweet children, from Patty to Chubby – all, with their mother's eyes – all, except Patty, looking up with a vague fear at their father as he entered. Patty understood the great sorrow that was come upon them, and tried to check her sobs as she heard her papa's footsteps.

'My children,' said Amos, taking Chubby in his arms, 'God is going to take away your dear mamma from us. She wants to see you to say good-bye. You must try to be very good and not cry.'

He could say no more, but turned round to see

if Nanny was there with Walter, and then led the way up-stairs, leading Dickey with the other hand. Mrs Hackit followed with Sophy and Patty, and then came Nanny with Walter and Fred.

It seemed as if Milly had heard the little footsteps on the stairs, for when Amos entered her eyes were wide open, eagerly looking towards the door. They all stood by the bedside – Amos nearest to her, holding Chubby and Dickey. But she motioned for Patty to come first, and clasping the poor pale child by the hand, said, –

'Patty, I'm going away from you. Love your papa. Comfort him; and take care of your little brothers and sisters. God will help you.'

Patty stood perfectly quiet, and said, 'Yes, mamma.'

The mother motioned with her pallid lips for the dear child to lean towards her and kiss her; and then Patty's great anguish overcame her, and she burst into sobs. Amos drew her towards him and pressed her head gently to him, while Milly beckoned Fred and Sophy, and said to them more faintly, –

'Patty will try to be your mamma when I am gone, my darlings. You will be good, and not vex her.'

They leaned towards her, and she stroked their fair heads, and kissed their tear-stained cheeks. They cried because mamma was ill and papa looked so unhappy; but they thought, perhaps next week things would be as they used to be again.

The little ones were lifted on the bed to kiss her. Little Walter said, 'Mamma, mamma,' and stretched out his fat arms and smiled; and Chubby seemed gravely wondering; but Dickey, who had been looking fixedly at her, with lip hanging down, ever since he came into the room, now seemed suddenly pierced with the idea that mamma was going away somewhere; his little heart swelled and he cried aloud.

Then Mrs Hackit and Nanny took them all away. Patty at first begged to stay at home and not go to Mrs Bond's again; but when Nanny reminded her that she had better go to take care of the younger ones, she submitted at once, and they were all packed in the pony-carriage once more.

Milly kept her eyes shut for some time after the children were gone. Amos had sunk on his knees, and was holding her hand while he watched her face. By-and-by she opened her eyes, and, drawing him close to her, whispered slowly, –

'My dear – dear – husband – you have been – very – good to me. You – have – made me – very – happy.'

She spoke no more for many hours. They watched her breathing becoming more and more difficult, until evening deepened into night, and until midnight was past. About half-past twelve she seemed to be trying to speak, and they leaned to catch her words.

'Music – music – didn't you hear it?'

Amos knelt by the bed and held her hand in his.

He did not believe in his sorrow. It was a bad dream. He did not know when she was gone. But Mr Brand, whom Mrs Hackit had sent for before twelve o'clock, thinking that Mr Barton might probably need his help, now came up to him and said, –

'She feels no more pain now. Come, my dear sir, come with me.'

'She isn't *dead?*' shrieked the poor desolate man, struggling to shake off Mr Brand, who had taken him by the arm. But his weary, weakened frame was not equal to resistance, and he was dragged out of the room.

CHAPTER 9

They laid her in the grave – the sweet mother with her baby in her arms – while the Christmas snow lay thick upon the graves. It was Mr Cleves who buried her. On the first news of Mr Barton's calamity, he had ridden over from Tripplegate to beg that he might be made of some use, and his silent grasp of Amos's hand had penetrated like the painful thrill of life-recovering warmth to the poor benumbed heart of the stricken man.

The snow lay thick upon the graves, and the day was cold and dreary; but there was many a sad eye watching that black procession as it passed from the vicarage to the church, and from the church to the open grave. There were men and women standing in that churchyard who had bandied vulgar jests about their pastor, and who had lightly charged him with sin; but now, when they saw him following the coffin, pale and haggard, he was consecrated anew by his great sorrow, and they looked at him with respectful pity.

All the children were there, for Amos had willed it so, thinking that some dim memory of that sacred moment might remain even with little Walter, and link itself with what he would hear of his sweet mother in after years. He himself led Patty and Dickey; then came Sophy and Fred; Mr Brand had begged to carry Chubby, and Nanny followed with Walter. They made a circle round the grave while the coffin was being lowered. Patty alone of all the children felt that mamma was in that coffin, and that a new and sadder life had begun for papa and herself. She was pale and trembling, but she clasped his hand more firmly as the coffin went down, and gave no sob. Fred and Sophy, though they were only two and three years younger, and though they had seen mamma in her coffin, seemed to themselves to be looking at some strange show. They had not learned to decipher that terrible handwriting of human destiny, illness and death. Dickey had rebelled against his black clothes, until he was told that it would be naughty to mamma not to put them on, when he at once submitted; and now, though he had heard Nanny say that mamma was in heaven, he had a vague notion that she would come home again to-morrow, and say he had been a good boy, and let him empty her work-box. He stood close to his father, with great rosy cheeks, and wide open blue eyes, looking first up at Mr Cleves and then down at the coffin, and thinking he and Chubby would play at that, when they got home.

The burial was over, and Amos turned with his children to re-enter the house – the house where, an hour ago, Milly's dear body lay, where the windows were half-darkened, and sorrow seemed to have a hallowed precinct for itself, shut out from the world. But now she was gone; the broad snow-reflected daylight was in all the rooms; the Vicarage again seemed part of the common working-day world, and Amos, for the first time, felt that he was alone – that day after day, month after month, year after year, would have to be lived through without Milly's love. Spring would come, and she would not be there; summer, and she would not be there; and he would never have her again with him by the fireside in the long evenings. The seasons all seemed irksome to his thoughts; and how dreary the sunshiny days that would be sure to come! She was gone from him; and he could never show her his love any more, never make up for omissions in the past by filling future days with tenderness.

O the anguish of that thought, that we can never atone to our dead for the stinted affection we gave them, for the light answers we returned to their plaints or their pleadings, for the little reverence we showed to that sacred human soul that lived so close to us, and was the divinest thing God had given us to know.

Amos Barton had been an affectionate husband, and while Milly was with him, he was never visited by the thought that perhaps his sympathy with her was not quick and watchful enough; but now he relived all their life together, with that terrible keenness of memory and imagination which bereavement gives, and he felt as if his very love needed a pardon for its poverty and selfishness.

No outward solace could counteract the bitterness of this inward woe. But outward solace came. Cold faces looked kind again, and parishioners turned over in their minds what they could best do to help their pastor. Mr Oldinport wrote to express his sympathy, and enclosed another twenty-pound note, begging that he might be permitted to contribute in this way to the relief of Mr Barton's mind from pecuniary anxieties, under the pressure of a grief which all his parishioners must share; and offering his interest towards placing the two eldest girls in a school expressly founded for clergymen's daughters. Mr Cleves succeeded in collecting thirty pounds among his richer clerical brethren, and, adding ten pounds himself, sent the sum to Amos, with the kindest and most delicate words of Christian fellowship and manly friendship. Miss Jackson forgot old grievances, and came to stay some months with Milly's children, bringing such material aid as she could spare from her small income. These were substantial helps, which relieved Amos from the pressure of his money difficulties; and the friendly attentions, the kind pressure of the hand, the cordial looks he met with everywhere in his parish, made him feel that the fatal frost which had settled on his pastoral duties, during the Countess's residence at the Vicarage, was completely thawed, and that the hearts of his parishioners were once more open to him.

No one breathed the Countess's name now; for Milly's memory hallowed her husband, as of old the place was hallowed on which an angel from God had alighted.

When the spring came, Mrs Hackit begged that she might have Dickey to stay with her, and great was the enlargement of Dickey's experience from that visit. Every morning he was allowed – being well wrapt up as to his chest, by Mrs Hackit's own hands, but very bare and red as to his legs – to run loose in the cow and poultry yard, to persecute the turkey-cock by satirical imitations of his gobble-gobble, and to put difficult questions to the groom as to the reasons why horses had four legs, and other transcendental matters. Then Mr Hackit would take Dickey up on horseback when he rode round his farm, and Mrs Hackit had a large plumcake in cut, ready to meet incidental attacks of hunger. So that Dickey had considerably modified his views as to the desirability of Mrs Hackit's kisses.

The Miss Farquhars made particular pets of Fred and Sophy, to whom they undertook to give lessons twice a-week in writing and geography; and Mrs Farquhar devised many treats for the little ones. Patty's treat was to stay at home, or walk about with her papa; and when he sat by the fire in an evening, after the other children were gone to bed, she would bring a stool, and placing it against his feet, would sit down upon it and lean her head against his knee. Then his hand would rest on that fair head, and he would feel that Milly's love was not quite gone out of his life.

So the time wore on till it was May again, and the church was quite finished and reopened in all its new splendour, and Mr Barton was devoting himself with more vigour than ever to his parochial duties. But one morning – it was a very bright morning, and evil tidings sometimes like to fly in the finest weather – there came a letter for Mr Barton, addressed in the Vicar's handwriting. Amos opened it with some anxiety – somehow or other he had a presentiment of evil. The letter contained the announcement that Mr Carpe had resolved on coming to reside at Shepperton, and that, consequently, in six months from that time Mr Barton's duties as curate in that parish would be closed.

O, it was hard! Just when Shepperton had become the place where he most wished to stay – where he had friends who knew his sorrows – where he lived close to Milly's grave. To part from that grave seemed like parting with Milly a second time; for Amos was one who clung to all the material links between his mind and the past. His imagination was not vivid, and required the stimulus of actual perception.

It roused some bitter feeling, too, to think that Mr Carpe's wish to reside at Shepperton was merely a pretext for removing Mr Barton, in order that he might ultimately give the curacy of Shepperton to his own brother-in-law, who was known to be wanting a new position.

Still, it must be borne; and the painful business of seeking another curacy must be set about without loss of time. After the lapse of some months, Amos was obliged to renounce the hope of getting one at all near Shepperton, and he at length resigned himself to accepting one in a distant country. The parish was in a large manufacturing town, where his walks would lie among noisy streets and dingy alleys, and where the children would have no garden to play in, no pleasant farmhouses to visit.

It was another blow inflicted on the bruised man.

CHAPTER 10

At length the dreaded week was come, when Amos and his children must leave Shepperton. There was general regret among the parishioners at his departure: not that any one of them thought his spiritual gifts pre-eminent, or was conscious of great edification from his ministry. But his recent troubles had called out their better sympathies, and that is always a source of love. Amos failed to touch the spring of goodness by his sermons, but he touched it effectually by his sorrows; and there was now a real bond between him and his flock.

'My heart aches for them poor motherless children,' said Mrs Hackit to her husband, 'a-goin' among strangers, an' into a nasty town, where there's no good victuals to be had, and you must pay dear to get bad 'uns.'

Mrs Hackit had a vague notion of a town life as a combination of dirty backyards, measly pork, and dingy linen.

The same sort of sympathy was strong among the poorer class of parishioners. Old stiff-jointed Mr Tozer, who was still able to earn a little by

120

gardening 'jobs,' stopped Mrs Cramp, the charwoman, on her way home from the Vicarage, where she had been helping Nanny to pack up the day before the departure, and inquired very particularly into Mr Barton's prospects.

'Ah, poor mon,' he was heard to say, 'I'm surry fur 'un. He hedn't much here, but he'll be wuss off theer. Half a loaf's better nor ne'er 'un.'

The sad good-byes had all been said before that last evening; and after all the packing was done and all the arrangements were made, Amos felt the oppression of that blank interval in which one has nothing left to think of but the dreary future – the separation from the loved and familiar, and the chilling entrance on the new and strange. In every parting there is an image of death.

Soon after ten o'clock, when he had sent Nanny to bed, that she might have a good night's rest before the fatigues of the morrow, he stole softly out to pay a last visit to Milly's grave. It was a moonless night, but the sky was thick with stars, and their light was enough to show that the grass had grown long on the grave, and that there was a tombstone telling in bright letters, on a dark ground, that beneath were deposited the remains of Amelia, the beloved wife of Amos Barton, who died in the thirty-fifth year of her age, leaving a husband and six children to lament her loss. The final words of the inscription were, 'Thy will be done.'

The husband was now advancing towards the

121

dear mound from which he was so soon to be parted, perhaps for ever. He stood a few minutes reading over and over again the words on the tombstone, as if to assure himself that all the happy and unhappy past was a reality. For love is frightened at the intervals of insensibility and callousness that encroach by little and little on the dominion of grief, and it makes efforts to recall the keenness of the first anguish.

Gradually, as his eye dwelt on the words, 'Amelia, the beloved wife,' the waves of feeling swelled within his soul, and he threw himself on the grave, clasping it with his arms, and kissing the cold turf.

'Milly, Milly, dost thou hear me? I didn't love thee enough – I wasn't tender enough to thee – but I think of it all now.'

The sobs came and choked his utterance, and the warm tears fell.

CONCLUSION

Only once again in his life has Amos Barton visited Milly's grave. It was in the calm and softened light of an autumnal afternoon, and he was not alone. He held on his arm a young woman, with a sweet, grave face, which strongly recalled the expression of Mrs Barton's, but was less lovely in form and colour. She was about thirty, but there were some premature lines round her mouth and eyes, which told of early anxiety.

Amos himself was much changed. His thin circlet of hair was nearly white, and his walk was no longer firm and upright. But his glance was calm, and even cheerful, and his neat linen told of a woman's care. Milly did not take all her love from the earth when she died. She had left some of it in Patty's heart.

All the other children were now grown up, and had gone their several ways. Dickey, you will be glad to hear, had shown remarkable talents as an engineer. His cheeks are still ruddy, in spite of mixed mathematics, and his eyes are still large and blue; but in other respects his person would

123

present no marks of identification for his friend Mrs Hackit, if she were to see him; especially now that her eyes must be grown very dim, with the wear of more than twenty additional years. He is nearly six feet high, and has a proportionately broad chest; he wears spectacles, and rubs his large white hands through a mass of shaggy brown hair. But I am sure you have no doubt that Mr Richard Barton is a thoroughly good fellow, as well as a man of talent, and you will be glad any day to shake hands with him, for his own sake as well as his mother's.

Patty alone remains by her father's side, and makes the evening sunshine of his life.

MR GILFIL'S LOVE-STORY

CHAPTER 1

When old Mr Gilfil died, thirty years ago, there was general sorrow in Shepperton; and if black cloth had not been hung round the pulpit and reading-desk, by order of his nephew and principal legatee, the parishioners would certainly have subscribed the necessary sum out of their own pockets, rather than allow such a tribute of respect to be wanting. All the farmers' wives brought out their black bombasines; and Mrs Jennings, at the Wharf, by appearing the first Sunday after Mr Gilfil's death in her salmon-coloured ribbons and green shawl, excited the severest remark. To be sure, Mrs Jennings was a new-comer, and town-bred, so that she could hardly be expected to have very clear notions of what was proper; but, as Mrs Higgins observed in an under-tone to Mrs Parrot when they were coming out of church, 'Her husband, who'd been born i' the parish, might ha' told her better.' An unreadiness to put on black on all available occasions, or too great an alacrity in putting it off, argued, in Mrs Higgins's opinion, a dangerous levity of character, and an unnatural insensibility to the essential fitness of things.

'Some folks can't a-bear to put off their colours,' she remarked; 'but that was never the way i' *my* family. Why, Mrs Parrot, from the time I was married till Mr Higgins died, nine year ago come Candlemas, I niver was out o' black two year together!'

'Ah,' said Mrs Parrot, who was conscious of inferiority in this respect, 'there isn't many families as have had so many deaths as yours, Mrs Higgins.'

Mrs Higgins, who was an elderly widow 'well left,' reflected with complacency that Mrs Parrot's observation was no more than just, and that Mrs Jennings very likely belonged to a family which had had no funerals to speak of.

Even dirty Dame Fripp, who was a very rare church-goer, had been to Mrs Hackit to beg a bit of old crape, and with this sign of grief pinned on her little coal-scuttle bonnet, was seen dropping her curtsy opposite the reading-desk. This manifestation of respect towards Mr Gilfil's Mr Gilfil's memory on the part of Dame Fripp had no theological bearing whatever. It was due to an event which had occurred some years back, and which, I am sorry to say, had left that grimy old lady as indifferent to the means of grace as ever. Dame Fripp kept leeches, and was understood to have such remarkable influence over those wilful animals in inducing them to bite under the most unpromising circumstances, that though her own leeches were usually rejected, from a suspicion that they had lost their appetite, she herself was constantly called in to apply the more lively individuals furnished from Mr Pilgrim's surgery, when, as was very often the case, one of that clever man's paying patients was attacked with inflammation. Thus Dame Fripp, in addition to 'property' supposed to yield her no less than half-a-crown a-week, was in the receipt of professional fees, the gross amount of which was vaguely estimated by her neighbours as 'pouns an' pouns.' Moreover, she drove a brisk trade in lollipop with epicurean urchins, who recklessly purchased that luxury at the rate of two hundred per cent. Nevertheless, with all these notorious sources of income, the shameless old woman constantly pleaded poverty, and begged for scraps at Mrs Hackit's, who, though she always said Mrs Fripp was 'as false as two folks,' and no better than a miser and a heathen, had yet a leaning towards her as an old neighbour.

'There's that case-hardened old Judy a-coming after the tea-leaves again,' Mrs Hackit would say; 'an' I'm fool enough to give 'em her, though Sally wants 'em all the while to sweep the floors with!'

Such was Dame Fripp, whom Mr Gilfil, riding leisurely in top-boots and spurs from doing duty at Knebley one warm Sunday afternoon, observed sitting in the dry ditch near her cottage, and by her side a large pig, who, with that ease and confidence belonging to perfect friendship, was lying with his head in her lap, and making no effort to play the agreeable beyond an occasional grunt.

'Why, Mistress Fripp,' said the Vicar, 'I didn't know you had such a fine pig. You'll have some rare flitches at Christmas!'

'Eh, God forbid! My son gev him me two 'ear ago, an' he's been company to me iver sin'. I couldn't find i' my heart to part wi'm, if I niver knowed the taste o' bacon-fat again.'

'Why, he'll eat his head off, and yours too. How can you go on keeping a pig, and making nothing by him?'

'O, he picks a bit up hisself, wi' rootin', and I dooant mind doin' wi'out to gi' him summat. A bit o' coompany's meat an' drink too, an' he follers me about, an' grunts when I spake to'm, just like a Christian.'

Mr Gilfil laughed, and I am obliged to admit that he said good-bye to Dame Fripp without asking her why she had not been to church, or making the slightest effort for her spiritual edification. But the next day he ordered his man David to take her a great piece of bacon, with a message, saying, the parson wanted to make sure that Mrs Fripp would know the taste of bacon-fat again. So, when Mr Gilfil died, Dame Fripp manifested her gratitude and reverence in the simple dingy fashion I have mentioned.

You already suspect that the Vicar did not shine in the more spiritual functions of his office; and indeed, the utmost I can say for him in this respect is, that he performed those functions with undeviating attention to brevity and dispatch. He had a large heap of short sermons, rather yellow and worn at the edges, from which he took two every Sunday, securing perfect impartiality in the selection by taking them as they came without reference to topics; and having preached one of these sermons at Shepperton in the morning, he mounted his horse and rode hastily with the other in his pocket to Knebley, where he officiated in a wonderful little church, with a chequered pavement which had once rung to the iron tread of military monks, with coats of arms in clusters on the lofty roof, marble warriors and their wives without noses occupying a large proportion of the area, and the twelve apostles, with their heads very much on one side, holding didactic ribbons, painted in fresco on the walls. Here, in an absence of mind to which he was prone, Mr Gilfil would sometimes forget to take off his spurs before putting on his surplice, and only become aware of the omission by feeling something mysteriously tugging at the skirts of that garment as he stepped into the reading-desk. But the Knebley farmers would as soon have thought of criticizing the moon as their pastor. He belonged to the course of nature, like markets and toll-gates and dirty bank-notes; and being a vicar, his claim on their veneration had never been counteracted by an exasperating claim on their pockets. Some of them,

131

who did not indulge in the superfluity of a covered cart without springs, had dined half an hour earlier than usual – that is to say, at twelve o'clock – in order to have time for their long walk through miry lanes, and present themselves duly in their places at two o'clock, when Mr Oldinport and Lady Felicia, to whom Knebley Church was a sort of family temple, made their way among the bows and curtsies of their dependants to a carved and canopied pew in the chancel, diffusing as they went a delicate odour of Indian roses on the unsusceptible nostrils of the congregation.

The farmers' wives and children sat on the dark oaken benches, but the husbands usually chose the distinctive dignity of a stall under one of the twelve apostles, where, when the alternation of prayers and responses had given place to the agreeable monotony of the sermon, Paterfamilias might be seen or heard sinking into a pleasant doze, from which he infallibly woke up at the sound of the concluding doxology. And then they made their way back again through the miry lanes, perhaps almost as much the better for this simple weekly tribute to what they knew of good and right, as many a more wakeful and critical congregation of the present day.

Mr Gilfil, too, used to make his way home in the later years of his life, for he had given up the habit of dining at Knebley Abbey on a Sunday, having, I am sorry to say, had a very bitter quarrel with Mr Oldinport, the cousin and predecessor of the Mr Oldinport who flourished in the Rev. Amos Barton's time. That quarrel was a sad pity, for the two had had many a good day's hunting together when they were younger, and in those friendly times not a few members of the hunt envied Mr Oldinport the excellent terms he was on with his Vicar; for, as Sir Jasper Sitwell observed, 'next to a man's wife, there's nobody can be such an infernal plague to you as a parson, always under your nose on your own estate.'

I fancy the original difference which led to the rupture was very slight; but Mr Gilfil was of an extremely caustic turn, his satire having a flavour of originality which was quite wanting in his sermons; and as Mr Oldinport's armour of conscious virtue presented some considerable and conspicuous gaps, the Vicar's keen-edged retorts probably made a few incisions too deep to be forgiven. Such, at least, was the view of the case presented by Mr Hackit, who knew as much of the matter as any third person. For, the very week after the quarrel, when presiding at the annual dinner of the Association for the Prosecution of Felons, held at the Oldinport Arms, he contributed an additional zest to the conviviality on that occasion by informing the company that 'the parson had given the Squire a lick with the rough side of his tongue.' The detection of the person or persons who had driven off Mr Parrot's heifer, could hardly have been more welcome news to the Shepperton tenantry, with whom Mr Oldinport was in the worst odour as a landlord, having kept up his rents in spite of falling prices, and not being in the least stung to emulation by paragraphs in the provincial newspapers, stating that the Honourable Augustus Purwell, or Viscount Blethers, had made a return of ten per cent on their last rentday. The fact was, Mr Oldinport had not the slightest intention of standing for Parliament, whereas he had the strongest intention of adding to his unentailed estate. Hence, to the Shepperton farmers it was as good as lemon with their grog to know that the Vicar had thrown out sarcasms against the Squire's charities, as little better than those of the man who stole a goose, and gave away the giblets in alms. For Shepperton, you observe, was in a state of Attic culture compared with Knebley; it had turnpike roads and a public opinion, whereas, in the Bœotian Knebley, men's minds and wagons alike moved in the deepest of ruts, and the landlord was only grumbled at as a necessary and unalterable evil, like the weather, the weevils, and the turnip-fly.

Thus in Shepperton this breach with Mr Oldinport tended only to heighten that good understanding which the Vicar had always enjoyed with the rest of his parishioners, from the generation whose children he had christened a quarter of a century before, down to that hopeful generation represented by little Tommy Bond, who had recently quitted frocks and trousers for the severe simplicity of a tight suit of corduroys, relieved by numerous brass buttons. Tommy was a saucy boy, impervious to all impressions of reverence, and excessively addicted to humming-tops and marbles, with which recreative resources he was in the habit of immoderately distending the pockets of his corduroys. One day, spinning his top on the garden-walk, and seeing the Vicar advance directly towards it, at that exciting moment when it was beginning to 'sleep' magnificently, he shouted out with all the force of his lungs – 'Stop! don't knock my top down, now!' From that day 'little Corduroys' had been an especial favourite with Mr Gilfil, who delighted to provoke his ready scorn and wonder by putting questions which gave Tommy the meanest opinion of his intellect.

'Well, little Corduroys, have they milked the geese to-day?'

'Milked the geese! why, they don't milk the geese, you silly!'

'No! dear heart! why, how do the goslings live, then?'

The nutriment of goslings rather transcending Tommy's observations in natural history, he feigned to understand this question in an exclamatory rather than an interrogatory sense, and became absorbed in winding up his top.

'Ah, I see you don't know how the goslings live! But did you notice how it rained sugar-plums yesterday?' (Here Tommy became attentive.) 'Why, they fell into my pocket as I rode along. You look in my pocket and see if they didn't.'

Tommy, without waiting to discuss the alleged antecedent, lost no time in ascertaining the presence of the agreeable consequent, for he had a well-founded belief in the advantages of diving into the Vicar's pocket. Mr Gilfil called it his wonderful pocket, because, as he delighted to tell the 'young shavers' and 'two-shoes' – so he called all little boys and girls – whenever he put pennies into it, they turned into sugar-plums or ginger-bread, or some other nice thing. Indeed, little Bessie Parrot, a flaxen-headed 'two-shoes,' very white and fat as to her neck, always had the admirable directness and sincerity to salute him with the question – 'What zoo dot in zoo pottet?'

You can imagine, then, that the christening dinners were none the less merry for the presence of the parson. The farmers relished his society particularly, for he could not only smoke his pipe, and season the details of parish affairs with abundance of caustic jokes and proverbs, but, as Mr Bond often said, no man knew more than the Vicar about the breed of cows and horses. He had grazing-land of his own about five miles off, which a bailiff, ostensibly a tenant, farmed under his direction; and to ride backwards and forwards, and look after the buying and selling of stock, was the old gentleman's chief relaxation, now his hunting days were over. To hear him discussing the respective merits of the Devonshire breed and the short-horns, or the last foolish decision of the magistrates about a pauper, a superficial observer might have seen little difference, beyond his superior shrewdness, between the Vicar and his bucolic parishioners; for it was his habit to approximate his accent and mode of speech to theirs, doubtless because he thought it a mere frustration of the purpose of language to talk of 'shear-hogs' and 'ewes' to men who habitually said 'sharrags' and 'yowes.' Nevertheless the farmers themselves were perfectly aware of the distinction between them and the parson, and had not at all the less belief in him as a gentleman and a clergyman for his easy speech and familiar manners. Mrs Parrot smoothed her apron and set her cap right with the utmost solicitude when she saw the Vicar coming, made him her deepest curtsy, and every Christmas had a fat turkey ready to send him with her 'duty.' And in the most gossiping colloquies with Mr Gilfil, you might have observed that both men and women 'minded their words,' and never became indifferent to his approbation.

The same respect attended him in his strictly clerical functions. The benefits of baptism were supposed to be somehow bound up with Mr Gilfil's personality, so metaphysical a distinction as that between a man and his office being, as yet, quite foreign to the mind of a good Shepperton churchman, savouring, he would have thought, of Dissent on the very face of it. Miss Selina Parrot put off her marriage a whole month when Mr Gilfil had an attack of rheumatism, rather than be married in a makeshift manner by the Milby curate.

137

'We've had a very good sermon this morning,' was the frequent remark, after hearing one of the old yellow series, heard with all the more satisfaction because it had been heard for the twentieth time; for to minds on the Shepperton level it is repetition, not novelty, that produces the strongest effect; and phrases, like tunes, are a long time making themselves at home in the brain.

Mr Gilfil's sermons, as you may imagine, were not of a highly doctrinal, still less of a polemical, cast. They perhaps did not search the conscience very powerfully; for you remember that to Mrs Patten, who had listened to them thirty years, the announcement that she was a sinner appeared an uncivil heresy; but, on the other hand, they made no unreasonable demand on the Shepperton intellect – amounting, indeed, to little more than an expansion of the concise thesis, that those who do wrong will find it the worse for them, and those who do well will find it the better for them; the nature of wrong-doing being exposed in special sermons against lying, backbiting, anger, slothfulness, and the like; and well-doing being interpreted as honesty, truthfulness, charity, industry, and other common virtues, lying quite on the surface of life, and having very little to do with deep spiritual doctrine. Mrs Patten understood that if she turned out ill-crushed cheeses, a just retribution awaited her; though, I fear, she made no particular application of the sermon on backbiting. Mrs Hackit expressed herself greatly edified by the sermon on honesty, the allusion to the unjust weight and deceitful balance having a peculiar lucidity for her, owing to a recent dispute with her grocer; but I am not aware that she ever appeared to be much struck by the sermon on anger.

As to any suspicion that Mr Gilfil did not dispense the pure Gospel, or any strictures on his doctrine and mode of delivery, such thoughts never visited the minds of the Shepperton parish- ioners – of those very parishioners who, ten or fifteen years later, showed themselves extremely critical of Mr Barton's discourses and demeanour. But in the interim they had tasted that dangerous fruit of the tree of knowledge – innovation, which is well known to open the eyes, often in an uncomfortable manner. At present, to find fault with the sermon was regarded as almost equivalent to finding fault with religion itself. One Sunday, Mr Hackit's nephew, Master Tom Stokes, a flippant town youth, greatly scandalized his excellent relatives by declaring that he could write as good a sermon as Mr Gilfil's; whereupon Mr Hackit sought to reduce the presumptuous youth to utter confusion, by offering him a sovereign if he would fulfil his vaunt. The sermon was written, however; and though it was not admitted to be anywhere within reach of Mr Gilfil's, it was yet so astonishingly like a sermon, having a text, three divisions, and a concluding exhortation beginning 'and now, my brethren,' that the sovereign, though denied formally, was bestowed informally, and the sermon was pronounced, when Master Stokes's back was turned, to be 'an uncommon cliver thing.'

The Rev. Mr Pickard, indeed, of the Independent Meeting, had stated, in a sermon preached at Rotherby, for the reduction of a debt on New Zion, built, with an exuberance of faith and a deficiency of funds, by seceders from the original Zion, that he lived in a parish where the Vicar was very 'dark'; and in the prayers he addressed to his own congregation, he was in the habit of comprehensively alluding to the parishioners outside the chapel walls, as those who, 'Gallio-like, cared for none of these things.' But I need hardly say that no church-goer ever came within earshot of Mr Pickard.

It was not to the Shepperton farmers only that Mr Gilfil's society was acceptable; he was a welcome guest at some of the best houses in that part of the country. Old Sir Jasper Sitwell would have been glad to see him every week; and if you had seen him conducting Lady Sitwell in to dinner, or had heard him talking to her with quaint yet graceful gallantry, you would have inferred that the earlier period of his life had been passed in more stately society than could be found in Shepperton, and that his slipshod chat and homely manners were but like weather-stains on a fine old block of marble, allowing you still to see here and there the fineness of the grain, and the delicacy of the original tint. But in his later years these visits became a little too troublesome to the old gentleman, and he was rarely to be found anywhere of an evening beyond the bounds of his own parish – most frequently, indeed, by the side of his own sitting-room fire, smoking his pipe, and maintaining the pleasing antithesis of dryness and moisture by an occasional sip of gin-and-water.

Here I am aware that I have run the risk of alienating all my refined lady readers, and utterly annihilating any curiosity they may have felt to know the details of Mr Gilfil's love-story. 'Gin-and-water! foh! you may as well ask us to interest ourselves in the romance of a tallow-chandler, who mingles the image of his beloved with short dips and moulds.'

But in the first place, dear ladies, allow me to plead that gin-and-water, like obesity, or baldness, or the gout, does not exclude a vast amount of antecedent romance, any more than the neatly executed 'fronts' which you may some day wear, will exclude your present possession of less expensive braids. Alas, alas! we poor mortals are often little better than wood-ashes – there is small sign of the sap, and the leafy freshness, and the bursting buds that were once there; but wherever we see wood-ashes, we know that all that early fullness of life must have been. I, at least, hardly ever look at a bent old man, or a wizened old woman, but I see also, with my mind's eye, that Past of which they are the shrunken remnant, and the unfinished romance of rosy cheeks and bright eyes seems sometimes of feeble interest and significance, compared with that drama of hope and love which has long ago reached its catastrophe, and left the poor soul, like a dim and dusty stage, with all its sweet garden-scenes and fair perspectives overturned and thrust out of sight.

In the second place, let me assure you that Mr Gilfil's potations of gin-and-water were quite moderate. His nose was not rubicund; on the contrary, his white hair hung around a pale and venerable face. He drank it chiefly, I believe, because it was cheap; and here I find myself alighting on another of the Vicar's weaknesses, which, if I cared to paint a flattering portrait rather than a faithful one, I might have chosen to suppress. It is undeniable that, as the years advanced, Mr Gilfil became, as Mr Hackit observed, more and more 'close-fisted,' though the growing propensity showed itself rather in the parsimony of his personal habits, than in withholding help from the needy. He was saving – so he represented the matter to himself – for a nephew, the only son of a sister who had been the dearest object, all but one, in his life. 'The lad,' he thought, 'will have a nice little fortune to begin life with, and will bring his pretty young wife some day to see the spot where his old uncle lies. It will perhaps be all the better for *his* hearth that mine was lonely.'

Mr Gilfil was a bachelor, then?

That is the conclusion to which you would probably have come if you had entered his sitting-room, where the bare tables, the large old-fashioned horse-hair chairs, and the threadbare Turkey carpet perpetually fumigated with tobacco, seemed to tell a story of wifeless existence that was contradicted by no portrait, no piece of embroidery, no faded bit of pretty triviality, hinting of taper-fingers and small feminine ambitions. And it was here that Mr Gilfil passed his evenings, seldom with other society than that of Ponto, his old brown setter, who, stretched out at full length on the rug with his nose between his forepaws, would wrinkle his brows and lift up his eyelids every now and then, to exchange a glance of mutual understanding with his master. But there was a chamber in Shepperton Vicarage which told a different story from that bare and cheerless dining-room – a chamber never entered by any one besides Mr Gilfil and old Martha the housekeeper, who, with David her husband as groom and gardener, formed the Vicar's entire establishment. The blinds of this chamber were always down, except once a-quarter, when Martha entered that she might air and clean it. She always asked Mr Gilfil for the key, which he kept locked up in his bureau, and returned it to him when she had finished her task.

It was a touching sight that the daylight streamed in upon, as Martha drew aside the blinds and thick curtains, and opened the Gothic casement of the oriel window! On the little dressing-table there was a dainty looking-glass in a carved and gilt frame; bits of wax-candle were still in the branched sockets at the sides, and on one of these branches hung a little black lace kerchief; a faded satin pin-cushion, with the pins rusted in it, a scent-bottle, and a large green fan, lay on the table; and on a dressing-box by the side of the glass was a work-basket, and an unfinished baby-cap, yellow with age, lying in it. Two gowns, of a fashion long forgotten, were hanging on nails against the door, and a pair of tiny red slippers, with a bit of tarnished silver embroidery on them, were standing at the foot of the bed. Two or three water-colour drawings, views of Naples, hung upon the walls; and over the mantelpiece, above some bits of rare old china, two miniatures in oval frames. One of these miniatures represented a young man about seven-and-twenty, with a sanguine complexion, full lips, and clear candid grey eyes. The other was the likeness of a girl, probably not more than eighteen, with small features, thin cheeks, a pale southern-looking complexion, and large dark eyes. The gentleman wore powder; the lady had her dark hair gathered away from her face, and a little cap, with a cherry-coloured bow, set on the top of her head – a coquettish head-dress, but the eyes spoke of sadness rather than of coquetry.

Such were the things that Martha had dusted and let the air upon, four times a-year, ever since she was a blooming lass of twenty; and she was now, in this last decade of Mr Gilfil's life, unquestionably on the wrong side of fifty. Such was the locked-up chamber in Mr Gilfil's house:

a sort of visible symbol of the secret chamber in his heart, where he had long turned the key on early hopes and early sorrows, shutting up for ever all the passion and the poetry of his life.

There were not many people in the parish, besides Martha, who had any very distinct remembrance of Mr Gilfil's wife, or indeed who knew anything of her, beyond the fact that there was a marble tablet, with a Latin inscription in memory of her, over the vicarage pew. The parishioners who were old enough to remember her arrival were not generally gifted with descriptive powers, and the utmost you could gather from them was, that Mrs Gilfil looked like a 'furriner, wi' such eyes, you can't think, an' a voice as went through you when she sung at church.' The one exception was Mrs Patten, whose strong memory and taste for personal narrative made her a great source of oral tradition in Shepperton. Mr Hackit, who had not come into the parish until ten years after Mrs Gilfil's death, would often put old questions to Mrs Patten for the sake of getting the old answers, which pleased him in the same way as passages from a favourite book, or the scenes of a familiar play, please more accomplished people.

'Ah, you remember well the Sunday as Mrs Gilfil first come to church, eh, Mrs Patten?'

'To be sure I do. It was a fine bright Sunday as ever was seen, just at the beginnin' o' hay harvest. Mr Tarbett preached that day, and Mr Gilfil sat i' the pew wi' his wife. I think I see him now, a-leadin' her up th' aisle, an' her head not reachin' much above his elber: a little pale woman, wi' eyes as black as sloes, an' yet lookin' blank-like, as if she see'd nothin' wi' em.'

'I warrant she had her weddin' clothes on?' said Mr Hackit.

'Nothin' partickler smart – on'y a white hat tied down under her chin, an' a white Indy muslin gown. But you don't know what Mr Gilfil was in those times. He was fine an' altered afore you come into the parish. He'd a fresh colour then, an' a bright look wi' his eyes, as did your heart good to see. He looked rare an' happy that Sunday, but somehow, I'd a feelin' as it wouldn't last long. I've no opinion o' furriners, Mr Hackit, for I've travelled i' their country wi' my lady in my time, an' seen anuff o' their victuals an' their nasty ways.'

'Mrs Gilfil come from It'ly, didn't she?'

'I reckon she did, but I niver could rightly hear about that. Mr Gilfil was niver to be spoke to about her, and nobody else hereabout knowed anythin'. Howiver, she must ha' come over pretty young, for she spoke English as well as you an' me. It's them Italians as has such fine voices, an' Mrs Gilfil sung, you never heared the like. He brought her here to have tea wi' me one afternoon, and says he, in his jovial way, 'Now, Mrs Patten, I want Mrs Gilfil to see the neatest house, and drink the best cup o' tea, in all Shepperton; you must show her your dairy and your cheese-room, and then she shall sing you a song.'

146

An' so she did; an' her voice seemed sometimes to fill the room; an' then it went low an' soft, as if it was whisperin' close to your heart like.'

'You never heared her again, I reckon?'

'No; she was sickly then, an' she died in a few months after. She wasn't in the parish much more nor half a year altogether. She didn't seem lively that afternoon, an' I could see she didn't care about the dairy, nor the cheeses, on'y she pretended, to please him. As for him, I niver see'd a man so wrapt up in a woman. He looked at her as if he was worshippin' her, an' as if he wanted to lift her off the ground ivery minute, to save her the trouble o' walkin'. Poor man, poor man! It had like to ha' killed him when she died, though he niver gev way, but went on ridin' about and preachin'. But he was wore to a shadder, an' his eyes used to look as dead – you wouldn't ha' knowed 'em.'

'She brought him no fortin?'

'Not she. All Mr Gilfil's property come by his mother's side. There was blood an' money too, there. It's a thousand pities as he married a' that way – a fine man like him, as might ha' had the pick o' the county, an' had his grandchildren about him now. An' him so fond o' children, too.'

In this manner Mrs Pattern usually wound up her reminiscences of the Vicar's wife, of whom, you perceive, she knew but little. It was clear that the communicative old lady had nothing to tell of Mrs Gilfil's history previous to her arrival in

Shepperton, and that she was unacquainted with Mr Gilfil's love-story.

But I, dear reader, am quite as communicative as Mrs Patten, and much better informed; so that if you care to know more about the Vicar's courtship and marriage, you need only carry your imagination back to the latter end of the last century, and your attention forward into the next chapter.

CHAPTER 2

It is the evening of the 21st of June 1788. The day has been bright and sultry, and the sun will still be more than an hour above the horizon, but his rays, broken by the leafy fretwork of the elms that border the park, no longer prevent two ladies from carrying out their cushions and embroidery, and seating themselves to work on the lawn in front of Cheverel Manor. The soft turf gives way even under the fairy tread of the younger lady, whose small stature and slim figure rest on the tiniest of full-grown feet. She trips along before the elder, carrying the cushions, which she places in the favourite spot, just on the slope by a clump of laurels, where they can see the sunbeams sparkling among the water-lilies, and can be themselves seen from the dining-room windows. She has deposited the cushions, and now turns round, so that you may have a full view of her as she stands waiting the slower advance of the elder lady. You are at once arrested by her large dark eyes, which, in their inexpressive unconscious beauty, resemble the eyes of a fawn; and it is only by an effort of attention that you notice the absence of bloom on her young cheek, and the southern yellowish tint of her small neck and face, rising above the little black lace kerchief which prevents the too immediate comparison of her skin with her white muslin gown. Her large eyes seem all the more striking because the dark hair is gathered away from her face, under a little cap set at the top of her head, with a cherry-coloured bow on one side.

The elder lady, who is advancing towards the cushions, is cast in a very different mould of womanhood. She is tall, and looks the taller because her powdered hair is turned backward over a toupee, and surmounted by lace and ribbons. She is nearly fifty, but her complexion is still fresh and beautiful, with the beauty of an auburn blonde; her proud pouting lips, and her head thrown a little backward as she walks, give an expression of hauteur which is not contradicted by the cold grey eye. The tucked-in kerchief, rising full over the low tight bodice of her blue dress, sets off the majestic form of her bust, and she treads the lawn as if she were one of Sir Joshua Reynolds's stately ladies, who had suddenly stepped from her frame to enjoy the evening cool.

'Put the cushions lower, Caterina, that we may not have so much sun upon us,' she called out, in a tone of authority, when still at some distance.

Caterina obeyed, and they sat down, making two bright patches of red and white and blue on the green background of the laurels and the lawn, which would look none the less pretty in a picture because one of the women's hearts was rather cold and the other rather sad.

And a charming picture Cheverel Manor would have made that evening, if some English Watteau had been there to paint it: the castellated house of grey-tinted stone, with the flickering sunbeams sending dashes of golden light across the many-shaped panes in the mullioned windows, and a great beech leaning athwart one of the flanking towers, and breaking, with its dark flattened boughs, the too formal symmetry of the front; the broad gravel-walk winding on the right, by a row of tall pines, alongside the pool – on the left branching out among swelling grassy mounds, surmounted by clumps of trees, where the red trunk of the Scotch fir glows in the descending sunlight against the bright green of limes and acacias; the great pool, where a pair of swans are swimming lazily with one leg tucked under a wing, and where the open water-lilies lie calmly accepting the kisses of the fluttering light-sparkles; the lawn, with its smooth emerald greenness, sloping down to the rougher and browner herbage of the park, from which it is invisibly fenced by a little stream that winds away from the pool, and disappears under a wooden bridge in the distant pleasure-ground; and on this lawn our two ladies, whose part in the landscape the painter, standing at a favourable point of view in the park, would represent with a few little dabs of red and white and blue.

151

Seen from the great Gothic windows of the dining-room, they had much more definiteness of outline, and were distinctly visible to the three gentlemen sipping their claret there, as two fair women, in whom all three had a personal interest. These gentlemen were a group worth considering attentively; but any one entering that dining-room for the first time, would perhaps have had his attention even more strongly arrested by the room itself, which was so bare of furniture that it impressed one with its architectural beauty like a cathedral. A piece of matting stretched from door to door, a bit of worn carpet under the dining-table, and a sideboard in a deep recess, did not detain the eye for a moment from the lofty groined ceiling, with its richly-carved pendants, all of creamy white, relieved here and there by touches of gold. On one side, this lofty ceiling was supported by pillars and arches, beyond which a lower ceiling, a miniature copy of the higher one, covered the square projection which, with its three large pointed windows, formed the central feature of the building. The room looked less like a place to dine in than a piece of space enclosed simply for the sake of beautiful outline; and the small dining-table, with the party round it, seemed an odd and insignificant accident, rather than anything connected with the original purpose of the apartment.

But, examined closely, that group was far from insignificant; for the eldest, who was reading in the newspaper the last portentous proceedings of the French parliaments, and turning with occasional comments to his young companions, was as fine a specimen of the old English gentleman as could well have been found in those venerable days of cocked-hats and pigtails. His dark eyes sparkled under projecting brows, made more prominent by bushy grizzled eyebrows; but any apprehension of severity excited by these penetrating eyes, and by a somewhat aquiline nose, was allayed by the good-natured lines about the mouth, which retained all its teeth and its vigour of expression in spite of sixty winters. The forehead sloped a little from the projecting brows, and its peaked outline was made conspicuous by the arrangement of the profusely-powdered hair, drawn backward and gathered into a pigtail. He sat in a small hard chair, which did not admit the slightest approach to a lounge, and which showed to advantage the flatness of his back and the breadth of his chest. In fact, Sir Christopher Cheverel was a splendid old gentleman, as any one may see who enters the saloon at Cheverel Manor, where his full-length portrait, taken when he was fifty, hangs side by side with that of his wife, the stately lady seated on the lawn.

Looking at Sir Christopher, you would at once have been inclined to hope that he had a full-grown son and heir; but perhaps you would have wished that it might not prove to be the young man on his right hand, in whom a certain resemblance to the Baronet, in the contour of the nose and brow, seemed to indicate a family relationship. If this young man had been less elegant in his person, he would have been remarked for the elegance of his dress. But the perfections of his slim well-proportioned figure were so striking that no one but a tailor could notice the perfections of his velvet coat; and his small white hands, with their blue veins and taper fingers, quite eclipsed the beauty of his lace ruffles. The face, however – it was difficult to say why – was certainly not pleasing. Nothing could be more delicate than the blond complexion – its bloom set off by the powdered hair – than the veined overhanging eyelids, which gave an indolent expression to the hazel eyes; nothing more finely cut than the transparent nostril and the short upper-lip. Perhaps the chin and lower jaw were too small for an irreproach-able profile, but the defect was on the side of that delicacy and *finesse* which was the distinctive characteristic of the whole person, and which was carried out in the clear brown arch of the eyebrows, and the marble smoothness of the sloping forehead. Impossible to say that this face was not eminently handsome; yet, for the majority both of men and women, it was destitute of charm. Women disliked eyes that seemed to be indolently accepting admiration instead of rendering it; and men, especially if they had a tendency to clumsiness in the nose and ankles, were inclined to think this Antinous in a pigtail a 'confounded puppy.' I fancy that was frequently the inward interjection of the Rev. Maynard Gilfil, who was seated on the opposite side of the dining-table, though Mr Gilfil's legs and profile were not at all of a kind to make him peculiarly alive to the impertinence and frivolity of personal advantages. His healthy open face and robust limbs were after an excellent pattern for everyday wear, and in the opinion of Mr Bates, the north-country gardener, would have become regimentals 'a fain saight' better than the 'peaky' features and slight form of Captain Wybrow, notwithstanding. that this young gentleman, as Sir Christopher's nephew and destined heir, had the strongest hereditary claim on the gardener's respect, and was undeniably 'clean-limbed.' But alas! human longings are perversely obstinate; and to the man whose mouth is watering for a peach, it is of no use to offer the largest vegetable marrow. Mr Gilfil was not sensitive to Mr Bates's opinion, whereas he *was* sensitive to the opinion of another person, who by no means shared Mr Bates's preference.

Who the other person was it would not have required a very keen observer to guess, from a certain eagerness in Mr Gilfil's glance as that little figure in white tripped along the lawn with the cushions. Captain Wybrow, too, was looking in the same direction, but his handsome face remained handsome – and nothing more.

'Ah,' said Sir Christopher, looking up from his

paper, 'there's my lady. Ring for coffee, Anthony; we'll go and join her, and the little monkey Tina shall give us a song.'

The coffee presently appeared, brought not as usual by the footman, in scarlet and drab, but by the old butler, in threadbare but well-brushed black, who, as he was placing it on the table, said—

'If you please. Sir Christopher, there's the widow Hartopp a-crying i' the still-room, and begs leave to see your honour.'

'I have given Markham full orders about the widow Hartopp,' said Sir Christopher, in a sharp decided tone. 'I have nothing to say to her.'

'Your honour,' pleaded the butler, rubbing his hands, and putting on an additional coating of humility, 'the poor woman's dreadful overcome, and says she can't sleep a wink this blessed night without seeing your honour, and she begs you to pardon the great freedom she's took to come at this time. She cries fit to break her heart.'

'Aye, aye; water pays no tax. Well, show her into the library.'

Coffee dispatched, the two young men walked out through the open window, and joined the ladies on the lawn, while Sir Christopher made his way to the library, solemnly followed by Rupert, his pet bloodhound, who, in his habitual place at the Baronet's right hand, behaved with great urbanity during dinner; but when the cloth was drawn, invariably disappeared under the table, apparently regarding the claret-jug as a mere human weakness, which he winked at, but refused to sanction.

The library lay but three steps from the dining-room, on the other side of a cloistered and matted passage. The oriel window was overshadowed by the great beech, and this, with the flat heavily-carved ceiling and the dark hue of the old books that lined the walls, made the room look sombre, especially on entering it from the dining-room, with its aerial curves and cream-coloured fretwork touched with gold. As Sir Christopher opened the door, a jet of brighter light fell on a woman in a widow's dress, who stood in the middle of the room, and made the deepest of curtsies as he entered. She was a buxom woman approaching forty, her eyes red with the tears which had evidently been absorbed by the handkerchief gathered into a damp ball in her right hand.

'Now, Mrs Hartopp,' said Sir Christopher, taking out his gold snuff-box and tapping the lid, 'what have you to say to me? Markham has delivered you a notice to quit, I suppose?'

'O yis, your honour, an' that's the reason why I've come. I hope your honour 'll think better on it, an' not turn me an' my poor children out o' the farm, where my husband al'ys paid his rent as reglar as the day come.'

'Nonsense! I should like to know what good it

will do you and your children to stay on a farm and lose every farthing your husband has left you, instead of selling your stock and going into some little place where you can keep your money together. It is very well known to every tenant of mine that I never allow widows to stay on their husbands' farms.'

'O, Sir Christifer, if you *would* consider – when I've sold the hay, an' corn, an' all the live things, an' paid the debts, an' put the money out to use, I shall have hardly anuff to keep wer souls an' bodies together. An' how can I rear my boys and put 'em 'prentice? They must goo for dey -labourers, an' their father a man wi' as good belongings as any on your honour's estate, an' niver threshed his wheat afore it was well i' the rick, nor sold the straw off his farm, nor nothin'. Ask all the farmers round if there was a stiddier, soberer man than my husband as attended Ripstone market. An' he says, "Bessie," says he – them was his last words – "you'll mek a shift to manage the farm, if Sir Christifer 'ull let you stay on."'

'Pooh, pooh!' said Sir Christopher, Mrs Hartopp's sobs having interrupted her pleadings, 'now listen to me, and try to understand a little common-sense. You are about as able to manage the farm as your best milch cow. You'll be obliged to have some managing man, who will either cheat you out of your money or wheedle you into marrying him.'

'O, your honour, I was never that sort o' woman, an' nobody has known it on me.'

'Very likely not, because you were never a widow before. A woman's always silly enough, but she's never quite as great a fool as she can be until she puts on a widow's cap. Now, just ask yourself how much the better you will be for staying on your farm at the end of four years, when you've got through your money, and let your farm run down, and are in arrears for half your rent; or perhaps, have got some great hulky fellow for a husband, who swears at you and kicks your children.'

'Indeed, Sir Christifer, I know a deal o' farmin', an' was brought up i' the thick on it, as you may say. An' there was my husband's great-aunt managed a farm for twenty year, an' left legacies to all her nephys an' nieces, an' even to my husband, as was then a babe unborn.'

'Psha! a woman six feet high, with a squint and sharp elbows, I dare say – a man in petticoats. Not a rosy-cheeked widow like you, Mrs Hartopp.'

'Indeed, your honour, I never heard on her squintin', an' they said as she might ha' been married o'er and o'er again, to people as had no call to hanker after her money.'

'Aye, aye, that's what you all think. Every man that looks at you wants to marry you, and would like you the better the more children you have and the less money. But it is useless to talk and cry. I have good reasons for my plans, and never alter them. What you have to do is to make the best of

159

your stock, and to look out for some little place to go to, when you leave The Hollows. Now, go back to Mrs Bellamy's room, and ask her to give you a dish of tea.'

Mrs Hartopp, understanding from Sir Christopher's tone that he was not to be shaken, curtsied low and left the library, while the Baronet, seating himself at his desk in the oriel window, wrote the following letter:—

'MR MARKHAM, – Take no steps about letting Crowsfoot Cottage, as I intend to put in the widow Hartopp when she leaves her farm; and if you will be here at eleven on Saturday morning, I will ride round with you, and settle about making some repairs, and see about adding a bit of land to the take, as she will want to keep a cow and some pigs. – Yours faithfully,
    'CHRISTOPHER CHEVEREL.'

After ringing the bell and ordering this letter to be sent, Sir Christopher walked out to join the party on the lawn. But finding the cushions deserted, he walked on to the eastern front of the building, where, by the side of the grand entrance, was the large bow-window of the saloon, opening on to the gravel-sweep, and looking towards a long vista of undulating turf, bordered by tall trees, which, seeming to unite itself with the green of the meadows and a grassy road through a plantation, only terminated with the Gothic arch of a gateway in the far distance. The bow-window was open, and Sir Christopher, stepping in, found the group he sought, examining the progress of the unfinished ceiling. It was in the same style of florid pointed Gothic as the dining-room, but more elaborate in its tracery, which was like petrified lacework picked out with delicate and varied colouring. About a fourth of it still remained uncoloured, and under this part were scaffolding, ladders, and tools; otherwise the spacious saloon was empty of furniture, and seemed to be a grand Gothic canopy for the group of five human figures standing in the centre.

'Francesco has been getting on a little better the last day or two,' said Sir Christopher, as he joined the party: 'he's a sad lazy dog, and I fancy he has a knack of sleeping as he stands, with his brushes in his hands. But I must spur him on, or we may not have the scaffolding cleared away before the bride comes, if you show dexterous generalship in your wooing, eh, Anthony? and take your Magdeburg quickly.'

'Ah, sir, a siege is known to be one of the most tedious operations in war,' said Captain Wybrow, with an easy smile.

'Not when there's a traitor within the walls in the shape of a soft heart. And that there will be, if Beatrice has her mother's tenderness as well as her mother's beauty.'

'What do you think, Sir Christopher,' said Lady

161

Cheverel, who seemed to wince a little under her husband's reminiscences, 'of hanging Guercino's "Sibyl" over that door when we put up the pictures? It is rather lost in my sitting-room.'

'Very good, my love,' answered Sir Christopher, in a tone of punctiliously polite affection; 'if you like to part with the ornament from your own room, it will show admirably here. Our portraits, by Sir Joshua, will hang opposite the window, and the "Transfiguration" at that end. You see, Anthony, I am leaving no good places on the walls for you and your wife. We shall turn you with your faces to the wall in the gallery, and you may take your revenge on us by-and-by.'

While this conversation was going on, Mr Gilfil turned to Caterina and said,—

'I like the view from this window better than any other in the house.'

She made no answer, and he saw that her eyes were filling with tears; so he added, 'Suppose we walk out a little; Sir Christopher and my lady seem to be occupied.'

Caterina complied silently, and they turned down one of the gravel walks that led, after many windings under tall trees and among grassy openings, to a large enclosed flower-garden. Their walk was perfectly silent, for Maynard Gilfil knew that Caterina's thoughts were not with him, and she had been long used to make him endure the weight of those moods which she carefully hid from others.

They reached the flower-garden, and turned mechanically in at the gate that opened, through a high thick hedge, on an expanse of brilliant colour, which, after the green shades they had passed through, startled the eye like flames. The effect was assisted by an undulation of the ground, which gradually descended from the entrance-gate, and then rose again towards the opposite end, crowned by an orangery. The flowers were glowing with their evening splendours; verbenas and heliotropes were sending up their finest incense. It seemed a gala where all was happiness and brilliancy, and misery could find no sympathy. This was the effect it had on Caterina. As she wound among the beds of gold and blue and pink, where the flowers seemed to be looking at her with wondering elf-like eyes, knowing nothing of sorrow, the feeling of isolation in her wretchedness overcame her, and the tears, which had been before trickling slowly down her pale cheeks, now gushed forth accompanied with sobs. And yet there was a loving human being close beside her, whose heart was aching for hers, who was possessed by the feeling that she was miserable, and that he was helpless to soothe her. But she was too much irritated by the idea that his wishes were different from hers, that he rather regretted the folly of her hopes than the probability of their disappointment, to take any comfort in his sympathy. Caterina, like the rest of us, turned away from sympathy which she suspected to be mingled with criticism, as the

163

child turns away from the sweetmeat in which it suspects imperceptible medicine.

'Dear Caterina, I think I hear voices,' said Mr Gilfil; 'they may be coming this way.'

She checked herself like one accustomed to conceal her emotions, and ran rapidly to the other end of the garden, where she seemed occupied in selecting a rose. Presently Lady Cheverel entered, leaning on the arm of Captain Wybrow, and followed by Sir Christopher. The party stopped to admire the tiers of geraniums near the gate; and in the mean time Caterina tripped back with a moss rose-bud in her hand, and going up to Sir Christopher, said – 'There, Padroncello – there is a nice rose for your button-hole.'

'Ah, you black-eyed monkey,' he said, fondly stroking her cheek; 'so you have been running off with Maynard, either to torment or coax him an inch or two deeper into love. Come, come, I want you to sing us "*Ho perduto*" before we sit down to picquet. Anthony goes to-morrow, you know; you must warble him into the right sentimental lover's mood, that he may acquit himself well at Bath.' He put her little arm under his, and calling to Lady Cheverel, 'Come Henrietta!' led the way towards the house.

The party entered the drawing-room, which, with its oriel window, corresponded to the library in the other wing, and had also a flat ceiling heavy with carving and blazonry; but the window being unshaded, and the walls hung with full-length

164

portraits of knights and dames in scarlet, white, and gold, it had not the sombre effect of the library. Here hung the portrait of Sir Anthony Cheverel, who in the reign of Charles II. was the renovator of the family splendour, which had suffered some declension from the early brilliancy of that Chevreuil who came over with the Conqueror. A very imposing personage was this Sir Anthony, standing with one arm akimbo, and one fine leg and foot advanced, evidently with a view to the gratification of his contemporaries and posterity. You might have taken off his splendid peruke, and his scarlet cloak, which was thrown backward from his shoulders, without annihilating the dignity of his appearance. And he had known how to choose a wife, too, for his lady, hanging opposite to him, with her sunny brown hair drawn away in bands from her mild grave face, and falling in two large rich curls on her snowy gently-sloping neck, which shamed the harsher hue and outline of her white satin robe, was a fit mother of 'large-acred' heirs.

In this room tea was served; and here, every evening, as regularly as the great clock in the courtyard with deliberate bass tones struck nine, Sir Christopher and Lady Cheverel sat down to picquet until half-past ten, when Mr Gilfil read prayers to the assembled household in the chapel.

But now it was not near nine, and Caterina must sit down to the harpsichord and sing Sir

Christopher's favourite airs by Gluck and Paesiello, whose operas, for the happiness of that generation, were then to be heard on the London stage. It happened this evening that the sentiment of these airs, 'Che farò senza Eurydice?' and 'Ho perduto il bel sembiante,' in both of which the singer pours out his yearning after his lost love, came very close to Caterina's own feeling. But her emotion, instead of being a hindrance to her singing, gave her additional power. Her singing was what she could do best; it was her one point of superiority, in which it was probable she would excel the highborn beauty whom Anthony was to woo; and her love, her jealousy, her pride, her rebellion against her destiny, made one stream of passion which welled forth in the deep rich tones of her voice. She had a rare contralto, which Lady Cheverel, who had high musical taste, had been careful to preserve her from straining.

'Excellent, Caterina,' said Lady Cheverel, as there was a pause after the wonderful linked sweetness of 'Che farò.' 'I never heard you sing that so well. Once more!'

It was repeated; and then came 'Ho perduto,' which Sir Christopher encored, in spite of the clock, just striking nine. When the last note was dying out, he said—

'There's a clever black-eyed monkey. Now bring out the table for picquet.'

Caterina drew out the table, and placed the cards; then, with her rapid fairy suddenness of motion, threw herself on her knees, and clasped Sir Christopher's knee. He bent down, stroked her cheek, and smiled.

'Caterina, that is foolish,' said Lady Cheverel. 'I wish you would leave off those stage-players' antics.'

She jumped up, arranged the music on the harpsichord, and then, seeing the Baronet and his lady seated at picquet, quietly glided out of the room.

Captain Wybrow had been leaning near the harpsichord during the singing, and the chaplain had thrown himself on a sofa at the end of the room. They both now took up a book. Mr Gilfil chose the last number of the *Gentleman's Magazine*: Captain Wybrow, stretched on an ottoman near the door, opened *Faublas*; and there was perfect silence in the room which, ten minutes before, was vibrating to the passionate tones of Caterina.

She had made her way along the cloistered passages, now lighted here and there by a small oil-lamp, to the grand-staircase, which led directly to a gallery running along the whole eastern side of the building, where it was her habit to walk when she wished to be alone. The bright moonlight was streaming through the windows, throwing into strange light and shadow the heterogeneous objects that lined the long walls. Greek statues, and busts of Roman emperors; low cabinets filled with curiosities, natural and antiquarian; tropical birds, and huge horns of beasts; Hindoo gods and strange shells; swords and daggers, and bits of chain-armour; Roman lamps, and tiny models of Greek temples; and, above all these, queer old family portraits – of little boys and girls, once the hope of the Cheverels, with close-shaven heads imprisoned in stiff ruffs – of faded, pink-faced ladies, with rudimentary features and highly-developed head-dresses – of gallant gentlemen, with high hips, high shoulders, and red pointed beards.

Here, on rainy days, Sir Christopher and his lady took their promenade, and here billiards were played; but, in the evening, it was forsaken by all except Caterina – and, sometimes, one other person.

She paced up and down in the moonlight, her pale face and thin white-robed form making her look like the ghost of some former Lady Cheverel come to revisit the glimpses of the moon.

By-and-by she paused opposite the broad window above the portico, and looked out on the long vista of turf and trees now stretching chill and saddened in the moonlight.

Suddenly a breath of warmth and roses seemed to float towards her, and an arm stole gently round her waist, while a soft hand took up her tiny fingers. Caterina felt an electric thrill, and was motionless for one long moment; then she pushed away the arm and hand, and, turning round, lifted up to the face that hung over her, eyes full of tenderness and reproach. The fawn-like unconsciousness was gone, and in that one look were the ground tones of poor little Caterina's nature – intense love and fierce jealousy.

'Why do you push me away, Tina?' said Captain Wybrow in a half-whisper; 'are you angry with me for what a hard fate puts upon me? Would you have me cross my uncle – who has done so much for us both – in his dearest wish? You know I have duties – we both have duties – before which feeling must be sacrificed.'

'Yes, yes,' said Caterina, stamping her foot, and turning away her head; 'don't tell me what I know already.'

There was a voice speaking in Caterina's mind, to which she had never yet given vent. That voice said continually, 'Why did he make me love him – why did he let me know he loved me, if he knew all the while that he couldn't brave everything for my sake?' Then love answered, 'He was led on by the feeling of the moment, as you have been, Caterina; and now you ought to help him to do what is right.' Then the voice rejoined, 'It was a slight matter to him. He doesn't much mind giving you up. He will soon love that beautiful woman, and forget a poor little pale thing like you.'

Thus love, anger, and jealousy were struggling in that young soul.

'Besides, Tina,' continued Captain Wybrow in still gentler tones, 'I shall not succeed. Miss Assher very likely prefers some one else; and you know I have the best will in the world to fail. I shall come back a hapless bachelor – perhaps to find you already married to the good-looking chaplain, who is over head and ears in love with you. Poor Sir Christopher has made up his mind that you're to have Gilfil.'

'Why will you speak so? You speak from your own want of feeling. Go away from me.'

'Don't let us part in anger, Tina. All this may pass away. It's as likely as not that I may never marry any one at all. These palpitations may carry me off, and you may have the satisfaction of knowing that I shall never be anybody's bridegroom. Who knows what may happen? I may be my own master before I get into the bonds of holy matrimony, and be able to choose my little singing-bird. Why should we distress ourselves before the time?'

'It is easy to talk so when you are not feeling,' said Caterina, the tears flowing fast. 'It is bad to bear now, whatever may come after. But you don't care about my misery.'

'Don't I, Tina?' said Anthony in his tenderest tones, again stealing his arm round her waist, and drawing her towards him. Poor Tina was the slave of this voice and touch. Grief and resentment, retrospect and foreboding, vanished – all life before and after melted away in the bliss of that moment, as Anthony pressed his lips to hers.

Captain Wybrow thought, 'Poor little Tina! it would make her very happy to have me. But she is a mad little thing.'

At that moment a loud bell startled Caterina

from her trance of bliss. It was the summons to prayers in the chapel, and she hastened away, leaving Captain Wybrow to follow slowly.

It was a pretty sight, that family assembled to worship in the little chapel, where a couple of wax-candles threw a mild faint light on the figures kneeling there. In the desk was Mr Gilfil, with his face a shade graver than usual. On his right hand, kneeling on their red velvet cushions, were the master and mistress of the household, in their elderly dignified beauty. On his left, the youthful grace of Anthony and Caterina, in all the striking contrast of their colouring – he, with his exquisite outline and rounded fairness, like an Olympian god; she, dark and tiny, like a gypsy changeling. Then there were the domestics kneeling on red-covered forms, – the women headed by Mrs Bellamy, the natty little old housekeeper, in snowy cap and apron, and Mrs Sharp, my lady's maid, of somewhat vinegar aspect and flaunting attire; the men by Mr Bellamy the butler, and Mr Warren, Sir Christopher's venerable valet.

A few collects from the Evening Service was what Mr Gilfil habitually read, ending with the simple petition, 'Lighten our darkness.'

And then they all rose, the servants turning to curtsy and bow as they went out. The family returned to the drawing-room, said good-night to each other, and dispersed – all to speedy slumber except two. Caterina only cried herself to sleep after the clock had struck twelve. Mr Gilfil lay awake still longer, thinking that very likely Caterina was crying.

Captain Wybrow, having dismissed his valet at eleven, was soon in a soft slumber, his face looking like a fine cameo in high relief on the slightly-indented pillow.

CHAPTER 3

The last chapter has given the discerning reader sufficient insight into the state of things at Cheverel Manor in the summer of 1788. In that summer, we know, the great nation of France was agitated by conflicting thoughts and passions, which were but the beginning of sorrows. And in our Caterina's little breast, too, there were terrible struggles. The poor bird was beginning to flutter and vainly dash its soft breast against the hard iron bars of the inevitable, and we see too plainly the danger, if that anguish should go on heightening instead of being allayed, that the palpitating heart may be fatally bruised.

Meanwhile, if, as I hope, you feel some interest in Caterina and her friends at Cheverel Manor, you are perhaps asking, How came she to be there? How was it that this tiny, dark-eyed child of the south, whose face was immediately suggestive of olive-covered hills, and taper-lit shrines, came to have her home in that stately English manor-house, by the side of the blonde matron, Lady Cheverel – almost as if a humming-bird were found perched on one of the elm-trees in the park, by the side of her ladyship's handsomest pouter-pigeon? Speaking good English, too, and joining in Protestant prayers. Surely she must have been adopted and brought over to England at a very early age? She was.

During Sir Christopher's last visit to Italy with his lady, fifteen years before, they resided for some time at Milan, where Sir Christopher, who was an enthusiast for Gothic architecture, and was then entertaining the project of metamorphosing his plain brick family mansion into the model of a Gothic manor-house, was bent on studying the details of that marble miracle, the Cathedral. Here Lady Cheverel, as at other Italian cities where she made any protracted stay, engaged a *maestro* to give her lessons in singing, for she had then not only fine musical taste, but a fine soprano voice. Those were days when very rich people used manuscript music, and many a man who resembled Jean Jacques in nothing else, resembled him in getting a livelihood 'à copier la musique à tant la page.' Lady Cheverel having need of this service, Maestro Albani told her he would send her a *poveraccio* of his acquaintance, whose manuscript was the neatest and most correct he knew of. Unhappily, the *poveraccio* was not always in his best wits, and was sometimes rather slow in consequence; but it would be a work of Christian charity worthy of the beautiful Signora to employ poor Sarti.

The next morning, Mrs Sharp, then a blooming

abigail of three-and-thirty, entered her lady's private room, and said, 'If you please, my lady, there's the frowsiest, shabbiest man you ever saw outside, and he's told Mr Warren as the singing-master sent him to see your ladyship. But I think you'll hardly like him to come in here. Belike he's only a beggar.'

'O yes, show him in immediately.'

Mrs Sharp retired, muttering something about 'fleas and worse.' She had the smallest possible admiration for fair Ausonia and its natives, and even her profound deference for Sir Christopher and her lady could not prevent her from expressing her amazement at the infatuation of gentlefolks in choosing to sojourn among 'Papises, in countries where there was no getting to air a bit o' linen, and where the people smelt o' garlic fit to knock you down.'

However, she presently reappeared, ushering in a small meagre man, sallow and dingy, with a restless wandering look in his dull eyes, and an excessive timidity about his deep reverences, which gave him the air of a man who had been long a solitary prisoner. Yet through all this squalor and wretchedness there were some traces discernible of comparative youth and former good looks. Lady Cheverel, though not very tender-hearted, still less sentimental, was essentially kind, and liked to dispense benefits like a goddess, who looks down benignly on the halt, the maimed, and the blind that approach her shrine. She was smitten with some compassion at the sight of poor Sarti, who struck her as the mere battered wreck of a vessel that might have once floated gaily enough on its outward voyage, to the sound of pipes and tabors. She spoke gently as she pointed out to him the operatic selections she wished him to copy, and he seemed to sun himself in her auburn, radiant presence, so that when he made his exit with the music-books under his arm, his bow, though not less reverent, was less timid.

It was ten years at least since Sarti had seen anything so bright and stately and beautiful as Lady Cheverel. For the time was far off in which he had trod the stage in satin and feathers, the *primo tenore* of one short season. Alas! he had completely lost his voice in the following winter, and had ever since been little better than a cracked fiddle, which is good for nothing but firewood. For, like many Italian singers, he was too ignorant to teach, and if it had not been for his one talent of penmanship, he and his young helpless wife might have starved. Then, just after their third child was born, fever came, swept away the sickly mother and the two eldest children, and attacked Sarti himself, who rose from his sick-bed with enfeebled brain and muscle, and a tiny baby on his hands, scarcely four months old. He lodged over a fruit-shop kept by a stout virago, loud of tongue and irate in temper, but who had had children born to her, and so had taken care of the tiny yellow, black-eyed *bambinetta*, and tended

Sarti himself through his sickness. Here he continued to live, earning a meagre subsistence for himself and his little one by the work of copying music, put into his hands chiefly by Maestro Albani. He seemed to exist for nothing but the child: he tended it, he dandled it, he chatted to it, living with it alone in his one room above the fruit-shop, only asking his landlady to take care of the marmoset during his short absences in fetching and carrying home work. Customers frequenting that fruit-shop might often see the tiny Caterina seated on the floor with her legs in a heap of peas, which it was her delight to kick about; or perhaps deposited, like a kitten, in a large basket out of harm's way.

Sometimes, however, Sarti left his little one with another kind of protectress. He was very regular in his devotions, which he paid thrice a-week in the great cathedral, carrying Caterina with him. Here, when the high morning sun was warming the myriad glittering pinnacles without, and struggling against the massive gloom within, the shadow of a man with a child on his arm might be seen flitting across the more stationary shadows of pillar and mullion, and making its way towards a little tinsel Madonna hanging in a retired spot near the choir. Amid all the sublimities of the mighty cathedral, poor Sarti had fixed on this tinsel Madonna as the symbol of Divine mercy and protection, – just as a child, in the presence of a great landscape, sees none of the glories of wood and sky, but sets its heart on a floating feather or insect that happens to be on a level with its eye. Here, then, Sarti worshipped and prayed, setting Caterina on the floor by his side; and now and then, when the cathedral lay near some place where he had to call, and did not like to take her, he would leave her there in front of the tinsel Madonna, where she would sit, perfectly good, amusing herself with low crowing noises and see-sawings of her tiny body. And when Sarti came back, he always found that the Blessed Mother had taken good care of Caterina.

That was briefly the history of Sarti, who fulfilled so well the orders Lady Cheverel gave him, that she sent him away again with a stock of new work. But this time, week after week passed, and he neither reappeared nor sent home the music entrusted to him. Lady Cheverel began to be anxious, and was thinking of sending Warren to inquire at the address Sarti had given her, when one day, as she was equipped for driving out, the valet brought in a small piece of paper which he said had been left for her ladyship by a man who was carrying fruit. The paper contained only three tremulous lines, in Italian:—

'Will the Eccelentissima, for the love of God, have pity on a dying man, and come to him?'

Lady Cheverel recognized the handwriting as Sarti's in spite of its tremulousness, and, going down to her carriage, ordered the Milanese coachman to drive to Strada Quinquagesima,

178

Numero 10. The coach stopped in a dirty narrow street opposite La Pazzini's fruit-shop, and that large specimen of womanhood immediately presented herself at the door, to the extreme disgust of Mrs Sharp, who remarked privately to Mr Warren that La Pazzini was a 'hijeous porpis.' The fruit-woman, however, was all smiles and deep curtsies to the Eccelentissima, who, not very well understanding her Milanese dialect, abbreviated the conversation by asking to be shown at once to Signor Sarti. La Pazzini preceded her up the dark narrow stairs, and opened a door through which she begged her ladyship to enter. Directly opposite the door lay Sarti, on a low miserable bed. His eyes were glazed, and no movement indicated that he was conscious of their entrance.

On the foot of the bed was seated a tiny child, apparently not three years old, her head covered by a linen cap, her feet clothed with leather boots, above which her little yellow legs showed thin and naked. A frock, made of what had once been a gay flowered silk, was her only other garment. Her large dark eyes shone from out her queer little face, like two precious stones in a grotesque image carved in old ivory. She held an empty medicine-bottle in her hand, and was amusing herself with putting the cork in and drawing it out again, to hear how it would pop.

La Pazzini went up to the bed, and said, 'Ecco la nobilissima donna!' but directly after screamed out, 'Holy mother! he is dead!'

179

It was so. The entreaty had not been sent in time for Sarti to carry out his project of asking the great English lady to take care of his Caterina. That was the thought which haunted his feeble brain as soon as he began to fear that his illness would end in death. She had wealth – she was kind – she would surely do something for the poor orphan. And so, at last, he sent that scrap of paper, which won the fulfilment of his prayer, though he did not live to utter it. Lady Cheverel gave La Pazzini money that the last decencies might be paid to the dead man, and carried away Caterina, meaning to consult Sir Christopher as to what should be done with her. Even Mrs Sharp had been so smitten with pity by the scene she had witnessed when she was summoned up-stairs to fetch Caterina, as to shed a small tear, though she was not at all subject to that weak-ness; indeed, she abstained from it on principle, because, as she often said, it was known to be the worst thing in the world for the eyes.

On the way back to her hotel, Lady Cheverel turned over various projects in her mind regarding Caterina, but at last one gained the preference over all the rest. Why should they not take the child to England, and bring her up there? They had been married twelve years, yet Cheverel Manor was cheered by no children's voices, and the old house would be all the better for a little of that music. Besides, it would be a Christian work to train this little Papist into a good Protestant, and graft as much English fruit as possible on the Italian stem.

Sir Christopher listened to this plan with hearty acquiescence. He loved children, and took at once to the little black-eyed monkey – his name for Caterina all through her short life. But neither he nor Lady Cheverel had any idea of adopting her as their daughter, and giving her their own rank in life. They were much too English and aristocratic to think of anything so romantic. No! The child would be brought up at Cheverel Manor as a protegée, to be ultimately useful, perhaps, in sorting worsteds, keeping accounts, reading aloud, and otherwise supplying the place of spectacles when her ladyship's eyes should wax dim.

So Mrs Sharp had to procure new clothes, to replace the linen cap, flowered frock, and leathern boots; and now, strange to say, little Caterina, who had suffered many unconscious evils in her existence of thirty moons, first began to know conscious troubles. 'Ignorance,' says Ajax, 'is a painless evil;' so, I should think, is dirt, considering the merry faces that go along with it. At any rate, cleanliness is sometimes a painful good, as any one can vouch who has had his face washed the wrong way, by a pitiless hand with a gold ring on the third finger. If you, reader, have not known that initiatory anguish, it is idle to expect that you will form any approximate conception of what Caterina endured under Mrs Sharp's new dispensation of soap-and-water. Happily, this purgatory came presently to be associated in her tiny brain with a passage straightway to a seat of bliss – the sofa in Lady Cheverel's sitting-room, where there were toys to be broken, a ride was to be had on Sir Christopher's knee, and a spaniel of resigned temper was prepared to undergo small tortures without flinching.

CHAPTER 4

In three months from the time of Caterina's adoption – namely, in the late autumn of 1773 – the chimneys of Cheverel Manor were sending up unwonted smoke, and the servants were awaiting in excitement the return of their master and mistress after a two years' absence. Great was the astonishment of Mrs Bellamy, the housekeeper, when Mr Warren lifted a little black-eyed child out of the carriage, and great was Mrs Sharp's sense of superior information and experience, as she detailed Caterina's history, interspersed with copious comments, to the rest of the upper servants that evening, as they were taking a comfortable glass of grog together in the housekeeper's room.

A pleasant room it was, as any party need desire to muster in on a cold November evening. The fireplace alone was a picture: a wide and deep recess with a low brick altar in the middle, where great logs of dry wood sent myriad sparks up the dark chimney-throat; and over the front of this recess a large wooden entablature bearing this motto, finely carved in old English letters, **'Fear**

God and honour the King.' And beyond the party, who formed a half-moon with their chairs and well-furnished table round this bright fire-place, what a space of chiaroscuro for the imagination to revel in! Stretching across the far end of the room, what an oak table, high enough surely for Homer's gods, standing on four massive legs, bossed and bulging like sculptured urns! and, lining the distant wall, what vast cupboards, suggestive of inexhaustible apricot jam and promiscuous butler's perquisites! A stray picture or two had found their way down there, and made agreeable patches of dark brown on the buff-coloured walls. High over the loud-resounding double door hung one which, from some indications of a face looming out of blackness, might, by a great synthetic effort, be pronounced a Magdalen. Considerably lower down hung the similitude of a hat and feathers, with portions of a ruff, stated by Mrs Bellamy to represent Sir Francis Bacon, who invented gunpowder, and, in her opinion, 'might ha' been better emplyed.'

But this evening the mind is but slightly arrested by the great Verulam, and is in the humour to think a dead philosopher less interesting than a living gardener, who sits conspicuous in the half-circle round the fireplace. Mr Bates is habitually a guest in the housekeeper's room of an evening, preferring the social pleasures there – the feast of gossip and the flow of grog – to a bachelor's chair in his charming thatched cottage on a little island,

184

where every sound is remote but the cawing of rooks and the screaming of wild geese: poetic sounds, doubtless, but, humanly speaking, not convivial.

Mr Bates was by no means an average person, to be passed without special notice. He was a sturdy Yorkshireman, approaching forty, whose face Nature seemed to have coloured when she was in a hurry, and had no time to attend to *nuances*, for every inch of him visible above his neckcloth was of one impartial redness; so that when he was at some distance your imagination was at liberty to place his lips anywhere between his nose and chin. Seen closer, his lips were discerned to be of a peculiar cut, and I fancy this had something to do with the peculiarity of his dialect, which, as we shall see, was individual rather than provincial. Mr Bates was further distinguished from the common herd by a perpetual blinking of the eyes; and this, together with the red-rose tint of his complexion, and a way he had of hanging his head forward, and rolling it from side to side as he walked, gave him the air of a Bacchus in a blue apron, who, in the present reduced circumstances of Olympus, had taken to the management of his own vines. Yet, as gluttons are often thin, so sober men are often rubicund; and Mr Bates was sober, with that manly, British, churchman-like sobriety which can carry a few glasses of grog without any perceptible clarification of ideas.

'Dang my boottens!' observed Mr Bates, who, at the conclusion of Mrs Sharp's narrative, felt himself urged to his strongest interjection, 'it's what I shouldn't ha' looked for from Sir Cristhifer an' my ledy, to bring a furrin child into the coonthry; an' depend on't, whether you an' me lives to see't or noo, it'll coom to soom harm. The first sitiation iver I held – it was a hold, hancient habbey, wi' the biggest orchard o' apples an' pears you ever see – there was a French valet, an' he stool silk stoockins, an' shirts, an' rings, an' iverythin' he could ley his hans on, an' run awey at last wi' th' missis's jewl-box. They're all alaike, them furriners. It roons i' th' blood.'

'Well,' said Mrs Sharp, with the air of a person who held liberal views, but knew where to draw the line, 'I'm not a-going to defend the furriners, for I've as good reason to know what they are as most folks, an' nobody'll iver hear me say but what they're next door to heathens, and the hile they eat wi' their victuals is enough to turn any Christian's stomach. But for all that – an' for all as the trouble in respect o' washin' an' managin' has fell upo' me through the journey – I can't say but what I think as my Lady an' Sir Cristifer's done a right thing by a hinnicent child as doesn't know its right han' from its left, i' bringing it where it'll learn to speak summat better nor gibberish, and be brought up i' the true religion. For as for them furrin churches as Sir Cristifer is so unaccountable mad after, wi' picturs o' men an' women

186

a-showin' therselves just for all the world as God made 'em, I think, for my part, as it's welly a sin to go into 'em.'

'You're likely to have more foreigners, however,' said Mr Warren, who liked to provoke the gardener, 'for Sir Christopher has engaged some Italian workmen to help in the alterations in the house.'

'Olterations!' exclaimed Mrs Bellamy, in alarm. 'What olterations?'

'Why,' answered Mr Warren, 'Sir Christopher, as I understand, is going to make a clean new thing of the old Manor-house, both inside and out. And he's got portfolios full of plans and pictures coming. It is to be cased with stone, in the Gothic style – pretty near like the churches, you know, as far as I can make out; and the ceilings are to be beyond anything as has been seen in the country. Sir Christopher's been giving a deal of study to it.'

'Dear heart alive!' said Mrs Bellamy, 'we shall be pisined wi' lime an' plaster, an' hev the house full o' workmen colloguing wi' the maids, an' meckin' no end o' mischief.'

'That ye may ley your life on, Mrs Bellamy,' said Mr Bates. 'Howiver, I'll noot denay that the Goothic stayle's prithy anoof, an' it's woonderful how near them stoon-carvers cuts oot the shapes o' the pine apples, an' shamrucks, an' rooses. I dare sey Sir Cristhifer 'll meck a naice thing o' the Manor, an' there woont be many gentlemen's houses i' the coonthry as 'll coom up to't, wi' sich

187

a garden an' pleasure-groons an' wall-fruit as King George maight be prood on.'

'Well, I can't think as th' house can be better nor it is, Gothic or no Gothic,' said Mrs Bellamy; 'an' I've done the picklin' an' preservin' in it fourteen year Michaelmas was a three weeks. But what does my lady say to't?'

'My lady knows better than cross Sir Cristifer in what he's set his mind on,' said Mr Bellamy, who objected to the critical tone of the conversation. 'Sir Cristifer 'll hev his own way, *that* you may tek your oath. An' i' the right on't too. He's a gentleman born, an's got the money. But come, Mester Bates, fill your glass, an' we'll drink health an' happiness to his honour an' my lady, an' then you shall give us a sung. Sir Cristifer doesn't come hum from Italy ivery night.'

This demonstrable position was accepted without hesitation as ground for a toast; but Mr Bates, apparently thinking that his song was not an equally reasonable sequence, ignored the second part of Mr Bellamy's proposal. So Mrs Sharp, who had been heard to say that she had no thoughts at all of marrying Mr Bates, though he was 'a sensable fresh-coloured man as many a woman 'ud snap at for a husband,' enforced Mr Bellamy's appeal.

'Come, Mr Bates, let us hear "Roy's Wife." I'd rether hear a good old sung like that, nor all the fine 'talian toodlin'.'

Mr Bates, urged thus flatteringly, stuck his

thumbs into the armholes of his waistcoat, threw himself back in his chair with his head in that position in which he could look directly towards the zenith, and struck up a remarkably *staccato* rendering of 'Roy's Wife of Aldivalloch.' This melody may certainly be taxed with excessive iteration, but that was precisely its highest recommendation to the present audience, who found it all the easier to swell the chorus. Nor did it at all diminish their pleasure that the only particular concerning 'Roy's Wife' which Mr Bates's enunciation allowed them to gather, was that she 'chated' him, – whether in the matter of garden stuff or of some other commodity, or why her name should, in consequence, be repeatedly reiterated with exultation, remaining an agreeable mystery.

Mr Bates's song formed the climax of the evening's good-fellowship, and the party soon after dispersed – Mrs Bellamy, perhaps, to dream of quicklime flying among her preserving-pans, or of lovesick housemaids reckless of unswept corners – and Mrs Sharp to sink into pleasant visions of independent housekeeping in Mr Bates's cottage, with no bells to answer, and with fruit and vegetables *ad libitum*.

Caterina soon conquered all prejudices against her foreign blood; for what prejudices will hold out against helplessness and broken prattle? She became the pet of the household, thrusting Sir Christopher's favourite bloodhound of that day, Mrs Bellamy's two canaries, and Mr Bates's largest

Dorking hen, into a merely secondary position. The consequence was, that in the space of a summer's day she went through a great cycle of experiences, commencing with the somewhat acidulated goodwill of Mrs Sharp's nursery discipline. Then came the grave luxury of her ladyship's sitting-room, and, perhaps, the dignity of a ride on Sir Christopher's knee, sometimes followed by a visit with him to the stables, where Caterina soon learned to hear without crying the baying of the chained bloodhounds, and to say, with ostentatious bravery, clinging to Sir Christopher's leg all the while, 'Dey not hurt Tina.' Then Mrs Bellamy would perhaps be going out to gather the rose-leaves and lavender, and Tina was made proud and happy by being allowed to carry a handful in her pinafore; happier still, when they were spread out on sheets to dry, so that she could sit down like a frog among them, and have them poured over her in fragrant showers. Another frequent pleasure was to take a journey with Mr Bates through the kitchen-gardens and the hot-houses, where the rich bunches of green and purple grapes hung from the roof, far out of reach of the tiny yellow hand that couldn't help stretching itself out towards them; though the hand was sure at last to be satisfied with some delicate-flavoured fruit or sweet-scented flower. Indeed, in the long monotonous leisure of that great country-house, you may be sure there was always some one who had nothing better to do than to play with Tina.

So that the little southern bird had its northern nest lined with tenderness, and caresses, and pretty things. A loving sensitive nature was too likely, under such nurture, to have its susceptibility heightened into unfitness for an encounter with any harder experience; all the more, because there were gleams of fierce resistance to any discipline that had a harsh or unloving aspect. For the only thing in which Caterina showed any precocity was a certain ingenuity in vindictiveness. When she was five years old she had revenged herself for an unpleasant prohibition by pouring the ink into Mrs Sharp's workbasket; and once, when Lady Cheverel took her doll from her, because she was affectionately licking the paint off its face, the little minx straightway climbed on a chair and threw down a flower-vase that stood on a bracket. This was almost the only instance in which her anger overcame her awe of Lady Cheverel, who had the ascendancy always belonging to kindness that never melts into caresses, and is severely but uniformly beneficent.

By-and-by the happy monotony of Cheverel Manor was broken in upon in the way Mr Warren had announced. The roads through the park were cut up by wagons carrying loads of stone from a neighbouring quarry, the green courtyard became dusty with lime, and the peaceful house rang with the sound of tools. For the next ten years Sir Christopher was occupied with the architectural metamorphosis of his old family mansion; thus anticipating, through the prompting of his individual taste, that general reaction from the insipid imitation of the Palladian style, towards a restoration of the Gothic, which marked the close of the eighteenth century. This was the object he had set his heart on, with a singleness of determination which was regarded with not a little contempt by his fox-hunting neighbours, who wondered greatly that a man with some of the best blood in England in his veins, should be mean enough to economize in his cellar, and reduce his stud to two old coach-horses and a hack, for the sake of riding a hobby, and playing the architect. Their wives did not see so much to blame in the matter of the cellar and stables, but they were eloquent in pity for poor Lady Cheverel, who had to live in no more than three rooms at once, and who must be distracted with noises, and have her constitution undermined by unhealthy smells. It was as bad as having a husband with an asthma. Why did not Sir Christopher take a house for her at Bath, or, at least, if he must spend his time in overlooking workmen, somewhere in the neighbourhood of the Manor? This pity was quite gratuitous, as the most plentiful pity always is; for though Lady Cheverel did not share her husband's architectural enthusiasm, she had too rigorous a view of a wife's duties, and too profound a deference for Sir Christopher, to regard submission as a grievance. As for Sir Christopher, he was perfectly indifferent to criticism. 'An obstinate, crotchety man,' said his neighbours. But I, who have seen Cheverel Manor as he bequeathed it to his heirs, rather attribute that unswerving architectural purpose of his, conceived and carried out through long years of systematic personal exertion, to something of the fervour of genius, as well as inflexibility of will; and in walking through those rooms, with their splendid ceilings and their meagre furniture, which tell how all the spare money had been absorbed before personal comfort was thought of, I have felt that there dwelt in this old English baronet some of that sublime spirit which distinguishes art from luxury, and worships beauty apart from self-indulgence.

While Cheverel Manor was growing from ugliness into beauty, Caterina too was growing from a little yellow bantling into a whiter maiden, with no positive beauty indeed, but with a certain light airy grace, which, with her large appealing dark eyes, and a voice that, in its low-toned tenderness, recalled the love-notes of the stock-dove, gave her a more than usual charm. Unlike the building, however, Caterina's development was the result of no systematic or careful appliances. She grew up very much like the primroses, which the gardener is not sorry to see within his enclosure, but takes no pains to cultivate. Lady Cheverel taught her to read and write, and say her catechism; Mr Warren, being a good accountant, gave her lessons in arithmetic, by her ladyship's desire; and Mrs Sharp initiated her in all the mysteries of the needle. But, for a long time, there was no thought of giving her any more elaborate education. It is very likely that to her dying day Caterina thought the earth stood still, and that the sun and stars moved round it; but so, for the matter of that, did Helen, and Dido, and Desdemona, and Juliet; whence I hope you will not think my Caterina less worthy to be a heroine on that account. The truth is, that, with one exception, her only talent lay in loving; and there, it is probable, the most astronomical of women could not have surpassed her. Orphan and protegée though she was, this supreme talent of hers found plenty of exercise at Cheverel Manor, and Caterina had more people to love than many a small lady and gentleman affluent in silver mugs and blood relations. I think the first place in her childish heart was given to Sir Christopher, for little girls are apt to attach themselves to the finest-looking gentleman at hand, especially as he seldom has anything to do with discipline. Next to the Baronet came Dorcas, the merry rosy-cheeked damsel who was Mrs Sharp's lieutenant in the nursery, and thus played the part of the raisins in a dose of senna. It was a black day for Caterina when Dorcas married the coachman, and went, with a great sense of elevation in the world, to preside over a 'public' in the noisy town of Sloppeter. A little china box, bearing the motto 'Though lost to sight, to memory dear,' which Dorcas sent her as a remembrance, was among Caterina's treasures ten years after.

The one other exceptional talent, you already guess, was music. When the fact that Caterina had a remarkable ear for music, and a still more remarkable voice, attracted Lady Cheverel's notice, the discovery was very welcome both to her and Sir Christopher. Her musical education became at once an object of interest. Lady Cheverel devoted much time to it; and the rapidity of Tina's progress surpassing all hopes, an Italian singing-master was engaged, for several years, to spend some months together at Cheverel Manor. This unexpected gift made a great alteration in Caterina's position. After those first years in which little girls are petted like puppies and kittens, there comes a time when it seems less obvious what they can be good for, especially when, like Caterina, they give no particular promise of cleverness or beauty; and it is not surprising that in that uninteresting period there was no particular plan formed as to her future position. She could always help Mrs Sharp, supposing she were fit for nothing else, as she grew up; but now, this rare gift of song endeared her to Lady Cheverel, who loved music above all things, and it associated her at once with the pleasures of the drawing-room. Insensibly she came to be regarded as one of the family, and the servants began to understand that Miss Sarti was to be a lady after all.

'And the raight on't too,' said Mr Bates, 'for she hasn't the cut of a gell as must work for her bread; she's as neshan' dilicate as a paich-blossom – welly laike a linnet, wi' on'y joost body anoof to hold her voice.'

But long before Tina had reached this stage of her history, a new era had begun for her, in the arrival of a younger companion than any she had hitherto known. When she was no more than seven, a ward of Sir Christopher's – a lad of fifteen, Maynard Gilfil by name – began to spend his vacations at Cheverel Manor, and found there no playfellow so much to his mind as Caterina. Maynard was an affectionate lad, who retained a propensity to white rabbits, pet squirrels, and guinea-pigs, perhaps a little beyond the age at which young gentlemen usually look down on such pleasures as puerile. He was also much given to fishing, and to carpentry, considered as a fine art, without any base view to utility. And in all these pleasures it was his delight to have Caterina as his companion, to call her little pet names, answer her wondering questions, and have her toddling after him as you may have seen a Blenheim spaniel trotting after a large setter. Whenever Maynard went back to school, there was a little scene of parting.

'You won't forget me, Tina, before I come back again? I shall leave you all the whip-cord we've made; and don't you let Guinea die. Come, give me a kiss, and promise not to forget me.'

As the years wore on, and Maynard passed from school to college, and from a slim lad to a stalwart young man, their companionship in the vacations necessarily took a different form, but it retained a brotherly and sisterly familiarity. With Maynard the boyish affection had insensibly grown into ardent love. Among all the many kinds of first love, that which begins in childish companionship is the strongest and most enduring: when passion comes to unite its force to long affection, love is at its spring-tide. And Maynard Gilfil's love was of a kind to make him prefer being tormented by Caterina to any pleasure, apart from her, which the most benevolent magician could have devised for him. It is the way with those tall large-limbed men, from Samson downwards. As for Tina, the little minx was perfectly well aware that Maynard was her slave; he was the one person in the world whom she did as she pleased with; and I need not tell you that this was a symptom of her being perfectly heart-whole so far as he was concerned: for a passionate woman's love is always overshadowed by fear.

Maynard Gilfil did not deceive himself in his interpretation of Caterina's feelings, but he nursed the hope that some time or other she would at least care enough for him to accept his love. So he waited patiently for the day when he might venture to say, 'Caterina, I love you!' You see, he would have been content with very little, being one of those men who pass through life without making the least clamour about themselves; thinking neither the cut of his coat, nor the flavour of his soup, nor the precise depth of a servant's bow, at all momentous. He thought – foolishly enough, as lovers *will* think – that it was a good augury for him when he came to be domesticated at Cheverel Manor in the quality of chaplain there, and curate of a neighbouring parish; judging falsely, from his own case, that habit and affection were the likeliest avenues to love. Sir Christopher satisfied several feelings in installing Maynard as chaplain in his house. He liked the old-fashioned dignity of that domestic appendage; he liked his ward's companionship; and, as Maynard had some private fortune, he might take life easily in that agreeable home, keeping his hunter, and observing a mild regimen of clerical duty, until the Cumbermoor living should fall in, when he might be settled for life in the neighbourhood of the manor. 'With Caterina for a wife, too,' Sir Christopher soon began to think; for though the good Baronet was not at all quick to suspect what was unpleasant and opposed to his views of fitness, he was quick to see what would dovetail with his own plans; and he had first guessed, and then ascertained by direct inquiry, the state of Maynard's feelings. He at once leaped to the conclusion that Caterina was of the same mind, or at least would be, when she was old enough. But these were too early days for anything definite to be said or done.

Meanwhile, new circumstances were arising, which, though they made no change in Sir Christopher's plans and prospects, converted Mr Gilfil's hopes into anxieties, and made it clear to him not only that Caterina's heart was never likely to be his, but that it was given entirely to another.

Once or twice in Caterina's childhood, there had been another boy-visitor at the manor, younger than Maynard Gilfil – a beautiful boy with brown curls and splendid clothes, on whom Caterina had looked with shy admiration. This was Anthony Wybrow, the son of Sir Christopher's younger sister, and chosen heir of Cheverel Manor. The Baronet had sacrificed a large sum, and even straitened the resources by which he was to carry out his architectural schemes, for the sake of removing the entail from his estate, and making this boy his heir – moved to the step, I am sorry to say, by an implacable quarrel with his elder sister; for a power of forgiveness was not among Sir Christopher's virtues. At length, on the death of Anthony's mother, when he was no longer a curly-headed boy, but a tall young man, with a captain's commission, Cheverel Manor became *his* home too, whenever he was absent from his regiment. Caterina was then a little woman, between sixteen and seventeen, and I need not spend many words in explaining what you perceive to be the most natural thing in the world.

There was little company kept at the Manor, and Captain Wybrow would have been much duller if Caterina had not been there. It was pleasant to pay her attentions – to speak to her in gentle tones, to see her little flutter of pleasure, the blush that just lit up her pale cheek, and the momentary timid glance of her dark eyes, when he praised her singing, leaning at her side over the piano. Pleasant, too, to cut out that chaplain, with his large calves! What idle man can withstand the temptation of a woman to fascinate, and another man to eclipse? – especially when it is quite clear to himself that he means no mischief, and shall leave everything to come right again by-and-by. At the end of eighteen months, however, during which Captain Wybrow had spent much of his time at the Manor, he found that matters had reached a point which he had not at all contemplated. Gentle tones had led to tender words, and tender words had called forth a response of looks which made it impossible not to carry on the *crescendo* of love-making. To find oneself adored by a little, graceful, dark-eyed, sweet-singing woman, whom no one need despise, is an agreeable sensation, comparable to smoking the finest Latakia, and also imposes some return of tenderness as a duty.

Perhaps you think that Captain Wybrow, who knew that it would be ridiculous to dream of his marrying Caterina, must have been a reckless libertine to win her affections in this manner! Not at all. He was a young man of calm passions, who was rarely led into any conduct of which he could not give a plausible account to himself; and the tiny fragile Caterina was a woman who touched the imagination and the affections rather than the senses. He really felt very kindly towards her, and would very likely have loved her – if he had been able to love any one. But nature had not endowed him with that capability. She had given him an admirable figure, the whitest of hands, the most delicate of nostrils, and a large amount of serene self-satisfaction; but, as if to save such a delicate piece of work from any risk of being shattered, she had guarded him from the liability to a strong emotion. There was no list of youthful misdemeanours on record against him, and Sir Christopher and Lady Cheverel thought him the best of nephews, the most satisfactory of heirs, full of grateful deference to themselves, and, above all things, guided by a sense of duty. Captain Wybrow always did the thing easiest and most agreeable to him from a sense of duty: he dressed expensively, because it was a duty he owed to his position; from a sense of duty he adapted himself to Sir Christopher's inflexible will, which it would have been troublesome as well as useless to resist; and, being of a delicate constitution, he took care of his health from a sense of duty. His health was the only point on which he gave anxiety to his friends; and it was owing to this that Sir Christopher wished to see his nephew early married, the more so as a match after the Baronet's own heart appeared immediately attainable. Anthony had seen and admired Miss Assher, the only child of a lady who had been Sir Christopher's earliest love, but who, as things will happen in this world, had married another baronet instead of him. Miss

Assher's father was now dead, and she was in possession of a pretty estate. If, as was probable, she should prove susceptible to the merits of Anthony's person and character, nothing could make Sir Christopher so happy as to see a marriage which might be expected to secure the inheritance of Cheverel Manor from getting into the wrong hands. Anthony had already been kindly received by Lady Assher as the nephew of her early friend; why should he not go to Bath, where she and her daughter were then residing, follow up the acquaintance, and win a handsome, well-born, and sufficiently wealthy bride?

Sir Christopher's wishes were communicated to his nephew, who at once intimated his willingness to comply with them – from a sense of duty. Caterina was tenderly informed by her lover of the sacrifice demanded from them both; and three days afterwards occurred the parting scene you have witnessed in the gallery, on the eve of Captain Wybrow's departure for Bath.

CHAPTER 5

The inexorable ticking of the clock is like the throb of pain to sensations made keen by a sickening fear. And so it is with the great clock-work of nature. Daisies and buttercups give way to the brown waving grasses, tinged with the warm red sorrel; the waving grasses are swept away, and the meadows lie like emeralds set in the bushy hedgerows; the tawny-tipped corn begins to bow with the weight of the full ear; the reapers are bending amongst it, and it soon stands in sheaves; then, presently, the patches of yellow stubble lie side by side with streaks of dark red earth, which the plough is turning up in preparation for the new-thrashed seed. And this passage from beauty to beauty, which to the happy is like the flow of a melody, measures for many a human heart the approach of foreseen anguish – seems hurrying on the moment when the shadow of dread will be followed up by the reality of despair.

How cruelly hasty that summer of 1788 seemed to Caterina! Surely the roses vanished earlier, and the berries on the mountain-ash were more impatient to redden, and bring on the autumn, when she would be face to face with her misery, and witness Anthony giving all his gentle tones, tender words, and soft looks to another.

Before the end of July, Captain Wybrow had written word that Lady Assher and her daughter were about to fly from the heat and gaiety of Bath to the shady quiet of their place at Farleigh, and that he was invited to join the party there. His letters implied that he was on an excellent footing with both the ladies, and gave no hint of a rival; so that Sir Christopher was more than usually bright and cheerful after reading them. At length, towards the close of August, came the announcement that Captain Wybrow was an accepted lover, and after much complimentary and congratulatory correspondence between the two families, it was understood that in September Lady Assher and her daughter would pay a visit to Cheverel Manor, when Beatrice would make the acquaintance of her future relatives, and all needful arrangements could be discussed. Captain Wybrow would remain at Farleigh till then, and accompany the ladies on their journey.

In the interval, every one at Cheverel Manor had something to do by way of preparing for the visitors. Sir Christopher was occupied in consultations with his steward and lawyer, and in giving orders to every one else, especially in spurring on Francesco to finish the saloon. Mr Gilfil had the responsibility of procuring a lady's horse, Miss Assher being a great rider. Lady Cheverel had unwonted calls to make and invitations to deliver. Mr Bates's turf, and gravel, and flower-beds were always at such a point of neatness and finish that nothing extraordinary could be done in the garden, except a little extraordinary scolding of the under-gardener, and this addition Mr Bates did not neglect.

Happily for Caterina, she too had her task, to fill up the long dreary day-time: it was to finish a chair cushion which would complete the set of embroidered covers for the drawing-room, Lady Cheverel's year-long work, and the only noteworthy bit of furniture in the Manor. Over this embroidery she sat with cold lips and a palpitating heart, thankful that this miserable sensation throughout the day-time seemed to counteract the tendency to tears which returned with night and solitude. She was most frightened when Sir Christopher approached her. The Baronet's eye was brighter and his step more elastic than ever, and it seemed to him that only the most leaden or churlish souls could be otherwise than brisk and exulting in a world where everything went so well. Dear old gentleman! he had gone through life a little flushed with the power of his will, and now his latest plan was succeeding, and Cheverel Manor would be inherited by a grand-nephew, whom he might even yet live to see a fine young fellow with at least the down on his chin. Why not? one is still young at sixty.

Sir Christopher had always something playful to say to Caterina.

'Now, little monkey, you must be in your best voice; you're the minstrel of the Manor, you know, and be sure you have a pretty gown and a new ribbon. You must not be dressed in russet, though you are a singing-bird.' Or perhaps, 'It is your turn to be courted next, Tina. But don't you learn any naughty proud airs. I must have Maynard let off easily.'

Caterina's affection for the old Baronet helped her to summon up a smile as he stroked her cheek and looked at her kindly, but that was the moment at which she felt it most difficult not to burst out crying. Lady Cheverel's conversation and presence were less trying; for her ladyship felt no more than calm satisfaction in this family event; and besides, she was further sobered by a little jealousy at Sir Christopher's anticipation of pleasure in seeing Lady Assher, enshrined in his memory as a mild-eyed beauty of sixteen, with whom he had exchanged locks before he went on his first travels. Lady Cheverel would have died rather than confess it, but she couldn't help hoping that he would be disappointed in Lady Assher, and rather ashamed of having called her so charming.

Mr Gilfil watched Caterina through these days with mixed feelings. Her suffering went to his heart; but, even for her sake, he was glad that a love which could never come to good should be no longer fed by false hopes; and how could he help saying to himself, 'Perhaps, after a while, Caterina will be tired of fretting about that cold-hearted puppy, and then . . .'

At length the much-expected day arrived, and the brightest of September suns was lighting up the yellowing lime-trees, as about five o'clock Lady Assher's carriage drove under the portico. Caterina, seated at work in her own room, heard the rolling of the wheels, followed presently by the opening and shutting of doors, and the sound of voices in the corridors. Remembering that the dinner-hour was six, and that Lady Cheverel had desired her to be in the drawing-room early, she started up to dress, and was delighted to find herself feeling suddenly brave and strong. Curiosity to see Miss Assher – the thought that Anthony was in the house – the wish not to look unattractive, were feelings that brought some colour to her lips, and made it easy to attend to her toilette. They would ask her to sing this evening, and she would sing well. Miss Assher should not think her utterly insignificant. So she put on her grey silk gown and her cherry-coloured ribbon with as much care as if she had been herself the betrothed; not forgetting the pair of round pearl earrings which Sir Christopher had told Lady Cheverel to give her, because Tina's little ears were so pretty.

Quick as she had been, she found Sir Christopher and Lady Cheverel in the drawing-room, chatting with Mr Gilfil, and telling him how handsome

Miss Assher was, but how entirely unlike her mother – apparently resembling her father only.

'Aha!' said Sir Christopher, as he turned to look at Caterina, 'what do you think of this, Maynard? Did you ever see Tina look so pretty before? Why, that little grey gown has been made out of a bit of my lady's, hasn't it? It doesn't take anything much larger than a pocket-handkerchief to dress the little monkey.'

Lady Cheverel, too, serenely radiant in the assurance a single glance had given her of Lady Assher's inferiority, smiled approval, and Caterina was in one of those moods of self-possession and indifference which come as the ebb-tide between the struggles of passion. She retired to the piano, and busied herself with arranging her music, not at all insensible to the pleasure of being looked at with admiration the while, and thinking that, the next time the door opened, Captain Wybrow would enter, and she would speak to him quite cheerfully. But when she heard him come in, and the scent of roses floated towards her, her heart gave one great leap. She knew nothing till he was pressing her hand, and saying, in the old easy way, 'Well, Caterina, how do you do? You look quite blooming.'

She felt her cheeks reddening with anger that he could speak and look with such perfect nonchalance. Ah! he was too deeply in love with some one else to remember anything he had felt for *her*. But the next moment she was conscious of her folly; – 'as if he could show any feeling then!' This conflict of emotions stretched into a long interval the few moments that elapsed before the door opened again, and her own attention, as well as that of all the rest, was absorbed by the entrance of the two ladies.

The daughter was the more striking, from the contrast she presented to her mother, a round-shouldered, middle-sized woman, who had once had the transient pink-and-white beauty of a blonde, with ill-defined features and early embonpoint. Miss Assher was tall, and gracefully though substantially formed, carrying herself with an air of mingled graciousness and self-confidence; her dark brown hair, untouched by powder, hanging in bushy curls round her face, and falling behind in long thick ringlets nearly to her waist. The brilliant carmine tint of her well-rounded cheeks, and the finely-cut outline of her straight nose, produced an impression of splendid beauty, in spite of commonplace brown eyes, a narrow forehead, and thin lips. She was in mourning, and the dead black of her crape dress, relieved here and there by jet ornaments, gave the fullest effect to her complexion, and to the rounded whiteness of her arms, bare from the elbow. The first *coup d'œil* was dazzling, and as she stood looking down with a gracious smile on Caterina, whom Lady Cheverel was presenting to her, the poor little thing seemed to herself to feel, for the first time, all the folly of her former dream.

'We are enchanted with your place, Sir Christopher,' said Lady Assher, with a feeble kind of pompousness, which she seemed to be copying from some one else; 'I'm sure your nephew must have thought Farleigh wretchedly out of order. Poor Sir John was so very careless about keeping up the house and grounds. I often talked to him about it, but he said, 'Pooh, pooh! as long as my friends find a good dinner and a good bottle of wine, they won't care about my ceilings being rather smoky.' He was so very hospitable, was Sir John.'

'I think the view of the house from the park, just after we passed the bridge, particularly fine,' said Miss Assher, interposing rather eagerly, as if she feared her mother might be making infelicitous speeches, 'and the pleasure of the first glimpse was all the greater because Anthony would describe nothing to us beforehand. He would not spoil our first impressions by raising false ideas. I long to go over the house, Sir Christopher, and learn the history of all your architectural designs, which Anthony says have cost you so much time and study.'

'Take care how you set an old man talking about the past, my dear,' said the Baronet; 'I hope we shall find something pleasanter for you to do than turning over my old plans and pictures. Our friend Mr Gilfil here has found a beautiful mare for you, and you can scour the country to your heart's content. Anthony has sent us word what a horse-woman you are.'

Miss Assher turned to Mr Gilfil with her most beaming smile, and expressed her thanks with the elaborate graciousness of a person who means to be thought charming, and is sure of success.

'Pray do not thank me,' said Mr Gilfil, 'till you have tried the mare. She has been ridden by Lady Sara Linter for the last two years; but one lady's taste may not be like another's in horses, any more than in other matters.'

While this conversation was passing, Captain Wybrow was leaning against the mantelpiece, contenting himself with responding from under his indolent eyelids to the glances Miss Assher was constantly directing towards him as she spoke. 'She is very much in love with him,' thought Caterina. But she was relieved that Anthony remained passive in his attentions. She thought, too, that he was looking paler and more languid than usual. 'If he didn't love her very much – if he sometimes thought of the past with regret, I think I could bear it all, and be glad to see Sir Christopher made happy.'

During dinner there was a little incident which confirmed these thoughts. When the sweets were on the table, there was a mould of jelly just opposite Captain Wybrow, and being inclined to take some himself, he first invited Miss Assher, who coloured, and said, in rather a sharper key than usual, 'Have you not learned by this time that I never take jelly?'

'Don't you?' said Captain Wybrow, whose

211

perceptions were not acute enough for him to notice the difference of a semitone. 'I should have thought you were fond of it. There was always some on the table at Farleigh, I think.'

'You don't seem to take much interest in my likes and dislikes.'

'I'm too much possessed by the happy thought that you like me,' was the *ex officio* reply, in silvery tones.

This little episode was unnoticed by every one but Caterina. Sir Christopher was listening with polite attention to Lady Assher's history of her last man-cook, who was first-rate at gravies, and for that reason pleased Sir John – he was so particular about his gravies, was Sir John: and so they kept the man six years in spite of his bad pastry. Lady Cheverel and Mr Gilfil were smiling at Rupert the bloodhound, who had pushed his great head under his master's arm, and was taking a survey of the dishes, after snuffing at the contents of the Baronet's plate.

When the ladies were in the drawing-room again, Lady Assher was soon deep in a statement to Lady Cheverel of her views about burying people in woollen.

'To be sure, you must have a woollen dress, because it's the law, you know; but that need hinder no one from putting linen underneath. I always used to say, 'If Sir John died to-morrow, I would bury him in his shirt;' and I did. And let me advise you to do so by Sir Christopher. You never saw Sir John, Lady Cheverel. He was a large tall man, with a nose just like Beatrice, and so very particular about his shirts.'

Miss Assher, meanwhile, had seated herself by Caterina, and with that smiling affability which seems to say, 'I am really not at all proud, though you might expect it of me,' said,—

'Anthony tells me you sing so very beautifully. I hope we shall hear you this evening.'

'O yes,' said Caterina, quietly, without smiling; 'I always sing when I am wanted to sing.'

'I envy you such a charming talent. Do you know, I have no ear; I cannot hum the smallest tune, and I delight in music so. Is it not unfortunate? But I shall have quite a treat while I am here; Captain Wybrow says you will give us some music every day.'

'I should have thought you wouldn't care about music if you had no ear,' said Caterina, becoming epigrammatic by force of grave simplicity.

'O, I assure you, I dote on it; and Anthony is so fond of it; it would be so delightful if I could play and sing to him; though he says he likes me best not to sing, because it doesn't belong to his idea of me. What style of music do you like best?'

'I don't know. I like all beautiful music.'

'And are you as fond of riding as of music?'

'No; I never ride. I think I should be very frightened.'

'O no! indeed you would not, after a little practice. I have never been in the least timid. I think Anthony is more afraid for me than I am for myself; and since I have been riding with him, I have been obliged to be more careful, because he is so nervous about me.'

Caterina made no reply; but she said to herself, 'I wish she would go away, and not talk to me. She only wants me to admire her good-nature, and to talk about Anthony.'

Miss Assher was thinking at the same time, 'This Miss Sarti seems a stupid little thing. Those musical people often are. But she is prettier than I expected; Anthony said she was not pretty.'

Happily at this moment Lady Assher called her daughter's attention to the embroidered cushions, and Miss Assher, walking to the opposite sofa, was soon in conversation with Lady Cheverel about tapestry and embroidery in general, while her mother, feeling herself superseded there, came and placed herself beside Caterina.

'I hear you are the most beautiful singer,' was of course the opening remark. 'All Italians sing so beautifully. I travelled in Italy with Sir John when we were first married, and we went to Venice, where they go about in gondolas, you know. You don't wear powder, I see. No more will Beatrice; though many people think her curls would look all the better for powder. She has so much hair, hasn't she? Our last maid dressed it much better than this; but, do you know, she wore Beatrice's stockings before they went to the wash, and we couldn't keep her after that, could we?'

Caterina, accepting the question as a mere bit of rhetorical effect, thought it superfluous to reply, till Lady Assher repeated, 'Could we, now?' as if Tina's sanction were essential to her repose of mind. After a faint 'No,' she went on.

'Maids are so very troublesome, and Beatrice is so particular, you can't imagine. I often say to her, 'My dear, you can't have perfection.' That very gown she has on – to be sure, it fits her beautifully now – but it has been unmade and made up again twice. But she is like poor Sir John – he was so very particular about his own things, was Sir John. Is Lady Cheverel particular?'

'Rather. But Mrs Sharp has been her maid twenty years.'

'I wish there was any chance of our keeping Griffin twenty years. But I am afraid we shall have to part with her because her health is so delicate; and she is so obstinate, she will not take bitters as I want her. *You* look delicate, now. Let me recommend you to take camomile tea in a morning, fasting. Beatrice is so strong and healthy, she never takes any medicine; but if I had had twenty girls, and they had been delicate, I should have given them all camomile tea. It strengthens the constitution beyond anything. Now, will you promise me to take camomile tea?'

'Thank you; I'm not at all ill,' said Caterina. 'I've always been pale and thin.'

Lady Assher was sure camomile tea would make all the difference in the world – Caterina must see

215

if it wouldn't – and then went dribbling on like a leaky shower-bath, until the early entrance of the gentlemen created a diversion, and she fastened on Sir Christopher, who probably began to think that, for poetical purposes, it would be better not to meet one's first love again, after a lapse of forty years.

Captain Wybrow, of course, joined his aunt and Miss Assher, and Mr Gilfil tried to relieve Caterina from the awkwardness of sitting aloof and dumb, by telling her how a friend of his had broken his arm and staked his horse that morning, not at all appearing to heed that she hardly listened, and was looking towards the other side of the room. One of the tortures of jealousy is, that it can never turn away its eyes from the thing that pains it.

By-and-by every one felt the need of a relief from chit-chat – Sir Christopher perhaps the most of all – and it was he who made the acceptable proposition—

'Come, Tina, are we to have no music to-night before we sit down to cards? Your ladyship plays at cards, I think?' he added, recollecting himself, and turning to Lady Assher.

'O yes! Poor dear Sir John would have a whist-table every night.'

Caterina sat down to the harpsichord at once, and had no sooner begun to sing than she perceived with delight that Captain Wybrow was gliding towards the harpsichord, and soon standing in the old place. This consciousness gave fresh strength to her voice; and when she noticed that Miss

Assher presently followed him with that air of ostentatious admiration which belongs to the absence of real enjoyment, her closing *bravura* was none the worse for being animated by a little triumphant contempt.

'Why, you are in better voice than ever, Caterina,' said Captain Wybrow, when she had ended. 'This is rather different from Miss Hibbert's small piping that we used to be glad of at Farleigh, is it not, Beatrice?'

'Indeed it is. You are a most enviable creature, Miss Sarti – Caterina – may I not call you Caterina? for I have heard Anthony speak of you so often, I seem to know you quite well. You will let me call you Caterina?'

'O yes, every one calls me Caterina, only when they call me Tina.'

'Come, come, more singing, more singing, little monkey,' Sir Christopher called out from the other side of the room. 'We have not had half enough yet.'

Caterina was ready enough to obey, for while she was singing she was queen of the room, and Miss Assher was reduced to grimacing admiration. Alas! you see what jealousy was doing in this poor young soul. Caterina, who had passed her life as a little unobtrusive singing-bird, nestling so fondly under the wings that were outstretched for her, her heart beating only to the peaceful rhythm of love, or fluttering with some easily stifled fear, had begun to know the fierce palpitations of triumph and hatred.

When the singing was over, Sir Christopher and Lady Cheverel sat down to whist with Lady Assher and Mr Gilfil, and Caterina placed herself at the Baronet's elbow, as if to watch the game, that she might not appear to thrust herself on the pair of lovers. At first she was glowing with her little triumph, and felt the strength of pride; but her eye *would* steal to the opposite side of the fireplace, where Captain Wybrow had seated himself close to Miss Assher, and was leaning with his arm over the back of the chair, in the most lover-like position. Caterina began to feel a choking sensation. She could see, almost without looking, that he was taking up her arm to examine her bracelet; their heads were bending close together, her curls touching his cheek – now he was putting his lips to her hand. Caterina felt her cheeks burn – she could sit no longer. She got up, pretended to be gliding about in search of something, and at length slipped out of the room.

Outside, she took a candle, and, hurrying along the passages and up the stairs to her own room, locked the door.

'O, I cannot bear it, I cannot bear it!' the poor thing burst out aloud, clasping her little fingers, and pressing them back against her forehead, as if she wanted to break them.

Then she walked hurriedly up and down the room.

'And this must go on for days and days, and I must see it.'

She looked about nervously for something to clutch. There was a muslin kerchief lying on the table; she took it up and tore it into shreds as she walked up and down, and then pressed it into hard balls in her hand.

'And Anthony,' she thought, 'he can do this without caring for what I feel. O, he can forget everything: how he used to say he loved me – how he used to take my hand in his as we walked – how he used to stand near me in the evenings for the sake of looking into my eyes.'

'Oh, it is cruel, it is cruel!' she burst out again aloud, as all those love-moments in the past returned upon her. Then the tears gushed forth, she threw herself on her knees by the bed, and sobbed bitterly.

She did not know how long she had been there, till she was startled by the prayer-bell; when, thinking Lady Cheverel might perhaps send some one to inquire after her, she rose, and began hastily to undress, that there might be no possibility of her going down again. She had hardly unfastened her hair, and thrown a loose gown about her, before there was a knock at the door, and Mrs Sharp's voice said – 'Miss Tina, my lady wants to know if you're ill.'

Caterina opened the door and said, 'Thank you, dear Mrs Sharp; I have a bad headache; please tell my lady I felt it come on after singing.'

'Then, goodness me! why arn't you in bed, istid o' standing shivering there, fit to catch your death?

Come, let me fasten up your hair and tuck you up warm.'

'O no, thank you; I shall really be in bed very soon. Good-night, dear Sharpy; don't scold; I will be good, and get into bed.'

Caterina kissed her old friend coaxingly, but Mrs Sharp was not to be 'come over' in that way, and insisted on seeing her former charge in bed, taking away the candle which the poor child had wanted to keep as a companion.

But it was impossible to lie there long with that beating heart; and the little white figure was soon out of bed again, seeking relief in the very sense of chill and uncomfort. It was light enough for her to see about her room, for the moon, nearly at full, was riding high in the heavens among scattered hurrying clouds. Caterina drew aside the window-curtain; and, sitting with her forehead pressed against the cold pane, looked out on the wide stretch of park and lawn.

How dreary the moonlight is! robbed of all its tenderness and repose by the hard driving wind. The trees are harassed by that tossing motion, when they would like to be at rest; the shivering grass makes her quake with sympathetic cold; and the willows by the pool, bent low and white under that invisible harshness, seem agitated and helpless like herself. But she loves the scene the better for its sadness: there is some pity in it. It is not like that hard unfeeling happiness of lovers, flaunting in the eyes of misery.

She set her teeth tight against the window-frame, and the tears fell thick and fast. She was so thankful she could cry, for the mad passion she had felt when her eyes were dry, frightened her. If that dreadful feeling were to come on when Lady Cheverel was present, she should never be able to contain herself.

Then there was Sir Christopher – so good to her – so happy about Anthony's marriage; and all the while she had these wicked feelings.

'O, I cannot help it, I cannot help it!' she said in a loud whisper between her sobs. 'O God, have pity upon me!'

In this way Tina wore out the long hours of the windy moonlight, till at last, with weary aching limbs, she lay down in bed again, and slept from mere exhaustion.

While this poor little heart was being bruised with a weight too heavy for it, Nature was holding on her calm inexorable way, in unmoved and terrible beauty. The stars were rushing in their eternal courses; the tides swelled to the level of the last expectant weed; the sun was making brilliant day to busy nations on the other side of the swift earth. The stream of human thought and deed was hurrying and broadening onward. The astronomer was at his telescope; the great ships were labouring over the waves; the toiling eagerness of commerce, the fierce spirit of revolution, were only ebbing in brief rest; and sleepless statesmen were dreading the possible crisis of the morrow.

What were our little Tina and her trouble in this mighty torrent, rushing from one awful unknown to another? Lighter than the smallest centre of quivering life in the water-drop, hidden and uncared for as the pulse of anguish in the breast of the tiniest bird that has fluttered down to its nest with the long-sought food, and has found the nest torn and empty.

CHAPTER 6

The next morning, when Caterina was waked from her heavy sleep by Martha bringing in the warm water, the sun was shining, the wind had abated, and those hours of suffering in the night seemed unreal and dreamlike, in spite of weary limbs and aching eyes. She got up and began to dress with a strange feeling of insensibility, as if nothing could make her cry again; and she even felt a sort of longing to be down stairs in the midst of company, that she might get rid of this benumbed condition by contact.

There are few of us that are not rather ashamed of our sins and follies as we look out on the blessed morning sunlight, which comes to us like a bright-winged angel beckoning us to quit the old path of vanity that stretches its dreary length behind us; and Tina, little as she knew about doctrines and theories, seemed to herself to have been both foolish and wicked yesterday. To-day she would try to be good; and when she knelt down to say her short prayer – the very form she had learned by heart when she was ten years old – she added, 'O God, help me to bear it!'

That day the prayer seemed to be answered, for after some remarks on her pale looks at breakfast, Caterina passed the morning quietly, Miss Assher and Captain Wybrow being out on a riding excursion. In the evening there was a dinner-party, and after Caterina had sung a little, Lady Cheverel, remembering that she was ailing, sent her to bed, where she soon sank into a deep sleep. Body and mind must renew their force to suffer as well as to enjoy.

On the morrow, however, it was rainy, and every one must stay indoors; so it was resolved that the guests should be taken over the house by Sir Christopher, to hear the story of the architectural alterations, the family portraits, and the family relics. All the party, except Mr Gilfil, were in the drawing-room when the proposition was made; and when Miss Assher rose to go, she looked towards Captain Wybrow, expecting to see him rise too; but he kept his seat near the fire, turning his eyes towards the newspaper which he had been holding unread in his hand.

'Are you not coming, Anthony?' said Lady Cheverel, noticing Miss Assher's look of expectation.

'I think not, if you'll excuse me,' he answered, rising and opening the door; 'I feel a little chilled this morning, and I am afraid of the cold rooms and draughts.'

Miss Assher reddened, but said nothing, and passed on, Lady Cheverel accompanying her.

Caterina was seated at work in the oriel window. It was the first time she and Anthony had been alone together, and she had thought before that he wished to avoid her. But now, surely, he wanted to speak to her – he wanted to say something kind. Presently he rose from his seat near the fire, and placed himself on the ottoman opposite to her.

'Well, Tina, and how have you been all this long time?'

Both the tone and the words were an offence to her; the tone was so different from the old one, the words were so cold and unmeaning. She answered, with a little bitterness,—

'I think you needn't ask. It doesn't make much difference to you.'

'Is that the kindest thing you have to say to me after my long absence?'

'I don't know why you should expect me to say kind things.'

Captain Wybrow was silent. He wished very much to avoid allusions to the past or comments on the present. And yet he wished to be well with Caterina. He would have liked to caress her, make her presents, and have her think him very kind to her. But these women are so plaguy perverse! There's no bringing them to look rationally at anything. At last he said, 'I hoped you would think all the better of me, Tina, for doing as I have done, instead of bearing malice towards me. I hoped you would see that it is the best thing for every one – the best for your happiness too.'

'O pray don't make love to Miss Assher for the sake of my happiness,' answered Tina.

At this moment the door opened, and Miss Assher entered, to fetch her reticule, which lay on the harpsichord. She gave a keen glance at Caterina, whose face was flushed, and saying to Captain Wybrow with a slight sneer, 'Since you are so chill, I wonder you like to sit in the window,' left the room again immediately.

The lover did not appear much discomposed, but sat quiet a little longer, and then, seating himself on the music-stool, drew it near to Caterina, and, taking her hand, said, 'Come, Tina, look kindly at me, and let us be friends. I shall always be your friend.'

'Thank you,' said Caterina, drawing away her hand. 'You are very generous. But pray move away. Miss Assher may come in again.'

'Miss Assher be hanged!' said Anthony, feeling the fascination of old habit returning on him in his proximity to Caterina. He put his arm round her waist, and leaned his cheek down to hers. The lips couldn't help meeting after that; but the next moment, with heart swelling and tears rising, Caterina burst away from him, and rushed out of the room.

CHAPTER 7

Caterina tore herself from Anthony with the desperate effort of one who has just self-recollection enough left to be conscious that the fumes of charcoal will master his senses unless he bursts a way for himself to the fresh air; but when she reached her own room, she was still too intoxicated with that momentary revival of old emotions, too much agitated by the sudden return of tenderness in her lover, to know whether pain or pleasure predominated. It was as if a miracle had happened in her little world of feeling, and made the future all vague – a dim morning haze of possibilities, instead of the sombre wintry daylight and clear rigid outline of painful certainty.

She felt the need of rapid movement. She must walk out in spite of the rain. Happily, there was a thin place in the curtain of clouds which seemed to promise that now, about noon, the day had a mind to clear up. Caterina thought to herself, 'I will walk to the Mosslands, and carry Mr Bates the comforter I have made for him, and then Lady Cheverel will not wonder so much at my going out.' At the hall door she found Rupert, the old bloodhound, stationed on the mat, with the determination that the first person who was sensible enough to take a walk that morning should have the honour of his approbation and society. As he thrust his great black and tawny head under her hand, and wagged his tail with vigorous eloquence, and reached the climax of his welcome by jumping up to lick her face, which was at a convenient licking height for him, Caterina felt quite grateful to the old dog for his friendliness. Animals are such agreeable friends – they ask no questions, they pass no criticisms.

The 'Mosslands' was a remote part of the grounds, encircled by the little stream issuing from the pool; and certainly, for a wet day, Caterina could hardly have chosen a less suitable walk, for though the rain was abating, and presently ceased altogether, there was still a smart shower falling from the trees which arched over the greater part of her way. But she found just the desired relief from her feverish excitement in labouring along the wet paths with an umbrella that made her arm ache. This amount of exertion was to her tiny body what a day's hunting often was to Mr Gilfil, who at times had *his* fits of jealousy and sadness to get rid of, and wisely had recourse to nature's innocent opium – fatigue.

When Caterina reached the pretty arched wooden bridge which formed the only entrance to the Mosslands for any but webbed feet, the sun had mastered the clouds, and was shining through the boughs of the tall elms that made a deep nest for the gardener's cottage – turning the raindrops into diamonds, and inviting the nasturtium flowers creeping over the porch and low-thatched roof to lift up their flame-coloured heads once more. The rooks were cawing with many-voiced monotony, apparently – by a remarkable approximation to human intelligence – finding great conversational resources in the change of weather. The mossy turf, studded with the broad blades of marsh-loving plants, told that Mr Bates's nest was rather damp in the best of weather; but he was of opinion that a little external moisture would hurt no man who was not perversely neglectful of that obvious and providential antidote, rum-and-water.

Caterina loved this nest. Every object in it, every sound that haunted it, had been familiar to her from the days when she had been carried thither on Mr Bates's arm, making little cawing noises to imitate the rooks, clapping her hands at the green frogs leaping in the moist grass, and fixing grave eyes on the gardener's fowls cluck-clucking under their pens. And now the spot looked prettier to her than ever; it was so out of the way of Miss Assher, with her brilliant beauty, and personal claims, and small civil remarks. She thought Mr Bates would not be come in to his dinner yet, so she would sit down and wait for him.

But she was mistaken. Mr Bates was seated in his arm-chair, with his pocket-handkerchief thrown over his face, as the most eligible mode of passing away those superfluous hours between meals when the weather drives a man in-doors. Roused by the furious barking of his chained bulldog, he descried his little favourite approaching, and forthwith presented himself at the doorway, looking disproportionately tall compared with the height of his cottage. The bulldog, meanwhile, unbent from the severity of his official demeanour, and commenced a friendly interchange of ideas with Rupert.

Mr Bates's hair was now grey, but his frame was none the less stalwart, and his face looked all the redder, making an artistic contrast with the deep blue of his cotton neckerchief, and of his linen apron twisted into a girdle round his waist.

'Why, dang my boottons, Miss Tiny,' he exclaimed, 'hoo coom ye to coom oot dabblin' your faet laike a little Muscovy duck, sich a day as this? Not but what ai'm delaighted to sae ye. Here Hesther,' he called to his old humpbacked housekeeper, 'tek the yoong ledy's oombrella an' spread it oot to dray. Coom, coom in, Miss Tiny, an' set ye doon by the faire an' dray yer faet, an' hev summat warm to kape ye from ketchin' coold.'

Mr Bates led the way, stooping under the door-places, into his small sitting-room, and, shaking the patch-work cushion in his arm-chair, moved it to within a good roasting distance of the blazing fire.

'Thank you, uncle Bates' (Caterina kept up her childish epithets for her friends, and this was one of them); 'not quite so close to the fire, for I am warm with walking.'

'Eh, but yer shoes are faine an' wet, an' ye must put up yer faet on the finder. Rare big faet, baint 'em? – aboot the saize of a good big spoon. I woonder ye can mek a shift to stan' on 'em. Now, what'll ye hev to warm yer insaide? a drop o' hot elder-wain, now?'

'No, not anything to drink, thank you; it isn't very long since breakfast,' said Caterina, drawing out the comforter from her deep pocket. Pockets were capacious in those days. 'Look here, uncle Bates; here is what I came to bring you. I made it on purpose for you. You must wear it this winter, and give your red one to old Brooks.'

'Eh, Miss Tiny, this *is* a beauty. An' ye made it all wi' yer little fingers for an old feller laike mae! I tek it very kaind on ye, an' I belave ye I'll wear it, and be prood on't too. These sthraipes, blue an' whaite, now, they mek it uncommon pritty.'

'Yes, that will suit your complexion, you know, better than the old scarlet one. I know Mrs Sharp will be more in love with you than ever when she sees you in the new one.'

'My complexion, ye little roogue! ye're alaughin' at me. But talkin' o' complexions, what a beautiful cooler the bride as is to be hes on her cheeks! Dang my boottons! she looks faine an' handsome o' hossback – sits as upraight as a dart, wi' a figure like a statty! Misthress Sharp has promised to put me behaind one o' the doors when the

231

ladies are comin' doon to dinner, so as I may sae the young un i' full dress, wi' all her curls an' that. Misthress Sharp says she's a'most beautifuller nor my ledy was when she was yoong; an' I think ye'll noot faind many i' the counthry as'll coom up to that.'

'Yes, Miss Assher is very handsome,' said Caterina, rather faintly, feeling the sense of her own insignificance returning at this picture of the impression Miss Assher made on others.

'Well, an' I hope she's good too, an'll mek a good naice to Sir Cristhifer an' my ledy. Misthress Griffin, the maid, says as she's rether tatchy and find-fautin' aboot her cloothes, laike. But she's yoong – she's yoong; that'll wear off when she's got a hoosband, an' children, an' summat else to think on. Sir Cristhifer's fain an' delaighted, I can see. He says to me th' other mornin', says he, "Well, Bates, what do you think of your young misthress as is to be?" An' I says, "Whay, yer honour, I think she's as fain a lass as iver I set eyes on; an' I wish the Captain luck in a fain family, an' your honour laife an' health to see't." Mr Warren says as the masther's all for forrardin' the weddin', an' it'll very laike be afore the autumn's oot.'

As Mr Bates ran on, Caterina felt something like a painful contraction at her heart. 'Yes,' she said, rising, 'I dare say it will. Sir Christopher is very anxious for it. But I must go, uncle Bates; Lady Cheverel will be wanting me, and it is your dinner-time.'

'Nay, my dinner doont sinnify a bit; but I moosn't kaep ye if my ledy wants ye. Though I hevn't thanked ye half anoof for the comfiter – the wrap-raskil, as they call't. My feckins, it's a beauty. But ye look very whaite and sadly, Miss Tiny; I doubt ye're poorly; an' this walkin' i' th' wet isn't good for ye.'

'O yes, it is indeed,' said Caterina, hastening out, and taking up her umbrella from the kitchen floor. 'I must really go now; so good-bye.'

She tripped off, calling Rupert, while the good gardener, his hands thrust deep in his pockets, stood looking after her and shaking his head with rather a melancholy air.

'She gets moor nesh and dillicat than iver,' he said, half to himself and half to Hester. 'I shouldn't woonder if she fades away, laike them cyclamens as I transplanted. She puts me i' maind on 'em somehow, hangin' on their little thin stalks, so whaite an' tinder.'

The poor little thing made her way back, no longer hungering for the cold moist air as a counteractive of inward excitement, but with a chill at her heart which made the outward chill only depressing. The golden sunlight beamed through the dripping boughs like a Shechinah, or visible divine presence, and the birds were chirping and trilling their new autumnal songs so sweetly, it seemed as if their throats, as well as the air, were all the clearer for the rain; but Caterina moved through all this joy and beauty like a poor wounded leveret painfully dragging its little body through the sweet clover-tufts – for it, sweet in vain. Mr Bates's words about Sir Christopher's joy, Miss Assher's beauty, and the nearness of the wedding, had come upon her like the pressure of a cold hand, rousing her from confused dozing to a perception of hard, familiar realities. It is so with emotional natures, whose thoughts are no more than the fleeting shadows cast by feeling: to them words are facts, and, even when known to be false, have a mastery over their smiles and tears. Caterina entered her own room again, with no other change from her former state of despondency and wretchedness than an additional sense of injury from Anthony. His behaviour towards her in the morning was a new wrong. To snatch a caress when she justly claimed an expression of penitence, of regret, of sympathy, was to make more light of her than ever.

CHAPTER 8

That evening Miss Assher seemed to carry herself with unusual haughtiness, and was coldly observant of Caterina. There was unmistakably thunder in the air. Captain Wybrow appeared to take the matter very easily, and was inclined to brave it out by paying more than ordinary attention to Caterina. Mr Gilfil had induced her to play a game at draughts with him, Lady Assher being seated at picquet with Sir Christopher, and Miss Assher in determined conversation with Lady Cheverel. Anthony, thus left as an odd unit, sauntered up to Caterina's chair, and leaned behind her, watching the game. Tina, with all the remembrances of the morning thick upon her, felt her cheeks becoming more and more crimson, and at last said impatiently, 'I wish you would go away.'

This happened directly under the view of Miss Assher, who saw Caterina's reddening cheeks, saw that she said something impatiently, and that Captain Wybrow moved away in consequence. There was another person, too, who had noticed this incident with strong interest, and who was moreover aware that Miss Assher not only saw, but keenly observed what was passing. That other person was Mr Gilfil, and he drew some painful conclusions which heightened his anxiety for Caterina.

The next morning, in spite of the fine weather, Miss Assher declined riding, and Lady Cheverel, perceiving that there was something wrong between the lovers, took care that they should be left together in the drawing-room. Miss Assher, seated on the sofa near the fire, was busy with some fancy-work, in which she seemed bent on making great progress this morning. Captain Wybrow sat opposite with a newspaper in his hand, from which he obligingly read extracts with an elaborately easy air, wilfully unconscious of the contemptuous silence with which she pursued her filigree work. At length he put down the paper, which he could no longer pretend not to have exhausted, and Miss Assher then said,—

'You seem to be on very intimate terms with Miss Sarti.'

'With Tina? oh yes; she has always been the pet of the house, you know. We have been quite brother and sister together.'

'Sisters don't generally colour so very deeply when their brothers approach them.'

'Does she colour? I never noticed it. But she's a timid little thing.'

'It would be much better if you would not be so hypocritical, Captain Wybrow. I am confident there has been some flirtation between you. Miss Sarti, in her position, would never speak to you with the petulance she did last night, if you had not given her some kind of claim on you.'

'My dear Beatrice, now do be reasonable; do ask yourself what earthly probability there is that I should think of flirting with poor little Tina. *Is* there anything about her to attract that sort of attention? She is more child than woman. One thinks of her as a little girl to be petted and played with.'

'Pray, what were you playing at with her yesterday morning, when I came in unexpectedly, and her cheeks were flushed, and her hands trembling?'

'Yesterday morning? – O, I remember. You know I always tease her about Gilfil, who is over head and ears in love with her; and she is angry at that, – perhaps, because she likes him. They were old playfellows years before I came here, and Sir Christopher has set his heart on their marrying.'

'Captain Wybrow, you are very false. It had nothing to do with Mr Gilfil that she coloured last night when you leaned over her chair. You might just as well be candid. If your own mind is not made up, pray do no violence to yourself. I am quite ready to give way to Miss Sarti's superior attractions. Understand that, so far as I am concerned, you are perfectly at liberty. I decline any share in the affection of a man who forfeits my respect by duplicity.'

In saying this, Miss Assher rose, and was sweeping haughtily out of the room, when Captain Wybrow placed himself before her, and took her hand.

'Dear, dear Beatrice, be patient; do not judge me so rashly. Sit down again, sweet,' he added in a pleading voice, pressing both her hands between his, and leading her back to the sofa, where he sat down beside her. Miss Assher was not unwilling to be led back or to listen, but she retained her cold and haughty expression.

'Can you not trust me, Beatrice? Can you not believe me, although there may be things I am unable to explain?'

'Why should there be anything you are unable to explain? An honourable man will not be placed in circumstances which he cannot explain to the woman he seeks to make his wife. He will not ask her to *believe* that he acts properly; he will let her *know* that he does so. Let me go, sir.'

She attempted to rise, but he passed his hand round her waist and detained her.

'Now, Beatrice dear,' he said imploringly, 'can you not understand that there are things a man doesn't like to talk about – secrets that he must keep for the sake of others, and not for his own sake? Everything that relates to myself you may ask me, but do not ask me to tell other people's secrets. Don't you understand me?'

'O yes,' said Miss Assher scornfully, 'I understand. Whenever you make love to a woman – that is her secret, which you are bound to keep for her. But it is folly to be talking in this way, Captain Wybrow. It is very plain that there is some relation more than friendship between you and Miss Sarti. Since you cannot explain that relation, there is no more to be said between us.'

'Confound it, Beatrice! you'll drive me mad. Can a fellow help a girl's falling in love with him? Such things are always happening, but men don't talk of them. These fancies will spring up without the slightest foundation, especially when a woman sees few people; they die out again when there is no encouragement. If you could like me, you ought not to be surprised that other people can; you ought to think the better of them for it.'

'You mean to say, then, that Miss Sarti is in love with you, without your ever having made love to her.'

'Do not press me to say such things, dearest. It is enough that you know I love you – that I am devoted to you. You naughty queen you, you know there is no chance for any one else where you are. You are only tormenting me, to prove your power over me. But don't be too cruel; for you know they say I have another heart-disease besides love, and these scenes bring on terrible palpitations.'

'But I must have an answer to this one question,' said Miss Assher, a little softened: 'Has there been, or is there, any love on your side towards Miss Sarti? I have nothing to do with her feelings, but I have a right to know yours.'

'I like Tina very much; who would not like such a little simple thing? You would not wish me not to like her? But love – that is a very different affair. One has a brotherly affection for such a woman as Tina; but it is another sort of woman that one loves.'

These last words were made doubly significant by a look of tenderness, and a kiss imprinted on the hand Captain Wybrow held in his. Miss Assher was conquered. It was so far from probable that Anthony should love that pale insignificant little thing – so highly probable that he should adore the beautiful Miss Assher. On the whole, it was rather gratifying that other women should be languishing for her handsome lover; he really was an exquisite creature. Poor Miss Sarti! Well, she would get over it.

Captain Wybrow saw his advantage. 'Come, sweet love,' he continued, 'let us talk no more about unpleasant things. You will keep Tina's secret, and be very kind to her – won't you? – for my sake. But you will ride out now? See what a glorious day it is for riding. Let me order the horses. I'm terribly in want of the air. Come, give me one forgiving kiss, and say you will go.'

Miss Assher complied with the double request, and then went to equip herself for the ride, while her lover walked to the stables.

CHAPTER 9

Meanwhile Mr Gilfil, who had a heavy weight on his mind, had watched for the moment when, the two elder ladies having driven out, Caterina would probably be alone in Lady Cheverel's sitting-room. He went up and knocked at the door.

'Come in,' said the sweet mellow voice, always thrilling to him as the sound of rippling water to the thirsty.

He entered and found Caterina standing in some confusion, as if she had been startled from a reverie. She felt relieved when she saw it was Maynard, but, the next moment, felt a little pettish that he should have come to interrupt and frighten her.

'Oh, it is you, Maynard! Do you want Lady Cheverel?'

'No, Caterina,' he answered gravely; 'I want you. I have something very particular to say to you. Will you let me sit down with you for half an hour?'

'Yes, dear old preacher,' said Caterina, sitting down with an air of weariness; 'what is it?'

Mr Gilfil placed himself opposite to her, and said, 'I hope you will not be hurt, Caterina, by what I am going to say to you. I do not speak from any other feelings than real affection and anxiety for you. I put everything else out of the question. You know you are more to me than all the world; but I will not thrust before you a feeling which you are unable to return. I speak to you as a brother – the old Maynard that used to scold you for getting your fishing-line tangled ten years ago. You will not believe that I have any mean, selfish motive in mentioning things that are painful to you?'

'No; I know you are very good,' said Caterina abstractedly.

'From what I saw yesterday evening,' Mr Gilfil went on, hesitating and colouring slightly, 'I am led to fear – pray forgive me if I am wrong, Caterina – that you – that Captain Wybrow is base enough still to trifle with your feelings, that he still allows himself to behave to you as no man ought who is the declared lover of another woman.'

'What do you mean, Maynard?' said Caterina, with anger flashing from her eyes. 'Do you mean that I let him make love to me? What right have you to think that of me? What do you mean that you saw yesterday evening?'

'Do not be angry, Caterina. I don't suspect you of doing wrong. I only suspect that heartless puppy of behaving so as to keep awake feelings in you that not only destroy your own peace of mind, but may lead to very bad consequences with regard to others. I want to warn you that Miss Assher has her eyes open on what passes between you and Captain Wybrow, and I feel sure she is getting jealous of you. Pray be very careful, Caterina, and try to behave with politeness and indifference to him. You must see by this time that he is not worth the feeling you have given him. He's more disturbed at his pulse beating one too many in a minute, than at all the misery he has caused you by his foolish trifling.'

'You ought not to speak so of him, Maynard,' said Caterina, passionately. 'He is not what you think. He *did* care for me; he *did* love me; only he wanted to do what his uncle wished.'

'O to be sure! I know it is only from the most virtuous motives that he does what is convenient to himself.'

Mr Gilfil paused. He felt that he was getting irritated, and defeating his own object. Presently he continued in a calm and affectionate tone.

'I will say no more about what I think of him, Caterina. But whether he loved you or not, his position now with Miss Assher is such that any love you may cherish for him can bring nothing but misery. God knows, I don't expect you to leave off loving him at a moment's notice. Time and absence, and trying to do what is right, are the only cures. If it were not that Sir Christopher and Lady Cheverel would be displeased and puzzled at your wishing to leave home just now, I would beg you to pay a visit to my sister. She and her husband are good creatures, and would make their house a home to you. But I could not urge the thing just now without giving a special reason; and what is most of all to be dreaded is the raising of any suspicion in Sir Christopher's mind of what has happened in the past, or of your present feelings. You think so too, don't you, Tina?'

Mr Gilfil paused again, but Caterina said nothing. She was looking away from him, out of the window, and her eyes were filling with tears. He rose, and, advancing a little towards her, held out his hand and said,—

'Forgive me, Caterina, for intruding on your feelings in this way. I was so afraid you might not be aware how Miss Assher watched you. Remember, I entreat you, that the peace of the whole family depends on your power of governing yourself. Only say you forgive me before I go.'

'Dear, good Maynard,' she said, stretching out her little hand, and taking two of his large fingers in her grasp, while her tears flowed fast; 'I am very cross to you. But my heart is breaking. I don't know what I do. Good-bye.'

He stooped down, kissed the little hand, and then left the room.

'The cursed scoundrel!' he muttered between his teeth, as he closed the door behind him. 'If it were not for Sir Christopher, I should like to pound him into paste to poison puppies like himself!'

CHAPTER 10

That evening Captain Wybrow, returning from a long ride with Miss Assher, went up to his dressing-room, and seated himself with an air of considerable lassitude before his mirror. The reflection there presented of his exquisite self was certainly paler and more worn than usual, and might excuse the anxiety with which he first felt his pulse, and then laid his hand on his heart.

'It's a devil of a position this for a man to be in,' was the train of his thought, as he kept his eyes fixed on the glass, while he leaned back in his chair, and crossed his hands behind his head; 'between two jealous women, and both of them as ready to take fire as tinder. And in my state of health too! I should be glad enough to run away from the whole affair, and go off to some lotos-eating place or other where there are no women, or only women who are too sleepy to be jealous. Here am I, doing nothing to please myself, trying to do the best thing for everybody else, and all the comfort I get is to have fire shot at me from women's eyes, and venom spirted at me from women's tongues.

If Beatrice takes another jealous fit into her head – and it's likely enough, Tina is so unmanageable – I don't know what storm she may raise. And any hitch in this marriage, especially of that sort, might be a fatal business for the old gentleman. I wouldn't have such a blow fall upon him for a great deal. Besides, a man must be married some time in his life, and I could hardly do better than marry Beatrice. She's an uncommonly fine woman, and I'm really very fond of her; and as I shall let her have her own way, her temper won't signify much. I wish the wedding was over and done with, for this fuss doesn't suit me at all. I haven't been half so well lately. That scene about Tina this morning quite upset me. Poor little Tina! What a little simpleton it was, to set her heart on me in that way! But she ought to see how impossible it is that things should be different. If she would but understand how kindly I feel towards her, and make up her mind to look on me as a friend; – but that is what one never can get a woman to do. Beatrice is very good-natured; I'm sure she would be kind to the little thing. It would be a great comfort if Tina would take to Gilfil, if it were only in anger against me. He'd make her a capital husband, and I should like to see the little grasshopper happy. If I had been in a different position, I would certainly have married her myself; but that was out of the question with my responsibilities to Sir Christopher. I think a little persuasion from my uncle would bring her to accept Gilfil; I know she would never be able to oppose my uncle's wishes. And if they were once married, she's such a loving little thing, she would soon be billing and cooing with him as if she had never known me. It would certainly be the best thing for her happiness if that marriage were hastened. Heigho! Those are lucky fellows that have no women falling in love with them. It's a confounded responsibility.'

At this point in his meditations he turned his head a little, so as to get a three-quarter view of his face. Clearly it was the '*dono infelice della bellezza*' that laid these onerous duties upon him – an idea which naturally suggested that he should ring for his valet.

For the next few days, however, there was such a cessation of threatening symptoms as to allay the anxiety both of Captain Wybrow and Mr Gilfil. All earthly things have their lull: even on nights when the most unappeasable wind is raging, there will be a moment of stillness before it crashes among the boughs again, and storms against the windows, and howls like a thousand lost demons through the keyholes.

Miss Assher appeared to be in the highest good-humour; Captain Wybrow was more assiduous than usual, and was very circumspect in his behaviour to Caterina, on whom Miss Assher bestowed unwonted attentions. The weather was brilliant; there were riding excursions in the mornings and dinner-parties in the evenings.

Consultations in the library between Sir Christopher and Lady Assher seemed to be leading to a satisfactory result; and it was understood that this visit at Cheverel Manor would terminate in another fortnight, when the preparations for the wedding would be carried forward with all dispatch at Farleigh. The Baronet seemed every day more radiant. Accustomed to view people who entered into his plans by the pleasant light which his own strong will and bright hopefulness were always casting on the future, he saw nothing but personal charms and promising domestic qualities in Miss Assher, whose quickness of eye and taste in externals formed a real ground of sympathy between her and Sir Christopher. Lady Cheverel's enthusiasm never rose above the temperate mark of calm satisfaction, and having quite her share of the critical acumen which characterizes the mutual estimates of the fair sex, she had a more moderate opinion of Miss Assher's qualities. She suspected that the fair Beatrice had a sharp and imperious temper; and being herself, on principle and by habitual self-command, the most deferential of wives, she noticed with disapproval Miss Assher's occasional air of authority towards Captain Wybrow. A proud woman who has learned to submit, carries all her pride to the reinforcement of her submission, and looks down with severe superiority on all feminine assumption as 'unbecoming.' Lady Cheverel, however, confined her criticisms to the privacy of her own thoughts, and, with a reticence which I fear may seem incredible, did not use them as a means of disturbing her husband's complacency.

And Caterina? How did she pass these sunny autumn days, in which the skies seemed to be smiling on the family gladness? To her the change in Miss Assher's manner was unaccountable. Those compassionate attentions, those smiling condescensions, were torture to Caterina, who was constantly tempted to repulse them with anger. She thought, 'Perhaps Anthony has told her to be kind to poor Tina. This was an insult. He ought to have known that the mere presence of Miss Assher was painful to her, that Miss Assher's smiles scorched her, that Miss Assher's kind words were like poison stings inflaming her to madness. And he – Anthony – he was evidently repenting of the tenderness he had been betrayed into that morning in the drawing-room. He was cold and distant and civil to her, to ward off Beatrice's suspicions, and Beatrice could be so gracious now, because she was sure of Anthony's entire devotion. Well! and so it ought to be – and she ought not to wish it otherwise. And yet – oh, he *was* cruel to her. She could never have behaved so to him. To make her love him so – to speak such tender words – to give her such caresses, and then to behave as if such things had never been. He had given her the poison that seemed so sweet while she was drinking it, and now it was in her blood, and she was helpless.'

With this tempest pent up in her bosom, the poor child went up to her room every night, and there it all burst forth. There, with loud whispers and sobs, restlessly pacing up and down, lying on the hard floor, courting cold and weariness, she told to the pitiful listening night the anguish which she could pour into no mortal ear. But always sleep came at last, and always in the morning the reactive calm that enabled her to live through the day.

It is amazing how long a young frame will go on battling with this sort of secret wretchedness, and yet show no traces of the conflict for any but sympathetic eyes. The very delicacy of Caterina's usual appearance, her natural paleness and habitually quiet mouse-like ways, made any symptoms of fatigue and suffering less noticeable. And her singing – the one thing in which she ceased to be passive, and became prominent – lost none of its energy. She sometimes wondered herself how it was that, whether she felt sad or angry, crushed with the sense of Anthony's indifference, or burning with impatience under Miss Assher's attentions, it was always a relief to her to sing. Those full deep notes she sent forth seemed to be lifting the pain from her heart – seemed to be carrying away the madness from her brain.

Thus Lady Cheverel noticed no change in Caterina, and it was only Mr Gilfil who discerned with anxiety the feverish spot that sometimes rose on her cheek, the deepening violet tint under her eyes, and the strange absent glance, the unhealthy glitter of the beautiful eyes themselves.

But, alas! those agitated nights were producing a more fatal effect than was represented by these slight outward changes.

CHAPTER 11

The following Sunday, the morning being rainy, it was determined that the family should not go to Cumbermoor Church as usual, but that Mr Gilfil, who had only an afternoon service at his curacy, should conduct the morning service in the chapel.

Just before the appointed hour of eleven, Caterina came down into the drawing-room, looking so unusually ill as to call forth an anxious inquiry from Lady Cheverel, who, on learning that she had a severe headache, insisted that she should not attend service, and at once packed her up comfortably on a sofa near the fire, putting a volume of Tillotson's Sermons into her hands, as appropriate reading, if Caterina should feel equal to that means of edification.

Excellent medicine for the mind are the good archbishop's sermons, but a medicine, unhappily, not suited to Tina's case. She sat with the book open on her knees, her dark eyes fixed vacantly on the portrait of that handsome Lady Cheverel, wife of the notable Sir Anthony. She gazed at the picture without thinking of it, and the fair blonde

252

dame seemed to look down on her with that benignant unconcern, that mild wonder, with which happy self-possessed women are apt to look down on their agitated and weaker sisters.

Caterina was thinking of the near future – of the wedding that was so soon to come – of all she would have to live through in the next months.

'I wish I could be very ill, and die before then,' she thought. 'When people get very ill, they don't mind about things. Poor Patty Richards looked so happy when she was in a decline. She didn't seem to care any more about her lover that she was engaged to be married to, and she liked the smell of the flowers so that I used to take her. O, if I could but like anything – if I could but think about anything else! If these dreadful feelings would go away, I wouldn't mind about not being happy. I wouldn't want anything – and I could do what would please Sir Christopher and Lady Cheverel. But when that rage and anger comes into me, I don't know what to do. I don't feel the ground under me; I only feel my head and heart beating, and it seems as if I must do something dreadful. O! I wonder if any one ever felt like me before. I must be very wicked. But God will have pity on me; He knows all I have to bear.'

In this way the time wore on till Tina heard the sound of voices along the passage, and became conscious that the volume of Tillotson had slipped on the floor. She had only just picked it up, and seen with alarm that the pages were bent, when

Lady Assher, Beatrice, and Captain Wybrow entered, all with that brisk and cheerful air which a sermon is often observed to produce when it is quite finished.

Lady Assher at once came and seated herself by Caterina. Her ladyship had been considerably refreshed by a doze, and was in great force for monologue.

'Well, my dear Miss Sarti, and how do you feel now? – a little better, I see. I thought you would be, sitting quietly here. These headaches, now, are all from weakness. You must not over-exert yourself, and you must take bitters. I used to have just the same sort of headaches when I was your age, and old Dr Samson used to say to my mother, 'Madam, what your daughter suffers from is weakness.' He was such a curious old man, was Dr Samson. But I wish you could have heard the sermon this morning. Such an excellent sermon! It was about the ten virgins: five of them were foolish, and five were clever, you know; and Mr Gilfil explained all that. What a very pleasant young man he is! – so very quiet and agreeable, and such a good hand at whist. I wish we had him at Farleigh. Sir John would have liked him beyond anything; he is so good-tempered at cards, and he was such a man for cards, was Sir John. And our rector is a very irritable man; he can't bear to lose his money at cards. I don't think a clergyman ought to mind about losing his money; do you? – do you now?'

'O pray, Lady Assher,' interposed Beatrice, in her usual tone of superiority, 'do not weary poor Caterina with such uninteresting questions. Your head seems very bad still, dear,' she continued, in a condoling tone, to Caterina; 'do take my vinaigrette, and keep it in your pocket. It will perhaps refresh you now and then.'

'No, thank you,' answered Caterina; 'I will not take it away from you.'

'Indeed, dear, I never use it; you must take it,' Miss Assher persisted, holding it close to Tina's hand. Tina coloured deeply, pushed the vinaigrette away with some impatience, and said, 'Thank you, I never use those things. I don't like vinaigrettes.'

Miss Assher returned the vinaigrette to her pocket in surprised and haughty silence, and Captain Wybrow, who had looked on in some alarm, said hastily, 'See! it is quite bright out of doors now. There is time for a walk before luncheon. Come, Beatrice, put on your hat and cloak, and let us have half an hour's walk on the gravel.'

'Yes, do, my dear,' said Lady Assher, 'and I will go and see if Sir Christopher is having his walk in the gallery.'

As soon as the door had closed behind the two ladies, Captain Wybrow, standing with his back to the fire, turned towards Caterina, and said in a tone of earnest remonstrance, 'My dear Caterina, let me beg of you to exercise more control over your feelings; you are really rude to Miss Assher, and I can see that she is quite hurt. Consider how strange your behaviour must appear to her. She will wonder what can be the cause of it. Come, dear Tina,' he added, approaching her, and attempting to take her hand; 'for your own sake, let me entreat you to receive her attentions politely. She really feels very kindly towards you, and I should be so happy to see you friends.'

Caterina was already in such a state of diseased susceptibility that the most innocent words from Captain Wybrow would have been irritating to her, as the whirr of the most delicate wing will afflict a nervous patient. But this tone of benevolent remonstrance was intolerable. He had inflicted a great and unrepented injury on her, and now he assumed an air of benevolence towards her. This was a new outrage. His profession of goodwill was insolence.

Caterina snatched away her hand and said indignantly, 'Leave me to myself, Captain Wybrow! I do not disturb you.'

'Caterina, why will you be so violent – so unjust to me? It is for you that I feel anxious. Miss Assher has already noticed how strange your behaviour is both to her and me, and it puts me into a very difficult position. What can I say to her?'

'Say?' Caterina burst forth, with intense bitterness, rising, and moving towards the door; 'say that I am a poor silly girl, and have fallen in love with you, and am jealous of her; but that you have never had any feeling but pity for me – you have never behaved with anything more than friendliness to me. Tell her that, and she will think all the better of you.'

Tina uttered this as the bitterest sarcasm her ideas would furnish her with, not having the faintest suspicion that the sarcasm derived any of its bitterness from truth. Underneath all her sense of wrong, which was rather instinctive than reflective – underneath all the madness of her jealousy, and her ungovernable impulses of resentment and vindictiveness – underneath all this scorching passion there were still left some hidden crystal dews of trust, of self-reproof, of belief that Anthony was trying to do the right. Love had not all gone to feed the fires of hatred. Tina still trusted that Anthony felt more for her than he seemed to feel; she was still far from suspecting him of a wrong which a woman resents even more than inconstancy. And she threw out this taunt simply as the most intense expression she could find for the anger of the moment.

As she stood nearly in the middle of the room, her little body trembling under the shock of passions too strong for it, her very lips pale, and her eyes gleaming, the door opened, and Miss Assher appeared, tall, blooming, and splendid, in her walking costume. As she entered, her face wore the smile appropriate to the exits and entrances of a young lady who feels that her presence is an interesting fact; but the next moment she looked at Caterina with grave surprise, and then threw a glance of angry suspicion at Captain Wybrow, who wore an air of weariness and vexation.

'Perhaps you are too much engaged to walk out, Captain Wybrow? I will go alone.'

'No, no, I am coming,' he answered, hurrying towards her, and leading her out of the room; leaving poor Caterina to feel all the reaction of shame and self-reproach after her outburst of passion.

CHAPTER 12

'Pray', what is likely to be the next scene in the drama between you and Miss Sarti?' said Miss Assher to Captain Wybrow as soon as they were out on the gravel. 'It would be agreeable to have some idea of what is coming.'

Captain Wybrow was silent. He felt out of humour, wearied, annoyed. There come moments when one almost determines never again to oppose anything but dead silence to an angry woman. 'Now then, confound it,' he said to himself, 'I'm going to be battered on the other flank.' He looked resolutely at the horizon, with something more like a frown on his face than Beatrice had ever seen there.

After a pause of two or three minutes, she continued in a still haughtier tone, 'I suppose you are aware, Captain Wybrow, that I expect an explanation of what I have just seen.'

'I have no explanation, my dear Beatrice,' he answered at last, making a strong effort over himself, 'except what I have already given you. I hoped you would never recur to the subject.'

'Your explanation, however, is very far from

satisfactory. I can only say that the airs Miss Sarti thinks herself entitled to put on towards you, are quite incompatible with your position as regards me. And her behaviour to me is most insulting. I shall certainly not stay in the house under such circumstances, and mamma must state the reasons to Sir Christopher.'

'Beatrice,' said Captain Wybrow, his irritation giving way to alarm, 'I beseech you to be patient, and exercise your good feelings in this affair. It is very painful, I know, but I am sure you would be grieved to injure poor Caterina – to bring down my uncle's anger upon her. Consider what a poor little dependent thing she is.'

'It is very adroit of you to make these evasions, but do not suppose that they deceive me. Miss Sarti would never dare to behave to you as she does, if you had not flirted with her, or made love to her. I suppose she considers your engagement to me a breach of faith to her. I am much obliged to you, certainly, for making me Miss Sarti's rival. You have told me a falsehood, Captain Wybrow.'

'Beatrice, I solemnly declare to you that Caterina is nothing more to me than a girl I naturally feel kindly to – as a favourite of my uncle's, and a nice little thing enough. I should be glad to see her married to Gilfil to-morrow; that's a good proof that I'm not in love with her, I should think. As to the past, I may have shown her little attentions, which she has exaggerated and misinterpreted. What man is not liable to that sort of thing?'

'But what can she found her behaviour on? What had she been saying to you this morning to make her tremble and turn pale in that way?'

'O, I don't know. I just said something about her behaving peevishly. With that Italian blood of hers, there's no knowing how she may take what one says. She's a fierce little thing, though she seems so quiet generally.'

'But she ought to be made to know how unbecoming and indelicate her conduct is. For my part, I wonder Lady Cheverel has not noticed her short answers and the airs she puts on.'

'Let me beg of you, Beatrice, not to hint anything of the kind to Lady Cheverel. You must have observed how strict my aunt is. It never enters her head that a girl can be in love with a man who has not made her an offer.'

'Well, I shall let Miss Sarti know myself that I have observed her conduct. It will be only a charity to her.'

'Nay, dear, that will be doing nothing but harm. Caterina's temper is peculiar. The best thing you can do will be to leave her to herself as much as possible. It will all wear off. I've no doubt she'll be married to Gilfil before long. Girls' fancies are easily diverted from one object to another. By Jove, what a rate my heart is galloping at! These confounded palpitations get worse instead of better.'

Thus ended the conversation, so far as it concerned Caterina, not without leaving a distinct resolution in Captain Wybrow's mind – a resolution carried into effect the next day, when he was in the library with Sir Christopher for the purpose of discussing some arrangements about the approaching marriage.

'By the by,' he said carelessly, when the business came to a pause, and he was sauntering round the room with his hands in his coat-pockets, surveying the backs of the books that lined the walls, 'when is the wedding between Gilfil and Caterina to come off, sir? I've a fellow-feeling for a poor devil so many fathoms deep in love as Maynard. Why shouldn't their marriage happen as soon as ours? I suppose he has come to an understanding with Tina?'

'Why,' said Sir Christopher, 'I did think of letting the thing be until old Crichley died; he can't hold out very long, poor fellow; and then Maynard might have entered into matrimony and the Rectory both at once. But, after all, that really is no good reason for waiting. There is no need for them to leave the Manor when they are married. The little monkey is quite old enough. It would be pretty to see her a matron, with a baby about the size of a kitten in her arms.'

'I think that system of waiting is always bad. And if I can further any settlement you would like to make on Caterina, I shall be delighted to carry out your wishes.'

'My dear boy, that's very good of you; but Maynard will have enough; and from what I know of him – and I know him well – I think he would rather provide for Caterina himself. However, now you have put this matter into my head, I begin to blame myself for not having thought of it before. I've been so wrapt up in Beatrice and you, you rascal, that I had really forgotten poor Maynard. And he's older than you – it's high time he was settled in life as a family man.'

Sir Christopher paused, took snuff in a meditative manner, and presently said, more to himself than to Anthony, who was humming a tune at the far end of the room, 'Yes, yes. It will be a capital plan to finish off all our family business at once.'

Riding out with Miss Assher the same morning, Captain Wybrow mentioned to her incidentally, that Sir Christopher was anxious to bring about the wedding between Gilfil and Caterina as soon as possible, and that he, for his part, should do all he could to further the affair. It would be the best thing in the world for Tina, in whose welfare he was really interested.

With Sir Christopher there was never any long interval between purpose and execution. He made up his mind promptly, and he acted promptly. On rising from luncheon, he said to Mr Gilfil, 'Come with me into the library, Maynard. I want to have a word with you.'

'Maynard, my boy,' he began, as soon as they were seated, tapping his snuff-box, and looking radiant at the idea of the unexpected pleasure he was about to give, 'why shouldn't we have two happy couples instead of one, before the autumn is over, eh?'

'Eh?' he repeated, after a moment's pause, lengthening out the monosyllable, taking a slow pinch, and looking up at Maynard with a sly smile.

'I'm not quite sure that I understand you, sir,' answered Mr Gilfil, who felt annoyed at the consciousness that he was turning pale.

'Not understand me, you rogue? You know very well whose happiness lies nearest to my heart after Anthony's. You know you let me into your secrets long ago, so there's no confession to make. Tina's quite old enough to be a grave little wife now; and though the Rectory's not ready for you, that's no matter. My lady and I shall feel all the more comfortable for having you with us. We should miss our little singing-bird if we lost her all at once.'

Mr Gilfil felt himself in a painfully difficult position. He dreaded that Sir Christopher should surmise or discover the true state of Caterina's feelings, and yet he was obliged to make those feelings the ground of his reply.

'My dear sir,' he at last said with some effort, 'you will not suppose that I am not alive to your goodness – that I am not grateful for your fatherly interest in my happiness; but I fear that Caterina's feelings towards me are not such as to warrant the hope that she would accept a proposal of marriage from me.'

'Have you ever asked her?'

'No, sir. But we often know these things too well without asking.'

'Pooh, pooh! The little monkey *must* love you. Why, you were her first playfellow; and I remember she used to cry if you cut your finger. Besides, she has always silently admitted that you were her lover. You know I have always spoken of you to her in that light. I took it for granted you had settled the business between yourselves; so did Anthony. Anthony thinks she's in love with you, and he has young eyes, which are apt enough to see clearly in these matters. He was talking to me about it this morning, and pleased me very much by the friendly interest he showed in you and Tina.'

The blood – more than was wanted – rushed back to Mr Gilfil's face; he set his teeth and clenched his hands in the effort to repress a burst of indignation. Sir Christopher noticed the flush, but thought it indicated the fluctuation of hope and fear about Caterina. He went on:—

'You're too modest by half, Maynard. A fellow who can take a five-barred gate as you can, ought not to be so faint-hearted. If you can't speak to her yourself, leave me to talk to her.'

'Sir Christopher,' said poor Maynard earnestly, 'I shall really feel it the greatest kindness you can possibly show me, not to mention this subject to Caterina at present. I think such a proposal, made prematurely, might only alienate her from me.'

Sir Christopher was getting a little displeased at this contradiction. His tone became a little sharper

265

as he said, 'Have you any grounds to state for this opinion, beyond your general notion that Tina is not enough in love with you?'

'I can state none beyond my own very strong impression that she does not love me well enough to marry me.'

'Then I think that ground is worth nothing at all. I am tolerably correct in my judgment of people; and if I am not very much deceived in Tina, she looks forward to nothing else but to your being her husband. Leave me to manage the matter as I think best. You may rely on me that I shall do no harm to your cause, Maynard.'

Mr Gilfil, afraid to say more, yet wretched in the prospect of what might result from Sir Christopher's determination, quitted the library in a state of mingled indignation against Captain Wybrow, and distress for himself and Caterina. What would she think of him? She might suppose that *he* had instigated or sanctioned Sir Christopher's proceeding. He should perhaps not have an opportunity of speaking to her on the subject in time; he would write her a note, and carry it up to her room after the dressing-bell had rung. No; that would agitate her, and unfit her for appearing at dinner, and passing the evening calmly. He would defer it till bedtime. After prayers, he contrived to lead her back to the drawing-room, and to put a letter in her hand. She carried it up to her own room, wondering, and there read,—

'DEAR CATERINA, – Do not suspect for a moment that anything Sir Christopher may say to you about our marriage has been prompted by me. I have done all I dare do to dissuade him from urging the subject, and have only been prevented from speaking more strongly by the dread of provoking questions which I could not answer without causing you fresh misery. I write this, both to prepare you for anything Sir Christopher may say, and to assure you – but I hope you already believe it – that your feelings are sacred to me. I would rather part with the dearest hope of my life than be the means of adding to your trouble.

'It is Captain Wybrow who has prompted Sir Christopher to take up the subject at this moment. I tell you this, to save you from hearing it suddenly when you are with Sir Christopher. You see now what sort of stuff that dastard's heart is made of. Trust in me always, dearest Caterina, as – whatever may come – your faithful friend and brother.

'MAYNARD GILFIL.'

Caterina was at first too terribly stung by the words about Captain Wybrow to think of the difficulty which threatened her – to think either of what Sir Christopher would say to her, or of what she could say in reply. Bitter sense of injury, fierce resentment, left no room for fear. With the poisoned garment upon him, the victim writhes under the torture – he has no thought of the coming death.

Anthony could do this! – Of this there could be no explanation but the coolest contempt for her feelings, the basest sacrifice of all the consideration and tenderness he owed her to the ease of his position with Miss Assher. No. It was worse than that; it was deliberate, gratuitous cruelty. He wanted to show her how he despised her; he wanted to make her feel her folly in having ever believed that he loved her.

The last crystal drops of trust and tenderness, she thought, were dried up; all was parched, fiery hatred. Now she need no longer check her resentment by the fear of doing him an injustice; he *had* trifled with her, as Maynard had said; he *had* been reckless of her; and now he was base and cruel. She had cause enough for her bitterness and anger; they were not so wicked as they had seemed to her.

As these thoughts were hurrying after each other like so many sharp throbs of fevered pain, she shed no tear. She paced restlessly to and fro, as her habit was – her hands clenched, her eyes gleaming fiercely and wandering uneasily, as if in search of something on which she might throw herself like a tigress.

'If I could speak to him,' she whispered, 'and tell him I hate him, I despise him, I loathe him!'

268

Suddenly, as if a new thought had struck her, she drew a key from her pocket, and unlocking an inlaid desk where she stored up her keepsakes, took from it a small miniature. It was in a very slight gold frame, with a ring to it, as if intended to be worn on a chain; and under the glass at the back were two locks of hair, one dark and the other auburn, arranged in a fantastic knot. It was Anthony's secret present to her a year ago – a copy he had had made specially for her. For the last month she had not taken it from its hiding-place: there was no need to heighten the vividness of the past. But now she clutched it fiercely, and dashed it across the room against the bare hearthstone.

Will she crush it under her feet, and grind it under her high-heeled shoe, till every trace of those false cruel features is gone?

Ah, no! She rushed across the room; but when she saw the little treasure she had cherished so fondly, so often smothered with kisses, so often laid under her pillow, and remembered with the first return of consciousness in the morning – when she saw this one visible relic of the too happy past lying with the glass shivered, the hair fallen out, the thin ivory cracked, there was a revulsion of the overstrained feeling: relenting came, and she burst into tears.

Look at her stooping down to gather up her treasure, searching for the hair and replacing it, and then mournfully examining the crack that disfigures the once-loved image. Alas! there is no glass now to guard either the hair or the portrait; but see how carefully she wraps delicate paper round it, and locks it up again in its old place. Poor child! God send the relenting may always come before the worst irrevocable deed!

This action had quieted her, and she sat down to read Maynard's letter again. She read it two or three times without seeming to take in the sense; her apprehension was dulled by the passion of the last hour, and she found it difficult to call up the ideas suggested by the words. At last she began to have a distinct conception of the impending interview with Sir Christopher. The idea of displeasing the Baronet, of whom every one at the Manor stood in awe, frightened her so much that she thought it would be impossible to resist his wish. He believed that she loved Maynard; he had always spoken as if he were quite sure of it. How could she tell him he was deceived – and what if he were to ask her whether she loved anybody else? To have Sir Christopher looking angrily at her, was more than she could bear, even in imagination. He had always been so good to her! Then she began to think of the pain she might give him, and the more selfish distress of fear gave way to the distress of affection. Unselfish tears began to flow, and sorrowful gratitude to Sir Christopher helped to awaken her sensibility to Mr Gilfil's tenderness and generosity.

'Dear, good Maynard! – what a poor return I make him! If I could but have loved him instead – but I can never love or care for anything again. My heart is broken.'

CHAPTER 13

The next morning the dreaded moment came. Caterina, stupefied by the suffering of the previous night, with that dull mental aching which follows on acute anguish, was in Lady Cheverel's sitting-room, copying out some charity lists, when her ladyship came in, and said, —

'Tina, Sir Christopher wants you; go down into the library.'

She went down trembling. As soon as she entered, Sir Christopher, who was seated near his writing-table, said, 'Now, little monkey, come and sit down by me; I have something to tell you.'

Caterina took a footstool, and seated herself on it at the Baronet's feet. It was her habit to sit on these low stools, and in this way she could hide her face better. She put her little arm round his leg, and leaned her cheek against his knee.

'Why, you seem out of spirits this morning, Tina. What's the matter, eh?'

'Nothing, Padroncello, only my head is bad.'

'Poor monkey! Well, now wouldn't it do the head good if I were to promise you a good husband,

and smart little wedding-gowns, and by-and-by a house of your own, where you would be a little mistress, and Padroncello would come and see you sometimes?'

'O no, no! I shouldn't like ever to be married. Let me always stay with you!'

'Pooh, pooh, little simpleton. I shall get old and tiresome, and there will be Anthony's children putting your nose out of joint. You will want some one to love you best of all, and you must have children of your own to love. I can't have you withering away into an old maid. I hate old maids. They make me dismal to look at them. I never see Sharp without shuddering. My little black-eyed monkey was never meant for anything so ugly. And there's Maynard Gilfil, the best man in the county, worth his weight in gold, heavy as he is; he loves you better than his eyes. And you love him too, you silly monkey, whatever you may say about not being married.'

'No, no, dear Padroncello, do not say so; I could not marry him.'

'Why not, you foolish child? You don't know your own mind. Why, it is plain to everybody that you love him. My lady has all along said she was sure you loved him – she has seen what little princess airs you put on to him; and Anthony too, *he* thinks you are in love with Gilfil. Come, what has made you take it into your head that you wouldn't like to marry him?'

Caterina was now sobbing too deeply to make

any answer. Sir Christopher patted her on the back and said, 'Come, come; why, Tina, you are not well this morning. Go and rest, little one. You will see things in quite another light when you are well. Think over what I have said, and remember there is nothing, after Anthony's marriage, that I have set my heart on so much as seeing you and Maynard settled for life. I must have no whims and follies – no nonsense.' This was said with a slight severity; but he presently added, in a soothing tone, 'There, there, stop crying, and be a good little monkey. Go and lie down and get to sleep.'

Caterina slipped from the stool on to her knees, took the old Baronet's hand, covered it with tears and kisses, and then ran out of the room.

Before the evening, Captain Wybrow had heard from his uncle the result of the interview with Caterina. He thought, 'If I could have a long quiet talk with her, I could perhaps persuade her to look more reasonably at things. But there's no speaking to her in the house without being interrupted, and I can hardly see her anywhere else without Beatrice's finding it out.' At last he determined to make it a matter of confidence with Miss Assher – to tell her that he wished to talk to Caterina quietly for the sake of bringing her to a calmer state of mind, and persuade her to listen to Gilfil's affection. He was very much pleased with this judicious and candid plan, and in the course of the evening he had arranged with himself the time and place of meeting, and had communicated his purpose to Miss Assher, who gave her entire approval. Anthony, she thought, would do well to speak plainly and seriously to Miss Sarti. He was really very patient and kind to her, considering how she behaved.

Tina had kept her room all that day, and had been carefully tended as an invalid, Sir Christopher having told her ladyship how matters stood. This tendance was so irksome to Caterina, she felt so uneasy under attentions and kindness that were based on a misconception, that she exerted herself to appear at breakfast the next morning, and declared herself well, though head and heart were throbbing. To be confined in her own room was intolerable; it was wretched enough to be looked at and spoken to, but it was more wretched to be left alone. She was frightened at her own sensations: she was frightened at the imperious vividness with which pictures of the past and future thrust themselves on her imagination. And there was another feeling, too, which made her want to be down stairs and moving about. Perhaps she might have an opportunity of speaking to Captain Wybrow alone – of speaking those words of hatred and scorn that burned on her tongue. That opportunity offered itself in a very unexpected manner.

Lady Cheverel having sent Caterina out of the drawing-room to fetch some patterns of embroidery from her sitting-room, Captain Wybrow presently walked out after her, and met her as she was returning down stairs.

'Caterina,' he said, laying his hand on her arm as she was hurrying on without looking at him, 'will you meet me in the Rookery at twelve o'clock? I must speak to you, and we shall be in privacy there. I cannot speak to you in the house.'

To his surprise, there was a flash of pleasure across her face; she answered shortly and decidedly, 'Yes,' then snatched her arm away from him, and passed down stairs.

Miss Assher was this morning busy winding silks, being bent on emulating Lady Cheverel's embroidery, and Lady Assher chose the passive amusement of holding the skeins. Lady Cheverel had now all her working apparatus about her, and Caterina, thinking she was not wanted, went away and sat down to the harpsichord in the sitting-room. It seemed as if playing massive chords – bringing out volumes of sound, would be the easiest way of passing the long feverish moments before twelve o'clock. Handel's 'Messiah' stood open on the desk, at the chorus 'All we like sheep,' and Caterina threw herself at once into the impetuous intricacies of that magnificent fugue. In her happiest moments she could never have played it so well; for now all the passion that made her misery was hurled by a convulsive effort into her music, just as pain gives new force to the clutch of the sinking wrestler, and as terror gives far-sounding intensity to the shriek of the feeble.

But at half-past eleven she was interrupted by Lady Cheverel, who said, 'Tina, go down, will you, and hold Miss Assher's silks for her. Lady Assher and I have decided on having our drive before luncheon.'

Caterina went down, wondering how she should escape from the drawing-room in time to be in the Rookery at twelve. Nothing should prevent her from going; nothing should rob her of this one precious moment – perhaps the last – when she could speak out the thoughts that were in her. After that, she would be passive; she would bear anything.

But she had scarcely sat down with a skein of yellow silk on her hands, when Miss Assher said, graciously,—

'I know you have an engagement with Captain Wybrow this morning. You must not let me detain you beyond the time.'

'So he has been talking to her about me,' thought Caterina. Her hands began to tremble as she held the skein.

Miss Assher continued, in the same gracious tone: 'It is tedious work holding these skeins. I am sure I am very much obliged to you.'

'No, you are not obliged to me,' said Caterina, completely mastered by her irritation; 'I have only done it because Lady Cheverel told me.'

The moment was come when Miss Assher could no longer suppress her long latent desire to 'let Miss Sarti know the impropriety of her conduct.' With the malicious anger that assumes the tone of compassion, she said,—

277

'Miss Sarti, I am really sorry for you, that you are not able to control yourself better. This giving way to unwarrantable feelings is lowering you – it is indeed.'

'What unwarrantable feelings?' said Caterina, letting her hands fall, and fixing her great dark eyes steadily on Miss Assher.

'It is quite unnecessary for me to say more. You must be conscious what I mean. Only summon a sense of duty to your aid. You are paining Captain Wybrow extremely by your want of self-control.'

'Did he tell you I pained him?'

'Yes, indeed, he did. He is very much hurt that you should behave to me as if you had a sort of enmity towards me. He would like you to make a friend of me. I assure you we both feel very kindly towards you, and are sorry you should cherish such feelings.'

'He is very good,' said Caterina, bitterly. 'What feelings did he say I cherished?'

This bitter tone increased Miss Assher's irritation. There was still a lurking suspicion in her mind, though she would not admit it to herself, that Captain Wybrow had told her a falsehood about his conduct and feelings towards Caterina. It was this suspicion, more even than the anger of the moment, which urged her to say something that would test the truth of his statement. That she would be humiliating Caterina at the same time, was only an additional temptation.

'These are things I do not like to talk of, Miss Sarti. I cannot even understand how a woman can indulge a passion for a man who has never given her the least ground for it, as Captain Wybrow assures me is the case.'

'He told you that, did he?' said Caterina, in clear low tones, her lips turning white as she rose from her chair.

'Yes, indeed, he did. He was bound to tell it me after your strange behaviour.'

Caterina said nothing, but turned round suddenly and left the room.

See how she rushes noiselessly, like a pale meteor, along the passages and up the gallery stairs! Those gleaming eyes, those bloodless lips, that swift silent tread, make her look like the incarnation of a fierce purpose, rather than a woman. The mid-day sun is shining on the armour in the gallery, making mimic suns on bossed sword-hilts and the angles of polished breastplates. Yes, there are sharp weapons in the gallery. There is a dagger in that cabinet; she knows it well. And as a dragon-fly wheels in its flight to alight for an instant on a leaf, she darts to the cabinet, takes out the dagger, and thrusts it into her pocket. In three minutes more she is out, in hat and cloak, on the gravel-walk, hurrying along towards the thick shades of the distant Rookery. She threads the windings of the plantations, not feeling the golden leaves that rain upon her, not feeling the earth beneath her feet. Her hand is in her pocket, clenching the handle of the dagger, which she holds half out of its sheath.

She has reached the Rookery, and is under the gloom of the interlacing boughs. Her heart throbs as if it would burst her bosom – as if every next leap must be its last. Wait, wait, O heart! till she has done this one deed. He will be there – he will be before her in a moment. He will come towards her with that false smile, thinking she does not know his baseness – she will plunge that dagger into his heart.

Poor child! poor child! she who used to cry to have the fish put back into the water – who never willingly killed the smallest living thing – dreams now, in the madness of her passion, that she can kill the man whose very voice unnerves her.

But what is that lying among the dank leaves on the path three yards before her?

Good God! it is he – lying motionless – his hat fallen off. He is ill, then – he has fainted. Her hand lets go the dagger, and she rushes towards him. His eyes are fixed; he does not see her. She sinks down on her knees, takes the dear head in her arms, and kisses the cold forehead.

'Anthony, Anthony! speak to me – it is Tina – speak to me! O God, he is dead!'

CHAPTER 14

'Yes, Maynard,' said Sir Christopher, chatting with Mr Gilfil in the library, 'it really is a remarkable thing that I never in my life laid a plan, and failed to carry it out. I lay my plans well, and I never swerve from them – that's it. A strong will is the only magic. And next to striking out one's plans, the pleasantest thing in the world is to see them well accomplished. This year, now, will be the happiest of my life, all but the year '53, when I came into possession of the Manor, and married Henrietta. The last touch is given to the old house; Anthony's marriage – the thing I had nearest my heart – is settled to my entire satisfaction; and by-and-by you will be buying a little wedding-ring for Tina's finger. Don't shake your head in that forlorn way; – when I make prophecies, they generally come to pass. But there's a quarter after twelve striking. I must be riding to the High Ash to meet Markham about felling some timber. My old oaks will have to groan for this wedding, but'—

The door burst open, and Caterina, ghastly and panting, her eyes distended with terror, rushed in,

281

threw her arms round Sir Christopher's neck, and gasping out – 'Anthony . . . the Rookery . . . dead . . . in the Rookery,' fell fainting on the floor.

In a moment Sir Christopher was out of the room, and Mr Gilfil was bending to raise Caterina in his arms. As he lifted her from the ground he felt something hard and heavy in her pocket. What could it be? The weight of it would be enough to hurt her as she lay. He carried her to the sofa, put his hand in her pocket, and drew forth the dagger.

Maynard shuddered. Did she mean to kill herself, then, or . . . or . . . a horrible suspicion forced itself upon him. 'Dead – in the Rookery.' He hated himself for the thought that prompted him to draw the dagger from its sheath. No! there was no trace of blood, and he was ready to kiss the good steel for its innocence. He thrust the weapon into his own pocket; he would restore it as soon as possible to its well-known place in the gallery. Yet, why had Caterina taken this dagger? What was it that had happened in the Rookery? Was it only a delirious vision of hers?

He was afraid to ring – afraid to summon any one to Caterina's assistance. What might she not say when she awoke from this fainting fit? She might be raving. He could not leave her, and yet he felt as if he were guilty for not following Sir Christopher to see what was the truth. It took but a moment to think and feel all this, but that moment seemed such a long agony to him, that he began to reproach himself for letting it pass without seeking some means of reviving Caterina. Happily the decanter of water on Sir Christopher's table was untouched. He would at least try the effect of throwing that water over her. She might revive without his needing to call any one else.

Meanwhile Sir Christopher was hurrying at his utmost speed towards the Rookery; his face, so lately bright and confident, now agitated by a vague dread. The deep alarmed bark of Rupert, who ran by his side, had struck the ear of Mr Bates, then on his way homeward, as something unwonted, and, hastening in the direction of the sound, he met the Baronet just as he was approaching the entrance of the Rookery. Sir Christopher's look was enough. Mr Bates said nothing, but hurried along by his side, while Rupert dashed forward among the dead leaves with his nose to the ground. They had scarcely lost sight of him a minute, when a change in the tone of his bark told them that he had found something, and in another instant he was leaping back over one of the large planted mounds. They turned aside to ascend the mound, Rupert leading them; the tumultuous cawing of the rooks, the very rustling of the leaves, as their feet plunged among them, falling like an evil omen on the Baronet's ear.

They have reached the summit of the mound, and have begun to descend. Sir Christopher sees something purple down on the path below among the yellow leaves. Rupert is already beside it, but Sir Christopher cannot move faster. A tremor has taken hold of the firm limbs. Rupert comes back and licks the trembling hand, as if to say 'Courage!' and then is down again snuffing the body. Yes, it is a body . . . Anthony's body. There is the white hand with its diamond ring clutching the dark leaves. His eyes are half open, but do not heed the gleam of sunlight that darts itself directly on them from between the boughs.

Still he might only have fainted; it might only be a fit. Sir Christopher knelt down, unfastened the cravat, unfastened the waistcoat, and laid his hand on the heart. It might be syncope; it might not – it could not be death. No! that thought must be kept far off.

'Go, Bates, get help; we'll carry him to your cottage. Send some one to the house to tell Mr Gilfil and Warren. Bid them send off for Doctor Hart, and break it to my lady and Miss Assher that Anthony is ill.'

Mr Bates hastened away, and the Baronet was left alone kneeling beside the body. The young and supple limbs, the rounded cheeks, the delicate ripe lips, the smooth white hands, were lying cold and rigid; and the aged face was bending over them in silent anguish; the aged deep-veined hands were seeking with tremulous inquiring touches for some symptom that life was not irrevocably gone.

Rupert was there too, waiting and watching;

licking first the dead and then the living hands; then running off on Mr Bates's track as if he would follow and hasten his return, but in a moment turning back again, unable to quit the scene of his master's sorrow.

CHAPTER 15

It is a wonderful moment, the first time we stand by one who has fainted, and witness the fresh birth of consciousness spreading itself over the blank features, like the rising sunlight on the alpine summits that lay ghastly and dead under the leaden twilight. A slight shudder, and the frost-bound eyes recover their liquid light; for an instant they show the inward semi-consciousness of an infant's; then, with a little start, they open wider and begin to *look*; the present is visible, but only as a strange writing, and the interpreter Memory is not yet there.

Mr Gilfil felt a trembling joy as this change passed over Caterina's face. He bent over her, rubbing her chill hands, and looking at her with tender pity as her dark eyes opened on him wonderingly. He thought there might be some wine in the dining-room close by. He left the room, and Caterina's eyes turned towards the window – towards Sir Christopher's chair. *There* was the link at which the chain of consciousness had snapped, and the events of the morning were beginning to recur dimly like a half-remembered dream, when Maynard returned with some wine.

He raised her, and she drank it; but still she was silent, seeming lost in the attempt to recover the past, when the door opened, and Mr Warren appeared with looks that announced terrible tidings. Mr Gilfil, dreading lest he should tell them in Caterina's presence, hurried towards him with his finger on his lips, and drew him away into the dining-room on the opposite side of the passage.

Caterina, revived by the stimulant, was now recovering the full consciousness of the scene in the Rookery. Anthony was lying there dead; she had left him to tell Sir Christopher; she must go and see what they were doing with him; perhaps he was not really dead – only in a trance; people did fall into trances sometimes. While Mr Gilfil was telling Warren how it would be best to break the news to Lady Cheverel and Miss Assher, anxious himself to return to Caterina, the poor child had made her way feebly to the great entrance-door, which stood open. Her strength increased as she moved and breathed the fresh air, and with every increase of strength came increased vividness of emotion, increased yearning to be where her thought was – in the Rookery with Anthony. She walked more and more swiftly, and at last, gathering the artificial strength of passionate excitement, began to run.

But soon she hears the tread of heavy steps, and under the yellow shade near the wooden bridge, she sees men slowly carrying something. Now she is face to face with them. Anthony is no longer in the Rookery: they are carrying him stretched on a door, and there behind him is Sir Christopher, with the firmly-set mouth, the deathly paleness, and the concentrated expression of suffering in the eye, which mark the suppressed grief of the strong man. The sight of this face, on which Caterina had never before beheld the signs of anguish, caused a rush of new feeling which for the moment submerged all the rest. She went gently up to him, put her little hand in his, and walked in silence by his side. Sir Christopher could not tell her to leave him, and so she went on with that sad procession to Mr Bates's cottage in the Mosslands, and sat there in silence, waiting and watching to know if Anthony were really dead.

She had not yet missed the dagger from her pocket; she had not yet even thought of it. At the sight of Anthony lying dead, her nature had rebounded from its new bias of resentment and hatred to the old sweet habit of love. The earliest and the longest has still the mastery over us; and the only past that linked itself with those glazed unconscious eyes, was the past when they beamed on her with tenderness. She forgot the interval of wrong and jealousy and hatred – all his cruelty, and all her thoughts of revenge – as the exile forgets the stormy passage that lay between home and happiness, and the dreary land in which he finds himself desolate.

CHAPTER 16

Before night all hope was gone. Dr Hart had said it was death; Anthony's body had been carried to the house, and every one there knew the calamity that had fallen on them.

Caterina had been questioned by Dr Hart, and had answered briefly that she found Anthony lying in the Rookery. That she should have been walking there just at that time was not a coincidence to raise conjectures in any one besides Mr Gilfil. Except in answering this question, she had not broken her silence. She sat mute in a corner of the gardener's kitchen, shaking her head when Maynard entreated her to return with him, and apparently unable to think of anything but the possibility that Anthony might revive, until she saw them carrying away the body to the house. Then she followed by Sir Christopher's side again, so quietly, that even Dr Hart did not object to her presence.

It was decided to lay the body in the library until after the coroner's inquest to-morrow; and when Caterina saw the door finally closed, she turned up the gallery stairs on her way to her own room, the place where she felt at home with her sorrows. It was the first time she had been in the gallery since that terrible moment in the morning, and now the spot and the objects around began to reawaken her half-stunned memory. The armour was no longer glittering in the sunlight, but there it hung dead and sombre above the cabinet from which she had taken the dagger. Yes! now it all came back to her – all the wretchedness and all the sin. But where was the dagger now? She felt in her pocket; it was not there. Could it have been her fancy – all that about the dagger? She looked in the cabinet; it was not there. Alas! no; it could not have been her fancy, and she *was* guilty of that wickedness. But where could the dagger be now? Could it have fallen out of her pocket? She heard steps ascending the stairs, and hurried on to her room, where, kneeling by the bed, and burying her face to shut out the hateful light, she tried to recall every feeling and incident of the morning.

It all came back; everything Anthony had done, and everything she had felt for the last month – for many months – ever since that June evening when he had last spoken to her in the gallery. She looked back on her storms of passion, her jealousy and hatred of Miss Assher, her thoughts of revenge on Anthony. O how wicked she had been! It was she who had been sinning; it was she who had driven him to do and say those things that had made her so angry. And if he had wronged her, what had she been on the verge of doing to him? She was too wicked ever to be pardoned. She would like to confess how wicked she had been, that they might punish her; she would like to humble herself to the dust before every one – before Miss Assher even. Sir Christopher would send her away – would never see her again, if he knew all; and she would be happier to be punished and frowned on, than to be treated tenderly while she had that guilty secret in her breast. But then, if Sir Christopher were to know all, it would add to his sorrow, and make him more wretched than ever. No! she could not confess it – she should have to tell about Anthony. But she could not stay at the Manor; she must go away; she could not bear Sir Christopher's eye, could not bear the sight of all these things that reminded her of Anthony and of her sin. Perhaps she should die soon; she felt very feeble; there could not be much life in her. She would go away and live humbly, and pray to God to pardon her, and let her die.

The poor child never thought of suicide. No sooner was the storm of anger passed than the tenderness and timidity of her nature returned, and she could do nothing but love and mourn. Her inexperience prevented her from imagining the consequences of her disappearance from the Manor; she foresaw none of the terrible details of alarm and distress and search that must ensue. 'They will think I am dead,' she said to herself, 'and by-and-by they will forget me, and Maynard will get happy again, and love some one else.'

291

She was roused from her absorption by a knock at the door. Mrs Bellamy was there. She had come by Mr Gilfil's request to see how Miss Sarti was, and to bring her some food and wine.

'You look sadly, my dear,' said the old housekeeper, 'an' you're all of a quake wi' cold. Get you to bed, now do. Martha shall come an' warm it, an' light your fire. See now, here's some nice arrowroot, wi' a drop o' wine in it. Tek that, an' it'll warm you. I must go down again, for I can't awhile to stay. There's so many things to see to; an' Miss Assher's in hysterics constant, an' her maid's ill i' bed – a poor creachy thing – an' Mrs Sharp's wanted every minute. But I'll send Martha up, an' do you get ready to go to bed, there's a dear child, an' tek care o' yourself.'

'Thank you, dear mammy,' said Tina, kissing the little old woman's wrinkled cheek; 'I shall eat the arrowroot, and don't trouble about me any more to-night. I shall do very well when Martha has lighted my fire. Tell Mr Gilfil I'm better. I shall go to bed by-and-by, so don't you come up again, because you may only disturb me.'

'Well, well, tek care o' yourself, there's a good child, an' God send you may sleep.'

Caterina took the arrowroot quite eagerly, while Martha was lighting her fire. She wanted to get strength for her journey, and she kept the plate of biscuits by her that she might put some in her pocket. Her whole mind was now bent on going away from the Manor, and she was thinking of all the ways and means her little life's experience could suggest.

It was dusk now; she must wait till early dawn, for she was too timid to go away in the dark, but she must make her escape before any one was up in the house. There would be people watching Anthony in the library, but she could make her way out of a small door leading into the garden, against the drawing-room on the other side of the house.

She laid her cloak, bonnet, and veil ready; then she lighted a candle, opened her desk, and took out the broken portrait wrapped in paper. She folded it again in two little notes of Anthony's, written in pencil, and placed it in her bosom. There was the little china box, too – Dorcas's present, the pearl earrings, and a silk purse, with fifteen seven-shilling pieces in it, the presents Sir Christopher had made her on her birthday, ever since she had been at the Manor. Should she take the earrings and the seven-shilling pieces? She could not bear to part with them; it seemed as if they had some of Sir Christopher's love in them. She would like them to be buried with her. She fastened the little round earrings in her ears, and put the purse with Dorcas's box in her pocket. She had another purse there, and she took it out to count her money, for she would never spend her seven-shilling pieces. She had a gumea and eight-shillings; that would be plenty.

So now she sat down to wait for the morning,

afraid to lay herself on the bed lest she should sleep too long. If she could but see Anthony once more, and kiss his cold forehead! But that could not be. She did not deserve it. She must go away from him, away from Sir Christopher, and Lady Cheverel, and Maynard, and everybody who had been kind to her, and thought her good while she was so wicked.

CHAPTER 17

Some of Mrs Sharp's earliest thoughts, the next morning, were given to Caterina, whom she had not been able to visit the evening before, and whom, from a nearly equal mixture of affection and self-importance, she did not at all like resigning to Mrs Bellamy's care. At half-past eight o'clock she went up to Tina's room, bent on benevolent dictation as to doses and diet and lying in bed. But on opening the door she found the bed smooth and empty. Evidently it had not been slept in. What could this mean? Had she sat up all night, and was she gone out to walk? The poor thing's head might be touched by what had happened yesterday; it was such a shock – finding Captain Wybrow in that way; she was perhaps gone out of her mind. Mrs Sharp looked anxiously in the place where Tina kept her hat and cloak; they were not there, so that she had had at least the presence of mind to put them on. Still the good woman felt greatly alarmed, and hastened away to tell Mr Gilfil, who, she knew, was in his study.

'Mr Gilfil,' she said, as soon as she had closed

the door behind her, 'my mind misgives me dreadful about Miss Sarti.'

'What is it?' said poor Maynard, with a horrible fear that Caterina had betrayed something about the dagger.

'She's not in her room, an' her bed's not been slept in this night, an' her hat an' cloak's gone.'

For a minute or two Mr Gilfil was unable to speak. He felt sure the worst had come: Caterina had destroyed herself. The strong man suddenly looked so ill and helpless that Mrs Sharp began to be frightened at the effect of her abruptness.

'O, sir, I'm grieved to my heart to shock you so; but I didn't know who else to go to.'

'No, no, you were quite right.'

He gathered some strength from his very despair. It was all over, and he had nothing now to do but to suffer and to help the suffering. He went on in a firmer voice:

'Be sure not to breathe a word about it to any one. We must not alarm Lady Cheverel and Sir Christopher. Miss Sarti may be only walking in the garden. She was terribly excited by what she saw yesterday, and perhaps was unable to lie down from restlessness. Just go quietly through the empty rooms, and see whether she is in the house. I will go and look for her in the grounds.'

He went down, and, to avoid giving any alarm in the house, walked at once towards the Mosslands in search of Mr Bates, whom he met returning from his breakfast. To the gardener he confided his fear about Caterina, assigning as a reason for this fear the probability that the shock she had undergone yesterday had unhinged her mind, and begging him to send men in search of her through the gardens and park, and inquire if she had been seen at the lodges; and if she were not found or heard of in this way, to lose no time in dragging the waters round the Manor.

'God forbid it should be so, Bates, but we shall be the easier for having searched everywhere.'

'Troost to mae, troost to mae, Mr Gilfil. Eh! but I'd ha' worked for day-wage all the rest o' my life, rether than anythin' should ha' happened to her.'

The good gardener, in deep distress, strode away to the stables that he might send the grooms on horseback through the park.

Mr Gilfil's next thought was to search the Rookery: she might be haunting the scene of Captain Wybrow's death. He went hastily over every mound, looked round every large tree, and followed every winding of the walks. In reality he had little hope of finding her there; but the bare possibility fenced off for a time the fatal conviction that Caterina's body would be found in the water. When the Rookery had been searched in vain, he walked fast to the border of the little stream that bounded one side of the grounds. The stream was almost everywhere hidden among trees, and there was one place where it was broader and deeper than elsewhere – she would be more likely to come to that spot than to the pool. He hurried along with strained eyes, his imagination continually creating what he dreaded to see.

There is something white behind that overhanging bough. His knees tremble under him. He seems to see part of her dress caught on a branch, and her dear dead face upturned. O God, give strength to thy creature, on whom thou hast laid this great agony! He is nearly up to the bough, and the white object is moving. It is a waterfowl, that spreads its wings and flies away screaming. He hardly knows whether it is a relief or a disappointment that she is not there. The conviction that she is dead presses its cold weight upon him none the less heavily.

As he reached the great pool in front of the Manor, he saw Mr Bates, with a group of men already there, preparing for the dreadful search which could only displace his vague despair by a definite horror; for the gardener, in his restless anxiety, had been unable to defer this until other means of search had proved vain. The pool was not now laughing with sparkles among the water-lilies. It looked black and cruel under the sombre sky, as if its cold depths held relentlessly all the murdered hope and joy of Maynard Gilfil's life.

Thoughts of the sad consequences for others as well as himself were crowding on his mind. The blinds and shutters were all closed in front of the Manor, and it was not likely that Sir Christopher would be aware of anything that was passing outside; but Mr Gilfil felt that Caterina's disappearance could not long be concealed from him. The coroner's inquest would be held shortly; she would be inquired for, and then it would be inevitable that the Baronet should know all.

CHAPTER 18

At twelve o'clock, when all search and inquiry had been in vain, and the coroner was expected every moment, Mr Gilfil could no longer defer the hard duty of revealing this fresh calamity to Sir Christopher, who must otherwise have it discovered to him abruptly.

The Baronet was seated in his dressing-room, where the dark window-curtains were drawn so as to admit only a sombre light. It was the first time Mr Gilfil had had an interview with him this morning, and he was struck to see how a single day and night of grief had aged the fine old man. The lines in his brow and about his mouth were deepened; his complexion looked dull and withered; there was a swollen ridge under his eyes; and the eyes themselves, which used to cast so keen a glance on the present, had the vacant expression which tells that vision is no longer a sense, but a memory.

He held out his hand to Maynard, who pressed it, and sat down beside him in silence. Sir Christopher's heart began to swell at this unspoken sympathy; the tears *would* rise, *would* roll in great drops down his cheeks. The first tears he had shed since boyhood were for Anthony.

Maynard felt as if his tongue were glued to the roof of his mouth. He could not speak first: he must wait until Sir Christopher said something which might lead on to the cruel words that must be spoken.

At last the Baronet mastered himself enough to say, 'I'm very weak, Maynard – God help me! I didn't think anything would unman me in this way; but I'd built everything on that lad. Perhaps I've been wrong in not forgiving my sister. She lost one of *her* sons a little while ago. I've been too proud and obstinate.'

'We can hardly learn humility and tenderness enough except by suffering,' said Maynard; 'and God sees we are in need of suffering, for it is falling more and more heavily on us. We have a new trouble this morning.'

'Tina?' said Sir Christopher, looking up anxiously – 'is Tina ill?'

'I am in dreadful uncertainty about her. She was very much agitated yesterday – and with her delicate health – I am afraid to think what turn the agitation may have taken.'

'Is she delirious, poor dear little one?'

'God only knows how she is. We are unable to find her. When Mrs Sharp went up to her room this morning, it was empty. She had not been in bed. Her hat and cloak were gone. I have had search made for her everywhere – in the house and garden, in the park, and – in the water. No one has seen her since Martha went up to light her fire at seven o'clock in the evening.'

While Mr Gilfil was speaking, Sir Christopher's eyes, which were eagerly turned on him, recovered some of their old keenness, and some sudden painful emotion, as at a new thought, flitted rapidly across his already agitated face, like the shadow of a dark cloud over the waves. When the pause came, he laid his hand on Mr Gilfil's arm, and said in a lower voice,—

'Maynard, did that poor thing love Anthony?'

'She did.'

Maynard hesitated after these words, struggling between his reluctance to inflict a yet deeper wound on Sir Christopher, and his determination that no injustice should be done to Caterina. Sir Christopher's eyes were still fixed on him in solemn inquiry, and his own sunk towards the ground, while he tried to find the words that would tell the truth least cruelly.

'You must not have any wrong thoughts about Tina,' he said at length. 'I must tell you now, for her sake, what nothing but this should ever have caused to pass my lips. Captain Wybrow won her affections by attentions which, in his position, he was bound not to show her. Before his marriage was talked of, he had behaved to her like a lover.'

Sir Christopher relaxed his hold of Maynard's arm, and looked away from him. He was silent for some minutes, evidently attempting to master himself, so as to be able to speak calmly.

'I must see Henrietta immediately,' he said at last, with something of his old sharp decision; 'she must know all; but we must keep it from every one else as far as possible. My dear boy,' he continued in a kinder tone, 'the heaviest burden has fallen on you. But we may find her yet; we must not despair: there has not been time enough for us to be certain. Poor dear little one! God help me! I thought I saw everything, and was stone-blind all the while.'

CHAPTER 19

The sad slow week was gone by at last. At the coroner's inquest a verdict of sudden death had been pronounced. Dr Hart, acquainted with Captain Wybrow's previous state of health, had given his opinion that death had been imminent from long-established disease of the heart, though it had probably been accelerated by some unusual emotion. Miss Assher was the only person who positively knew the motive that had led Captain Wybrow to the Rookery; but she had not mentioned Caterina's name, and all painful details or inquiries were studiously kept from her. Mr Gilfil and Sir Christopher, however, knew enough to conjecture that the fatal agitation was due to an appointed meeting with Caterina.

All search and inquiry after her had been fruitless, and were the more likely to be so because they were carried on under the prepossession that she had committed suicide. No one noticed the absence of the trifles she had taken from her desk; no one knew of the likeness, or that she had hoarded her seven-shilling pieces, and it was not remarkable that she should have happened to be wearing the pearl earrings. She had left the house, they thought, taking nothing with her; it seemed impossible she could have gone far; and she must have been in a state of mental excitement, that made it too probable she had only gone to seek relief in death. The same places within three or four miles of the Manor were searched again and again – every pond, every ditch in the neighbourhood was examined.

Sometimes Maynard thought that death might have come on unsought, from cold and exhaustion; and not a day passed but he wandered through the neighbouring woods, turning up the heaps of dead leaves, as if it were possible her dear body could be hidden there. Then another horrible thought recurred, and before each night came he had been again through all the uninhabited rooms of the house, to satisfy himself once more that she was not hidden behind some cabinet, or door, or curtain – that he should not find her there with madness in her eyes, looking and looking, and yet not seeing him.

But at last those five long days and nights were at an end, the funeral was over, and the carriages were returning through the park. When they had set out, a heavy rain was falling; but now the clouds were breaking up, and a gleam of sunshine was sparkling among the dripping boughs under which they were passing. This gleam fell upon a man on horseback who was jogging slowly along, and whom Mr Gilfil recognized, in spite of diminished rotundity, as Daniel Knott, the coachman who had married the rosy-cheeked Dorcas ten years before.

Every new incident suggested the same thought to Mr Gilfil; and his eye no sooner fell on Knott than he said to himself, 'Can he be come to tell us anything about Caterina?' Then he remembered that Caterina had been very fond of Dorcas, and that she always had some present ready to send her when Knott paid an occasional visit to the Manor. Could Tina have gone to Dorcas? But his heart sank again as he thought, very likely Knott had only come because he had heard of Captain Wybrow's death, and wanted to know how his old master had borne the blow.

As soon as the carriage reached the house, he went up to his study and walked about nervously, longing, but afraid, to go down and speak to Knott, lest his faint hope should be dissipated. Any one looking at that face, usually so full of calm goodwill, would have seen that the last week's suffering had left deep traces. By day he had been riding or wandering incessantly, either searching for Caterina himself, or directing inquiries to be made by others. By night he had not known sleep – only intermittent dozing, in which he seemed to be finding Caterina dead, and woke up with a start from this unreal agony to the real anguish of believing that he should see her no more. The clear grey eyes looked sunken and restless, the full careless lips had a strange tension about them, and the brow, formerly so smooth and open, was contracted as if with pain. He had not lost the object of a few months' passion; he had lost the being who was bound up with his power of loving, as the brook we played by or the flowers we gathered in childhood are bound up with our sense of beauty. Love meant nothing for him but to love Caterina. For years, the thought of her had been present in everything, like the air and the light; and now she was gone, it seemed as if all pleasure had lost its vehicle: the sky, the earth, the daily ride, the daily talk might be there, but the loveliness and the joy that were in them had gone for ever.

Presently, as he still paced backwards and forwards, he heard steps along the corridor, and there was a knock at his door. His voice trembled as he said, 'Come in,' and the rush of renewed hope was hardly distinguishable from pain when he saw Warren enter with Daniel Knott behind him.

'Knott is come, sir, with news of Miss Sarti. I thought it best to bring him to you first.'

Mr Gilfil could not help going up to the old coachman and wringing his hand; but he was unable to speak, and only motioned to him to take a chair, while Warren left the room. He hung upon Daniel's moonface, and listened to his small piping voice, with the same solemn yearning expectation with which he would have given ear to the most awful messenger from the land of shades.

'It war Dorkis, sir, would hev me come; but we

307

knowed nothin' o' what's happened at the Manor. She's frightened out on her wits about Miss Sarti, an' she would hev me saddle Blackbird this mornin', an' leave the ploughin', to come an' let Sir Christifer an' my lady know. P'raps you've heared, sir, we don't keep the Cross Keys at Sloppeter now; a uncle o' mine died three 'ear ago, an' left me a leggicy. He was bailiff to Squire Ramble, as hed them there big farms on his hans; an' so we took a little farm o' forty acres or thereabouts, becos Dorkis didn't like the public when she got moithered wi' children. As pritty a place as iver you see, sir, wi' water at the back convenent for the cattle.'

'For God's sake,' said Maynard, 'tell me what it is about Miss Sarti. Don't stay to tell me anything else now.'

'Well, sir,' said Knott, rather frightened by the parson's vehemence, 'she come t' our house i' the carrier's cart o' Wednesday, when it was welly nine o'clock at night; and Dorkis run out, for she heared the cart stop, an' Miss Sarti throwed her arms roun' Dorkis's neck an' says, 'Tek me in, Dorkis, tek me in,' an' went off into a swoond, like. An' Dorkis calls out to me, – 'Dannel,' she calls – an' I run out and carried the young miss in, an' she come roun' arter a bit, an' opened her eyes, and Dorkis got her to drink a spoonful o' rum-an'-water – we've got some capital rum as we brought from the Cross Keys, an' Dorkis won't let nobody drink it. She says she keeps it for sickness; but for my part, I think it's a pity to drink good rum when your mouth's out o' taste; you may just as well hev doctor's stuff. Howiver, Dorkis got her to bed, an' there she's lay iver sin', stoopid like, an' niver speaks, an' on'y teks little bits an' sups when Dorkis coaxes her. An' we begun to be frightened, and couldn't think what had made her come away from the Manor, and Dorkis was afeard there was summat wrong. So this mornin' she could hold no longer, an' would hev no nay but I must come an' see; an' so I've rode twenty mile upo' Blackbird, as thinks all the while he's a ploughin', an' turns sharp roun, ivery thirty yards, as if he was at the end of a furrow. I've hed a sore time wi' him, I can tell you, sir.'

'God bless you, Knott, for coming!' said Mr Gilfil, wringing the old coachman's hand again. 'Now go down and have something and rest yourself. You will stay here to-night, and by-and-by I shall come to you to learn the nearest way to your house. I shall get ready to ride there immediately, when I have spoken to Sir Christopher.'

In an hour from that time Mr Gilfil was galloping on a stout mare towards the little muddy village of Callam, five miles beyond Sloppeter. Once more he saw some gladness in the afternoon sunlight; once more it was a pleasure to see the hedgerow trees flying past him, and to be conscious of a 'good seat' while his black Kitty bounded beneath him, and the air whistled to the rhythm of her pace. Caterina was not dead; he had found her; his love and tenderness and long-suffering seemed so strong, they must recall her to life and happiness. After that week of despair, the rebound was so violent that it carried his hopes at once as far as the utmost mark they had ever reached. Caterina would come to love him at last; she would be his. They had been carried through all that dark and weary way that she might know the depth of his love. How he would cherish her – his little bird with the timid bright eye, and the sweet throat that trembled with love and music! She would nestle against him, and the poor little breast which had been so ruffled and bruised should be safe for evermore. In the love of a brave and faithful man there is always a strain of maternal tenderness; he gives out again those beams of protecting fondness which were shed on him as he lay on his mother's knee.

It was twilight as he entered the village of Callam, and, asking a home -bound labourer the way to Daniel Knott's, learned that it was by the church, which showed its stumpy ivy-clad spire on a slight elevation of ground; a useful addition to the means of identifying that desirable homestead afforded by Daniel's description – 'the prittiest place iver you see' – though a small cow-yard full of excellent manure, and leading right up to the door, without any frivolous interruption from garden or railing, might perhaps have been enough to make that description unmistakably specific.

Mr Gilfil had no sooner reached the gate leading into the cow-yard, than he was descried by a flaxen-haired lad of nine, prematurely invested with the *toga virilis*, or smock-frock, who ran forward to let in the unusual visitor. In a moment Dorcas was at the door, the roses on her cheeks apparently all the redder for the three pair of cheeks which formed a group round her, and for the very fat baby who stared in her arms, and sucked a long crust with calm relish.

'Is it Mr Gilfil, sir?' said Dorcas, curtsying low as he made his way through the damp straw, after tying up his horse.

'Yes, Dorcas; I'm grown out of your knowledge. How is Miss Sarti?'

'Just for all the world the same, sir, as I suppose Dannel's told you; for I reckon you've come from the Manor, though you're come uncommon quick, to be sure.'

'Yes, he got to the Manor about one o'clock, and I set off as soon as I could. She's not worse, is she?'

'No change, sir, for better or wuss. Will you please to walk in, sir? She lies there teckin' no notice o' nothin', no more nor a baby as is on'y a wick old, an' looks at me as blank as if she didn't know me. O what can it be, Mr Gilfil? How come she to leave the Manor? How's his honour an' my lady?'

'In great trouble, Dorcas. Captain Wybrow, Sir Christopher's nephew, you know, has died suddenly. Miss Sarti found him lying dead, and I think the shock has affected her mind.'

'Eh, dear! that fine young gentleman as was to be th' heir, as Dannel told me about. I remember seein' him when he was a little un, a-visitin' at the Manor. Well-a-day, what a grief to his honour and my lady. But that poor Miss Tina – an' she found him a-lyin' dead? O dear, O dear!'

Dorcas had led the way into the best kitchen, as charming a room as best kitchens used to be in farmhouses which had no parlours – the fire reflected in a bright row of pewter plates and dishes; the sand-scoured deal tables so clean you longed to stroke them; the salt-coffer in one chimney-corner, and a three-cornered chair in the other, the walls behind handsomely tapestried with flitches of bacon, and the ceiling ornamented with pendant hams.

'Sit ye down, sir – do,' said Dorcas, moving the three-cornered chair, 'an' let me get you somethin' after your long journey. Here, Becky, come an' tek the baby.'

Becky, a red-armed damsel, emerged from the adjoining back-kitchen, and possessed herself of baby, whose feelings or fat made him conveniently apathetic under the transference.

'What'll you please to tek, sir, as I can give you? I'll get you a rasher o' bacon i' no time, an' I've got some tea, or belike you'd tek a glass o' rum-an'-water. I know we've got nothin' as you're used t' eat and drink; but such as I hev, sir, I shall be proud to give you.'

'Thank you, Dorcas; I can't eat or drink anything.

I'm not hungry or tired. Let us talk about Tina. Has she spoken at all?'

'Niver since the fust words. 'Dear Dorkis,' says she, "tek me in;" an' then went off into a faint, an' not a word has she spoke since. I get her t' eat little bits an' sups o' things, but she teks no notice o' nothin'. I've took up Bessie wi' me now an' then' – here Dorcas lifted to her lap a curly-headed little girl of three, who was twisting a corner of her mother's apron, and opening round eyes at the gentleman – 'folks 'll tek notice o' children sometimes when they won't o' nothin' else. An' we gethered th' autumn crocuses out o' th' orchard, an' Bessie carried 'em up in her hand, an' put 'em on the bed. I knowed how fond Miss Tina was o' flowers an' them things, when she was a little un. But she looked at Bessie an' the flowers just the same as if she didn't see 'em. It cuts me to th' heart to look at them eyes o' hers: I think they're bigger nor iver, an' they look like my poor baby's as died, when it got so thin – O dear, its little hands, you could see thro' 'em. But I've great hopes if she was to see you, sir, as come from the Manor, it might bring back her mind, like.'

Maynard had that hope too, but he felt cold mists of fear gathering round him after the few bright warm hours of joyful confidence which had passed since he first heard that Caterina was alive. The thought *would* urge itself upon him that her mind and body might never recover from the strain that had been put upon them – that her delicate thread of life had already nearly spun itself out.

'Go now, Dorcas, and see how she is, but don't say anything about my being here. Perhaps it would be better for me to wait till daylight before I see her, and yet it would be very hard to pass another night in this way.'

Dorcas set down little Bessie, and went away. The three other children, including young Daniel in his smock-frock, were standing opposite to Mr Gilfil, watching him still more shyly now they were without their mother's countenance. He drew little Bessie towards him, and set her on his knee. She shook her yellow curls out of her eyes, and looked up at him as she said,—

'Zoo tome to tee ze yady? Zoo mek her peak? What zoo do to her? Tiss her?'

'Do you like to be kissed, Bessie?'

'Det,' said Bessie, immediately ducking down her head very low, in resistance to the expected rejoinder.

'We've got two pups,' said young Daniel, emboldened by observing the gentleman's amenities towards Bessie. 'Shall I show 'em yer? One's got white spots.'

'Yes, let me see them.'

Daniel ran out, and presently reappeared with two blind puppies, eagerly followed by the mother, affectionate though mongrel, and an exciting scene was beginning when Dorcas returned and said,—

'There's niver any difference in her hardly. I think you needn't wait, sir. She lies very still, as she al'ys does. I've put two candles i' the room, so as she may see you well. You'll please t' excuse the room, sir, an' the cap as she hes on; it's one o' mine.'

Mr Gilfil nodded silently, and rose to follow her up-stairs. They turned in at the first door, their footsteps making little noise on the plaster floor. The red-chequered linen curtains were drawn at the head of the bed, and Dorcas had placed the candles on this side of the room, so that the light might not fall oppressively on Caterina's eyes. When she had opened the door, Dorcas whispered, 'I'd better leave you, sir, I think?'

Mr Gilfil motioned assent, and advanced beyond the curtain. Caterina lay with her eyes turned the other way, and seemed unconscious that any one had entered. Her eyes, as Dorcas had said, looked larger than ever, perhaps because her face was thinner and paler, and her hair quite gathered away under one of Dorcas's thick caps. The small hands, too, that lay listlessly on the outside of the bed-clothes, were thinner than ever. She looked younger than she really was, and any one seeing the tiny face and hands for the first time, might have thought they belonged to a little girl of twelve, who was being taken away from coming instead of past sorrow.

When Mr Gilfil advanced and stood opposite to her, the light fell full upon his face. A slight startled expression came over Caterina's eyes; she looked at him earnestly for a few moments, then lifted up her hand as if to beckon him to stoop down towards her, and whispered 'Maynard!'

He seated himself on the bed, and stooped down towards her. She whispered again—

'Maynard, did you see the dagger?'

He followed his first impulse in answering her, and it was a wise one.

'Yes,' he whispered, 'I found it in your pocket, and put it back again in the cabinet.'

He took her hand in his and held it gently, awaiting what she would say next. His heart swelled so with thankfulness that she had recognized him, he could hardly repress a sob. Gradually her eyes became softer and less intense in their gaze. The tears were slowly gathering, and presently some large hot drops rolled down her cheek. Then the flood-gates were opened, and the heart-easing stream gushed forth; deep sobs came; and for nearly an hour she lay without speaking, while the heavy icy pressure that withheld her misery from utterance was thus melting away. How precious these tears were to Maynard, who day after day had been shuddering at the continually recurring image of Tina with the dry scorching stare of insanity!

By degrees the sobs subsided, she began to breathe calmly, and lay quiet with her eyes shut. Patiently Maynard sat, not heeding the flight of the hours, not heeding the old clock that ticked loudly on the landing. But when it was nearly ten,

Dorcas, impatiently anxious to know the result of Mr Gilfil's appearance, could not help stepping in on tip-toe. Without moving, he whispered in her ear to supply him with candles, see that the cow-boy had shaken down his mare, and go to bed – he would watch with Caterina – a great change had come over her.

Before long, Tina's lips began to move. 'Maynard,' she whispered again. He leaned towards her, and she went on.

'You know how wicked I am, then? You know what I meant to do with the dagger?'

'Did you mean to kill yourself, Tina?'

She shook her head slowly, and then was silent for a long while. At last, looking at him with solemn eyes, she whispered, 'To kill *him*.'

'Tina, my loved one, you would never have done it. God saw your whole heart; He knows you would never harm a living thing. He watches over His children, and will not let them do things they would pray with their whole hearts not to do. It was the angry thought of a moment, and He forgives you.'

She sank into silence again till it was nearly midnight. The weary enfeebled spirit seemed to be making its slow way with difficulty through the windings of thought; and when she began to whisper again, it was in reply to Maynard's words.

'But I had had such wicked feelings for a long while. I was so angry, and I hated Miss Assher so,

317

and I didn't care what came to anybody, because I was so miserable myself. I was full of bad passions. No one else was ever so wicked.'

'Yes, Tina, many are just as wicked. I often have very wicked feelings, and am tempted to do wrong things; but then my body is stronger than yours, and I can hide my feelings, and resist them better. They do not master me so. You have seen the little birds when they are very young and just begin to fly, how all their feathers are ruffled when they are frightened or angry; they have no power over themselves left, and might fall into a pit from mere fright. You were like one of those little birds. Your sorrow and suffering had taken such hold of you, you hardly knew what you did.'

He would not speak long, lest he should tire her, and oppress her with too many thoughts. Long pauses seemed needful for her before she could concentrate her feelings in short words.

'But when I meant to do it,' was the next thing she whispered, 'it was as bad as if I had done it.'

'No, my Tina,' answered Maynard slowly, waiting a little between each sentence; 'we mean to do wicked things that we never could do, just as we mean to do good or clever things that we never could do. Our thoughts are often worse than we are, just as they are often better than we are. And God sees us as we are altogether, not in separate feelings or actions, as our fellow-men see us. We are always doing each other injustice, and thinking better or worse of each other than we deserve, because we only hear and see separate words and actions. We don't see each other's whole nature. But God sees that you could not have committed that crime.'

Caterina shook her head slowly, and was silent. After a while,

'I don't know,' she said; 'I seemed to see him coming towards me, just as he would really have looked, and I meant – I meant to do it.'

'But when you saw him – tell me how it was, Tina?'

'I saw him lying on the ground, and thought he was ill. I don't know how it was then; I forgot everything. I knelt down and spoke to him, and – and he took no notice of me, and his eyes were fixed, and I began to think he was dead.'

'And you have never felt angry since?'

'O no, no; it is I who have been more wicked than any one; it is I who have been wrong all through.'

'No, my Tina; the fault has not all been yours; *he* was wrong; he gave you provocation. And wrong makes wrong. When people use us ill, we can hardly help having ill feeling towards them. But that second wrong is more excusable. I am more sinful than you, Tina; I have often had very bad feelings towards Captain Wybrow; and if he had provoked me as he did you, I should perhaps have done something more wicked.'

'O, it was not so wrong in him; he didn't know how he hurt me. How was it likely he could love me as I loved him? And how could he marry a poor little thing like me?'

Maynard made no reply to this, and there was again silence, till Tina said,

'Then I was so deceitful; they didn't know how wicked I was. Padroncello didn't know; his good little monkey he used to call me; and if he had known, O how naughty he would have thought me!'

'My Tina, we have all our secret sins; and if we knew ourselves, we should not judge each other harshly. Sir Christopher himself has felt, since this trouble came upon him, that he has been too severe and obstinate.'

In this way – in these broken confessions and answering words of comfort – the hours wore on, from the deep black night to the chill early twilight, and from early twilight to the first yellow streak of morning parting the purple cloud. Mr Gilfil felt as if in the long hours of that night the bond that united his love for ever and alone to Caterina had acquired fresh strength and sanctity. It is so with the human relations that rest on the deep emotional sympathy of affection: every new day and night of joy or sorrow is a new ground, a new consecration, for the love that is nourished by memories as well as hopes – the love to which perpetual repetition is not a weariness but a want, and to which a separated joy is the beginning of pain.

The cocks began to crow; the gate swung; there was a tramp of footsteps in the yard, and Mr Gilfil heard Dorcas stirring. These sounds seemed to affect Caterina, for she looked anxiously at him and said, 'Maynard, are you going away?'

'No, I shall stay here at Callam until you are better, and then you will go away too.'

'Never to the Manor again, O no! I shall live poorly, and get my own bread.'

'Well, dearest, you shall do what you would like best. But I wish you could go to sleep now. Try to rest quietly, and by-and-by you will perhaps sit up a little. God has kept you in life in spite of all this sorrow; it will be sinful not to try and make the best of His gift. Dear Tina, you *will* try; – and little Bessie brought you some crocuses once; you didn't notice the poor little thing; but you will notice her when she comes again, will you not?'

'I will try,' whispered Tina humbly, and then closed her eyes.

By the time the sun was above the horizon, scattering the clouds, and shining with pleasant morning warmth through the little leaded window, Caterina was asleep. Maynard gently loosed the tiny hand, cheered Dorcas with the good news, and made his way to the village inn, with a thankful heart that Tina had been so far herself again. Evidently the sight of him had blended naturally with the memories in which her mind was absorbed, and she had been led on to an unburdening of herself that might be the beginning of a complete restoration. But her body was so enfeebled – her soul so bruised – that the utmost tenderness and care would be necessary. The next thing to be done was to send tidings to Sir Christopher and Lady Cheverel; then to write and summon his sister, under whose care he had determined to place Caterina. The Manor, even if she had been wishing to return thither, would, he knew, be the most undesirable home for her at present: every scene, every object there, was associated with still unallayed anguish. If she were domesticated for a time with his mild gentle sister, who had a peaceful home and a prattling little boy, Tina might attach herself anew to life, and recover, partly at least, the shock that had been given to her constitution. When he had written his letters and taken a hasty breakfast, he was soon in his saddle again, on his way to Sloppeter, where he would post them, and seek out a medical man, to whom he might confide the moral causes of Caterina's enfeebled condition.

CHAPTER 20

In less than a week from that time, Caterina was persuaded to travel in a comfortable carriage, under the care of Mr Gilfil and his sister, Mrs Heron, whose soft blue eyes and mild manners were very soothing to the poor bruised child – the more so as they had an air of sisterly equality, which was quite new to her. Under Lady Cheverel's uncaressing authoritative goodwill, Tina had always retained a certain constraint and awe; and there was a sweetness before unknown in having a young and gentle woman, like an elder sister, bending over her caressingly, and speaking in low loving tones.

Maynard was almost angry with himself for feeling happy while Tina's mind and body were still trembling on the verge of irrecoverable decline; but the new delight of acting as her guardian angel, of being with her every hour of the day, of devising everything for her comfort, of watching for a ray of returning interest in her eyes, was too absorbing to leave room for alarm or regret.

On the third day the carriage drove up to the door of Foxholm Parsonage, where the Rev. Arthur

Heron presented himself on the door-step, eager to greet his returning Lucy, and holding by the hand a broad-chested tawny-haired boy of five, who was smacking a miniature hunting-whip with great vigour.

Nowhere was there a lawn more smooth-shaven, walks better swept, or a porch more prettily festooned with creepers, than at Foxholm Parsonage, standing snugly sheltered by beeches and chestnuts halfway down the pretty green hill which was surmounted by the church, and over-looking a village that straggled at its ease among pastures and meadows, surrounded by wild hedge-rows and broad shadowing trees, as yet unthreat-ened by improved methods of farming.

Brightly the fire shone in the great parlour, and brightly in the little pink bedroom, which was to be Caterina's, because it looked away from the churchyard, and on to a farm homestead, with its little cluster of beehive ricks, and placid groups of cows, and cheerful matin sounds of healthy labour. Mrs Heron, with the instinct of a delicate, impress-ible woman, had written to her husband to have this room prepared for Caterina. Contented speckled hens, industriously scratching for the rarely-found corn, may sometimes do more for a sick heart than a grove of nightingales; there is something irresistibly calming in the unsentimental cheeriness of top-knotted pullets, unpetted sheep-dogs, and patient cart-horses enjoying a drink of muddy water.

324

In such a home as this parsonage, a nest of comfort, without any of the stateliness that would carry a suggestion of Cheverel Manor, Mr Gilfil was not unreasonable in hoping that Caterina might gradually shake off the haunting vision of the past, and recover from the languor and feebleness which were the physical sign of that vision's blighting presence. The next thing to be done was to arrange an exchange of duties with Mr Heron's curate, that Maynard might be constantly near Caterina, and watch over her progress. She seemed to like him to be with her, to look uneasily for his return; and though she seldom spoke to him, she was most contented when he sat by her, and held her tiny hand in his large protecting grasp. But Oswald, *alias* Ozzy, the broad-chested boy, was perhaps her most beneficial companion. With something of his uncle's person, he had inherited also his uncle's early taste for a domestic menagerie, and was very imperative in demanding Tina's sympathy in the welfare of his guinea-pigs, squirrels, and dormice. With him she seemed now and then to have gleams of her childhood coming athwart the leaden clouds, and many hours of winter went by the more easily for being spent in Ozzy's nursery.

Mrs Heron was not musical, and had no instrument; but one of Mr Gilfil's cares was to procure a harpsichord, and have it placed in the drawing-room, always open, in the hope that some day the spirit of music would be reawakened in Caterina, and she would be attracted towards the instrument. But the winter was almost gone by, and he had waited in vain. The utmost improvement in Tina had not gone beyond passiveness and acquiescence – a quiet grateful smile, compliance with Oswald's whims, and an increasing consciousness of what was being said and done around her. Sometimes she would take up a bit of woman's work, but she seemed too languid to persevere in it; her fingers soon dropped, and she relapsed into motionless reverie.

At last – it was one of those bright days in the end of February, when the sun is shining with a promise of approaching spring. Maynard had been walking with her and Oswald round the garden to look at the snowdrops, and she was resting on the sofa after the walk. Ozzy, roaming about the room in quest of a forbidden pleasure, came to the harpsichord, and struck the handle of his whip on a deep bass note.

The vibration rushed through Caterina like an electric shock: it seemed as if at that instant a new soul were entering into her, and filling her with a deeper, more significant life. She looked round, rose from the sofa, and walked to the harpsichord. In a moment her fingers were wandering with their old sweet method among the keys, and her soul was floating in its true familiar element of delicious sound, as the water-plant that lies withered and shrunken on the ground expands into freedom and beauty when once more bathed in its native flood.

Maynard thanked God. An active power was reawakened, and must make a new epoch in Caterina's recovery.

Presently there were low liquid notes blending themselves with the harder tones of the instrument, and gradually the pure voice swelled into predominance. Little Ozzy stood in the middle of the room, with his mouth open and his legs very wide apart, struck with something like awe at this new power in 'Tin-Tin,' as he called her, whom he had been accustomed to think of as a playfellow not at all clever, and very much in need of his instruction on many subjects. A genie soaring with broad wings out of his milk-jug would not have been more astonishing.

Caterina was singing the very air from the *Orfeo* which we heard her singing so many months ago at the beginning of her sorrows. It was *Che faro*, Sir Christopher's favourite, and its notes seemed to carry on their wings all the tenderest memories of her life, when Cheverel Manor was still an untroubled home. The long happy days of childhood and girlhood recovered all their rightful predominance over the short interval of sin and sorrow.

She paused, and burst into tears – the first tears she had shed since she had been at Foxholm. Maynard could not help hurrying towards her, putting his arm round her, and leaning down to kiss her hair. She nestled to him, and put up her little mouth to be kissed.

The delicate-tendrilled plant must have something to cling to. The soul that was born anew to music was born anew to love.

CHAPTER 21

O
n the 30th of May 1790, a very pretty sight was seen by the villagers assembled near the door of Foxholm church. The sun was bright upon the dewy grass, the air was alive with the murmur of bees and the trilling of birds, the bushy blossoming chestnuts and the foamy flowering hedgerows seemed to be crowding round to learn why the church-bells were ringing so merrily, as Maynard Gilfil, his face bright with happiness, walked out of the old Gothic doorway with Tina on his arm. The little face was still pale, and there was a subdued melancholy in it, as of one who sups with friends for the last time, and has his ear open for the signal that will call him away. But the tiny hand rested with the pressure of contented affection on Maynard's arm, and the dark eyes met his downward glance with timid answering love.

There was no train of bridesmaids; only pretty Mrs Heron leaning on the arm of a dark-haired young man hitherto unknown in Foxholm, and holding by the other hand little Ozzy, who exulted less in his new velvet cap and tunic, than in the notion that he was bridesman to Tin-Tin.

Last of all came a couple whom the villagers eyed yet more eagerly than the bride and bridegroom: a fine old gentleman, who looked round with keen glances that cowed the conscious scapegraces among them, and a stately lady in blue-and-white silk robes, who must surely be like Queen Charlotte.

'Well, that theer's whut I coall a pictur,' said old 'Mester' Ford, a true Staffordshire patriarch, who leaned on a stick and held his head very much on one side, with the air of a man who had little hope of the present generation, but would at all events give it the benefit of his criticism. 'Th' yoong men noo-a-deys, the'r poor squashy things – the' looke well anoof, but the' woon't wear, the' woon't wear. Theer's neer un'll carry his 'ears like that Sir Cris'fer Chuvrell.'

''Ull bet ye two pots,' said another of the seniors, 'as that yoongster a-walkin' wi' th' parson's wife'll be Sir Cris'fer's son – he fevours him.'

'Nay, yae'll bet that wi' as big a fule as yersen; hae's noo son at oall. As I oonderstan', hae's the nevey as is t' heir th' esteate. The coochman as puts oop at th' White Hoss tellt me as theer war another nevey, a dell finer chap t' looke at nor this un, as died in a fit, oall on a soodden, an' soo this here yoong un's got upo' th' perch istid.'

At the church gate Mr Bates was standing in a new suit, ready to speak words of good omen as the bride and bridegroom approached. He had come all the way from Cheverel Manor on purpose to see Miss Tiny happy once more, and would have been in a state of unmixed joy but for the inferiority of the wedding nosegays to what he could have furnished from the garden at the Manor.

'God A' maighty bless ye both, an' send ye long laife an' happiness,' were the good gardener's rather tremulous words.

'Thank you, uncle Bates; always remember Tina,' said the sweet low voice, which fell on Mr Bates's ear for the last time.

The wedding journey was to be a circuitous route to Shepperton, where Mr Gilfil had been for several months inducted as vicar. This small living had been given him through the interest of an old friend who had some claim on the gratitude of the Oldinport family; and it was a satisfaction both to Maynard and Sir Christopher that a home to which he might take Caterina had thus readily presented itself at a distance from Cheverel Manor. For it had never yet been thought safe that she should revisit the scene of her sufferings, her health continuing too delicate to encourage the slightest risk of painful excitement. In a year or two, perhaps, by the time old Mr Crichley, the rector of Cumbermoor, should have left a world of gout, and when Caterina would very likely be a happy mother, Maynard might safely take up his abode at Cumbermoor, and Tina would feel nothing but content at seeing a new 'little black-eyed monkey' running up and down the gallery and gardens of the Manor. A mother dreads no memories – those shadows have all melted away in the dawn of baby's smile.

In these hopes, and in the enjoyment of Tina's nestling affection, Mr Gilfil tasted a few months of perfect happiness. She had come to lean entirely on his love, and to find life sweet for his sake. Her continual languor and want of active interest was a natural consequence of bodily feebleness, and the prospect of her becoming a mother was a new ground for hoping the best.

But the delicate plant had been too deeply bruised, and in the struggle to put forth a blossom it died.

Tina died, and Maynard Gilfil's love went with her into deep silence for evermore.

EPILOGUE

This was Mr Gilfil's love-story, which lay far back from the time when he sat, worn and grey, by his lonely fireside in Shepperton Vicarage. Rich brown locks, passionate love, and deep early sorrow, strangely different as they seem from the scanty white hairs, the apathetic content, and the unexpectant quiescence of old age, are but part of the same life's journey; as the bright Italian plains, with the sweet *Addio* of their beckoning maidens, are part of the same day's travel that brings us to the other side of the mountain, between the sombre rocky walls and among the guttural voices of the Valais.

To those who were familiar only with the grey-haired Vicar, jogging leisurely along on his old chestnut cob, it would perhaps have been hard to believe that he had ever been the Maynard Gilfil who, with a heart full of passion and tenderness, had urged his black Kitty to her swiftest gallop on the way to Callam, or that the old gentleman of caustic tongue, and bucolic tastes, and sparing

333

habits, had known all the deep secrets of devoted love, had struggled through its days and nights of anguish, and trembled under its unspeakable joys. And indeed the Mr Gilfil of those late Shepperton days had more of the knots and ruggednesses of poor human nature than there lay any clear hint of in the open-eyed loving Maynard. But it is with men as with trees: if you lop off their finest branches, into which they were pouring their young life-juice, the wounds will be healed over with some rough boss, some odd excrescence; and what might have been a grand tree expanding into liberal shade, is but a whimsical misshapen trunk. Many an irritating fault, many an unlovely oddity, has come of a hard sorrow, which has crushed and maimed the nature just when it was expanding into plenteous beauty; and the trivial erring life which we visit with our harsh blame, may be but as the unsteady motion of a man whose best limb is withered.

And so the dear old Vicar, though he had something of the knotted whimsical character of the poor lopped oak, had yet been sketched out by nature as a noble tree. The heart of him was sound, the grain was of the finest, and in the grey-haired man who filled his pocket with sugar-plums for the little children, whose most biting words were directed against the evil-doing of the rich man, and who, with all his social pipes and slipshod talk, never sank below the highest level of his parishioners' respect, there was the main trunk of the same brave, faithful, tender nature that had poured out the finest, freshest forces of its life-current in a first and only love – the love of Tina.

JANET'S REPENTANCE

CHAPTER 1

'No!' said lawyer Dempster, in a loud, rasping, oratorical tone, struggling against chronic huskiness, 'as long as my Maker grants me power of voice and power of intellect, I will take every legal means to resist the introduction of demoralizing, methodistical doctrine into this parish; I will not supinely suffer an insult to be inflicted on our venerable pastor, who has given us sound instruction for half a century.'

It was very warm everywhere that evening, but especially in the bar of the Red Lion at Milby, where Mr Dempster was seated mixing his third glass of brandy-and-water. He was a tall and rather massive man, and the front half of his large surface was so well dredged with snuff, that the cat, having inadvertently come near him, had been seized with a severe fit of sneezing – an accident which, being cruelly misunderstood, had caused her to be driven contumeliously from the bar. Mr Dempster habitually held his chin tucked in, and his head hanging forward, weighed down, perhaps, by a preponderant occiput and a bulging forehead, between which his closely-clipped coronal surface lay like a flat and new-mown table-land. The only other observable features were puffy cheeks and a protruding yet lipless mouth. Of his nose I can only say that it was snuffy, and as Mr Dempster was never caught in the act of looking at anything in particular, it would have been difficult to swear to the colour of his eyes.

'Well! I'll not stick at giving *myself* trouble to put down such hypocritical cant,' said Mr Tomlinson, the rich miller. 'I know well enough what your Sunday-evening lectures are good for – for wenches to meet their sweethearts, and brew mischief. There's work enough with the servant-maids as it is – such as I never heared the like of in my mother's time, and it's all along o' your schooling and newfangled plans. Give me a servant as can nayther read nor write, I say, and doesn't know the year o' the Lord as she was born in. I should like to know what good those Sunday schools have done, now. Why, the boys used to go a birds'-nesting of a Sunday morning; and a capital thing, too – ask any farmer; and very pritty it was to see the strings o' heggs hanging up in poor people's houses. You'll not see 'em nowhere now.'

'Pooh!' said Mr Luke Byles, who piqued himself on his reading, and was in the habit of asking casual acquaintances if they knew anything of Hobbes; 'it is right enough that the lower orders should be instructed. But this sectarianism within the Church ought to be put down. In point of fact, these Evangelicals are not Churchmen at all; they're no better than Presbyterians.'

'Presbyterans? what are they?' inquired Mr Tomlinson, who often said his father had given him 'no eddication, and he didn't care who knowed it; he could buy up most o' th' eddicated men he'd ever come across.'

'The Presbyterians,' said Mr Dempster, in rather a louder tone than before, holding that every appeal for information must naturally be addressed to him, 'are a sect founded in the reign of Charles I., by a man named John Presbyter, who hatched all the brood of Dissenting vermin that crawl about in dirty alleys, and circumvent the lord of the manor in order to get a few yards of ground for their pigeon-house conventicles.'

'No, no, Dempster,' said Mr Luke Byles, 'you're out there. Presbyterianism is derived from the word presbyter, meaning an elder.'

'Don't contradict *me*, sir!' stormed Dempster. 'I say the word presbyterian is derived from John Presbyter, a miserable fanatic who wore a suit of leather, and went about from town to village, and from village to hamlet, inoculating the vulgar with the asinine virus of Dissent.'

'Come, Byles, that seems a deal more liker,' said Mr Tomlinson, in a conciliatory tone, apparently of opinion that history was a process of ingenious guessing.

'It's not a question of likelihood; it's a known

fact. I could fetch you my Encyclopædia, and show it you this moment.'

'I don't care a straw, sir, either for you or your Encyclopædia,' said Mr Dempster; 'a farrago of false information, of which you picked up an imperfect copy in a cargo of waste paper. Will you tell *me*, sir, that I don't know the origin of Presbyterianism? I, sir, a man known through the county, entrusted with the affairs of half a score parishes; while you, sir, are ignored by the very fleas that infest the miserable alley in which you were bred.'

A loud and general laugh, with 'You'd better let him alone, Byles;' 'you'll not get the better of Dempster in a hurry,' drowned the retort of the too well-informed Mr Byles, who, white with rage, rose and walked out of the bar.

'A meddlesome, upstart, Jacobinical fellow, gentlemen,' continued Mr Dempster. 'I was determined to be rid of him. What does he mean by thrusting himself into our company? A man with about as much principle as he has property, which, to my knowledge, is considerably less than none. An insolvent atheist, gentlemen. A deistical prater, fit to sit in the chimney-corner of a pot-house, and make blasphemous comments on the one greasy newspaper fingered by beer-swilling tinkers. I will not suffer in my company a man who speaks lightly of religion. The signature of a fellow like Byles would be a blot on our protest.'

'And how do you get on with your signatures?'

said Mr Pilgrim, the doctor, who had presented his large top-booted person within the bar while Mr Dempster was speaking. Mr Pilgrim had just returned from one of his long day's rounds among the farmhouses, in the course of which he had sat down to two hearty meals that might have been mistaken for dinners, if he had not declared them to be 'snaps;' and as each snap had been followed by a few glasses of 'mixture,' containing a less liberal proportion of water than the articles he himself labelled with that broadly generic name, he was in that condition which his groom indicated with poetic ambiguity, by saying that 'master had been in the sunshine.' Under these circumstances, after a hard day, in which he had really had no regular meal, it seemed a natural relaxation to step into the bar of the Red Lion, where, as it was Saturday evening, he should be sure to find Dempster, and hear the latest news about the protest against the evening lecture.

'Have you hooked Ben Landor yet?' he continued, as he took two chairs, one for his body, and the other for his right leg.

'No,' said Mr Budd, the churchwarden, shaking his head, 'Ben Landor has a way of keeping himself neutral in everything, and he doesn't like to oppose his father. Old Landor is a regular Tryanite. But we haven't got your name yet, Pilgrim.'

'Tut tut, Budd,' said Mr Dempster sarcastically, 'you don't expect Pilgrim to sign? He's got a dozen Tryanite livers under his treatment. Nothing like cant and methodism for producing a superfluity of bile.'

'O, I thought, as Pratt had declared himself a Tryanite, we should be sure to get Pilgrim on our side.'

Mr Pilgrim was not a man to sit quiet under a sarcasm, nature having endowed him with a considerable share of self-defensive wit. In his most sober moments he had an impediment in his speech, and as copious gin-and-water stimulated not the speech but the impediment, he had time to make his retort sufficiently bitter.

'Why, to tell you the truth, Budd,' he spluttered, 'there's a report all over the town that Deb Traunter swears you shall take her with you as one of the delegates, and they say there's to be a fine crowd at your door the morning you start, to see the row. Knowing your tenderness for that member of the fair sex, I thought you might find it impossible to deny her. I hang back a little from signing on that account, as Prendergast might not take the protest well if Deb Traunter went with you.'

Mr Budd was a small, sleek-headed bachelor of five-and-forty, whose scandalous life had long furnished his more moral neighbours with an after-dinner joke. He had no other striking characteristic, except that he was a currier of choleric temperament, so that you might wonder why he had been chosen as clergyman's churchwarden, if I did not tell you that he had recently been elected through Mr Dempster's exertions, in order that his zeal against the threatened evening lecture might be backed by the dignity of office.

'Come, come, Pilgrim,' said Mr Tomlinson, covering Mr Budd's retreat, 'you know you like to wear the crier's coat, green o' one side and red o' the other. You've been to hear Tryan preach at Paddiford Common – you know you have.'

'To be sure I have; and a capital sermon too. It's a pity you were not there. It was addressed to those "void of understanding."'

'No, no, you'll never catch me there,' returned Mr Tomlinson, not in the least stung, 'he preaches without book, they say, just like a Dissenter. It must be a rambling sort of a concern.'

'That's not the worst,' said Mr Dempster, 'he preaches against good works; says good works are not necessary to salvation – a sectarian, antinomian, anabaptist doctrine. Tell a man he is not to be saved by his works, and you open the floodgates of all immorality. You see it in all these canting innovators; they're all bad ones by the sly; smooth-faced, drawling, hypocritical fellows, who pretend ginger isn't hot in their mouths, and cry down all innocent pleasures; their hearts are all the blacker for their sanctimonious outsides. Haven't we been warned against those who make clean the outside of the cup and the platter? There's this Tryan, now, he goes about praying with old women, and singing with charity children; but what has he really got his eye on all the while? A domineering ambitious Jesuit, gentlemen; all he wants is to get his foot far enough into the parish to step into Crewe's shoes when the old gentleman dies. Depend upon it, whenever you see a man pretending to be better than his neighbours, that man has either some cunning end to serve, or his heart is rotten with spiritual pride.'

As if to guarantee himself against this awful sin, Mr Dempster seized the brandy bottle, and poured out a larger quantity than usual.

'Have you fixed on your third delegate yet?' said Mr Pilgrim, whose taste was for detail rather than for dissertation.

'That's the man,' answered Dempster, pointing to Mr Tomlinson. 'We start for Elmstoke Rectory on Tuesday morning; so, if you mean to give us your signature, you must make up your mind pretty quickly, Pilgrim.'

Mr Pilgrim did not in the least mean it, so he only said, 'I shouldn't wonder if Tryan turns out too many for you, after all. He's got a well-oiled tongue of his own, and has perhaps talked over Prendergast into a determination to stand by him.'

'Ve-ry little fear of that,' said Dempster, in a confident tone. 'I'll soon bring him round. Tryan has got his match. I've plenty of rods in pickle for Tryan.'

At this moment Boots entered the bar, and put a letter into the lawyer's hands, saying, 'There's

Trower's man just come into the yard wi' a gig, sir, an' he's brought this here letter.'

Mr Dempster read the letter and said, 'Tell him to turn the gig – I'll be with him in a minute. Here, run to Gruby's and get this snuff-box filled – quick!'

'Trower's worse, I suppose; eh, Dempster? Wants you to alter his will, eh?' said Mr Pilgrim.

'Business – business – business – I don't know exactly what,' answered the cautious Dempster, rising deliberately from his chair, thrusting on his low-crowned hat, and walking with a slow but not unsteady step out of the bar.

'I never see Dempster's equal; if I did I'll be shot,' said Mr Tomlinson, looking after the lawyer admiringly. 'Why, he's drunk the best part of a bottle o' brandy since here we've been sitting, and I'll bet a guinea, when he's got to Trower's his head 'll be as clear as mine. He knows more about law when he's drunk than all the rest on 'em when they're sober.'

'Aye, and other things too besides law,' said Mr Budd. 'Did you notice how he took up Byles about the Presbyterians? Bless your heart, he knows everything, Dempster does. He studied very hard when he was a young man.'

CHAPTER 2

The conversation just recorded is not, I am aware, remarkably refined or witty; but if it had been, it could hardly have taken place in Milby when Mr Dempster flourished there, and old Mr Crewe, the curate, was yet alive.

More than a quarter of a century has slipped by since then, and in the interval Milby has advanced at as rapid a pace as other market-towns in her Majesty's dominions. By this time it has a handsome railway station, where the drowsy London traveller may look out by the brilliant gas-light and see perfectly sober papas and husbands alighting with their leather-bags after transacting their day's business at the county town. There is a resident rector, who appeals to the consciences of his hearers with all the immense advantages of a divine who keeps his own carriage; the church is enlarged by at least five hundred sittings; and the grammar-school, conducted on reformed principles, has its upper forms crowded with the genteel youth of Milby. The gentlemen there fall into no other excess at dinner-parties than the perfectly well-bred and virtuous excess of stupidity; and though the ladies are still said sometimes to take too much upon themselves, they are never known to take too much in any other way. The conversation is sometimes quite literary, for there is a flourishing book-club, and many of the younger ladies have carried their studies so far as to have forgotten a little German. In short, Milby is now a refined, moral, and enlightened town; no more resembling the Milby of former days than the huge, long-skirted, drab greatcoat that embarrassed the ankles of our grandfathers resembled the light paletot in which we tread jauntily through the muddiest streets, or than the bottle-nosed Britons, rejoicing over a tankard, in the old sign of the Two Travellers at Milby, resembled the severe-looking gentlemen in straps and high collars whom a modern artist has represented as sipping the imaginary port of that well-known commercial house.

But pray, reader, dismiss from your mind all the refined and fashionable ideas associated with this advanced state of things, and transport your imagination to a time when Milby had no gas-lights; when the mail drove up dusty or bespattered to the door of the Red Lion; when old Mr Crewe, the curate, in a brown Brutus wig, delivered inaudible sermons on a Sunday, and on a week-day imparted the education of a gentleman – that is to say, an arduous inacquaintance with Latin through the medium of the Eton grammar – to three pupils in the upper grammar-school.

If you had passed through Milby on the coach at that time, you would have had no idea what important people lived there, and how very high a sense of rank was prevalent among them. It was a dingy-looking town, with a strong smell of tanning up one street, and a great shaking of handlooms up another; and even in that focus of aristocracy, Friar's Gate, the houses would not have seemed very imposing to the hasty and superficial glance of a passenger. You might still less have suspected that the figure in light fustian and large grey whiskers, leaning against the grocer's door-post in High Street, was no less a person than Mr Lowme, one of the most aristocratic men in Milby, said to have been 'brought up a gentleman,' and to have had the gay habits accordant with that station, keeping his harriers and other expensive animals. He was now quite an elderly Lothario, reduced to the most economical sins; the prominent form of his gaiety being this of lounging at Mr Gruby's door, embarrassing the servant-maids who came for grocery, and talking scandal with the rare passers-by. Still, it was generally understood that Mr Lowme belonged to the highest circle of Milby society; his sons and daughters held up their heads very high indeed; and in spite of his condescending way of chatting and drinking with inferior people, he would himself have scorned any closer identification with them. It must be admitted that he was of some service to the town in this station at

Mr Gruby's door, for he and Mr Landor's Newfoundland dog, who stretched himself and gaped on the opposite causeway, took something from the lifeless air that belonged to the High Street on every day except Saturday.

Certainly, in spite of three assemblies and a charity ball in the winter, the occasional advent of a ventriloquist, or a company of itinerant players, some of whom were very highly thought of in London, and the annual three-days' fair in June, Milby might be considered dull by people of a hypochondriacal temperament, and perhaps this was one reason why many of the middle-aged inhabitants, male and female, often found it impossible to keep up their spirits without a very abundant supply of stimulants. It is true there were several substantial men who had a reputation for exceptional sobriety, so that Milby habits were really not as bad as possible; and no one is warranted in saying that old Mr Crewe's flock could not have been worse without any clergyman at all.

The well-dressed parishioners generally were very regular church-goers, and to the younger ladies and gentlemen I am inclined to think that the Sunday morning service was the most exciting event of the week; for few places could present a more brilliant show of out-door toilettes than might be seen issuing from Milby church at one o'clock. There were the four tall Miss Pittmans, old Lawyer Pittman's daughters, with cannon curls surmounted by large hats, and long, drooping ostrich feathers of parrot green. There was Miss Phipps, with a crimson bonnet, very much tilted up behind, and a cockade of stiff feathers on the summit. There was Miss Landor, the belle of Milby, clad regally in purple and ermine, with a plume of feathers neither drooping nor erect, but maintaining a discreet medium. There were the three Miss Tomlinsons, who imitated Miss Landor, and also wore ermine and feathers; but their beauty was considered of a coarse order, and their square forms were quite unsuited to the round tippet which fell with such remarkable grace on Miss Landor's sloping shoulders. Looking at this plumed procession of ladies, you would have formed rather a high idea of Milby wealth; yet there was only one closed carriage in the place, and that was old Mr Landor's, the banker, who, I think, never drove more than one horse. These sumptuously-attired ladies flashed past the vulgar eye in one-horse chaises, by no means of a superior build.

The young gentlemen, too, were not without their little Sunday displays of costume, of a limited masculine kind. Mr Eustace Landor, being nearly of age, had recently acquired a diamond ring, together with the habit of rubbing his hand through his hair. He was tall and dark, and thus had an advantage which Mr Alfred Phipps, who, like his sister, was blond and stumpy, found it difficult to overtake, even by the severest attention to shirt studs, and the particular shade of brown that was best relieved by gilt buttons.

The respect for the Sabbath, manifested in this attention to costume, was unhappily counterbalanced by considerable levity of behaviour during the prayers and sermon; for the young ladies and gentlemen of Milby were of a very satirical turn, Miss Landor especially being considered remarkably clever, and a terrible quiz; and the large congregation necessarily containing many persons inferior in dress and demeanour to the distinguished aristocratic minority, divine service offered irresistible temptations to joking, through the medium of telegraphic communications from the galleries to the aisles and back again. I remember blushing very much, and thinking Miss Landor was laughing at me, because I was appearing in coat-tails for the first time, when I saw her look down slyly towards where I sat, and then turn with a titter to handsome Mr Bob Lowme, who had such beautiful whiskers meeting under his chin. But perhaps she was not thinking of me after all; for our pew was near the pulpit, and there was almost always something funny about old Mr Crewe. His brown wig was hardly ever put on quite right, and he had a way of raising his voice for three or four words, and lowering it again to a mumble, so that we could scarcely make out a word he said; though, as my mother observed, that was of no consequence in the prayers, since every one had a prayer-book; and as for the sermon, she continued with some causticity, we all of us heard more of it than we could remember when we got home.

This youthful generation was not particularly literary. The young ladies who frizzed their hair, and gathered it all into large barricades in front of their heads, leaving their occipital region exposed without ornament, as if that, being a back view, was of no consequence, dreamed as little that their daughters would read a selection of German poetry, and be able to express an admiration for Schiller, as that they would turn all their hair the other way – that instead of threatening us with barricades in front, they would be most killing in retreat,

'And, like the Parthian, wound us as they fly.'

Those charming well-frizzed ladies spoke French indeed with considerable facility, unshackled by any timid regard to idiom, and were in the habit of conducting conversations in that language in the presence of their less instructed elders; for according to the standard of those backward days, their education had been very lavish, such young ladies as Miss Landor, Miss Phipps, and the Miss Pittmans, having been 'finished' at distant and expensive schools.

Old lawyer Pittman had once been a very important person indeed, having in his earlier days managed the affairs of several gentlemen in those parts, who had subsequently been obliged to sell everything and leave the country, in which crisis Mr Pittman accommodatingly stepped in as a purchaser of their estates, taking on himself the risk and trouble of a more leisurely sale; which, however, happened to turn out very much to his advantage. Such opportunities occur quite unexpectedly in the way of business. But I think Mr Pittman must have been unlucky in his later speculations, for now, in his old age, he had not the reputation of being very rich; and though he rode slowly to his office in Milby every morning on an old white hackney, he had to resign the chief profits, as well as the active business of the firm, to his younger partner, Dempster. No one in Milby considered old Pittman a virtuous man, and the elder townspeople were not at all backward in narrating the least advantageous portions of his biography in a very round unvarnished manner. Yet I could never observe that they trusted him any the less, or liked him any the worse. Indeed, Pittman and Dempster were the popular lawyers of Milby and its neighbourhood, and Mr Benjamin Landor, whom no one had anything particular to say against, had a very meagre business in comparison. Hardly a landholder, hardly a farmer, hardly a parish within ten miles of Milby, whose affairs were not under the legal guardianship of Pittman and Dempster, and I think the clients were proud of their lawyers' unscrupulousness, as the patrons of the fancy are proud of their champion's 'condition.' It was not, to be sure, the thing for ordinary life, but it was the thing to bet on in a lawyer. Dempster's talent in 'bringing through' a client was a very common topic of conversation with the farmers, over an incidental glass of grog at the Red Lion. 'He's a long-headed feller, Dempster; why, it shows yer what a head-piece Dempster has, as he can drink a bottle o' brandy at a sittin', an' yit see further through a stone wall when he's done, than other folks 'll see through a glass winder.' Even Mr Jerome, chief member of the congregation at Salem Chapel, an elderly man of very strict life, was one of Dempster's clients, and had quite an exceptional indulgence for his attorney's foibles, perhaps attributing them to the inevitable incompatibility of law and gospel.

The standard of morality at Milby, you perceive, was not inconveniently high in those good old times, and an ingenuous vice or two was what every man expected of his neighbour. Old Mr Crewe, the curate, for example, was allowed to enjoy his avarice in comfort, without fear of sarcastic parish demagogues; and his flock liked him all the better for having scraped together a large fortune out of his school and curacy, and the proceeds of the three thousand pounds he had with his little deaf wife. It was clear he must be a learned man, for he had once had a large private school in connection with the grammar school, and had even numbered a young nobleman or two among his pupils. The fact that he read nothing at all now, and that his mind seemed absorbed in the commonest matters, was doubtless due to his having exhausted the resources of erudition earlier in life. It is true he was not spoken of in terms of high respect, and old Crewe's stingy housekeeping was a frequent subject of jesting; but this was a good old-fashioned characteristic in a parson who had been part of Milby life for half a century: it was like the dents and disfigurements in an old family tankard, which no one would like to part with for a smart new piece of plate fresh from Birmingham. The parishioners saw no reason at all why it should be desirable to venerate the parson or any one else: they were much more comfortable to look down a little on their fellow-creatures.

Even the Dissent in Milby was then of a lax and indifferent kind. The doctrine of adult baptism, struggling under a heavy load of debt, had let off half its chapel area as a ribbon-shop; and Methodism was only to be detected, as you detect curious larvae, by diligent search in dirty corners. The Independents were the only Dissenters of whose existence Milby gentility was at all conscious, and it had a vague idea that the salient points of their creed were prayer without book, red brick, and hypocrisy. The Independent chapel, known as Salem, stood red and conspicuous in a broad street; more than one pewholder kept a brass-bound gig; and Mr Jerome, a retired corn-factor, and the most eminent member of the congregation, was one of the richest men in the parish. But in spite of this apparent prosperity, together with the usual amount of extemporaneous preaching mitigated by furtive notes, Salem belied its name, and was not always the abode of peace. For some reason or other, it was unfortunate in the choice of its ministers. The Rev. Mr Horner, elected with brilliant hopes, was discovered to be given to tippling and quarrelling with his wife; the Rev. Mr Rose's doctrine was a little too 'high,' verging on Antinomianism; the Rev. Mr Stickney's gift as a preacher was found to be less striking on a more extended acquaintance; and the Rev. Mr Smith, a distinguished minister much sought after in the iron districts, with a talent for poetry, became objectionable from an inclination to exchange verses with the young ladies of his congregation. It was reasonably argued that such verses as Mr Smith's must take a long time for their composition, and the habit alluded to might intrench seriously on his pastoral duties. These reverend gentlemen, one and all, gave it as their opinion that the Salem church members were among the least enlightened of the Lord's people, and that Milby was a low place, where they would have found it a severe lot to have their lines fall for any long period; though, to see the smart and crowded congregation assembled on occasion of the annual charity sermon, any one might have supposed that the minister of Salem had rather a brilliant position in the ranks of Dissent. Several Church families used to attend on that occasion, for Milby, in those uninstructed days, had not yet heard that the schismatic ministers of Salem were obviously typified by Korah, Dathan, and Abiram; and many Church people there were of opinion that Dissent might be a weakness, but, after all, had no great harm in it. These lax Episcopalians were, I believe, chiefly tradespeople, who held that, inasmuch as Congregationalism consumed candles, it ought to be supported, and accordingly made a point of presenting themselves at Salem for the afternoon charity sermon, with the expectation of being asked to hold a plate. Mr Pilgrim, too, was always there with his half-sovereign; for as there was no Dissenting doctor in Milby, Mr Pilgrim looked with great tolerance on all shades of religious opinion that did not include a belief in cures by miracle.

On this point he had the concurrence of Mr Pratt, the only other medical man of the same standing in Milby. Otherwise, it was remarkable how strongly these two clever men were contrasted. Pratt was middle-sized, insinuating, and silvery-voiced; Pilgrim was tall, heavy, rough-mannered, and spluttering. Both were considered to have great powers of conversation, but Pratt's anecdotes were of the fine old crusted quality to be procured only of Joe Miller; Pilgrim's had the full fruity flavour of the most recent scandal. Pratt elegantly referred all diseases to debility, and with a proper contempt for symptomatic treatment, went to the root of the matter with port wine and bark; Pilgrim was persuaded that the evil principle in the human system was plethora, and he made war against it with cupping, blistering, and cathartics. They had both been long established in Milby, and as each had a sufficient practice, there was no very malignant rivalry between them; on the contrary, they had that sort of friendly contempt for each other which is always conducive to a good understanding between professional men; and when any new surgeon attempted, in an ill-advised hour, to settle himself in the town, it was strikingly demonstrated how slight and trivial are theoretic differences compared with the broad basis of common human feeling. There was the most perfect unanimity between Pratt and Pilgrim in the determination to drive away the obnoxious and too probably unqualified intruder as soon as possible. Whether the first wonderful cure he effected was on a patient of Pratt's or of Pilgrim's, one was as ready as the other to pull the interloper by the nose, and both alike directed their remarkable powers of conversation towards making the town too hot for him. But by their respective patients these two distinguished men were pitted against each other with great virulence. Mrs Lowme could not conceal her amazement that Mrs Phipps should trust her life in the hands of Pratt, who let her feed herself up to that degree, it was really shocking to hear how short her breath was; and Mrs Phipps had no patience with Mrs Lowme, living, as she did, on tea and broth, and looking as yellow as any crow-flower, and yet letting Pilgrim bleed and blister her and give her lowering medicine till her clothes hung on her like a scarecrow's. On the whole, perhaps, Mr Pilgrim's reputation was at the higher pitch, and when any lady under Mr Pratt's care was doing ill, she was half disposed to think that a little more 'active treatment' might suit her better. But without very definite provocation no one would take so serious a step as to part with the family doctor, for in those remote days there were few varieties of human hatred more formidable than the medical. The doctor's estimate, even of a confiding patient, was apt to rise and fall with the entries in the day-book; and I have known Mr Pilgrim discover the most unexpected virtues in a patient seized with a promising illness. At such times you might have been glad to perceive that there were some of Mr Pilgrim's fellow-creatures of whom he entertained a high opinion, and that he was liable to the amiable weakness of a too admiring estimate. A good inflammation fired his enthusiasm, and a lingering dropsy dissolved him into charity. Doubtless this *crescendo* of benevolence was partly due to feelings not at all represented by the entries in the day-book; for in Mr Pilgrim's heart, too, there was a latent store of tenderness and pity which flowed forth at the sight of suffering. Gradually, however, as his patients became convalescent, his view of their characters became more dispassionate;

361

when they could relish mutton-chops, he began to admit that they had foibles, and by the time they had swallowed their last dose of tonic, he was alive to their most inexcusable faults. After this, the thermometer of his regard rested at the moderate point of friendly backbiting, which sufficed to make him agreeable in his morning visits to the amiable and worthy persons who were yet far from convalescent.

Pratt's patients were profoundly uninteresting to Pilgrim: their very diseases were despicable, and he would hardly have thought their bodies worth dissecting. But of all Pratt's patients, Mr Jerome was the one on whom Mr Pilgrim heaped the most unmitigated contempt. In spite of the surgeon's wise tolerance, Dissent became odious to him in the person of Mr Jerome. Perhaps it was because that old gentleman, being rich, and having very large yearly bills for medical attendance on himself and his wife, nevertheless employed Pratt – neglected all the advantages of 'active treatment,' and paid away his money without getting his system lowered. On any other ground it is hard to explain a feeling of hostility to Mr Jerome, who was an excellent old gentleman, expressing a great deal of goodwill towards his neighbours, not only in imperfect English, but in loans of money to the ostensibly rich, and in sacks of potatoes to the obviously poor.

Assuredly Milby had that salt of goodness which keeps the world together, in greater abundance than was visible on the surface: innocent babes were born there, sweetening their parents' hearts with simple joys; men and women withering in disappointed worldliness, or bloated with sensual ease, had better moments in which they pressed the hand of suffering with sympathy, and were moved to deeds of neighbourly kindness. In church and in chapel there were honest-hearted worshippers who strove to keep a conscience void of offence; and even up the dimmest alleys you might have found here and there a Wesleyan to whom Methodism was the vehicle of peace on earth, and goodwill to men. To a superficial glance, Milby was nothing but dreary prose: a dingy town, surrounded by flat fields, lopped elms, and sprawling manufacturing villages, which crept on and on with their weaving-shops, till they threatened to graft themselves on the town. But the sweet spring came to Milby notwithstanding: the elm-tops were red with buds; the churchyard was starred with daisies; the lark showered his love-music on the flat fields; the rainbows hung over the dingy town, clothing the very roofs and chimneys in a strange transfiguring beauty. And so it was with the human life there, which at first seemed a dismal mixture of griping worldliness, vanity, ostrich feathers, and the fumes of brandy: looking closer, you found some purity, gentleness, and unselfishness, as you may have observed a scented geranium giving forth its wholesome odours amidst blasphemy and gin in a noisy pot-house. Little deaf Mrs Crewe would often carry half her own spare dinner to the sick and hungry; Miss Phipps, with her cockade of red feathers, had a filial heart, and lighted her father's pipe with a pleasant smile; and there were grey-haired men in drab gaiters, not at all noticeable as you passed them in the street, whose integrity had been the basis of their rich neighbour's wealth.

Such as the place was, the people there were entirely contented with it. They fancied life must be but a dull affair for that large portion of mankind who were necessarily shut out from an acquaintance with Milby families, and that it must be an advantage to London and Liverpool, that Milby gentlemen occasionally visited those places on business. But the inhabitants became more intensely conscious of the value they set upon all their advantages, when innovation made its appearance in the person of the Rev. Mr Tryan, the new curate at the chapel-of-ease on Paddiford Common. It was soon notorious in Milby that Mr Tryan held peculiar opinions; that he preached extempore; that he was founding a religious lending library in his remote corner of the parish; that he expounded the Scriptures in cottages; and that his preaching was attracting the Dissenters, and filling the very aisles of his church. The rumour sprang up that Evangelicalism had invaded Milby parish; – a murrain or blight all the more terrible, because its nature was but dimly conjectured. Perhaps Milby was one of the last spots to be reached by the wave of a new movement; and it was only now, when the tide was just on the turn, that the limpets there got a sprinkling. Mr Tryan was the first Evangelical clergyman who had risen above the Milby horizon: hitherto that obnoxious adjective had been unknown to the towns-people of any gentility; and there were even many Dissenters who considered 'evangelical' simply a sort of baptismal name to the magazine which circulated among the congregation of Salem Chapel. But now, at length, the disease had been imported, when the parishioners were expecting it as little as the innocent Red Indians expected small-pox. As long as Mr Tryan's hearers were confined to Paddiford Common – which, by the by, was hardly recognizable as a common at all, but was a dismal district where you heard the rattle of the hand-loom, and breathed the smoke of coal-pits – the 'canting parson' could be treated as a joke. Not so when a number of single ladies in the town appeared to be infected, and even one or two men of substantial property, with old Mr Landor, the banker, at their head, seemed to be 'giving in' to the new movement – when Mr Tryan was known to be well received in several good houses, where he was in the habit of finishing the evening with exhortation and prayer. Evangelicalism was no longer a nuisance existing merely in by-corners, which any well-clad person could avoid; it was invading the very drawing-rooms, mingling itself with the comfortable fumes of port-wine and brandy, threatening to deaden with its murky breath all the splendour of the ostrich feathers, and to stifle Milby ingenuousness, not pretending to be better than its neighbours, with a cloud of cant and lugubrious hypocrisy. The alarm reached its climax when it was reported that Mr Tryan was endeavouring to obtain authority from Mr Prendergast, the non-resident rector, to establish a Sunday evening lecture in the parish church, on the ground that old Mr Crewe did not preach the Gospel.

It now first appeared how surprisingly high a value Milby in general set on the ministrations of Mr Crewe; how convinced it was that Mr Crewe was the model of a parish priest, and his sermons the soundest and most edifying that had ever remained unheard by a church-going population. All allusions to his brown wig were suppressed, and by a rhetorical figure his name was associated with venerable grey hairs; the attempted intrusion of Mr Tryan was an insult to a man deep in years and learning; moreover, it was an insolent effort to thrust himself forward in a parish where he was clearly distasteful to the superior portion of its inhabitants. The town was divided into two zealous parties, the Tryanites and anti-Tryanites; and by the exertions of the eloquent Dempster, the anti-Tryanite virulence was soon developed into an organized opposition. A protest against the meditated evening lecture was framed by that orthodox attorney, and after being numerously signed, was to be carried to Mr Prendergast by three delegates representing the intellect, morality, and wealth of Milby. The intellect, you perceive, was to be personified in Mr Dempster, the morality in Mr Budd, and the wealth in Mr Tomlinson; and the distinguished triad was to set out on its great mission, as we have seen, on the third day from that warm Saturday evening when the conversation recorded in the previous chapter took place in the bar of the Red Lion.

CHAPTER 3

It was quite as warm on the following Thursday evening, when Mr Dempster and his colleagues were to return from their mission to Elmstoke Rectory; but it was much pleasanter in Mrs Linnet's parlour than in the bar of the Red Lion. Through the open window came the scent of mignonette and honeysuckle; the grass-plot in front of the house was shaded by a little plantation of Gueldres roses, syringas, and laburnums; the noise of looms and carts and unmelodious voices reached the ear simply as an agreeable murmur, for Mrs Linnet's house was situated quite on the outskirts of Paddiford Common; and the only sound likely to disturb the serenity of the feminine party assembled there, was the occasional buzz of intrusive wasps, apparently mistaking each lady's head for a sugar-basin. No sugar-basin was visible in Mrs Linnet's parlour, for the time of tea was not yet, and the round table was littered with books which the ladies were covering with black canvas as a reinforcement of the new Paddiford Lending Library. Miss Linnet, whose manuscript was the neatest type of zigzag, was seated at a

368

small table apart, writing on green paper tickets, which were to be pasted on the covers. Miss Linnet had other accomplishments besides that of a neat manuscript, and an index to some of them might be found in the ornaments of the room. She had always combined a love of serious and poetical reading with her skill in fancy-work, and the neatly-bound copies of Dryden's *Virgil*, Hannah More's *Sacred Dramas*, Falconer's *Shipwreck*, Mason *On Self-Knowledge, Rasselas*, and Burke *On the Sublime and Beautiful*, which were the chief ornaments of the book-case, were all inscribed with her name, and had been bought with her pocket-money when she was in her teens. It must have been at least fifteen years since the latest of those purchases, but Miss Linnet's skill in fancy-work appeared to have gone through more numerous phases than her literary taste; for the japanned boxes, the alum and sealing-wax baskets, the fan-dolls, the 'transferred' landscapes on the fire-screens, and the recent bouquets of wax-flowers, showed a disparity in freshness which made them referable to widely different periods. Wax-flowers presuppose delicate fingers and robust patience, but there are still many points of mind and person which they leave vague and problematic; so I must tell you that Miss Linnet had dark ringlets, a sallow complexion, and an amiable disposition. As to her features, there was not much to criticize in them, for she had little nose, less lip, and no eyebrow; and as to her intellect, her friend Mrs Pettifer often said: 'She didn't know a more sensible person to talk to than Mary Linnet. There was no one she liked better to come and take a quiet cup of tea with her, and read a little of Klopstock's *Messiah*. Mary Linnet had often told her a great deal of her mind when they were sitting together: she said there were many things to bear in every condition of life, and nothing should induce her to marry without a prospect of happiness. Once, when Mrs Pettifer admired her wax-flowers, she said, "Ah, Mrs Pettifer, think of the beauties of nature!" She always spoke very prettily, did Mary Linnet; very different, indeed, from Rebecca.'

Miss Rebecca Linnet, indeed, was not a general favourite. While most people thought it a pity that a sensible woman like Mary had not found a good husband – and even her female friends said nothing more ill-natured of her, than that her face was like a piece of putty with two Scotch pebbles stuck in it – Rebecca was always spoken of sarcastically, and it was a customary kind of banter with young ladies to recommend her as a wife to any gentleman they happened to be flirting with – her fat, her finery, and her thick ankles, sufficing to give piquancy to the joke, notwithstanding the absence of novelty. Miss Rebecca, however, possessed the accomplishment of music, and her singing of 'Oh no, we never mention her,' and 'The Soldier's Tear,' was so desirable an accession to the pleasures of a tea-party, that no one cared to offend her, especially as Rebecca had a high spirit of her own, and in spite of her expansively rounded contour, had a particularly sharp tongue. Her reading had been more extensive than her sister's, embracing most of the fiction in Mr Procter's circulating library, and nothing but an acquaintance with the course of her studies could afford a clue to the rapid transitions in her dress, which were suggested by the style of beauty, whether sentimental, sprightly, or severe, possessed by the heroine of the three volumes actually in perusal. A piece of lace, which drooped round the edge of her white bonnet one week, had been rejected by the next; and her cheeks, which, on Whitsunday, loomed through a Turnerian haze of net-work, were, on Trinity Sunday, seen reposing in distinct red outline on her shelving bust, like the sun on a fog-bank. The black velvet, meeting with a crystal clasp, which one evening encircled her head, had on another descended to her neck, and on a third to her wrist, suggesting to an active imagination, either a magical contraction of the ornament, or a fearful ratio of expansion in Miss Rebecca's person. With this constant application of art to dress, she could have had little time for fancy-work, even if she had not been destitute of her sister's taste for that delightful and truly feminine occupation. And here, at least, you perceive the justice of the Milby opinion as to the relative suit-ability of the two Miss Linnets for matrimony. When a man is happy enough to win the affections of a sweet girl, who can soothe his cares with *crochet*, and respond to all his most cherished ideas with beaded urn-rugs and chair-covers in German wool, he has, at least, a guarantee of domestic comfort, whatever trials may await him out of doors. What a resource it is under fatigue and irritation to have your drawing-room well supplied with small mats, which would always be ready if you ever wanted to set anything on them! And what styptic for a bleeding heart can equal copious squares of *crochet*, which are useful for slipping down the moment you touch them? How our fathers managed without *crochet* is the wonder; but I believe some small and feeble substitute existed in their time under the name of 'tatting.' Rebecca Linnet, however, had neglected tatting as well as other forms of fancy-work. At school, to be sure, she had spent a great deal of time in acquiring flower-painting, according to the ingenious method then fashionable, of applying the shapes of leaves and flowers cut out in cardboard, and scrubbing a brush over the surface thus conveniently marked out; but even the spill-cases and hand-screens which were her last half-year's performances in that way, were not considered eminently successful and had long been consigned to the retirement of the best bedroom. Thus, there was a good deal of family unlikeness between Rebecca and her sister, and I am afraid there was also a little family dislike; but Mary's disapproval had usually been kept imprisoned behind her thin lips, for Rebecca was not only of a headstrong disposition, but was her mother's pet; the old lady being herself stout, and preferring a more showy style of cap than she could prevail on her daughter Mary to make up for her.

But I have been describing Miss Rebecca as she was in former days only, for her appearance this evening, as she sits pasting on the green tickets, is in striking contrast with what it was three or four months ago. Her plain grey gingham dress and plain white collar could never have belonged to her wardrobe before that date; and though she is not reduced in size, and her brown hair will do nothing but hang in crisp ringlets down her large cheeks, there is a change in her air and expression which seems to shed a softened light over her person, and make her look like a peony in the shade, instead of the same flower flaunting in a parterre in the hot sunlight.

No one could deny that Evangelicalism had wrought a change for the better in Rebecca Linnet's person – not even Miss Pratt, the thin, stiff lady in spectacles, seated opposite to her, who always had a peculiar repulsion for 'females with a gross habit of body.' Miss Pratt was an old maid; but that is a no more definite description than if I had said she was in the autumn of life. Was it autumn when the orchards are fragrant with apples, or autumn when the oaks are brown, or autumn when the last yellow leaves are fluttering in the chill breeze? The young ladies in Milby

373

would have told you that the Miss Linnets were old maids; but the Miss Linnets were to Miss Pratt what the apple-scented September is to the bare, nipping days of late November. The Miss Linnets were in that temperate zone of old-maidism, when a woman will not say but that if a man of suitable years and character were to offer himself, she might be induced to tread the remainder of life's vale in company with him; Miss Pratt was in that arctic region where a woman is confident that at no time of life would she have consented to give up her liberty, and that she has never seen the man whom she would engage to honour and obey. If the Miss Linnets were old maids, they were old maids with natural ringlets and embonpoint, not to say obesity; Miss Pratt was an old maid with a cap, a braided 'front,' a backbone and appendages. Miss Pratt was the one blue-stocking of Milby, possessing, she said, no less than five hundred volumes, competent, as her brother the doctor often observed, to conduct a conversation on any topic whatever, and occasionally dabbling a little in authorship, though it was understood that she had never put forth the full powers of her mind in print. Her *Letters to a Young Man on his Entrance into Life*, and *De Courcy, or the Rash Promise, a Tale for Youth*, were mere trifles which she had been induced to publish because they were calculated for popular utility, but they were nothing to what she had for years had by her in manuscript. Her latest production had been Six Stanzas, addressed to the Rev. Edgar Tryan, printed on glazed paper with a neat border, and beginning, 'Forward, young wrestler for the truth!'

Miss Pratt having kept her brother's house during his long widowhood, his daughter, Miss Eliza, had had the advantage of being educated by her aunt, and thus of imbibing a very strong antipathy to all that remarkable woman's tastes and opinions. The silent handsome girl of two-and-twenty, who is covering the *Memoirs of Felix Neff*, is Miss Eliza Pratt; and the small elderly lady in dowdy clothing, who is also working diligently, is Mrs Pettifer, a superior-minded widow, much valued in Milby, being such a very respectable person to have in the house in case of illness, and of quite too good a family to receive any money-payment – you could always send her garden-stuff that would make her ample amends. Miss Pratt has enough to do in commenting on the heap of volumes before her, feeling it a responsibility entailed on her by her great powers of mind to leave nothing without the advantage of her opinion. Whatever was good must be sprinkled with the chrism of her approval; whatever was evil must be blighted by her condemnation.

'Upon my word,' she said, in a deliberate high voice, as if she were dictating to an amanuensis, 'it is a most admirable selection of works for popular reading, this that our excellent Mr Tryan has made. I do not know whether, if the task had been confided to me, I could have made a selection, combining in a higher degree religious instruction and edification, with a due admixture of the purer species of amusement. This story of *Father Clement* is a library in itself on the errors of Romanism. I have ever considered fiction a suitable form for conveying moral and religious instruction, as I have shown in my little work *De Courcy*, which, as a very clever writer in the *Crompton Argus* said at the time of its appearance, is the light vehicle of a weighty moral.'

'One 'ud think,' said Mrs Linnet, who also had her spectacles on, but chiefly for the purpose of seeing what the others were doing, 'there didn't want much to drive people away from a religion as makes 'em walk barefoot over stone floors, like that girl in *Father Clement* – sending the blood up to the head frightful. Anybody might see that was an unnat'ral creed.'

'Yes,' said Miss Pratt, 'but asceticism is not the root of the error, as Mr Tryan was telling us the other evening – it is the denial of the great doctrine of justification by faith. Much as I had reflected on all subjects in the course of my life, I am indebted to Mr Tryan for opening my eyes to the full importance of that cardinal doctrine of the Reformation. From a child I had a deep sense of religion, but in my early days the Gospel light was obscured in the English Church, notwithstanding the possession of our incomparable Liturgy, than which I know no human composition more faultless and sublime. As I tell Eliza, I was

376

not blest as she is at the age of two-and-twenty, in knowing a clergyman who unites all that is great and admirable in intellect with the highest spiritual gifts. I am no contemptible judge of a man's acquirements, and I assure you I have tested Mr Tryan's by questions which are a pretty severe touchstone. It is true, I sometimes carry him a little beyond the depth of the other listeners. Profound learning,' continued Miss Pratt, shutting her spectacles, and tapping them on the book before her, 'has not many to estimate it in Milby.'

'Miss Pratt,' said Rebecca, 'will you please give me *Scott's Force of Truth?* There – that small book lying against the *Life of Legh Richmond*.'

'That's a book I'm very fond of – the *Life of Legh Richmond*,' said Mrs Linnet. 'He found out all about that woman at Tutbury as pretended to live without eating. Stuff and nonsense!'

Mrs Linnet had become a reader of religious books since Mr Tryan's advent, and as she was in the habit of confining her perusal to the purely secular portions, which bore a very small proportion to the whole, she could make rapid progress through a large number of volumes. On taking up the biography of a celebrated preacher, she immediately turned to the end to see what disease he died of; and if his legs swelled, as her own occasionally did, she felt a stronger interest in ascertaining any earlier facts in the history of the dropsical divine – whether he had ever fallen off a stage coach, whether he had married more than one wife, and, in general, any adventures or repartees recorded of him previous to the epoch of his conversion. She then glanced over the letters and diary, and wherever there was a predominance of Zion, the River of Life, and notes of exclamation, she turned over to the next page; but any passage in which she saw such promising nouns as 'small-pox,' 'pony,' or 'boots and shoes,' at once arrested her.

'It is half-past six now,' said Miss Linnet, looking at her watch as the servant appeared with the tea-tray. 'I suppose the delegates are come back by this time. If Mr Tryan had not so kindly promised to call and let us know, I should hardly rest without walking to Milby myself to know what answer they have brought back. It is a great privilege for us, Mr Tryan living at Mrs Wagstaff's, for he is often able to take us on his way backwards and forwards into the town.'

'I wonder if there's another man in the world who has been brought up as Mr Tryan has, that would choose to live in those small close rooms on the common, among heaps of dirty cottages, for the sake of being near the poor people,' said Mrs Pettifer. 'I'm afraid he hurts his health by it; he looks to me far from strong.'

'Ah,' said Miss Pratt, 'I understand he is of a highly respectable family indeed, in Huntingdonshire. I heard him myself speak of his father's carriage – quite incidentally you know – and Eliza tells me what very fine cambric handkerchiefs he uses. My eyes are not good enough to see such things, but I know what breeding is as well as most people, and it is easy to see that Mr Tryan is quite *comme il faw*, to use a French expression.'

'I should like to tell him better nor use fine cambric i' this place, where there's such washing, it's a shame to be seen,' said Mrs Linnet; 'he'll get 'em tore to pieces. Good lawn 'ud be far better. I saw what a colour his linen looked at the sacrament last Sunday. Mary's making him a black silk case to hold his bands, but I told her she'd more need wash 'em for him.'

'O mother!' said Rebecca, with solemn severity, 'pray don't think of pocket-handkerchiefs and linen, when we are talking of such a man. And at this moment, too, when he is perhaps having to bear a heavy blow. We have more need to help him by prayer, as Aaron and Hur held up the hands of Moses. We don't know but wickedness may have triumphed, and Mr Prendergast may have consented to forbid the lecture. There have been dispensations quite as mysterious, and Satan is evidently putting forth all his strength to resist the entrance of the Gospel into Milby Church.'

'You niver spoke a truer word than that, my dear,' said Mrs Linnet, who accepted all religious phrases, but was extremely rationalistic in her interpretation; 'for if iver Old Harry appeared in a human form, it's that Dempster. It was all through him as we got cheated out o' Pye's Croft, making out as the title wasn't good. Such lawyer's villainy! As if paying good money wasn't title enough to anything. If your father as is dead and gone had been worthy to know it! But he'll have a fall some day, Dempster will. Mark my words.'

'Ah, out of his carriage, you mean,' said Miss Pratt, who, in the movement occasioned by the clearing of the table, had lost the first part of Mrs Linnet's speech. 'It certainly is alarming to see him driving home from Rotherby, flogging his galloping horse like a madman. My brother has often said he expected every Thursday evening to be called in to set some of Dempster's bones; but I suppose he may drop that expectation now, for we are given to understand from good authority that he has forbidden his wife to call my brother in again either to herself or her mother. He swears no Tryanite doctor shall attend his family. I have reason to believe that Pilgrim was called in to Mrs Dempster's mother the other day.'

'Poor Mrs Raynor! she's glad to do anything for the sake of peace and quietness,' said Mrs Pettifer; 'but it's no trifle at her time of life to part with a doctor as knows her constitution.'

'What trouble that poor woman has to bear in her old age!' said Mary Linnet, 'to see her daughter leading such a life! – an only daughter, too, that she dotes on.'

'Yes, indeed,' said Miss Pratt. 'We, of course, know more about it than most people, my brother having attended the family so many years. For my part, I never thought well of the marriage; and I endeavoured to dissuade my brother when Mrs Raynor asked him to give Janet away at the wedding. 'If you will take my advice, Richard,' I said, 'you will have nothing to do with that marriage.' And he has seen the justice of my opinion since. Mrs Raynor herself was against the connection at first; but she always spoiled Janet, and I fear, too, she was won over by a foolish pride in having her daughter marry a professional man. I fear it was so. No one but myself, I think, foresaw the extent of the evil.'

'Well,' said Mrs Pettifer, 'Janet had nothing to look to but being a governess; and it was hard for Mrs Raynor to have to work at millinering – a woman well brought up, and her husband a man who held his head as high as any man in Thurston. And it isn't everybody that sees everything fifteen years beforehand. Robert Dempster was the cleverest man in Milby; and there weren't many young men fit to talk to Janet.'

'It is a thousand pities,' said Miss Pratt, choosing to ignore Mrs Pettifer's slight sarcasm, 'for I certainly did consider Janet Raynor the most promising young woman of my acquaintance; – a little too much lifted up, perhaps, by her superior education, and too much given to satire, but able to express herself very well indeed about any book I recommended to her perusal. There is no young woman in Milby now who can be compared with what Janet was when she was married, either in mind or person. I consider Miss Landor far, far below her. Indeed, I cannot say much for the mental superiority of the young ladies in our first families. They are superficial – very superficial.'

'She made the handsomest bride that ever came out of Milby church, too,' said Mrs Pettifer. 'Such a very fine figure! and it showed off her white poplin so well. And what a pretty smile Janet always had! Poor thing, she keeps that now for all her old friends. I never see her but she has some-thing pretty to say to me – living in the same street, you know, I can't help seeing her often, though I've never been to the house since Dempster broke out on me in one of his drunken fits. She comes to me sometimes, poor thing, looking so strange, anybody passing her in the street may see plain enough what's the matter; but she's always got some little good-natured plan in her head for all that. Only last night when I met her, I saw five yards off she wasn't fit to be out; but she had a basin in her hand, full of something she was carrying to Sally Martin, the deformed girl that's in a consumption.'

'But she is just as bitter against Mr Tryan as her husband is, I understand,' said Rebecca. 'Her heart is very much set against the truth, for I understand she bought Mr Tryan's sermons on purpose to ridicule them to Mrs Crewe.'

'Well, poor thing,' said Mrs Pettifer, 'you know she stands up for everything her husband says and does. She never will admit to anybody that he's not a good husband.'

'That is her pride,' said Miss Pratt. 'She married him in opposition to the advice of her best friends, and now she is not willing to admit that she was wrong. Why, even to my brother – and a medical attendant, you know, can hardly fail to be acquainted with family secrets – she has always pretended to have the highest respect for her husband's qualities. Poor Mrs Raynor, however, is well aware that every one knows the real state of things. Latterly, she has not even avoided the subject with me. The very last time I called on her she said, 'Have you been to see my poor daughter?' and burst into tears.'

'Pride or no pride,' said Mrs Pettifer, 'I shall always stand up for Janet Dempster. She sat up with me night after night when I had that attack of rheumatic fever six years ago. There's great excuses for her. When a woman can't think of her husband coming home without trembling, it's enough to make her drink something to blunt her feelings – and no children either, to keep her from it. You and me might do the same, if we were in her place.'

'Speak for yourself, Mrs Pettifer,' said Miss Pratt. 'Under no circumstances can I imagine myself resorting to a practice so degrading. A woman should find support in her own strength of mind.'

'I think,' said Rebecca, who considered Miss Pratt still very blind in spiritual things, notwithstanding her assumption of enlightenment, 'she will find poor support if she trusts only to her own strength. She must seek aid elsewhere than in herself.'

Happily the removal of the tea-things just then created a little confusion, which aided Miss Pratt to repress her resentment at Rebecca's presumption in correcting her – a person like Rebecca Linnet! who six months ago was as flighty and vain a woman as Miss Pratt had ever known – so very unconscious of her unfortunate person!

The ladies had scarcely been seated at their work another hour, when the sun was sinking, and the clouds that flecked the sky to the very zenith were every moment taking on a brighter gold. The gate of the little garden opened, and Miss Linnet, seated at her small table near the window, saw Mr Tryan enter.

'There is Mr Tryan,' she said, and her pale cheek was lighted up with a little blush that would have made her look more attractive to almost any one except Miss Eliza Pratt, whose fine grey eyes allowed few things to escape her silent observation. 'Mary Linnet gets more and more in love with Mr Tryan,' thought Miss Eliza; 'it is really pitiable to see such feelings in a woman of her age, with those old-maidish little ringlets. I dare say she flatters herself Mr Tryan may fall in love with her, because he makes her useful among the poor.' At the same time, Miss Eliza, as she bent her handsome head and large cannon curls with apparent calmness over her work, felt a considerable internal flutter when she heard the knock at the door. Rebecca had less self-command. She felt too much agitated to go on with her pasting, and clutched the leg of the table to counteract the trembling in her hands.

Poor women's hearts! Heaven forbid that I should laugh at you, and make cheap jests on your susceptibility towards the clerical sex, as if it had nothing deeper or more lovely in it than the mere vulgar angling for a husband. Even in these enlightened days, many a curate who, considered abstractedly, is nothing more than a sleek bimanous animal in a white neckcloth, with views more or less Anglican, and furtively addicted to the flute, is adored by a girl who has coarse brothers, or by a solitary woman who would like to be a helpmate in good works beyond her own means, simply because he seems to them the model of refinement and of public usefulness. What wonder, then, that in Milby society, such as I have told you it was a very long while ago, a zealous Evangelical clergyman, aged thirty-three, called forth all the little agitations that belong to the divine necessity of loving, implanted in the Miss Linnets, with their seven or eight lustrums and their unfashionable ringlets, no less than in Miss Eliza Pratt, with her youthful bloom and her ample cannon curls.

But Mr Tryan has entered the room, and the strange light from the golden sky falling on his light brown hair, which is brushed high up round his head, makes it look almost like an auréole. His grey eyes, too, shine with unwonted brilliancy this evening. They were not remarkable eyes, but they accorded completely in their changing light with the changing expression of his person, which indicated the paradoxical character often observable in a large-limbed sanguine blond; at once mild and irritable, gentle and overbearing, indolent and resolute, self-conscious and dreamy. Except that the well-filled lips had something of the artificially compressed look which is often the sign of a struggle to keep the dragon undermost, and that the complexion was rather pallid, giving the idea of imperfect health, Mr Tryan's face in repose was that of an ordinary whiskerless blond, and it seemed difficult to refer a certain air of distinction about him to anything in particular, unless it were his delicate hands and well-shapen feet.

It was a great anomaly to the Milby mind that a canting evangelical parson, who would take tea with tradespeople, and make friends of vulgar women like the Linnets, should have so much the air of a gentleman, and be so little like the splay-footed Mr Stickney of Salem, to whom he approximated so closely in doctrine. And this want of correspondence between the physique and the creed had excited no less surprise in the larger town of Laxeter, where Mr Tryan had formerly held a curacy; for of the two other Low Church clergymen in the neighbourhood, one was a Welshman of globose figure and unctuous complexion, and the other a man of atrabiliar aspect, with lank black hair, and a redundance of limp cravat – in fact, the sort of thing you might expect in men who distributed the publications of the Religious Tract Society and introduced Dissenting hymns into the Church.

Mr Tryan shook hands with Mrs Linnet, bowed with rather a preoccupied air to the other ladies, and seated himself in the large horse-hair easy-chair which had been drawn forward for him, while the ladies ceased from their work, and fixed their eyes on him, awaiting the news he had to tell them.

'It seems,' he began, in a low and silvery tone, 'I need a lesson of patience; there has been something wrong in my thought or action about this evening lecture. I have been too much bent on doing good to Milby after my own plan – too reliant on my own wisdom.'

Mr Tryan paused. He was struggling against inward irritation.

'The delegates are come back, then?' 'Has Mr Prendergast given way?' 'Has Dempster succeeded?' – were the eager questions of three ladies at once.

'Yes; the town is in an uproar. As we were sitting in Mr Landor's drawing-room we heard a loud cheering, and presently Mr Thrupp, the clerk at the bank, who had been waiting at the Red Lion to hear the result, came to let us know. He said Dempster had been making a speech to the mob out of the window. They were distributing drink to the people, and hoisting placards in great letters, – 'Down with the Tryanites!' 'Down with cant!'

They had a hideous caricature of me being tripped-up and pitched head foremost out of the pulpit. Good old Mr Landor would insist on sending me round in the carriage; he thought I should not be safe from the mob; but I got down at the Crossways. The row was evidently preconcerted by Dempster before he set out. He made sure of succeeding.'

Mr Tryan's utterance had been getting rather louder and more rapid in the course of this speech, and he now added, in the energetic chest-voice, which, both in and out of the pulpit, alternated continually with his more silvery notes,—

'But his triumph will be a short one. If he thinks he can intimidate me by obloquy or threats, he has mistaken the man he has to deal with. Mr Dempster and his colleagues will find themselves checkmated after all. Mr Prendergast has been false to his own conscience in this business. He knows as well as I do that he is throwing away the souls of the people by leaving things as they are in the parish. But I shall appeal to the Bishop – I am confident of his sympathy.'

'The Bishop will be coming shortly, I suppose,' said Miss Pratt, 'to hold a confirmation?'

'Yes; but I shall write to him at once, and lay the case before him. Indeed, I must hurry away now, for I have many matters to attend to. You, ladies, have been kindly helping me with your labours, I see,' continued Mr Tryan, politely, glancing at the canvas-covered books as he rose from his seat. Then, turning to Mary Linnet: 'Our library is really getting on, I think. You and your sister have quite a heavy task of distribution now.'

Poor Rebecca felt it very hard to bear that Mr Tryan did not turn towards her too. If he knew how much she entered into his feelings about the lecture, and the interest she took in the library. Well! perhaps it was her lot to be overlooked – and it might be a token of mercy. Even a good man might not always know the heart that was most with him. But the next moment poor Mary had a pang, when Mr Tryan turned to Miss Eliza Pratt, and the preoccupied expression of his face melted into that beaming timidity with which a man almost always addresses a pretty woman.

'I have to thank you, too, Miss Eliza, for seconding me so well in your visits to Joseph Mercer. The old man tells me how precious he finds your reading to him, now he is no longer able to go to church.'

Miss Eliza only answered by a blush, which made her look all the handsomer, but her aunt said,

'Yes, Mr Tryan, I have ever inculcated on my dear Eliza the importance of spending her leisure in being useful to her fellow-creatures. Your example and instruction have been quite in the spirit of the system which I have always pursued, though we are indebted to you for a clearer view of the motives that should actuate us in our pursuit of good works. Not that I can accuse myself of having ever had a self-righteous spirit, but my humility was rather instinctive than based on a firm ground of doctrinal knowledge, such as you so admirably impart to us.'

Mrs Linnet's usual entreaty that Mr Tryan would 'have something – some wine-and-water and a biscuit,' was just here a welcome relief from the necessity of answering Miss Pratt's oration.

'Not anything, my dear Mrs Linnet, thank you. You forget what a Rechabite I am. By the by, when I went this morning to see a poor girl in Butcher's Lane, whom I had heard of as being in a consumption, I found Mrs Dempster there. I had often met her in the street, but did not know it was Mrs Dempster. It seems she goes among the poor a good deal. She is really an interesting-looking woman. I was quite surprised, for I have heard the worst account of her habits – that she is almost as bad as her husband. She went out hastily as soon as I entered. But,' (apologetically) 'I am keeping you all standing, and I must really hurry away. Mrs Pettifer, I have not had the pleasure of calling on you for some time; I shall take an early opportunity of going your way. Good evening, good evening.'

CHAPTER 4

Mr Tryan was right in saying that the 'row' in Milby had been preconcerted by Dempster. The placards and the caricature were prepared before the departure of the delegates; and it had been settled that Mat Paine, Dempster's clerk, should ride out on Thursday morning to meet them at Whitlow, the last place where they would change horses, that he might gallop back and prepare an ovation for the triumvirate in case of their success. Dempster had determined to dine at Whitlow: so that Mat Paine was in Milby again two hours before the entrance of the delegates, and had time to send a whisper up the back streets that there was promise of a 'spree' in the Bridge Way, as well as to assemble two knots of picked men – one to feed the flame of orthodox zeal with gin-and-water, at the Green Man, near High Street; the other to solidify their church principles with heady beer at the Bear and Ragged Staff, in the Bridge Way.

The Bridge Way was an irregular straggling street, where the town fringed off raggedly into the Whitlow road: rows of new red-brick houses, in which ribbon-looms were rattling behind long lines of window, alternating with old, half-thatched, half-tiled cottages – one of those dismal wide streets where dirt and misery have no long shadows thrown on them to soften their ugliness. Here, about half-past five o'clock, Silly Caleb, an idiot well known in Dog Lane, but more of a stranger in the Bridge Way, was seen slouching along with a string of boys hooting at his heels; presently another group, for the most part out at elbows, came briskly in the same direction, looking round them with an air of expectation; and at no long interval, Deb Traunter, in a pink flounced gown and floating ribbons, was observed talking with great affability to two men in seal-skin caps and fustian, who formed her cortège. The Bridge Way began to have a presentiment of something in the wind. Phib Cook left her evening wash-tub and appeared at her door in soap-suds, a bonnet-poke, and general dampness; three narrow-chested ribbon-weavers, in rusty black streaked with shreds of many-coloured silk, sauntered out with their hands in their pockets; and Molly Beale, a brawny old virago, descrying wiry Dame Ricketts peeping out from her entry, seized the opportunity of renewing the morning's skirmish. In short, the Bridge Way was in that state of excitement which is understood to announce a 'demonstration' on the part of the British public; and the afflux of remote townsmen increasing, there was soon so large a crowd that it was time for Bill Powers, a plethoric Goliath, who presided over the knot of beer-drinkers at the Bear and Ragged Staff, to issue forth with his companions, and, like the enunciator of the ancient myth, make the assemblage distinctly conscious of the common sentiment that had drawn them together. The expectation of the delegates' chaise, added to the fight between Molly Beale and Dame Ricketts, and the ill-advised appearance of a lean bull-terrier, were a sufficient safety-valve to the popular excitement during the remaining quarter of an hour; at the end of which, the chaise was seen approaching along the Whitlow road, with oak boughs ornamenting the horses' heads, and, to quote the account of this interesting scene which was sent to the *Rotherby Guardian*, 'loud cheers immediately testified to the sympathy of the honest fellows collected there, with the public-spirited exertions of their fellow-townsmen.' Bill Powers, whose bloodshot eyes, bent hat, and protuberant altitude, marked him out as the natural leader of the assemblage, undertook to interpret the common sentiment by stopping the chaise, advancing to the door with raised hat, and begging to know of Mr Dempster, whether the Rector had forbidden the 'canting lecture.'

'Yes, yes,' said Mr Dempster. 'Keep up a jolly good hurray.'

No public duty could have been more easy and agreeable to Mr Powers and his associates, and the chorus swelled all the way to the High Street, where, by a mysterious coincidence often observable in these spontaneous 'demonstrations,' large placards on long poles were observed to shoot upwards from among the crowd, principally in the direction of Tucker's Lane, where the Green Man was situated. One bore, 'Down with the Tryanites!' another, 'No Cant!' another, 'Long live our venerable Curate!' and one in still larger letters, 'Sound Church Principles and no Hypocrisy!' But a still more remarkable impromptu was a huge caricature of Mr Tryan in gown and band, with an enormous auréole of yellow hair and upturned eyes, standing on the pulpit stairs and trying to pull down old Mr Crewe. Groans, yells, and hisses – hisses, yells, and groans – only stemmed by the appearance of another caricature representing Mr Tryan being pitched head-foremost from the pulpit stairs by a hand which the artist, either from subtilty of intention or want of space, had left unindicated. In the midst of the tremendous cheering that saluted this piece of symbolical art, the chaise had reached the door of the Red Lion, and loud cries of 'Dempster for ever!' with a feebler cheer now and then for Tomlinson and Budd, were presently responded to by the appearance of the public-spirited attorney at the large upper window, where also were visible a little in the background the small sleek head of Mr Budd, and the blinking countenance of Mr Tomlinson.

Mr Dempster held his hat in his hand, and poked his head forward with a butting motion by way of

bow. A storm of cheers subsided at last into dropping sounds of 'Silence!' 'Hear him!' 'Go it,
Dempster!' and the lawyer's rasping voice became
distinctly audible.

'Fellow Townsmen! It gives us the sincerest
pleasure – I speak for my respected colleagues as
well as myself – to witness these strong proofs of
your attachment to the principles of our excellent
Church, and your zeal for the honour of our venerable pastor. But it is no more than I expected of
you. I know you well. I've known you for the last
twenty years to be as honest and respectable a set
of rate-payers as any in this county. Your hearts
are sound to the core! No man had better try to
thrust his cant and hypocrisy down *your* throats.
You're used to wash them with liquor of a better
flavour. This is the proudest moment in my own
life, and I think I may say in that of my colleagues,
in which I have to tell you that our exertions in
the cause of sound religion and manly morality
have been crowned with success. Yes, my fellow
Townsmen! I have the gratification of announcing
to you thus formally what you have already learned
indirectly. The pulpit from which our venerable
pastor has fed us with sound doctrine for half a
century is not to be invaded by a fanatical,
sectarian, double-faced, Jesuitical interloper! We
are not to have our young people demoralized and
corrupted by the temptations to vice, notoriously
connected with Sunday evening lectures! We are
not to have a preacher obtruding himself upon us,

395

who decries good works, and sneaks into our homes perverting the faith of our wives and daughters! We are not to be poisoned with doctrines which damp every innocent enjoyment, and pick a poor man's pocket of the sixpence with which he might buy himself a cheerful glass after a hard day's work, under pretence of paying for bibles to send to the Chicktaws!

'But I'm not going to waste your valuable time with unnecessary words. I am a man of deeds' ('Aye, damn you, that you are, and you charge well for 'em too,' said a voice from the crowd, probably that of a gentleman who was immediately afterwards observed with his hat crushed over his head.) 'I shall always be at the service of my fellow-townsmen, and whoever dares to hector over you, or interfere with your innocent pleasures, shall have an account to settle with Robert Dempster.

'Now, my boys! you can't do better than disperse and carry the good news to all your fellow-townsmen, whose hearts are as sound as your own. Let some of you go one way and some another, that every man, woman, and child in Milby may know what you know yourselves. But before we part, let us have three cheers for True Religion, and down with Cant!'

When the last cheer was dying, Mr Dempster closed the window, and the judiciously instructed placards and caricatures moved off in divers directions, followed by larger or smaller divisions of the crowd. The greatest attraction apparently lay in the direction of Dog Lane, the outlet towards Paddiford Common, whither the caricatures were moving; and you foresee, of course, that those works of symbolical art were consumed with a liberal expenditure of dry gorse-bushes and vague shouting.

After these great public exertions, it was natural that Mr Dempster and his colleagues should feel more in need than usual of a little social relaxation; and a party of their friends was already beginning to assemble in the large parlour of the Red Lion, convened partly by their own curiosity, and partly by the invaluable Mat Paine. The most capacious punch-bowl was put in requisition; and that born gentleman, Mr Lowme, seated opposite Mr Dempster as 'Vice,' undertook to brew the punch, defying the criticisms of the envious men out of office, who, with the readiness of irresponsibility, ignorantly suggested more lemons. The social festivities were continued till long past midnight, when several friends of sound religion were conveyed home with some difficulty, one of them showing a dogged determination to seat himself in the gutter.

Mr Dempster had done as much justice to the punch as any of the party; and his friend Boots, though aware that the lawyer could 'carry his liquor like Old Nick,' with whose social demeanour Boots seemed to be particularly well acquainted, nevertheless thought it might be as well to see so good a customer in safety to his own door, and walked quietly behind his elbow out of the innyard. Dempster, however, soon became aware of him, stopped short, and, turning slowly round upon him, recognized the well-known drab waistcoat sleeves, conspicuous enough in the starlight.

'You twopenny scoundrel! What do you mean by dogging a professional man's footsteps in this way? I'll break every bone in your skin if you attempt to track me, like a beastly cur sniffing at one's pocket. Do you think a gentleman will make his way home any the better for having the scent of your blacking-bottle thrust up his nostrils?'

Boots slunk back, in more amusement than ill-humour, thinking the lawyer's 'rum talk' was doubtless part and parcel of his professional ability; and Mr Dempster pursued his slow way alone.

His house lay in Orchard Street, which opened on the prettiest outskirt of the town – the church, the parsonage, and a long stretch of green fields. It was an old-fashioned house, with an overhanging upper story; outside, it had a face of rough stucco, and casement windows with green frames and shutters; inside, it was full of long passages, and rooms with low ceilings. There was a large heavy knocker on the green door, and though Mr Dempster carried a latch-key, he sometimes chose to use the knocker. He chose to do so now. The thunder resounded through Orchard Street, and, after a single minute, there was a second clap louder than the first. Another minute, and still the door was not opened; whereupon Mr Dempster, muttering, took out his latch-key, and, with less difficulty than might have been expected, thrust it into the door. When he opened the door the passage was dark.

'Janet!' in the loudest rasping tone, was the next sound that rang through the house.

'Janet!' again – before a slow step was heard on the stairs, and a distant light began to flicker on the wall of the passage.

'Curse you! you creeping idiot! Come faster, can't you?'

Yet another few seconds, and the figure of a tall woman, holding aslant a heavy-plated drawing-room candlestick, appeared at the turning of the passage that led to the broader entrance.

See, she has on a light dress which sits loosely about her figure, but does not disguise its liberal, graceful outline. A heavy mass of straight jet-black hair has escaped from its fastening, and hangs over her shoulders. Her grandly-cut features, pale with the natural paleness of a brunette, have premature lines about them telling that the years have been lengthened by sorrow, and the delicately-curved nostril, which seems made to quiver with the proud consciousness of power and beauty, must have quivered to the heart-piercing griefs which have given that worn look to the corners of the mouth. Her wide open black eyes have a strangely fixed, sightless gaze, as she pauses at the turning, and stands silent before her husband.

'I'll teach you to keep me waiting in the dark,

you pale staring fool!' advancing with his slow drunken step. 'What, you've been drinking again, have you? I'll beat you into your senses.'

He laid his hand with a firm grip on her shoulder, turned her round, and pushed her slowly before him along the passage and through the dining-room door which stood open on their left hand.

There was a portrait of Janet's mother, a grey-haired, dark-eyed old woman, in a neatly-fluted cap, hanging over the mantelpiece. Surely the aged eyes take on a look of anguish as they see Janet – not trembling, no! it would be better if she trembled – standing stupidly unmoved in her great beauty, while the heavy arm is lifted to strike her. The blow falls – another – and another. Surely the mother hears that cry – 'O Robert! pity! pity!'

Poor grey-haired woman! Was it for this you suffered a mother's pangs in your lone widow-hood five-and-thirty years ago? Was it for this you kept the little worn morocco shoes Janet had first run in, and kissed them day by day when she was away from you, a tall girl at school? Was it for this you looked proudly at her when she came back to you in her rich pale beauty, like a tall white arum that has just unfolded its grand pure curves to the sun?

The mother lies sleepless and praying in her lonely house, weeping the hard tears of age, because she dreads this may be a cruel night for her child.

She too has a picture over her mantelpiece, drawn in chalk by Janet long years ago. She looked at it before she went to bed. It is a head bowed beneath a cross, and wearing a crown of thorns.

CHAPTER 5

It was half-past nine o'clock in the morning. The midsummer sun was already warm on the roofs and weathercocks of Milby. The churchbells were ringing, and many families were conscious of Sunday sensations, chiefly referable to the fact that the daughters had come down to breakfast in their best frocks, and with their hair particularly well dressed. For it was not Sunday, but Wednesday; and though the Bishop was going to hold a Confirmation, and to decide whether or not there should be a Sunday evening lecture in Milby, the sunbeams had the usual working-day look to the haymakers already long out in the fields, and to laggard weavers just 'setting up' their week's 'piece.' The notion of its being Sunday was the strongest in young ladies like Miss Phipps, who was going to accompany her younger sister to the confirmation, and to wear a 'sweetly pretty' transparent bonnet with marabout feathers on the interesting occasion, thus throwing into relief the suitable simplicity of her sister's attire, who was, of course, to appear in a new white frock; or in the pupils at Miss Townley's, who were absolved from all lessons, and were going to church to see the Bishop, and to hear the Honourable and Reverend Mr Prendergast, the rector, read prayers – a high intellectual treat, as Miss Townley assured them. It seemed only natural that a rector, who was honourable, should read better than old Mr Crewe, who was only a curate, and not honourable; and when little Clara Robins wondered why some clergymen were rectors and others not, Ellen Marriott assured her with great confidence that it was only the clever men who were made rectors. Ellen Marriott was going to be confirmed. She was a short, fair, plump girl, with blue eyes and sandy hair, which was this morning arranged in taller cannon curls than usual, for the reception of the Episcopal benediction, and some of the young ladies thought her the prettiest girl in the school; but others gave the preference to her rival, Maria Gardner, who was much taller, and had a lovely 'crop' of dark-brown ringlets, and who, being also about to take upon herself the vows made in her name at her baptism, had oiled and twisted her ringlets with especial care. As she seated herself at the breakfast-table before Miss Townley's entrance to dispense the weak coffee, her crop excited so strong a sensation that Ellen Marriott was at length impelled to look at it, and to say with suppressed but bitter sarcasm, 'Is that Miss Gardner's head?' 'Yes,' said Maria, amiable and stuttering, and no match for Ellen in retort; 'Th – th – this is my head.' 'Then I don't

403

admire it at all!' was the crushing rejoinder of Ellen, followed by a murmur of approval among her friends. Young ladies, I suppose, exhaust their sac of venom in this way at school. That is the reason why they have such a harmless tooth for each other in after life.

The only other candidate for confirmation at Miss Townley's was Mary Dunn, a draper's daughter in Milby, and a distant relation of the Miss Linnets. Her pale lanky hair could never be coaxed into permanent curl, and this morning the heat had brought it down to its natural condition of lankiness earlier than usual. But that was not what made her sit melancholy and apart at the lower end of the form. Her parents were admirers of Mr Tryan, and had been persuaded, by the Miss Linnets' influence, to insist that their daughter should be prepared for confirmation by him, over and above the preparation given to Miss Townley's pupils by Mr Crewe. Poor Mary Dunn! I am afraid she thought it too heavy a price to pay for these spiritual advantages, to be excluded from every game at ball, to be obliged to walk with none but little girls – in fact, to be the object of an aversion that nothing short of an incessant supply of plumcakes would have neutralized. And Mrs Dunn was of opinion that plumcake was unwholesome. The anti-Tryanite spirit, you perceive, was very strong at Miss Townley's, imported probably by day scholars, as well as encouraged by the fact that that clever woman was herself strongly opposed to innovation, and remarked every Sunday that Mr Crewe had preached an 'excellent discourse.' Poor Mary Dunn dreaded the moment when school-hours would be over, for then she was sure to be the butt of those very explicit remarks which, in young ladies' as well as young gentlemen's seminaries, constitute the most subtle and delicate form of the innuendo. 'I'd never be a Tryanite, would you?' 'O here comes the lady that knows so much more about religion than we do!' 'Some people think themselves so very pious!'

It is really surprising that young ladies should not be thought competent to the same curriculum as young gentlemen. I observe that their powers of sarcasm are quite equal; and if there had been a genteel academy for young gentlemen at Milby, I am inclined to think that, notwithstanding Euclid and the classics, the party spirit there would not have exhibited itself in more pungent irony, or more incisive satire, than was heard in Miss Townley's seminary. But there was no such academy, the existence of the grammar-school under Mr Crewe's superintendence probably discouraging speculations of that kind; and the genteel youths of Milby were chiefly come home for the midsummer holidays from distant schools. Several of us had just assumed coat-tails, and the assumption of new responsibilities apparently following as a matter of course, we were among the candidates for confirmation. I wish I could say that the solemnity of our feelings was on a level with the solemnity of the occasion; but unimaginative boys find it difficult to recognize apostolical institutions in their developed form, and I fear our chief emotion concerning the ceremony was a sense of sheepishness, and our chief opinion, the speculative and heretical position, that it ought to be confined to the girls. It was a pity, you will say; but it is the way with us men in other crises, that come a long while after confirmation. The golden moments in the stream of life rush past us, and we see nothing but sand; the angels come to visit us, and we only know them when they are gone.

But, as I said, the morning was sunny, the bells were ringing, the ladies of Milby were dressed in their Sunday garments.

And who is this bright-looking woman walking with hasty step along Orchard Street so early, with a large nosegay in her hand? Can it be Janet Dempster, on whom we looked with such deep pity, one sad midnight, hardly a fortnight ago? Yes; no other woman in Milby has those searching black eyes, that tall graceful unconstrained figure, set off by her simple muslin dress and black lace shawl, that massy black hair now so neatly braided in glossy contrast with the white satin ribbons of her modest cap and bonnet. No other woman has that sweet speaking smile, with which she nods to Jonathan Lamb, the old parish clerk. And, ah! – now she comes nearer – there are those sad lines about the mouth and eyes on which that sweet smile plays like sunbeams on the storm-beaten beauty of the full and ripened corn.

She is turning out of Orchard Street, and making her way as fast as she can to her mother's house, a pleasant cottage facing a roadside meadow from which the hay is being carried. Mrs Raynor has had her breakfast, and is seated in her arm-chair reading, when Janet opens the door, saying, in her most playful voice,—

'Please, mother, I'm come to show myself to you before I go to the Parsonage. Have I put on my pretty cap and bonnet to satisfy you?'

Mrs Raynor looked over her spectacles, and met her daughter's glance with eyes as dark and loving as her own. She was a much smaller woman than Janet, both in figure and feature, the chief resemblance lying in the eyes and the clear brunette complexion. The mother's hair had long been grey, and was gathered under the neatest of caps, made by her own clever fingers, as all Janet's caps and bonnets were too. They were well-practised fingers, for Mrs Raynor had supported herself in her widowhood by keeping a millinery establishment, and in this way had earned money enough to give her daughter what was then thought a first-rate education, as well as to save a sum which, eked out by her son-in-law, sufficed to support her in her solitary old age. Always the same clean, neat old lady, dressed in black silk, was Mrs Raynor: a patient, brave woman, who bowed with resignation under the burden of remembered sorrow, and bore with meek fortitude the new load that the new days brought with them.

'Your bonnet wants pulling a trifle forwarder, my child,' she said, smiling, and taking off her spectacles, while Janet at once knelt down before her, and waited to be 'set to rights,' as she would have done when she was a child. 'You're going straight to Mrs Crewe's, I suppose? Are those flowers to garnish the dishes?'

'No, indeed, mother. This is a nosegay for the middle of the table. I've sent up the dinner-service and the ham we had cooked at our house yesterday, and Betty is coming directly with the garnish and the plate. We shall get our good Mrs Crewe through her troubles famously. Dear tiny woman! You should have seen her lift up her hands yesterday, and pray heaven to take her before ever she should have another collation to get ready for the Bishop. She said, 'It's bad enough to have the Archdeacon, though he doesn't want half so many jelly-glasses. I wouldn't mind, Janet, if it was to feed all the old hungry cripples in Milby; but so much trouble and expense for people who eat too much every day of their lives!' We had such a cleaning and furbishing-up of the sitting-room yesterday! Nothing will ever do away with the smell of Mr Crewe's pipes, you know; but we have thrown it into the background, with yellow soap and dry lavender. And now I must run away. You will come to church, mother?'

'Yes, my dear, I wouldn't lose such a pretty sight.

It does my old eyes good to see so many fresh young faces. Is your husband going?'

'Yes, Robert will be there. I've made him as neat as a new pin this morning, and he says the Bishop will think him too buckish by half. I took him into Mammy Dempster's room to show himself. We hear Tryan is making sure of the Bishop's support; but we shall see. I would give my crooked guinea, and all the luck it will ever bring me, to have him beaten, for I can't endure the sight of the man coming to harass dear old Mr and Mrs Crewe in their last days. Preaching the Gospel indeed! That is the best Gospel that makes everybody happy and comfortable, isn't it, mother?'

'Ah, child, I'm afraid there's no Gospel will do that here below.'

'Well, I can do something to comfort Mrs Crewe, at least; so give me a kiss, and good-bye till church-time.'

The mother leaned back in her chair when Janet was gone, and sank into a painful reverie. When our life is a continuous trial, the moments of respite seem only to substitute the heaviness of dread for the heaviness of actual suffering: the curtain of cloud seems parted an instant only that we may measure all its horror as it hangs low, black, and imminent, in contrast with the transient brightness; the water-drops that visit the parched lips in the desert, bear with them only the keen imagination of thirst. Janet looked glad and tender now – but what scene of misery was coming next?

She was too like the cistus flowers in the little garden before the window, that, with the shades of evening, might lie with the delicate white and glossy dark of their petals trampled in the roadside dust. When the sun had sunk, and the twilight was deepening, Janet might be sitting there, heated, maddened, sobbing out her griefs with selfish passion, and wildly wishing herself dead.

Mrs Raynor had been reading about the lost sheep, and the joy there is in heaven over the sinner that repenteth. Surely the eternal love she believed in through all the sadness of her lot, would not leave her child to wander farther and farther into the wilderness till there was no turning – the child so lovely, so pitiful to others, so good – till she was goaded into sin by woman's bitterest sorrows! Mrs Raynor had her faith and her spiritual comforts, though she was not in the least evangelical, and knew nothing of doctrinal zeal. I fear most of Mr Tryan's hearers would have considered her destitute of saving knowledge, and I am quite sure she had no well-defined views on justification. Nevertheless, she read her Bible a great deal, and thought she found divine lessons there – how to bear the cross meekly, and be merciful. Let us hope that there is a saving ignorance, and that Mrs Raynor was justified without knowing exactly how.

She tried to have hope and trust, though it was hard to believe that the future would be anything else than the harvest of the seed that was being sown before her eyes. But always there is seed being sown silently and unseen, and everywhere there come sweet flowers without our foresight or labour. We reap what we sow, but Nature has love over and above that justice, and gives us shadow and blossom and fruit that spring from no planting of ours.

CHAPTER 6

Most people must have agreed with Mrs Raynor that the Confirmation that day was a pretty sight, at least when those slight girlish forms and fair young faces moved in a white rivulet along the aisles, and flowed into kneeling semicircles under the light of the great chancel window, softened by patches of dark old painted glass; and one would think that to look on while a pair of venerable hands pressed such young heads, and a venerable face looked upward for a blessing on them, would be very likely to make the heart swell gently, and to moisten the eyes. Yet I remember the eyes seemed very dry in Milby church that day, notwithstanding that the Bishop was an old man, and probably venerable (for though he was not an eminent Grecian, he was the brother of a Whig lord); and I think the eyes must have remained dry, because he had small delicate womanish hands adorned with ruffles, and, instead of laying them on the girls' heads, just let them hover over each in quick succession, as if it were not etiquette to touch them, and as if the laying on of hands were like the theatrical embrace – part of the play, and not to be really believed in. To be sure, there were a great many heads, and the Bishop's time was limited. Moreover, a wig can, under no circumstances, be affecting, except in rare cases of illusion; and copious lawn-sleeves cannot be expected to go directly to any heart except a washer-woman's.

I know Ned Phipps, who knelt against me and I am sure made me behave much worse than I should have done without him, whispered that he thought the Bishop was a 'guy,' and I certainly remember thinking that Mr Prendergast looked much more dignified with his plain white surplice and black hair. He was a tall commanding man, and read the Liturgy in a strikingly sonorous and uniform voice, which I tried to imitate the next Sunday at home, until my little sister began to cry, and said I was 'yoaring at her.'

Mr Tryan sat in a pew near the pulpit with several other clergymen. He looked pale, and rubbed his hand over his face and pushed back his hair oftener than usual. Standing in the aisle close to him, and repeating the responses with edifying loudness, was Mr Budd, churchwarden and delegate, with a white staff in his hand and a backward bend of his small head and person, such as, I suppose, he considered suitable to a friend of sound religion. Conspicuous in the gallery, too, was the tall figure of Mr Dempster, whose professional avocations rarely allowed him to occupy his place at church.

413

'There's Dempster,' said Mrs Linnet to her daughter Mary, 'looking more respectable than usual, I declare. He's got a fine speech by heart to make to the Bishop, I'll answer for it. But he'll be pretty well sprinkled with snuff before service is over, and the Bishop won't be able to listen to him for sneezing, that's one comfort.'

At length, the last stage in the long ceremony was over, the large assembly streamed warm and weary into the open afternoon sunshine, and the Bishop retired to the Parsonage, where, after honouring Mrs Crewe's collation, he was to give audience to the delegates and Mr Tryan on the great question of the evening lecture.

Between five and six o'clock the Parsonage was once more as quiet as usual under the shadow of its tall elms, and the only traces of the Bishop's recent presence there were the wheel-marks on the gravel, and the long table with its garnished dishes awry, its damask sprinkled with crumbs, and its decanters without their stoppers. Mr Crewe was already calmly smoking his pipe in the opposite sitting-room, and Janet was agreeing with Mrs Crewe that some of the blanc-mange would be a nice thing to take to Sally Martin, while the little old lady herself had a spoon in her hand ready to gather the crumbs into a plate, that she might scatter them on the gravel for the little birds.

Before that time, the Bishop's carriage had been seen driving through the High Street on its way to Lord Trufford's, where he was to dine. The question of the lecture was decided, then?

The nature of the decision may be gathered from the following conversation which took place in the bar of the Red Lion that evening.

'So you're done, eh, Dempster?' was Mr Pilgrim's observation, uttered with some gusto. He was not glad Mr Tryan had gained his point, but he was not sorry Dempster was disappointed.

'Done, sir? Not at all. It is what I anticipated. I knew we had nothing else to expect in these days, when the Church is infested by a set of men who are only fit to give out hymns from an empty cask, to tunes set by a journeyman cobbler. But I was not the less to exert myself in the cause of sound Churchmanship for the good of the town. Any coward can fight a battle when he's sure of winning; but give me the man who has pluck to fight when he's sure of losing. That's my way, sir; and there are many victories worse than a defeat, as Mr Tryan shall learn to his cost.'

'He must be a poor shuperannyated sort of a bishop, that's my opinion,' said Mr Tomlinson, 'to go along with a sneaking Methodist like Tryan. And, for my part, I think we should be as well wi'out bishops, if they're no wiser than that. Where's the use o' havin' thousands a-year an' livin' in a pallis, if they don't stick to the Church?'

'No. There you're going out of your depth, Tomlinson,' said Mr Dempster. 'No one shall hear me say a word against Episcopacy – it is a safeguard of the Church; we must have ranks and dignities there as well as everywhere else. No, sir! Episcopacy is a good thing; but it may happen that a bishop is not a good thing. Just as brandy is a good thing, though this particular bottle is British, and tastes like sugared rainwater caught down the chimney. Here, Ratcliffe, let me have something to drink, a little less like a decoction of sugar and soot.'

'*I* said nothing again' Episcopacy,' returned Mr Tomlinson. 'I only said I thought we should do as well wi'out bishops; an' I'll say it again for the matter o' that. Bishops never brought ony grist to my mill.'

'Do you know when the lectures are to begin?' said Mr Pilgrim.

'They are to *begin* on Sunday next,' said Mr Dempster in a significant tone; 'but I think it will not take a long-sighted prophet to foresee the end of them. It strikes me Mr Tryan will be looking out for another curacy shortly.'

'He'll not get many Milby people to go and hear his lectures after a while, I'll bet a guinea,' observed Mr Budd. 'I know I'll not keep a single workman on my ground who either goes to the lecture himself or lets anybody belonging to him go.'

'Nor me nayther,' said Mr Tomlinson. 'No Tryanite shall touch a sack or drive a wagon o' mine, that you may depend on. An' I know more besides me as are o' the same mind.'

'Tryan has a good many friends in the town,

though, and friends that are likely to stand by him too,' said Mr Pilgrim. 'I should say it would be as well to let him and his lectures alone. If he goes on preaching as he does, with such a constitution as his, he'll get a relaxed throat by-and-by, and you'll be rid of him without any trouble.'

'We'll not allow him to do himself that injury,' said Mr Dempster. 'Since his health is not good, we'll persuade him to try change of air. Depend upon it, he'll find the climate of Milby too hot for him.'

CHAPTER 7

Mr Dempster did not stay long at the Red Lion that evening. He was summoned home to meet Mr Armstrong, a wealthy client, and as he was kept in consultation till a late hour, it happened that this was one of the nights on which Mr Dempster went to bed tolerably sober. Thus the day, which had been one of Janet's happiest, because it had been spent by her in helping her dear old friend Mrs Crewe, ended for her with unusual quietude; and as a bright sunset promises a fair morning, so a calm lying down is a good augury for a calm waking. Mr Dempster, on the Thursday morning, was in one of his best humours, and though perhaps some of the good humour might result from the prospect of a lucrative and exciting bit of business in Mr Armstrong's probable lawsuit, the greater part of it was doubtless due to those stirrings of the more kindly, healthy sap of human feeling, by which goodness tries to get the upper hand in us whenever it seems to have the slightest chance – on Sunday mornings, perhaps, when we are set free from the grinding hurry of the week, and take the little three-year-old on our knee at break-fast to share our egg and muffin; in moments of trouble, when death visits our roof or illness makes us dependent on the tending hand of a slighted wife; in quiet talks with an aged mother, of the days when we stood at her knee with our first picture-book, or wrote her loving letters from school. In the man whose childhood has known caresses there is always a fibre of memory that can be touched to gentle issues, and Mr Dempster, whom you have hitherto seen only as the orator of the Red Lion, and the drunken tyrant of a dreary midnight home, was the first-born darling son of a fair little mother. That mother was living still, and her own large black easy-chair, where she sat knitting through the live-long day, was now set ready for her at the breakfast-table, by her son's side, a sleek tortoise-shell cat acting as provisional incumbent.

'Good morning, Mamsey! why, you're looking as fresh as a daisy this morning. You're getting young again,' said Mr Dempster, looking up from his newspaper when the little old lady entered. A very little old lady she was, with a pale, scarcely wrinkled face, hair of that peculiar white which tells that the locks have once been blond, a natty pure white cap on her head, and a white shawl pinned over her shoulders. You saw at a glance that she had been a mignonne blonde, strangely unlike her tall, ugly, dingy-complexioned son; unlike her daughter-in-law, too, whose

419

large-featured brunette beauty seemed always thrown into higher relief by the white presence of little Mamsey. The unlikeness between Janet and her mother-in-law went deeper than outline and complexion, and indeed there was little sympathy between them, for old Mrs Dempster had not yet learned to believe that her son, Robert, would have gone wrong if he had married the right woman – a meek woman like herself, who would have borne him children, and been a deft, orderly housekeeper. In spite of Janet's tenderness and attention to her, she had had little love for her daughter-in-law from the first, and had witnessed the sad growth of home-misery through long years, always with a disposition to lay the blame on the wife rather than on the husband, and to reproach Mrs Raynor for encouraging her daughter's faults by a too exclusive sympathy. But old Mrs Dempster had that rare gift of silence and passivity which often supplies the absence of mental strength; and, whatever were her thoughts, she said no word to aggravate the domestic discord. Patient and mute she sat at her knitting through many a scene of quarrel and anguish; resolutely she appeared unconscious of the sounds that reached her ears, and the facts she divined after she had retired to her bed; mutely she witnessed poor Janet's faults, only registering them as a balance of excuse on the side of her son. The hard, astute, domineering attorney was still that little old woman's pet, as he had been when she watched with triumphant pride his first tumbling effort to march alone across the nursery floor. 'See what a good son he is to me!' she often thought. 'Never gave me a harsh word. And so he might have been a good husband.'

O it is piteous – that sorrow of aged women! In early youth, perhaps, they said to themselves, 'I shall be happy when I have a husband to love me best of all;' then, when the husband was too careless, 'My child will comfort me;' then, through the mother's watching and toil, 'My child will repay me all when it grows up.' And at last, after the long journey of years has been wearily travelled through, the mother's heart is weighed down by a heavier burden, and no hope remains but the grave.

But this morning old Mrs Dempster sat down in her easy-chair without any painful, suppressed remembrance of the preceding night.

'I declare mammy looks younger than Mrs Crewe, who is only sixty-five,' said Janet. 'Mrs Crewe will come to see you to-day, mammy, and tell you all about her troubles with the Bishop and the collation. She'll bring her knitting, and you'll have a regular gossip together.'

'The gossip will be all on one side, then, for Mrs Crewe gets so very deaf, I can't make her hear a word. And if I motion to her, she always understands me wrong.'

'O, she will have so much to tell you to-day, you will not want to speak yourself. You, who have patience to knit those wonderful counterpanes, mammy, must not be impatient with dear Mrs Crewe. Good old lady! I can't bear her to think she's ever tiresome to people, and you know she's very ready to fancy herself in the way. I think she would like to shrink up to the size of a mouse, that she might run about and do people good without their noticing her.'

'It isn't patience I want, God knows; it's lungs to speak loud enough. But you'll be at home yourself, I suppose, this morning; and you can talk to her for me.'

'No, mammy; I promised poor Mrs Lowme to go and sit with her. She's confined to her room, and both the Miss Lowmes are out; so I'm going to read the newspaper to her and amuse her.'

'Couldn't you go another morning? As Mr Armstrong and that other gentleman are coming to dinner, I should think it would be better to stay at home. Can you trust Betty to see to everything? She's new to the place.'

'O I couldn't disappoint Mrs Lowme; I promised her. Betty will do very well, no fear.'

Old Mrs Dempster was silent after this, and began to sip her tea. The breakfast went on without further conversation for some time, Mr Dempster being absorbed in the papers. At length, when he was running over the advertisements, his eye seemed to be caught by something that suggested a new thought to him. He presently thumped the table with an air of exultation, and said, turning to Janet,—

'I've a capital idea, Gypsy!' (that was his name for his dark-eyed wife when he was in an extraordinarily good humour), 'and you shall help me. It's just what you're up to.'

'What is it?' said Janet, her face beaming at the sound of the pet name, now heard so seldom. 'Anything to do with conveyancing?'

'It's a bit of fun worth a dozen fees – a plan for raising a laugh against Tryan and his gang of hypocrites.'

'What is it? Nothing that wants a needle and thread, I hope, else I must go and tease mother.'

'No, nothing sharper than your wit – except mine. I'll tell you what it is. We'll get up a programme of the Sunday evening lecture, like a play-bill, you know – 'Grand Performance of the celebrated Mountebank,' and so on. We'll bring in the Tryanites – old Landor and the rest – in appropriate characters. Proctor shall print it, and we'll circulate it in the town. It will be a capital hit.'

'Bravo!' said Janet, clapping her hands. She would just then have pretended to like almost anything, in her pleasure at being appealed to by her husband, and she really did like to laugh at the Tryanites. 'We'll set about it directly, and sketch it out before you go to the office. I've got Tryan's sermons up-stairs, but I don't think there's anything in them we can use. I've only just

423

looked into them; they're not at all what I expected – dull, stupid things – nothing of the roaring fire-and-brimstone sort that I expected.'

'Roaring? No; Tryan's as soft as a sucking dove – one of your honey-mouthed hypocrites. Plenty of devil and malice in him, though, I could see that, while he was talking to the Bishop; but as smooth as a snake outside. He's beginning a single-handed fight with me, I can see – persuading my clients away from me. We shall see who will be the first to cry *peccavi*. Milby will do better without Mr Tryan than without Robert Dempster, I fancy! and Milby shall never be flooded with cant as long as I can raise a breakwater against it. But now, get the breakfast things cleared away, and let us set about the play-bill. Come, mamsey, come and have a walk with me round the garden, and let us see how the cucumbers are getting on. I've never taken you round the garden for an age. Come, you don't want a bonnet. It's like walking in a greenhouse this morning.'

'But she will want a parasol,' said Janet. 'There's one on the stand against the garden-door, Robert.'

The little old lady took her son's arm with placid pleasure. She could barely reach it so as to rest upon it, but he inclined a little towards her, and accommodated his heavy long-limbed steps to her feeble pace. The cat chose to sun herself too, and walked close beside them, with tail erect, rubbing her sleek sides against their legs, too well fed to be excited by the twittering birds. The garden was of the grassy, shady kind, often seen attached to old houses in provincial towns; the apple-trees had had time to spread their branches very wide, the shrubs and hardy perennial plants had grown into a luxuriance that required constant trimming to prevent them from intruding on the space for walking. But the farther end, which united with green fields, was open and sunny.

It was rather sad, and yet pretty, to see that little group passing out of the shadow into the sunshine, and out of the sunshine into the shadow again: sad, because this tenderness of the son for the mother was hardly more than a nucleus of healthy life in an organ hardening by disease, because the man who was linked in this way with an innocent past, had become callous in worldliness, fevered by sensuality, enslaved by chance impulses; pretty, because it showed how hard it is to kill the deep-down fibrous roots of human love and goodness – how the man from whom we make it our pride to shrink, has yet a close brotherhood with us through some of our most sacred feelings.

As they were returning to the house, Janet met them, and said, 'Now, Robert, the writing things are ready. I shall be clerk, and Mat Paine can copy it out after.'

Mammy once more deposited in her arm-chair, with her knitting in her hand, and the cat purring at her elbow, Janet seated herself at the table, while

Mr Dempster placed himself near her, took out his snuffbox, and plentifully suffusing himself with the inspiring powder, began to dictate.

What he dictated, we shall see by-and-by.

CHAPTER 8

The next day, Friday, at five o'clock by the sundial, the large bow-window of Mrs Jerome's parlour was open; and that lady herself was seated within its ample semicircle, having a table before her on which her best tea-tray, her best china, and her best urn-rug had already been standing in readiness for half an hour. Mrs Jerome's best tea-service was of delicate white fluted china, with gold sprigs upon it – as pretty a tea-service as you need wish to see, and quite good enough for chimney ornaments; indeed, as the cups were without handles, most visitors who had the distinction of taking tea out of them, wished that such charming china had already been promoted to that honorary position. Mrs Jerome was like her china, handsome and old-fashioned. She was a buxom lady of sixty, in an elaborate lace cap fastened by a frill under her chin, a dark, well-curled front concealing her forehead, a snowy neckerchief exhibiting its ample folds as far as her waist, and a stiff grey silk gown. She had a clean damask napkin pinned before her to guard her dress during the process of tea-making; her favourite geraniums in the bow-window were looking as healthy as she could desire; her own handsome portrait, painted when she was twenty years younger, was smiling down on her with agreeable flattery; and altogether she seemed to be in as peaceful and pleasant a position as a buxom, well-dressed elderly lady need desire. But, as in so many other cases, appearances were deceptive. Her mind was greatly perturbed and her temper ruffled by the fact that it was more than a quarter past five even by the losing timepiece, that it was half-past by her large gold watch, which she held in her hand as if she were counting the pulse of the afternoon, and that, by the kitchen clock, which she felt sure was not an hour too fast, it had already struck six. The lapse of time was rendered the more unendurable to Mrs Jerome by her wonder that Mr Jerome could stay out in the garden with Lizzie in that thoughtless way, taking it so easily that tea-time was long past, and that, after all the trouble of getting down the best tea-things, Mr Tryan would not come.

This honour had been shown to Mr Tryan, not at all because Mrs Jerome had any high appreciation of his doctrine or of his exemplary activity as a pastor, but simply because he was a 'Church clergyman,' and as such was regarded by her with the same sort of exceptional respect that a white woman who had married a native of the Society Islands might be supposed to feel towards a white-skinned visitor from the land of her youth.

For Mrs Jerome had been reared a Churchwoman, and having attained the age of thirty before she was married, had felt the greatest repugnance in the first instance to renouncing the religious forms in which she had been brought up. 'You know,' she said in confidence to her Church acquaintances, 'I wouldn't give no ear at all to Mr Jerome at fust; but after all, I begun to think as there was a maeny things wuss nor goin' to chapel, an' you'd better do that nor not pay your way. Mr Jerome had a very pleasant manner wi' him, an' there was niver another as kep a gig, an' 'ud make a settlement on me like him, chapel or no chapel. It seemed very odd to me for a lung while, the preachin' wi'out book, an' the stannin' up to one lung prayer, istid o' changin' yur postur. But la! there's nothin' as you mayn't get used to i' time; you can al'ys sit down, you know, afore the prayer's done. The ministers say welly the same things as the Church parsons, by what I could iver mek out, an' we're out o' chapel i' the mornin' a deal sooner nor they're out o' church. An' as for pews, ourn's a deal comfortabler nor aeny i' Milby church.'

Mrs Jerome, you perceive, had not a keen susceptibility to shades of doctrine, and it is probable that, after listening to Dissenting eloquence for thirty years, she might safely have re-entered the Establishment without performing any spiritual quarantine. Her mind, apparently, was of that non-porous flinty character which is not in the least danger from surrounding damp. But on the question of getting start of the sun in the day's business, and clearing her conscience of the necessary sum of meals and the consequent 'washing up' as soon as possible, so that the family might be well in bed at nine, Mrs Jerome *was* susceptible; and the present lingering pace of things, united with Mr Jerome's unaccountable obliviousness, was not to be borne any longer. So she rang the bell for Sally.

'Goodness me, Sally! go into the garden an' see after your master. Tell him it's goin' on for six, an' Mr Tryan 'ull niver think o' comin' now, an' it's time we got tea over. An' he's lettin' Lizzie stain her frock, I expect, among them strawberry beds. Mek her come in this minute.'

No wonder Mr Jerome was tempted to linger in the garden, for though the house was pretty and well deserved its name – 'the White House,' the tall damask roses that clustered over the porch being thrown into relief by rough stucco of the most brilliant white, yet the garden and orchards were Mr Jerome's glory, as well they might be; and there was nothing in which he had a more innocent pride – peace to a good man's memory! all his pride was innocent – than in conducting a hitherto uninitiated visitor over his grounds, and making him in some degree aware of the incomparable advantages possessed by the inhabitants of the White House in the matter of red-streaked apples, russets, northern greens (excellent for baking), swan-egg pears, and early vegetables, to say nothing of flowering 'srubs,' pink hawthorns, lavender bushes more than ever Mrs Jerome could use, and, in short, a superabundance of everything that a person retired from business could desire to possess himself or to share with his friends. The garden was one of those old-fashioned paradises which hardly exist any longer except as memories of our childhood: no finical separation between flower and kitchen garden there; no monotony of enjoyment for one sense to the exclusion of another; but a charming paradisiacal mingling of all that was pleasant to the eyes and good for food. The rich flower-border running along every walk, with its endless succession of spring flowers, anemones, auriculas, wall-flowers, sweet-williams, campanulas, snapdragons, and tiger-lilies, had its taller beauties, such as moss and Provence roses, varied with espalier apple-trees; the crimson of a carnation was carried out in the lurking crimson of the neighbouring strawberry-beds; you gathered a moss-rose one moment and a bunch of currants the next; you were in a delicious fluctuation between the scent of jasmine and the juice of gooseberries. Then what a high wall at one end, flanked by a summer-house so lofty, that after ascending its long flight of steps you could see perfectly well there was no view worth looking at; what alcoves and garden-seats in all directions; and along one side, what a hedge, tall, and firm, and unbroken, like a green wall!

It was near this hedge that Mr Jerome was

standing when Sally found him. He had set down the basket of strawberries on the gravel, and had lifted up little Lizzie in his arms to look at a bird's nest. Lizzie peeped, and then looked at her grandpa with round blue eyes, and then peeped again.

'D'ye see it, Lizzie?' he whispered.

'Yes,' she whispered in return, putting her lips very near grandpa's face. At this moment Sally appeared.

'Eh, eh, Sally, what's the matter? Is Mr Tryan come?'

'No, sir, an' Missis says she's sure he won't come now, an' she wants you to come in an' hev tea. Dear heart, Miss Lizzie, you've stained your pinafore, an' I shouldn't wonder if it's gone through to your frock. There'll be fine work! Come alonk wi' me, do.'

'Nay, nay, nay, we've done no harm, we've done no harm, hev we Lizzie? The wash-tub 'll mek all right again.'

Sally, regarding the wash-tub from a different point of view, looked sourly serious, and hurried away with Lizzie, who trotted submissively along, her little head in eclipse under a large nankin bonnet, while Mr Jerome followed leisurely with his full broad shoulders in rather a stooping posture, and his large good-natured features and white locks shaded by a broad-brimmed hat.

'Mr Jerome, I wonder at you,' said Mrs Jerome, in a tone of indignant remonstrance, evidently sustained by a deep sense of injury, as her husband opened the parlour door. 'When will you leave off invitin' people to meals an' not lettin' 'em know the time? I'll answer for't, you niver said a word to Mr Tryan as we should tek tea at five o'clock. It's just like you!'

'Nay, nay, Susan,' answered the husband in a soothing tone, 'there's nothin' amiss. I told Mr Tryan as we took tea at five punctial; mayhap summat's a detainin' on him. He's a deal to do an' to think on, remember.'

'Why, it's struck six i' the kitchen a'ready. It's nonsense to look for him comin' now. So you may's well ring for th' urn. Now Sally's got th' heater i' th' fire, we may's well hev th' urn in, though he doesn't come. I niver see the like o' you, Mr Jerome, for axin' people an' givin' me the trouble o' gettin' things down an' hevin' crumpets made, an' after all they don't come. I shall hev to wash every one o' these tea-things myself, for there's no trustin' Sally – she'd break a fortin i' crockery i' no time!'

'But why will you give yourself sich trouble, Susan? Our everyday tea-things would ha' done as well for Mr Tryan, an' they're a deal convenenter to hold.'

'Yes, that's just your way, Mr Jerome, you're al'ys a-findin' faut wi' my chany, because I bought it myself afore I was married. But let me tell you, I knowed how to choose chany if I didn't know how to choose a husband. An' where's Lizzie? You've niver left her i' the garden by herself, wi' her white frock on an' clean stockins?'

'Be easy, my dear Susan, be easy; Lizzie's come in wi' Sally. She's hevin' her pinafore took off, I'll be bound. Ah! There's Mr Tryan a-comin' through the gate.'

Mrs Jerome began hastily to adjust her damask napkin and the expression of her countenance for the reception of the clergyman, and Mr Jerome went out to meet his guest, whom he greeted outside the door.

'Mr Tryan, how do you do, Mr Tryan? Welcome to the White House! I'm glad to see you, sir, I'm glad to see you.'

If you had heard the tone of mingled goodwill, veneration, and condolence in which this greeting was uttered, even without seeing the face that completely harmonized with it, you would have no difficulty in inferring the ground-notes of Mr Jerome's character. To a fine ear that tone said as plainly as possible – 'Whatever recommends itself to me, Thomas Jerome, as piety and goodness, shall have my love and honour. Ah, friends, this pleasant world is a sad one, too, isn't it? Let us help one another, let us help one another.' And it was entirely owing to this basis of character, not at all from any clear and precise doctrinal discrimination, that Mr Jerome had very early in life become a Dissenter. In his boyish days he had been thrown where Dissent seemed to have the balance of piety, purity, and good works on its side, and to become a Dissenter seemed to him identical with choosing God instead of mammon. That race of Dissenters is extinct in these days, when opinion has got far ahead of feeling, and every chapel-going youth can fill our ears with the advantages of the Voluntary system, the corruptions of a State Church, and the Scriptural evidence that the first Christians were Congregationalists. Mr Jerome knew nothing of this theoretic basis for Dissent, and in the utmost extent of his polemical discussion he had not gone further than to question whether a Christian man was bound in conscience to distinguish Christmas and Easter by any peculiar observance beyond the eating of mince-pies and cheese-cakes. It seemed to him that all seasons were alike good for thanking God, departing from evil and doing well, whereas it might be desirable to restrict the period for indulging in unwholesome forms of pastry. Mr Jerome's dissent being of this simple, non-polemical kind, it is easy to understand that the report he heard of Mr Tryan as a good man and a powerful preacher, who was stirring the hearts of the people, had been enough to attract him to the Paddiford Church, and that having felt himself more edified there than he had of late been under Mr Stickney's discourses at Salem, he had driven thither repeatedly in the Sunday afternoons, and had sought an opportunity of making Mr Tryan's acquaintance. The evening lecture was a subject of warm interest with him, and the opposition Mr Tryan met with gave that interest a strong tinge of partisanship; for there was a store of irascibility in Mr Jerome's nature which must find a vent somewhere, and in so kindly and upright a man could only find it in indignation against those whom he held to be enemies of truth and goodness. Mr Tryan had not hitherto been to the White House, but yesterday, meeting Mr Jerome in the street, he had at once accepted the invitation to tea, saying there was something he wished to talk about. He appeared worn and fatigued now, and after shaking hands with Mrs Jerome, threw himself into a chair and looked out on the pretty garden with an air of relief.

'What a nice place you have here, Mr Jerome! I've not seen anything so quiet and pretty since I came to Milby. On Paddiford Common, where I live, you know, the bushes are all sprinkled with soot, and there's never any quiet except in the dead of night.'

'Dear heart! dear heart! That's very bad – and for you, too, as hev to study. Wouldn't it be better for you to be somewhere more out i' the country like?'

'O no! I should lose so much time in going to and fro, and besides I like to be *among* the people. I've no face to go and preach resignation to those poor things in their smoky air and comfortless homes, when I come straight from every luxury myself. There are many things quite lawful for other men, which a clergyman must forego if he would do any good in a manufacturing population like this.'

Here the preparations for tea were crowned by the simultaneous appearance of Lizzie and the crumpet. It is a pretty surprise, when one visits an elderly couple, to see a little figure enter in a white frock with a blond head as smooth as satin, round blue eyes, and a cheek like an apple blossom. A toddling little girl is a centre of common feeling which makes the most dissimilar people understand each other; and Mr Tryan looked at Lizzie with that quiet pleasure which is always genuine.

'Here we are, here we are!' said proud grandpapa. 'You didn't think we'd got such a little gell as this, did you, Mr Tryan? Why, it seems but th' other day since her mother was just such another. This is our little Lizzie, this is. Come an' shake hands wi' Mr Tryan, Lizzie; come.'

Lizzie advanced without hesitation, and put out one hand, while she fingered her coral necklace with the other, and looked up into Mr Tryan's face with a reconnoitring gaze. He stroked the satin head, and said in his gentlest voice, 'How do you do, Lizzie? will you give me a kiss?' She put up her little bud of a mouth, and then retreating a little and glancing down at her frock, said,

'Dit id my noo fock. I put it on 'tod you wad toming. Tally taid you wouldn't 'ook at it.'

'Hush, hush, Lizzie, little gells must be seen and not heard,' said Mrs Jerome; while grandpapa, winking significantly, and looking radiant with delight at Lizzie's extraordinary promise of cleverness, set her up on her high cane-chair by the side of grandma, who lost no time in shielding the beauties of the new frock with a napkin.

'Well now, Mr Tryan,' said Mr Jerome, in a very serious tone when tea had been distributed, 'let me hear how you're a-goin' on about the lectur. When I was i' the town yisterday, I heared as there was pessecutin' schemes a-bein' laid again' you. I fear me those raskills 'ull mek things very onpleasant to you.'

'I've no doubt they will attempt it; indeed, I quite expect there will be a regular mob got up on Sunday evening, as there was when the delegates returned, on purpose to annoy me and the congregation on our way to church.'

'Ah, they're capible o' anything, such men as Dempster an' Budd; an' Tomlinson backs 'em wi' money, though he can't wi' brains. Howiver, Dempster's lost one client by's wicked doins, an' I'm deceived if he won't lose more nor one. I little thought, Mr Tryan, when I put my affairs into his hands twenty 'ear ago this Michaelmas, as he was to turn out a pessecutor o' religion. I niver lighted on a cliverer, promisiner young man nor he was then. They talked of his bein' fond of a extry glass now an' then, but niver nothin' like what he's come to since. An' it's headpiece you must look for in a lawyer, Mr Tryan, it's headpiece. His wife, too, was al'ys an uncommon favourite o' mine – poor thing! I hear sad stories about her now. But she's

438

druv to it, she's druv to it, Mr Tryan. A tender-hearted woman to the poor, she is, as iver lived; an' as pretty-spoken a woman as you need wish to talk to. Yes! I'd al'ys a likin' for Dempster an' his wife, spite o' iverything. But as soon as iver I heared o' that dilegate business, I says, says I, that man shall hev no more to do wi' my affairs. It may put me t' inconvenience, but I'll encourage no man as pessecutes religion.'

'He is evidently the brain and hand of the persecution,' said Mr Tryan. 'There may be a strong feeling against me in a large number of the inhabitants – it must be so, from the great ignorance of spiritual things in this place. But I fancy there would have been no formal opposition to the lecture, if Dempster had not planned it. I am not myself the least alarmed at anything he can do; he will find I am not to be cowed or driven away by insult or personal danger. God has sent me to this place, and, by His blessing, I'll not shrink from anything I may have to encounter in doing His work among the people. But I feel it right to call on all those who know the value of the Gospel, to stand by me publicly. I think – and Mr Landor agrees with me – that it will be well for my friends to proceed with me in a body to the church on Sunday evening. Dempster, you know, has pretended that almost all the respectable inhabit-ants are opposed to the lecture. Now, I wish that falsehood to be visibly contradicted. What do you think of the plan? I have to-day been to see several

439

of my friends, who will make a point of being there to accompany me, and will communicate with others on the subject.'

'I'll mek one, Mr Tryan, I'll mek one. You shall not be wantin' in any support as I can give. Before you come to it, sir, Milby was a dead an' dark place; you are the fust man i' the Church to my knowledge as has brought the word o' God home to the people; an' I'll stan' by you, sir, I'll stan' by you. I'm a Dissenter, Mr Tryan, I've been a Dissenter iver sin' I was fifteen 'ear old; but show me good i' the Church, an' I'm a Churchman too. When I was a boy I lived at Tilston; you mayn't know the place; the best part o' the land there belonged to Squire Sandeman; he'd a club-foot, hed Squire Sandeman – lost a deal o' money by canal shares. Well, sir, as I was sayin', I lived at Tilston, an' the rector there was a terrible drinkin', fox-huntin' man; you niver see such a parish i' your time for wickedness; Milby's nothin' to it. Well, sir, my father was a workin' man, an' couldn't afford to gi' me ony eddication, so I went to a night-school as was kep by a Dissenter, one Jacob Wright; an' it was from that man, sir, as I got my little schoolin' an' my knowledge o' religion. I went to chapel wi' Jacob – he was a good man was Jacob – an' to chapel I've been iver since. But I'm no enemy o' the Church, sir, when the Church brings light to the ignorant and the sinful; an' that's what you're a-doin', Mr Tryan. Yes, sir, I'll stan' by you. I'll go to church wi' you o' Sunday evenin'.'

'You'd fur better stay at home, Mr Jerome, if I may give *my* opinion,' interposed Mrs Jerome. 'It's not as I hevn't ivery respect for you, Mr Tryan, but Mr Jerome 'ull do you no good by his interferin'. Dissenters are not at all looked on i' Milby, an' he's as nervous as iver he can be; he'll come back as ill as ill, an' niver let me hev a wink o' sleep all night.'

Mrs Jerome had been frightened at the mention of a mob, and her retrospective regard for the religious communion of her youth by no means inspired her with the temper of a martyr. Her husband looked at her with an expression of tender and grieved remonstrance, which might have been that of the patient patriarch on the memorable occasion when he rebuked *his* wife.

'Susan, Susan, let me beg on you not to oppose me, an' put stumblin'-blocks i' the way o' doin' what's right. I can't give up my conscience, let me give up what else I may.'

'Perhaps,' said Mr Tryan, feeling slightly uncomfortable, 'since you are not very strong, my dear sir, it will be well, as Mrs Jerome suggests, that you should not run the risk of any excitement.'

'Say no more, Mr Tryan. I'll stan' by you, sir. It's my duty. It's the cause o' God, sir; it's the cause o' God.'

Mr Tryan obeyed his impulse of admiration and gratitude, and put out his hand to the white-haired old man, saying, 'Thank you, Mr Jerome, thank you.'

Mr Jerome grasped the proffered hand in silence, and then threw himself back in his chair, casting a regretful look at his wife, which seemed to say, 'Why don't you feel with me, Susan?'

The sympathy of this simple-minded old man was more precious to Mr Tryan than any mere onlooker could have imagined. To persons possessing a great deal of that facile psychology which prejudges individuals by means of formulæ, and casts them, without further trouble, into duly lettered pigeon-holes, the Evangelical curate might seem to be doing simply what all other men like to do – carrying out objects which were identified not only with his theory, which is but a kind of secondary egoism, but also with the primary egoism of his feelings. Opposition may become sweet to a man when he has christened it persecution: a self-obtrusive, over-hasty reformer complacently disclaiming all merit, while his friends call him a martyr, has not in reality a career the most arduous to the fleshly mind. But Mr Tryan was not cast in the mould of the gratuitous martyr. With a power of persistence which had been often blamed as obstinacy, he had an acute sensibility to the very hatred or ridicule he did not flinch from provoking. Every form of disapproval jarred him painfully; and, though he fronted his opponents manfully, and often with considerable warmth of temper, he had no pugnacious pleasure in the contest. It was one of the weaknesses of his nature to be too keenly alive to every harsh wind of opinion; to wince under the frowns of the foolish; to be irritated by the injustice of those who could not possibly have the elements indispensable for judging him rightly; and with all this acute sensibility to blame, this dependence on sympathy, he had for years been constrained into a position of antagonism. No wonder, then, that good old Mr Jerome's cordial words were balm to him. He had often been thankful to an old woman for saying 'God bless you;' to a little child for smiling at him; to a dog for submitting to be patted by him.

Tea being over by this time, Mr Tryan proposed a walk in the garden as a means of dissipating all recollection of the recent conjugal dissidence. Little Lizzie's appeal, 'Me go, gandpa!' could not be rejected, so she was duly bonneted and pinafored, and then they turned out into the evening sunshine. Not Mrs Jerome, however; she had a deeply-meditated plan of retiring *ad interim* to the kitchen and washing up the best tea-things, as a mode of getting forward with the sadly-retarded business of the day.

'This way, Mr Tryan, this way,' said the old gentleman; 'I must take you to my pastur fust, an' show you our cow – the best milker i' the county. An' see here at these back-buildins, how convenent the dairy is; I planned it ivery bit myself. An' here I've got my little carpenter's shop an' my blacksmith's shop; I do no end o' jobs here myself. I niver could bear to be idle, Mr Tryan; I must al'ys be at somethin' or other. It was time for me to ley by business and mek room for younger folks. I'd got money enough, wi' only one daughter to leave it to, an' I says to myself, says I, it's time to leave off moitherin' myself wi' this world so much, an' give more time to thinkin' of another. But there's a many hours atween getting up an' lyin' down, an' thoughts are no cumber; you can move about wi' a good many on 'em in your head. See here's the pastur.'

A very pretty pasture it was, where the large-spotted short-horned cow quietly chewed the cud as she lay and looked sleepily at her admirers – a daintily-trimmed hedge all round, dotted here and there with a mountain-ash or a cherry-tree.

'I've a good bit more land besides this, worth your while to look at, but mayhap it's further nor you'd like to walk now. Bless you! I've welly an' acre o' potato-ground yonters; I've a good big family to supply, you know.' (Here Mr Jerome winked and smiled significantly.) 'An' that puts me i' mind, Mr Tryan, o' summat I wanted to say to you. Clergymen like you, I know, see a deal more poverty an' that, than other folks, an' hev a many claims on 'em more nor they can well meet; an' if you'll mek use o' my purse any time, or let me know where I can be o' any help, I'll tek it very kind on you.'

'Thank you, Mr Jerome, I will do so, I promise you. I saw a sad case yesterday; a collier – a fine broad-chested fellow about thirty – was killed by the falling of a wall in the Paddiford colliery. I was in one of the cottages near when they brought him home on a door, and the shriek of the wife has been ringing in my ears ever since. There are three little children. Happily the woman has her loom, so she will be able to keep out of the work-house; but she looks very delicate.'

'Give me her name, Mr Tryan,' said Mr Jerome, drawing out his pocket-book. 'I'll call an' see her, I'll call an' see her.'

Deep was the fountain of pity in the good old man's heart! He often ate his dinner stintingly, oppressed by the thought that there were men, women, and children, with no dinner to sit down to, and would relieve his mind by going out in the afternoon to look for some need that he could supply, some honest struggle in which he could lend a helping hand. That any living being should want, was his chief sorrow; that any rational being should waste, was the next. Sally, indeed, having been scolded by master for a too lavish use of sticks in lighting the kitchen fire, and various instances of recklessness with regard to candle ends, considered him 'as mean as aenythink;' but he had as kindly a warmth as the morning sunlight, and, like the sunlight, his goodness shone on all that came in his way, from the saucy rosy-cheeked lad whom he delighted to make happy with a Christmas box, to the pallid sufferers up dim entries, languishing under the tardy death of want and misery.

It was very pleasant to Mr Tryan to listen to the simple chat of the old man – to walk in the shade of the incomparable orchard, and hear the story of the crops yielded by the red-streaked apple-tree, and the quite embarrassing plentifulness of the summer-pears – to drink in the sweet evening breath of the garden, as they sat in the alcove – and so, for a short interval, to feel the strain of his pastoral task relaxed.

Perhaps he felt the return to that task through the dusty roads all the more painfully, perhaps something in that quiet shady home had reminded him of the time before he had taken on him the yoke of self-denial. The strongest heart will faint sometimes under the feeling that enemies are bitter, and that friends only know half its sorrows. The most resolute soul will now and then cast back a yearning look in treading the rough mountain-path, away from the greensward and laughing voices of the valley. However it was, in the nine o'clock twilight that evening, when Mr Tryan had entered his small study and turned the key in the door, he threw himself into the chair before his writing-table, and, heedless of the papers there, leaned his face low on his hand, and moaned heavily.

It is apt to be so in this life, I think. While we are coldly discussing a man's career, sneering at his mistakes, blaming his rashness, and labelling his opinions – 'he is Evangelical and narrow,' or 'Latitudinarian and Pantheistic,' or 'Anglican and supercilious' – that man, in his solitude, is perhaps shedding hot tears because his sacrifice is a hard one, because strength and patience are failing him to speak the difficult word, and do the difficult deed.

CHAPTER 9

Mr Tryan showed no such symptoms of weakness on the critical Sunday. He unhesitatingly rejected the suggestion that he should be taken to church in Mr Landor's carriage – a proposition which that gentleman made as an amendment on the original plan, when the rumours of meditated insult became alarming. Mr Tryan declared he would have no precautions taken, but would simply trust in God and his good cause. Some of his more timid friends thought this conduct rather defiant than wise, and reflecting that a mob has great talents for impromptu, and that legal redress is imperfect satisfaction for having one's head broken with a brickbat, were beginning to question their consciences very closely as to whether it was not a duty they owed to their families to stay at home on Sunday evening. These timorous persons, however, were in a small minority, and the generality of Mr Tryan's friends and hearers rather exulted in an opportunity of braving insult for the sake of a preacher to whom they were attached on personal as well as doctrinal grounds. Miss Pratt spoke of

Cranmer, Ridley, and Latimer, and observed that the present crisis afforded an occasion for emulating their heroism even in these degenerate times; while less highly instructed persons, whose memories were not well stored with precedents, simply expressed their determination, as Mr Jerome had done, to 'stan' by' the preacher and his cause, believing it to be the 'cause of God.'

On Sunday evening, then, at a quarter past six, Mr Tryan, setting out from Mr Landor's with a party of his friends who had assembled there, was soon joined by two other groups from Mr Pratt's and Mr Dunn's; and stray persons on their way to church naturally falling into rank behind this leading file, by the time they reached the entrance of Orchard Street, Mr Tryan's friends formed a considerable procession, walking three or four abreast. It was in Orchard Street, and towards the church gates, that the chief crowd was collected; and at Mr Dempster's drawing-room window, on the upper floor, a more select assembly of Anti-Tryanites were gathered, to witness the entertaining spectacle of the Tryanites walking to church amidst the jeers and hootings of the crowd.

To prompt the popular with with appropriate sobriquets, numerous copies of Mr Dempster's play-bill were posted on the walls, in suitably large and emphatic type. As it is possible that the most industrious collector of mural literature may not have been fortunate enough to possess himself of this production, which ought by all means to be preserved amongst the materials of our provincial religious history, I subjoin a faithful copy.

GRAND ENTERTAINMENT!!!
To be given at Milby on Sunday evening
next, by the
FAMOUS COMEDIAN, TRY-IT-ON!
And his first-rate company, including not only an
UNPARALLELED CAST FOR COMEDY!
But a Large Collection of *reclaimed and
converted Animals*;
Among the rest
A Bear, who used to *dance!*
A Parrot, once given to *swearing!!*
A Polygamous Pig!!!
and
A Monkey who used to *catch fleas
on a Sunday!!!!*
Together with a
Pair of *regenerated* LINNETS!
With an entirely new song, and *plumage*.
MR TRY-IT-ON
Will first pass through the streets, in procession,
with his unrivalled Company, warranted to have
their *eyes turned up higher*, and the *corners of their
mouths turned down lower*, than any other
company of Mountebanks in this circuit!
AFTER WHICH
The Theatre will be opened, and the
entertainment will
commence at HALF-PAST SIX,

When will be presented
A piece, never before performed on
any stage, entitled,
THE WOLF IN SHEEP'S CLOTHING;
or
THE METHODIST IN A MASK.

Mr Boanerges Soft Sawder,	. . . .	Mr TRY-IT-ON.
Old Ten-per-cent Godly,	. . . .	Mr GANDER.
Dr Feedemup,	. . . .	Mr TONIC.
Mr Lime-Twig Lady-winner,	. . . .	Mr TRY-IT-ON.
Miss Piety Bait-the-hook,	. . . .	Miss TONIC.
Angelica,	. . . .	Miss SERAPHINA TONIC.

After which
A miscellaneous Musical Interlude,
commencing with
The *Lamentations of Jerom-iah!*
In nasal recitative.
To be followed by
The favourite Cackling Quartette,
by
Two Hen-birds who are *no chickens!*
The well-known *counter*-tenor, Mr Done,
and a *Gander*,
lineally descended from the *Goose* that
laid golden eggs!
To conclude with a

GRAND CHORUS by the
Entire Orchestra of converted Animals!!
But owing to the unavoidable absence (from
illness) of the *Bull-dog, who has left off fighting,*
Mr Tonic has kindly undertaken, at a moment's
notice, to supply the '*bark!*'

The whole to conclude with a
Screaming Farce of
THE PULPIT SNATCHER

Mr Saintly Smooth-face,	. . . . . . Mr TRY-IT-ON!
Mr Worming Sneaker,	. . . . . Mr TRY-IT-ON!!
Mr All-grace No-works,	. . . . . . Mr TRY-IT-ON!!!
Mr Elect-and-Chosen Apewell,	. . . . . . Mr TRY-IT-ON!!!!
Mr Malevolent Prayerful,	. . . . . . Mr TRY-IT-ON!!!!!
Mr Foist-himself Everywhere,	. . . . . . Mr TRY-IT-ON!!!!!!
Mr Flout-the-aged Upstart,	. . . . . . Mr TRY-IT-ON!!!!!!!

Admission Free. A *Collection* will be made
at the Doors.
Vivat Rex!

This satire, though it presents the keenest edge of Milby wit, does not strike you as lacerating, I imagine. But hatred is like fire – it makes even light rubbish deadly. And Mr Dempster's sarcasms were not merely visible on the walls; they were reflected in the derisive glances, and audible in the jeering voices of the crowd. Through this pelting shower of nicknames and bad puns, with an *ad libitum* accompaniment of groans, howls, hisses, and hee-haws, but of no heavier missiles, Mr Tryan walked pale and composed, giving his arm to old Mr Landor, whose step was feeble. On the other side of him was Mr Jerome, who still walked firmly, though his shoulders were slightly bowed.

Outwardly Mr Tryan was composed, but inwardly he was suffering acutely from these tones of hatred and scorn. However strong his consciousness of right, he found it no stronger armour against such weapons as derisive glances and virulent words, than against stones and clubs: his conscience was in repose, but his sensibility was bruised.

Once more only did the Evangelical curate pass up Orchard Street followed by a train of friends; once more only was there a crowd assembled to witness his entrance through the church gates. But that second time no voice was heard above a whisper, and the whispers were words of sorrow and blessing.

That second time, Janet Dempster was not looking on in scorn and merriment; her eyes were worn with grief and watching, and she was following her beloved friend and pastor to the grave.

CHAPTER 10

History, we know, is apt to repeat herself, and to foist very old incidents upon us with only a slight change of costume. From the time of Xerxes downwards, we have seen generals playing the braggadocio at the outset of their campaigns, and conquering the enemy with the greatest ease in after-dinner speeches. But events are apt to be in disgusting discrepancy with the anticipations of the most ingenious tacticians; the difficulties of the expedition are ridiculously at variance with able calculations; the enemy has the impudence not to fall into confusion as had been reasonably expected of him; the mind of the gallant general begins to be distracted by news of intrigues against him at home, and, notwithstanding the handsome compliments he paid to Providence as his undoubted patron before setting out, there seems every probability that the *Te Deums* will be all on the other side.

So it fell out with Mr Dempster in his memorable campaign against the Tryanites. After all the premature triumph of the return from Elmstoke, the battle of the Evening Lecture had been lost;

455

the enemy was in possession of the field; and the utmost hope remaining was, that by a harassing guerilla warfare he might be driven to evacuate the country.

For some time this sort of warfare was kept up with considerable spirit. The shafts of Milby ridicule were made more formidable by being poisoned with calumny; and very ugly stories, narrated with circumstantial minuteness, were soon in circulation concerning Mr Tryan and his hearers, from which stories it was plainly deducible that Evangelicalism led by a necessary consequence to hypocritical indulgence in vice. Some old friendships were broken asunder, and there were near relations who felt that religious differences, unmitigated by any prospect of a legacy, were a sufficient ground for exhibiting their family antipathy. Mr Budd harangued his workmen, and threatened them with dismissal if they or their families were known to attend the evening lecture; and Mr Tomlinson, on discovering that his foreman was a rank Tryanite, blustered to a great extent, and would have cashiered that valuable functionary on the spot, if such a retributive procedure had not been inconvenient.

On the whole, however, at the end of a few months, the balance of substantial loss was on the side of the Anti-Tryanites. Mr Pratt, indeed, had lost a patient or two besides Mr Dempster's family; but as it was evident that Evangelicalism had not dried up the stream of his anecdote, or in the least altered his view of any lady's constitution, it is probable that a change accompanied by so few outward and visible signs, was rather the pretext than the ground of his dismissal in those additional cases. Mr Dunn was threatened with the loss of several good customers, Mrs Phipps and Mrs Lowme having set the example of ordering him to send in his bill; and the draper began to look forward to his next stock-taking with an anxiety which was but slightly mitigated by the parallel his wife suggested between his own case and that of Shadrach, Meshech, and Abednego, who were thrust into a burning fiery furnace. For, as he observed to her the next morning, with that perspicacity which belongs to the period of shaving, whereas their deliverance consisted in the fact that their linen and woollen goods were not consumed, his own deliverance lay in precisely the opposite result. But convenience, that admirable branch system from the main line of self-interest, makes us all fellow-helpers in spite of adverse resolutions. It is probable that no speculative or theological hatred would be ultimately strong enough to resist the persuasive power of convenience: that a latitudinarian baker, whose bread was honourably free from alum, would command the custom of any dyspeptic Puseyite; that an Arminian with the toothache would prefer a skilful Calvinistic dentist to a bungler stanch against the doctrines of Election and Final Perseverance, who would be likely to break the tooth in his head; and that a

Plymouth Brother, who had a well-furnished grocery-shop in a favourable vicinage, would occasionally have the pleasure of furnishing sugar or vinegar to orthodox families that found themselves unexpectedly 'out of' those indispensable commodities. In this persuasive power of convenience lay Mr Dunn's ultimate security from martyrdom. His drapery was the best in Milby; the comfortable use and wont of procuring satisfactory articles at a moment's notice proved too strong for Anti-Tryanite zeal; and the draper could soon look forward to his next stock-taking without the support of a Scriptural parallel.

On the other hand, Mr Dempster had lost his excellent client, Mr Jerome – a loss which galled him out of proportion to the mere monetary deficit it represented. The attorney loved money, but he loved power still better. He had always been proud of having early won the confidence of a conventicle-goer, and of being able to 'turn the prop of Salem round his thumb.' Like most other men, too, he had a certain kindness towards those who had employed him when he was only starting in life; and just as we do not like to part with an old weather-glass from our study, or a two-feet ruler that we have carried in our pocket ever since we began business, so Mr Dempster did not like having to erase his old client's name from the accustomed drawer in the bureau. Our habitual life is like a wall hung with pictures, which has been shone on by the suns of many years: take one of the pictures away, and it leaves a definite blank space, to which our eyes can never turn without a sensation of discomfort. Nay, the involuntary loss of any familiar object almost always brings a chill as from an evil omen; it seems to be the first finger-shadow of advancing death.

From all these causes combined, Mr Dempster could never think of his lost client without strong irritation, and the very sight of Mr Jerome passing in the street was wormwood to him.

One day, when the old gentleman was coming up Orchard Street on his roan mare, shaking the bridle, and tickling her flank with the whip as usual, though there was a perfect mutual understanding that she was not to quicken her pace, Janet happened to be on her own door-step, and he could not resist the temptation of stopping to speak to that 'nice little woman,' as he always called her, though she was taller than all the rest of his feminine acquaintances. Janet, in spite of her disposition to take her husband's part in all public matters, could bear no malice against her old friend; so they shook hands.

'Well, Mrs Dempster, I'm surry to my heart not to see you sometimes, that I am,' said Mr Jerome, in a plaintive tone. 'But if you've got any poor people as wants help, and you know's deservin', send 'em to me, send 'em to me, just the same.'

'Thank you, Mr Jerome, that I will. Good-bye.'

Janet made the interview as short as she could, but it was not short enough to escape the observation of her husband, who, as she feared, was on his mid-day return from his office at the other end of the street, and this offence of hers, in speaking to Mr Jerome, was the frequently recurring theme of Mr Dempster's objurgatory domestic eloquence.

Associating the loss of his old client with Mr Tryan's influence, Dempster began to know more distinctly why he hated the obnoxious curate. But a passionate hate, as well as a passionate love, demands some leisure and mental freedom. Persecution and revenge, like courtship and toadyism, will not prosper without a considerable expenditure of time and ingenuity, and these are not to spare with a man whose law-business and liver are both beginning to show unpleasant symptoms. Such was the disagreeable turn affairs were taking with Mr Dempster, and, like the general distracted by home intrigues, he was too much harassed himself to lay ingenious plans for harassing the enemy.

Meanwhile, the evening lecture drew larger and larger congregations; not, perhaps, attracting many from that select aristocratic circle in which the Lowmes and Pittmans were predominant, but winning the larger proportion of Mr Crewe's morning and afternoon hearers, and thinning Mr Stickney's evening audiences at Salem. Evangelicalism was making its way in Milby, and gradually diffusing its subtle odour into chambers that were bolted and barred against it. The movement, like all other religious 'revivals,' had a mixed effect. Religious ideas have the fate of melodies, which, once set afloat in the world, are taken up by all sorts of instruments, some of them woefully coarse, feeble, or out of tune, until people are in danger of crying out that the melody itself is detestable. It may be that some of Mr Tryan's hearers had gained a religious vocabulary rather than religious experience; that here and there a weaver's wife, who, a few months before, had been simply a silly slattern, was converted into that more complex nuisance, a silly and sanctimonious slattern; that the old Adam, with the pertinacity of middle age, continued to tell fibs behind the counter, notwithstanding the new Adam's addiction to Bible-reading and family prayer; that the children in the Paddiford Sunday-school had their memories crammed with phrases about the blood of cleansing, imputed righteousness, and justification by faith alone, which an experience lying principally in chuck-farthing, hop-scotch, parental slappings, and longings after unattainable lollipop, served rather to darken than to illustrate; and that at Milby, in those distant days, as in all other times and places where the mental atmosphere is changing, and men are inhaling the stimulus of new ideas, folly often mistook itself for wisdom, ignorance gave itself airs of knowledge, and selfishness, turning its eyes upward, called itself religion.

Nevertheless, Evangelicalism had brought into

palpable existence and operation in Milby society that idea of duty, that recognition of something to be lived for beyond the mere satisfaction of self, which is to the moral life what the addition of a great central ganglion is to animal life. No man can begin to mould himself on a faith or an idea without rising to a higher order of experience: a principle of subordination, of self-mastery, has been introduced into his nature; he is no longer a mere bundle of impressions, desires, and impulses. Whatever might be the weaknesses of the ladies who pruned the luxuriance of their lace and ribbons, cut out garments for the poor, distributed tracts, quoted Scripture, and defined the true Gospel, they had learned this – that there was a divine work to be done in life, a rule of goodness higher than the opinion of their neighbours; and if the notion of a heaven in reserve for themselves was a little too prominent, yet the theory of fitness for that heaven consisted in purity of heart, in Christ-like compassion, in the subduing of selfish desires. They might give the name of piety to much that was only puritanic egoism; they might call many things sin that were not sin; but they had at least the feeling that sin was to be avoided and resisted, and colour-blindness, which may mistake drab for scarlet, is better than total blindness which sees no distinction of colour at all. Miss Rebecca Linnet, in quiet attire, with a somewhat excessive solemnity of countenance, teaching at the Sunday School, visiting the poor, and striving after a standard of purity and goodness, had surely more moral loveliness than in those flaunting peony-days, when she had no other model than the costumes of the heroines in the circulating library. Miss Eliza Pratt, listening in rapt attention to Mr Tryan's evening lecture, no doubt found evangelical channels for vanity and egoism; but she was clearly in moral advance of Miss Phipps giggling under her feathers at old Mr Crewe's peculiarities of enunciation. And even elderly fathers and mothers, with minds, like Mrs Linnet's, too tough to imbibe much doctrine, were the better for having their hearts inclined towards the new preacher as a messenger from God. They became ashamed, perhaps, of their evil tempers, ashamed of their worldliness, ashamed of their trivial, futile past. The first condition of human goodness is something to love; the second, something to reverence. And this latter precious gift was brought to Milby by Mr Tryan and Evangelicalism.

Yes, the movement was good, though it had that mixture of folly and evil which often makes what is good an offence to feeble and fastidious minds, who want human actions and characters riddled through the sieve of their own ideas, before they can accord their sympathy or admiration. Such minds, I dare say, would have found Mr Tryan's character very much in need of that riddling process. The blessed work of helping the world forward, happily does not wait to be done by perfect men; and I should imagine that neither

Luther nor John Bunyan, for example, would have satisfied the modern demand for an ideal hero, who believes nothing but what is true, feels nothing but what is exalted, and does nothing but what is graceful. The real heroes, of God's making, are quite different: they have their natural heritage of love and conscience which they drew in with their mother's milk; they know one or two of those deep spiritual truths which are only to be won by long wrestling with their own sins and their own sorrows; they have earned faith and strength so far as they have done genuine work: but the rest is dry barren theory, blank prejudice, vague hearsay. Their insight is blended with mere opinion; their sympathy is perhaps confined in narrow conduits of doctrine, instead of flowing forth with the freedom of a stream that blesses every weed in its course; obstinacy or self-assertion will often inter-fuse itself with their grandest impulses; and their very deeds of self-sacrifice are sometimes only the rebound of a passionate egoism. So it was with Mr Tryan: and any one looking at him with the bird's-eye glance of a critic might perhaps say that he made the mistake of identifying Christianity with a too narrow doctrinal system; that he saw God's work too exclusively in antagonism to the world, the flesh, and the devil; that his intellectual culture was too limited – and so on; making Mr Tryan the text for a wise discourse on the characteristics of the Evangelical school in his day.

But I am not poised at that lofty height. I am

on the level and in the press with him, as he struggles his way along the stony road, through the crowd of unloving fellow-men. He is stumbling, perhaps; his heart now beats fast with dread, now heavily with anguish; his eyes are sometimes dim with tears, which he makes haste to dash away; he pushes manfully on, with fluctuating faith and courage, with a sensitive failing body; at last he falls, the struggle is ended, and the crowd closes over the space he has left.

'One of the Evangelical clergy, a disciple of Venn,' says the critic from his bird's-eye station. 'Not a remarkable specimen; the anatomy and habits of his species have been determined long ago.'

Yet surely, surely the only true knowledge of our fellow-man is that which enables us to feel with him – which gives us a fine ear for the heart-pulses that are beating under the mere clothes of circumstance and opinion. Our subtlest analysis of schools and sects must miss the essential truth, unless it be lit up by the love that sees in all forms of human thought and work, the life and death struggles of separate human beings.

CHAPTER 11

Mr Tryan's most unfriendly observers were obliged to admit that he gave himself no rest. Three sermons on Sunday, a night-school for young men on Tuesday, a cottage-lecture on Thursday, addresses to school-teachers, and catechizing of school-children, with pastoral visits, multiplying as his influence extended beyond his own district of Paddiford Common, would have been enough to tax severely the powers of a much stronger man. Mr Pratt remonstrated with him on his imprudence, but could not prevail on him so far to economize time and strength as to keep a horse. On some ground or other, which his friends found difficult to explain to themselves, Mr Tryan seemed bent on wearing himself out. His enemies were at no loss to account for such a course. The Evangelical curate's selfishness was clearly of too bad a kind to exhibit itself after the ordinary manner of a sound, respectable selfishness. 'He wants to get the reputation of a saint,' said one; 'He's eaten up with spiritual pride,' said another; 'He's got his eye on some fine living, and wants to creep up the bishop's sleeve,' said a third.

Mr Stickney, of Salem, who considered all voluntary discomfort as a remnant of the legal spirit, pronounced a severe condemnation on this self-neglect, and expressed his fear that Mr Tryan was still far from having attained true Christian liberty. Good Mr Jerome eagerly seized this doctrinal view of the subject as a means of enforcing the suggestions of his own benevolence; and one cloudy afternoon, in the end of November, he mounted his roan mare with the determination of riding to Paddiford and 'arguing' the point with Mr Tryan.

The old gentleman's face looked very mournful as he rode along the dismal Paddiford lanes, between rows of grimy houses, darkened with handlooms, while the black dust was whirled about him by the cold November wind. He was thinking of the object which had brought him on this afternoon ride, and his thoughts, according to his habit when alone, found vent every now and then in audible speech. It seemed to him, as his eyes rested on this scene of Mr Tryan's labours, that he could understand the clergyman's self-privation without resorting to Mr Stickney's theory of defective spiritual enlightenment. Do not philosophic doctors tell us that we are unable to discern so much as a tree, except by an unconscious cunning which combines many past and separate sensations; that no one sense is independent of another, so that in the dark we can hardly taste a fricassee, or tell whether our

467

pipe is alight or not, and the most intelligent boy, if accommodated with claws or hoofs instead of fingers, would be likely to remain on the lowest form? If so, it is easy to understand that our discernment of men's motives must depend on the completeness of the elements we can bring from our own susceptibility and our own experience. See to it, friend, before you pronounce a too hasty judgment, that your own moral sensibilities are not of a hoofed or clawed character. The keenest eye will not serve, unless you have the delicate fingers, with their subtle nerve filaments, which elude scientific lenses, and lose themselves in the invisible world of human sensations.

As for Mr Jerome, he drew the elements of his moral vision from the depths of his veneration and pity. If he himself felt so much for these poor things to whom life was so dim and meagre, what must the clergyman feel who had undertaken before God to be their shepherd?

'Ah!' he whispered, interruptedly, 'it's too big a load for his conscience, poor man! He wants to mek himself their brother, like; can't abide to preach to the fastin' on a full stomach. Ah! he's better nor we are, that's it – he's a deal better nor we are.'

Here Mr Jerome shook his bridle violently, and looked up with an air of moral courage, as if Mr Stickney had been present, and liable to take offence at this conclusion. A few minutes more brought him in front of Mrs Wagstaff's, where Mr

Tryan lodged. He had often been here before, so that the contrast between this ugly square brick house, with its shabby bit of grass-plot, stared at all round by cottage windows, and his own pretty white home, set in a paradise of orchard, and garden, and pasture, was not new to him; but he felt it with fresh force to-day, as he slowly fastened his roan by the bridle to the wooden paling, and knocked at the door. Mr Tryan was at home, and sent to request that Mr Jerome would walk up into his study, as the fire was out in the parlour below.

At the mention of a clergyman's study, perhaps, your too active imagination conjures up a perfect snuggery, where the general air of comfort is rescued from a secular character by strong ecclesiastical suggestions in the shape of the furniture, the pattern of the carpet, and the prints on the wall; where, if a nap is taken, it is in an easy-chair with a Gothic back, and the very feet rest on a warm and velvety simulation of church windows; where the pure art of rigorous English Protestantism smiles above the mantel-piece in the portrait of an eminent bishop, or a refined Anglican taste is indicated by a German print from Overbeck; where the walls are lined with choice divinity in sombre binding, and the light is softened by a screen of boughs with a grey church in the background.

But I must beg you to dismiss all such scenic prettinesses, suitable as they may be to a clergyman's character and complexion; for I have to confess that Mr Tryan's study was a very ugly little room indeed, with an ugly slap-dash pattern on the walls, an ugly carpet on the floor, and an ugly view of cottage-roofs and cabbage-gardens from the window. His own person, his writing-table, and his book-case, were the only objects in the room that had the slightest air of refinement; and the sole provision for comfort was a clumsy straight-backed arm-chair, covered with faded chintz. The man who could live in such a room, unconstrained by poverty, must either have his vision fed from within by an intense passion, or he must have chosen that least attractive form of self-mortification which wears no haircloth and has no meagre days, but accepts the vulgar, the commonplace and the ugly, whenever the highest duty seems to lie among them.

'Mr Tryan, I hope you'll excuse me disturbin' on you,' said Mr Jerome. 'But I'd summat partickler to say.'

'You don't disturb me at all, Mr Jerome; I'm very glad to have a visit from you,' said Mr Tryan, shaking him heartily by the hand, and offering him the chintz-covered 'easy' chair; 'it is some time since I've had an opportunity of seeing you, except on a Sunday.'

'Ah! sir! your time's so tecken up, I'm well awear o' that; it's not only what you hev to do, but it's goin' about from place to place; an' you don't keep

470

a hoss, Mr Tryan. You don't tek care enough o' yourself – you don't indeed, an' that's what I come to talk to y' about.'

'That's very good of you, Mr Jerome; but I assure you I think walking does me no harm. It is rather a relief to me after speaking or writing. You know I have no great circuit to make. The farthest distance I have to walk is to Milby church, and if ever I want a horse on a Sunday, I hire Radley's, who lives not many hundred yards from me.'

'Well, but now! the winter's comin' on, an' you'll get wet i' your feet, an' Pratt tells me as your constitution's dillicate, as anybody may see, for the matter o' that, wi'out bein' a doctor. An' this is the light I look at it in, Mr Tryan: who's to fill up your place, if you was to be disabled, as I may say? Consider what a valyable life yourn is. You've begun a great work i' Milby, an' so you might carry't on, if you'd your health and strength. The more care you tek o' yourself, the longer you'll live, belike, God willing, to do good to your fellow-creturs.'

'Why, my dear Mr Jerome, I think I should not be a long-lived man in any case; and if I were to take care of myself under the pretext of doing more good, I should very likely die and leave nothing done after all.'

'Well! but keepin' a hoss wouldn't hinder you from workin'. It 'ud help you to do more, though Pratt says as it's usin' your voice so constant as

471

does you the most harm. Now, isn't it – I'm no scholard, Mr Tryan, an' I'm not a-goin' to dictate to you – but isn't it a'most a-killin' o' yourself, to go on a' that way beyond your strength? We musn't fling wer lives away.'

'No, not fling them away lightly, but we are permitted to lay down our lives in a right cause. There are many duties, as you know, Mr Jerome, which stand before taking care of our own lives.'

'Ah! I can't arguy wi' you, Mr Tryan; but what I wanted to say 's this – There's my little chacenut hoss; I should tek it quite a kindness if you'd hev him through the winter an' ride him. I've thought o' sellin' him a maeny times, for Mrs Jerome can't abide him; and what do I want wi' two nags? But I'm fond o' the little chacenut, an' I shouldn't like to sell him. So if you'll only ride him for me, you'll do me a kindness – you will indeed, Mr Tryan.'

'Thank you, Mr Jerome. I promise you to ask for him, when I feel that I want a nag. There is no man I would more gladly be indebted to than you; but at present I would rather not have a horse. I should ride him very little, and it would be an inconvenience to me to keep him rather than otherwise.'

Mr Jerome looked troubled and hesitating, as if he had something on his mind that would not readily shape itself into words. At last he said, 'You'll excuse me, Mr Tryan, I wouldn't be teckin'

472

a liberty, but I know what great claims you hev on you as a clergyman. Is it th' expense, Mr Tryan? is it the money?'

'No, my dear sir. I have much more than a single man needs. My way of living is quite of my own choosing, and I am doing nothing but what I feel bound to do, quite apart from money considerations. We cannot judge for one another, you know; we have each our peculiar weaknesses and temptations. I quite admit that it might be right for another man to allow himself more luxuries, and I assure you I think it no superiority in myself to do without them. On the contrary, if my heart were less rebellious, and if I were less liable to temptation, I should not need that sort of self-denial. But,' added Mr Tryan, holding out his hand to Mr Jerome, 'I understand your kindness, and bless you for it. If I want a horse, I shall ask for the chestnut.'

Mr Jerome was obliged to rest contented with this promise, and rode home sorrowfully, reproaching himself with not having said one thing he meant to say when setting out, and with having 'clean forgot' the arguments he had intended to quote from Mr Stickney.

Mr Jerome's was not the only mind that was seriously disturbed by the idea that the curate was over-working himself. There were tender women's hearts in which anxiety about the state of his affections was beginning to be merged in anxiety about the state of his health. Miss Eliza

Pratt had at one time passed through much sleepless cogitation on the possibility of Mr Tryan's being attached to some lady at a distance – at Laxeter, perhaps, where he had formerly held a curacy; and her fine eyes kept close watch lest any symptom of engaged affections on his part should escape her. It seemed an alarming fact that his handkerchiefs were beautifully marked with hair, until she reflected that he had an unmarried sister of whom he spoke with much affection as his father's companion and comforter. Besides, Mr Tryan had never paid any distant visit, except one for a few days to his father, and no hint escaped him of his intending to take a house, or change his mode of living. No! he could not be engaged, though he might have been disappointed. But this latter misfortune is one from which a devoted clergyman has been known to recover, by the aid of a fine pair of grey eyes that beam on him with affectionate reverence. Before Christmas, however, her cogitations began to take another turn. She heard her father say very confidently that 'Tryan was consumptive, and if he didn't take more care of himself, his life would not be worth a year's purchase;' and shame at having speculated on suppositions that were likely to prove so false, sent poor Miss Eliza's feelings with all the stronger impetus into the one channel of sorrowful alarm at the prospect of losing the pastor who had opened to her a new life of piety and self-subjection. It is a sad weakness in us, after all, that the thought of a man's death hallows him anew to us; as if life were not sacred too – as if it were comparatively a light thing to fail in love and reverence to the brother who has to climb the whole toilsome steep with us, and all our tears and tenderness were due to the one who is spared that hard journey.

The Miss Linnets, too, were beginning to take a new view of the future, entirely uncoloured by jealousy of Miss Eliza Pratt.

'Did you notice,' said Mary, one afternoon when Mrs Pettifer was taking tea with them – 'did you notice that short dry cough of Mr Tryan's yesterday? I think he looks worse and worse every week, and I only wish I knew his sister; I would write to her about him. I'm sure something should be done to make him give up part of his work, and he will listen to no one here.'

'Ah,' said Mrs Pettifer, 'it's a thousand pities his father and sister can't come and live with him, if he isn't to marry. But I wish with all my heart he could have taken to some nice woman as would have made a comfortable home for him. I used to think he might take to Eliza Pratt; she's a good girl, and very pretty; but I see no likelihood of it now.'

'No, indeed,' said Rebecca, with some emphasis; 'Mr Tryan's heart is not for any woman to win; it is all given to his work; and I could never wish to see him with a young inexperienced wife who would be a drag on him instead of a helpmate.'

'He'd need have somebody, young or old,' observed Mrs Linnet, 'to see as he wears a flannel wescoat, an' changes his stockins when he comes in. It's my opinion he's got that cough wi' sittin' i' wet shoes an' stockins; an' that Mrs Wagstaff's a poor addle-headed thing; she doesn't half tek care on him.'

'O, mother!' said Rebecca, 'she's a very pious woman. And I'm sure she thinks it too great a privilege to have Mr Tryan with her, not to do the best she can to make him comfortable. She can't help her rooms being shabby.'

'I've nothing to say again' her piety, my dear; but I know very well I shouldn't like her to cook my victual. When a man comes in hungry an' tired, piety won't feed him, I reckon. Hard carrots 'ull lie heavy on his stomach, piety or no piety. I called in one day when she was dishin' up Mr Tryan's dinner, an' I could see the potatoes was as watery as watery. It's right enough to be speritial – I'm no enemy to that; but I like my potatoes mealy. I don't see as anybody 'ull go to heaven the sooner for not digestin' their dinner – providin' they don't die sooner, as mayhap Mr Tryan will, poor dear man!'

'It will be a heavy day for us all when that comes to pass,' said Mrs Pettifer. 'We shall never get anybody to fill up *that* gap. There's the new clergyman that's just come to Shepperton – Mr Parry; I saw him the other day at Mrs Bond's. He may be a very good man, and a fine preacher; they

476

say he is; but I thought to myself, what a difference between him and Mr Tryan! He's a sharp-sort-of-looking man, and hasn't that feeling way with him that Mr Tryan has. What is so wonderful to me in Mr Tryan is the way he puts himself on a level with one, and talks to one like a brother. I'm never afraid of telling him anything. He never seems to look down on anybody. He knows how to lift up those that are cast down, if ever man did.'

'Yes,' said Mary. 'And when I see all the faces turned up to him in Paddiford church, I often think how hard it would be for any clergyman who had to come after him; he has made the people love him so.'

CHAPTER 12

In her occasional visits to her near neighbour Mrs Pettifer, too old a friend to be shunned because she was a Tryanite, Janet was obliged sometimes to hear allusions to Mr Tryan, and even to listen to his praises, which she usually met with playful incredulity.

'Ah, well,' she answered one day, 'I like dear old Mr Crewe and his pipes a great deal better than your Mr Tryan and his Gospel. When I was a little toddle, Mr and Mrs Crewe used to let me play about in their garden, and have a swing between the great elm-trees, because mother had no garden. I like people who are kind; kindness is my religion; and that's the reason I like you, dear Mrs Pettifer, though you *are* a Tryanite.'

'But that's Mr Tryan's religion too – at least partly. There's nobody can give himself up more to doing good amongst the poor; and he thinks of their bodies too, as well as their souls.'

'O yes, yes; but then he talks about faith and grace, and all that, making people believe they are better than others, and that God loves them more than He does the rest of the world. I know he has

478

put a great deal of that into Sally Martin's head, and it has done her no good at all. She was as nice, honest, patient a girl as need be before; and now she fancies she has new light and new wisdom. I don't like those notions.'

'You mistake him, indeed you do, my dear Mrs Dempster; I wish you'd go and hear him preach.'

'Hear him preach! Why, you wicked woman, you would persuade me to disobey my husband, would you? O, shocking! I shall run away from you. Good-bye.'

A few days after this conversation, however, Janet went to Sally Martin's about three o'clock in the afternoon. The pudding that had been sent in for herself and 'Mammy,' struck her as just the sort of delicate morsel the poor consumptive girl would be likely to fancy, and in her usual impulsive way she had started up from the dinner-table at once, put on her bonnet, and set off with a covered plateful to the neighbouring street. When she entered the house there was no one to be seen; but in the little side-room where Sally lay, Janet heard a voice. It was one she had not heard before, but she immediately guessed it to be Mr Tryan's. Her first impulse was to set down her plate and go away, but Mrs Martin might not be in, and then there would be no one to give Sally that delicious bit of pudding. So she stood still, and was obliged to hear what Mr Tryan was saying. He was interrupted by one of the invalid's violent fits of coughing.

'It is very hard to bear, is it not?' he said, when she was still again. 'Yet God seems to support you under it wonderfully. Pray for me, Sally, that I may have strength too when the hour of great suffering comes. It is one of my worst weaknesses to shrink from bodily pain, and I think the time is perhaps not far off when I shall have to bear what you are bearing. But now I have tired you. We have talked enough. Good-bye.'

Janet was surprised, and forgot her wish not to encounter Mr Tryan; the tone and the words were so unlike what she had expected to hear. There was none of the self-satisfied unction of the teacher, quoting, or exhorting, or expounding, for the benefit of the hearer, but a simple appeal for help, a confession of weakness. Mr Tryan had his deeply-felt troubles, then? Mr Tryan, too, like herself, knew what it was to tremble at a foreseen trial – to shudder at an impending burden, heavier than he felt able to bear?

The most brilliant deed of virtue could not have inclined Janet's goodwill towards Mr Tryan so much as this fellowship in suffering, and the softening thought was in her eyes when he appeared in the doorway, pale, weary, and depressed. The sight of Janet standing there with the entire absence of self-consciousness which belongs to a new and vivid impression, made him start and pause a little. Their eyes met, and they looked at each other gravely for a few moments. Then they bowed, and Mr Tryan passed out.

There is a power in the direct glance of a sincere and loving human soul, which will do more to dissipate prejudice and kindle charity than the most elaborate arguments. The fullest exposition of Mr Tryan's doctrine might not have sufficed to convince Janet that he had not an odious self-complacency in believing himself a peculiar child of God; but one direct, pathetic look of his had dissociated him with that conception for ever.

This happened late in the autumn, not long before Sally Martin died. Janet mentioned her new impression to no one, for she was afraid of arriving at a still more complete contradiction of her former ideas. We have all of us considerable regard for our past self, and are not fond of casting reflections on that respected individual by a total negation of his opinions. Janet could no longer think of Mr Tryan without sympathy, but she still shrank from the idea of becoming his hearer and admirer. That was a reversal of the past which was as little accordant with her inclination as her circumstances.

And indeed this interview with Mr Tryan was soon thrust into the background of poor Janet's memory by the daily thickening miseries of her life.

CHAPTER 13

The loss of Mr Jerome as a client proved only the beginning of annoyances to Dempster. That old gentleman had in him the vigorous remnant of an energy and perseverance which had created his own fortune; and being, as I have hinted, given to chewing the cud of a righteous indignation with considerable relish, he was determined to carry on his retributive war against the persecuting attorney. Having some influence with Mr Pryme, who was one of the most substantial rate-payers in the neighbouring parish of Dingley, and who had himself a complex and long-standing private account with Dempster, Mr Jerome stirred up this gentleman to an investigation of some suspicious points in the attorney's conduct of the parish affairs. The natural consequence was a personal quarrel between Dempster and Mr Pryme; the client demanded his account, and then followed the old story of an exorbitant lawyer's bill, with the unpleasant anti-climax of taxing.

These disagreeables, extending over many months, ran along side by side with the pressing business of Mr Armstrong's lawsuit, which was threatening to take a turn rather depreciatory of Dempster's professional prevision; and it is not surprising that, being thus kept in a constant state of irritated excitement about his own affairs, he had little time for the further exhibition of his public spirit, or for rallying the forlorn hope of sound churchmanship against cant and hypocrisy. Not a few persons who had a grudge against him, began to remark, with satisfaction, that 'Dempster's luck was forsaking him;' particularly Mrs Linnet, who thought she saw distinctly the gradual ripening of a providential scheme, whereby a just retribution would be wrought on the man who had deprived her of Pye's Croft. On the other hand, Dempster's well-satisfied clients, who were of opinion that the punishment of his wickedness might conveniently be deferred to another world, noticed with some concern that he was drinking more than ever, and that both his temper and his driving were becoming more furious. Unhappily those additional glasses of brandy, that exasperation of loud-tongued abuse, had other effects than any that entered into the contemplation of anxious clients: they were the little superadded symbols that were perpetually raising the sum of home misery.

Poor Janet! how heavily the months rolled on for her, laden with fresh sorrows as the summer passed into autumn, the autumn into winter, and the winter into spring again. Every feverish morning, with its blank listlessness and despair, seemed more hateful than the last; every coming night more impossible to brave without arming herself in leaden stupor. The morning light brought no gladness to her: it seemed only to throw its glare on what had happened in the dim candle-light – on the cruel man seated immovable in drunken obstinacy by the dead fire and dying lights in the dining-room, rating her in harsh tones, reiterating old reproaches – or on a hideous blank of something unremembered, something that must have made that dark bruise on her shoulder, which aches as she dresses herself.

Do you wonder how it was that things had come to this pass – what offence Janet had committed in the early years of marriage to rouse the brutal hatred of this man? The seeds of things are very small: the hours that lie between sunrise and the gloom of midnight are travelled through by tiniest markings of the clock: and Janet, looking back along the fifteen years of her married life, hardly knew how or where this total misery began; hardly knew when the sweet wedded love and hope that had set for ever had ceased to make a twilight of memory and relenting, before the oncoming of the utter dark.

Old Mrs Dempster thought she saw the true beginning of it all in Janet's want of housekeeping skill and exactness. 'Janet,' she said to herself, 'was always running about doing things for other people, and neglecting her own house. That provokes a man: what use is it for a woman to be loving, and making a fuss with her husband, if she doesn't take care and keep his home just as he likes it; if she isn't at hand when he wants anything done; if she doesn't attend to all his wishes, let them be as small as they may? That was what I did when I was a wife, though I didn't make half so much fuss about loving my husband. Then, Janet had no children.' . . . Ah! there Mammy Dempster had touched a true spring, not perhaps of her son's cruelty, but of half Janet's misery. If she had had babes to rock to sleep – little ones to kneel in their nightdress and say their prayers at her knees – sweet boys and girls to put their young arms round her neck and kiss away her tears, her poor hungry heart would have been fed with strong love, and might never have needed that fiery poison to still its cravings. Mighty is the force of motherhood! says the great tragic poetto us across the ages, finding, as usual, the simplest words for the sublimest fact – δεινόν τὸ τίκτειν ἐστίν. It transforms all things by its vital heat: it turns timidity into fierce courage, and dreadless defiance into tremulous submission; it turns thoughtlessness into foresight, and yet stills all anxiety into calm content; it makes self-ishness become self-denial, and gives even to hard vanity the glance of admiring love. Yes; if Janet had been a mother, she might have been saved from much sin, and therefore from much of her sorrow.

But do not believe that it was anything either

present or wanting in poor Janet that formed the motive of her husband's cruelty. Cruelty, like every other vice, requires no motive outside itself – it only requires opportunity. You do not suppose Dempster had any motive for drinking beyond the craving for drink; the presence of brandy was the only necessary condition. And an unloving, tyrannous, brutal man needs no motive to prompt his cruelty; he needs only the perpetual presence of a woman he can call his own. A whole park full of tame or timid-eyed animals to torment at his will would not serve him so well to glut his lust of torture; they could not *feel* as one woman does; they could not throw out the keen retort which whets the edge of hatred.

Janet's bitterness would overflow in ready words; she was not to be made meek by cruelty; she would repent of nothing in the face of injustice, though she was subdued in a moment by a word or a look that recalled the old days of fondness; and in times of comparative calm would often recover her sweet woman's habit of caressing playful affection. But such days were become rare, and poor Janet's soul was kept like a vexed sea, tossed by a new storm before the old waves have fallen. Proud, angry resistance and sullen endurance were now almost the only alternations she knew. She would bear it all proudly to the world, but proudly towards him too; her woman's weakness might shriek a cry for pity under a heavy blow, but voluntarily she would do nothing to mollify him, unless he first relented.

What had she ever done to him but love him too well – but believe in him too foolishly? He had no pity on her tender flesh; he could strike the soft neck he had once asked to kiss. Yet she would not admit her wretchedness; she had married him blindly, and she would bear it out to the terrible end, whatever that might be. Better this misery than the blank that lay for her outside her married home.

But there was one person who heard all the plaints and all the outbursts of bitterness and despair which Janet was never tempted to pour into any other ear; and alas! in her worst moments, Janet would throw out wild reproaches against that patient listener. For the wrong that rouses our angry passions finds only a medium in us; it passes through us like a vibration, and we inflict what we have suffered.

Mrs Raynor saw too clearly all through the winter that things were getting worse in Orchard Street. She had evidence enough of it in Janet's visits to her; and, though her own visits to her daughter were so timed that she saw little of Dempster personally, she noticed many indications not only that he was drinking to greater excess, but that he was beginning to lose that physical power of supporting excess which had long been the admiration of such fine spirits as Mr Tomlinson. It seemed as if Dempster had some consciousness of this – some new distrust of himself; for, before winter was over, it was observed that he had renounced his habit of driving out alone, and was never seen in his gig without a servant by his side.

Nemesis is lame, but she is of colossal stature, like the gods; and sometimes, while her sword is not yet unsheathed, she stretches out her huge left arm and grasps her victim. The mighty hand is invisible, but the victim totters under the dire clutch.

The various symptoms that things were getting worse with the Dempsters afforded Milby gossip something new to say on an old subject. Mrs Dempster, every one remarked, looked more miserable than ever, though she kept up the old pretence of being happy and satisfied. She was scarcely ever seen, as she used to be, going about on her good-natured errands; and even old Mrs Crewe, who had always been wilfully blind to anything wrong in her favourite Janet, was obliged to admit that she had not seemed like herself lately. 'The poor thing's out of health,' said the kind little old lady, in answer to all gossip about Janet; 'her headaches always were bad, and I know what headaches are; why, they make one quite delirious sometimes.' Mrs Phipps, for her part, declared she would never accept an invitation to Dempster's again; it was getting so very disagreeable to go there, Mrs Dempster was often 'so strange.' To be sure, there were dreadful stories about the way Dempster used his wife; but in Mrs Phipps's opinion, it was six of one and half-a-dozen of the other. Mrs Dempster had never been like other women: she had always a flighty way with her, carrying parcels of snuff to old Mrs Tooke, and going to drink tea with Mrs Brinley, the carpenter's wife; and then never taking care of her clothes, always wearing the same things week-day or Sunday. A man has a poor look-out with a wife of that sort. Mr Phipps, amiable and laconic, wondered how it was women were so fond of running each other down.

Mr Pratt, having been called in provisionally to a patient of Mr Pilgrim's in a case of compound fracture, observed in a friendly colloquy with his brother surgeon the next day,

'So Dempster has left off driving himself, I see; he won't end with a broken neck after all. You'll have a case of meningitis and delirium tremens instead.'

'Ah,' said Mr Pilgrim, 'he can hardly stand it much longer at the rate he's going on, one would think. He's been confoundedly cut up about that business of Armstrong's, I fancy. It may do him some harm, perhaps, but Dempster must have feathered his nest pretty well; he can afford to lose a little business.'

'His business will outlast him, that's pretty clear,' said Pratt; 'he'll run down like a watch with a broken spring one of these days.'

Another prognostic of evil to Dempster came at the beginning of March. For then 'little Mamsey' died – died suddenly. The housemaid found her seated motionless in her arm-chair, her knitting fallen down, and the tortoise-shell cat reposing on it unreproved. The little white old woman had ended her wintry age of patient sorrow, believing to the last that 'Robert might have been a good husband as he had been a good son.'

When the earth was thrown on Mamsey's coffin, and the son, in crape scarf and hatband, turned away homeward, his good angel, lingering with outstretched wing on the edge of the grave, cast one despairing look after him, and took flight for ever.

CHAPTER 14

The last week in March – three weeks after old Mrs Dempster died – occurred the unpleasant winding-up of affairs between Dempster and Mr Pryme, and under this additional source of irritation the attorney's diurnal drunkenness had taken on its most ill-tempered and brutal phase. On the Friday morning, before setting out for Rotherby, he told his wife that he had invited 'four men' to dinner at half-past six that evening. The previous night had been a terrible one for Janet, and when her husband broke his grim morning silence to say these few words, she was looking so blank and listless that he added in a loud sharp key, 'Do you hear what I say? or must I tell the cook?' She started, and said 'Yes, I hear.'

'Then mind and have a dinner provided, and don't go mooning about like Crazy Jane.'

Half an hour afterwards Mrs Raynor, quietly busy in her kitchen with her household labours – for she had only a little twelve-year-old girl as a servant – heard with trembling the rattling of the garden gate and the opening of the outer door. She knew the step, and in one short moment she lived beforehand through the coming scene. She hurried out of the kitchen, and there in the passage, as she had felt, stood Janet, her eyes worn as if by night-long watching, her dress careless, her step languid. No cheerful morning greeting to her mother – no kiss. She turned into the parlour, and, seating herself on the sofa opposite her mother's chair, looked vacantly at the walls and furniture until the corners of her mouth began to tremble, and her dark eyes filled with tears that fell unwiped down her cheeks. The mother sat silently opposite to her, afraid to speak. She felt sure there was nothing new the matter – sure that the torrent of words would come sooner or later.

'Mother! why don't you speak to me?' Janet burst out at last; 'you don't care about my suffering; you are blaming me because I feel – because I am miserable.'

'My child, I am not blaming you – my heart is bleeding for you. Your head is bad this morning – you have had a bad night. Let me make you a cup of tea now. Perhaps you didn't like your breakfast.'

'Yes, that is what you always think, mother. It is the old story, you think. You don't ask me what it is I have had to bear. You are tired of hearing me. You are cruel, like the rest; every one is cruel in this world. Nothing but blame – blame – blame;

never any pity. God is cruel to have sent me into the world to bear all this misery.'

'Janet, Janet, don't say so. It is not for us to judge; we must submit; we must be thankful for the gift of life.'

'Thankful for life? Why should I be thankful? God has made me with a heart to feel, and He has sent me nothing but misery. How could I help it? How could I know what would come? Why didn't you tell me, mother? – why did you let me marry? You knew what brutes men could be; and there's no help for me – no hope. I can't kill myself; I've tried; but I can't leave this world and go to another. There may be no pity for me there, as there is none here.'

'Janet, my child, there *is* pity. Have I ever done anything but love you? And there is pity in God. Hasn't He put pity into your heart for many a poor sufferer? Where did it come from, if not from Him?'

Janet's nervous irritation now broke out into sobs instead of complainings; and her mother was thankful, for after that crisis there would very likely come relenting, and tenderness, and comparative calm. She went out to make some tea, and when she returned with the tray in her hands, Janet had dried her eyes and now turned them towards her mother with a faint attempt to smile; but the poor face, in its sad blurred beauty, looked all the more piteous.

'Mother will insist upon her tea,' she said, 'and

I really think I can drink a cup. But I must go home directly, for there are people coming to dinner. Could you go with me and help me, mother?'

Mrs Raynor was always ready to do that. She went to Orchard Street with Janet, and remained with her through the day – comforted, as evening approached, to see her become more cheerful and willing to attend to her toilette. At half-past five everything was in order; Janet was dressed; and when the mother had kissed her and said good-bye, she could not help pausing a moment in sorrowful admiration at the tall rich figure, looking all the grander for the plainness of the deep mourning dress, and the noble face with its massy folds of black hair, made matronly by a simple white cap. Janet had that enduring beauty which belongs to pure majestic outline and depth of tint. Sorrow and neglect leave their traces on such beauty, but it thrills us to the last, like a glorious Greek temple, which, for all the loss it has suffered from time and barbarous hands, has gained a solemn history, and fills our imagination the more because it is incomplete to the sense.

It was six o'clock before Dempster returned from Rotherby. He had evidently drunk a great deal, and was in an angry humour; but Janet, who had gathered some little courage and forbearance from the consciousness that she had done her best to-day, was determined to speak pleasantly to him.

'Robert,' she said gently, as she saw him seat himself in the dining-room in his dusty snuffy clothes, and take some documents out of his pocket, 'will you not wash and change your dress? It will refresh you.'

'Leave me alone, will you?' said Dempster, in his most brutal tone.

'Do change your coat and waistcoat, they are so dusty. I've laid all your things out ready.'

'O, you have, have you?' After a few minutes he rose very deliberately and walked up-stairs into his bedroom. Janet had often been scolded before for not laying out his clothes, and she thought now, not without some wonder, that this attention of hers had brought him to compliance.

Presently he called out, 'Janet!' and she went up-stairs.

'Here! Take that!' he said, as soon as she reached the door, flinging at her the coat she had laid out. 'Another time, leave me to do as I please, will you?'

The coat, flung with great force, only brushed her shoulder, and fell some distance within the drawing-room, the door of which stood open just opposite. She hastily retreated as she saw the waistcoat coming, and one by one the clothes she had laid out were all flung into the drawing-room.

Janet's face flushed with anger, and for the first time in her life her resentment overcame the long-cherished pride that made her hide her griefs from the world. There are moments when by some strange impulse we contradict our past selves – fatal moments, when a fit of passion, like a lava stream, lays low the work of half our lives. Janet thought, 'I will not pick up the clothes; they shall lie there until the visitors come, and he shall be ashamed of himself.'

There was a knock at the door, and she made haste to seat herself in the drawing-room, lest the servant should enter and remove the clothes, which were lying half on the table and half on the ground. Mr Lowme entered with a less familiar visitor, a client of Dempster's, and the next moment Dempster himself came in.

His eye fell at once on the clothes, and then turned for an instant with a devilish glance of concentrated hatred on Janet, who, still flushed and excited, affected unconsciousness. After shaking hands with his visitors he immediately rang the bell.

'Take those clothes away,' he said to the servant, not looking at Janet again.

During dinner, she kept up her assumed air of indifference, and tried to seem in high spirits, laughing and talking more than usual. In reality, she felt as if she had defied a wild beast within the four walls of his den, and he was crouching backward in preparation for his deadly spring.

Dempster affected to take no notice of her, talked obstreperously, and drank steadily.

About eleven the party dispersed, with the exception of Mr Budd, who had joined them after dinner, and appeared disposed to stay drinking a little longer. Janet began to hope that he would stay long enough for Dempster to become heavy and stupid, and so to fall asleep down stairs, which was a rare but occasional ending of his nights. She told the servants to sit up no longer, and she herself undressed and went to bed, trying to cheat her imagination into the belief that the day was ended for her. But when she lay down, she became more intensely awake than ever. Everything she had taken this evening seemed only to stimulate her senses and her apprehensions to new vividness. Her heart beat violently, and she heard every sound in the house.

At last, when it was twelve, she heard Mr Budd go out; she heard the door slam. Dempster had not moved. Was he asleep? Would he forget? The minute seemed long, while, with a quickening pulse, she was on the stretch to catch every sound.

'Janet!' The loud jarring voice seemed to strike her like a hurled weapon.

'Janet!' he called again, moving out of the dining-room to the foot of the stairs.

There was a pause of a minute.

'If you don't come, I'll kill you.'

Another pause, and she heard him turn back

497

into the dining-room. He was gone for a light – perhaps for a weapon. Perhaps he *would* kill her. Let him. Life was as hideous as death. For years she had been rushing on to some unknown but certain horror; and now she was close upon it. She was almost glad. She was in a state of flushed feverish defiance that neutralized her woman's terrors.

She heard his heavy step on the stairs; she saw the slowly advancing light. Then she saw the tall massive figure, and the heavy face, now fierce with drunken rage. He had nothing but the candle in his hand. He set it down on the table, and advanced close to the bed.

'So you think you'll defy me, do you? We'll see how long that will last. Get up, madam; out of bed this instant!'

In the close presence of the dreadful man – of this huge crushing force, armed with savage will – poor Janet's desperate defiance all forsook her, and her terrors came back. Trembling she got up, and stood helpless in her night-dress before her husband.

He seized her with his heavy grasp by the shoulder, and pushed her before him.

'I'll cool your hot spirit for you! I'll teach you to brave me!'

Slowly he pushed her along before him, down stairs and through the passage, where a small oil-lamp was still flickering. What was he going to do to her? She thought every moment he was going to dash her before him on the ground. But she gave no scream – she only trembled.

He pushed her on to the entrance, and held her firmly in his grasp, while he lifted the latch of the door. Then he opened the door a little way, thrust her out, and slammed it behind her.

For a short space, it seemed like a deliverance to Janet. The harsh north-east wind, that blew through her thin night-dress, and sent her long heavy black hair streaming, seemed like the breath of pity after the grasp of that threatening monster. But soon the sense of release from an overpowering terror gave way before the sense of the fate that had really come upon her.

This, then, was what she had been travelling towards through her long years of misery! Not yet death. O! if she had been brave enough for it, death would have been better. The servants slept at the back of the house; it was impossible to make them hear, so that they might let her in again quietly, without her husband's knowledge. And she would not have tried. He had thrust her out, and it should be for ever.

There would have been dead silence in Orchard Street but for the whistling of the wind and the swirling of the March dust on the pavement. Thick clouds covered the sky; every door was closed; every window was dark. No ray of light fell on the tall white figure that stood in lonely misery on the door-step; no eye rested on Janet as she sank down on the cold stone, and looked into the dismal night. She seemed to be looking into her own blank future.

CHAPTER 15

The stony street, the bitter north-east wind and darkness – and in the midst of them a tender woman thrust out from her husband's home in her thin night-dress, the harsh wind cutting her naked feet, and driving her long hair away from her half-clad bosom, where the poor heart is crushed with anguish and despair.

The drowning man, urged by the supreme agony, lives in an instant through all his happy and unhappy past: when the dark flood has fallen like a curtain, memory, in a single moment, sees the drama acted over again. And even in those earlier crises, which are but types of death – when we are cut off abruptly from the life we have known, when we can no longer expect to-morrow to resemble yesterday, and find ourselves by some sudden shock on the confines of the unknown – there is often the same sort of lightning-flash through the dark and unfrequented chambers of memory.

When Janet sat down shivering on the door-stone, with the door shut upon her past life, and the future black and unshapen before her as the night, the scenes of her childhood, her youth and her painful womanhood, rushed back upon her consciousness, and made one picture with her present desolation. The petted child taking her newest toy to bed with her – the young girl, proud in strength and beauty, dreaming that life was an easy thing, and that it was pitiful weakness to be unhappy – the bride, passing with trembling joy from the outer court to the inner sanctuary of woman's life – the wife, beginning her initiation into sorrow, wounded, resenting, yet still hoping and forgiving – the poor bruised woman, seeking through weary years the one refuge of despair, oblivion: – Janet seemed to herself all these in the same moment that she was conscious of being seated on the cold stone under the shock of a new misery. All her early gladness, all her bright hopes and illusions, all her gifts of beauty and affection, served only to darken the riddle of her life; they were the betraying promises of a cruel destiny which had brought out those sweet blossoms only that the winds and storms might have a greater work of desolation, which had nursed her like a pet fawn into tenderness and fond expectation, only that she might feel a keener terror in the clutch of the panther. Her mother had sometimes said that troubles were sent to make us better and draw us nearer to God. What mockery that seemed to Janet! *Her* troubles had been sinking her lower from year to year, pressing upon her like heavy fever-laden vapours, and perverting the very plenitude of her nature into a deeper source of disease. Her wretchedness had been a perpetually tightening instrument of torture, which had gradually absorbed all the other sensibilities of her nature into the sense of pain and the maddened craving for relief. Oh, if some ray of hope, of pity, of consolation, would pierce through the horrible gloom, she might believe *then* in a Divine love – in a heavenly Father who cared for His children! But now she had no faith, no trust. There was nothing she could lean on in the wide world, for her mother was only a fellow-sufferer in her own lot. The poor patient woman could do little more than mourn with her daughter: she had humble resignation enough to sustain her own soul, but she could no more give comfort and fortitude to Janet, than the withered ivy-covered trunk can bear up its strong, full-boughed offspring crashing down under an Alpine storm. Janet felt she was alone: no human soul had measured her anguish, had understood her self-despair, had entered into her sorrows and her sins with that deep-sighted sympathy which is wiser than all blame, more potent than all reproof – such sympathy as had swelled her own heart for many a sufferer. And if there was any Divine Pity, she could not feel it; it kept aloof from her, it poured no balm into her wounds, it stretched out no hand to bear up her weak resolve, to fortify her fainting courage.

Now, in her utmost loneliness, she shed no tear: she sat staring fixedly into the darkness, while inwardly she gazed at her own past, almost losing the sense that it was her own, or that she was anything more than a spectator at a strange and dreadful play.

The loud sound of the church clock striking one, startled her. She had not been there more than half an hour, then? And it seemed to her as if she had been there half the night. She was getting benumbed with cold. With that strong instinctive dread of pain and death which had made her recoil from suicide, she started up, and the disagreeable sensation of resting on her benumbed feet helped to recall her completely to the sense of the present. The wind was beginning to make rents in the clouds, and there came every now and then a dim light of stars that frightened her more than the darkness; it was like a cruel finger pointing her out in her wretchedness and humiliation; it made her shudder at the thought of the morning twilight. What could she do? Not go to her mother – not rouse her in the dead of night to tell her this. Her mother would think she was a spectre; it would be enough to kill her with horror. And the way there was so long . . . if she should meet some one . . . yet she must seek some shelter, somewhere to hide herself. Five doors off there was Mrs Pettifer's; that kind woman would take her in. It was of no use now to be proud and mind about the world's knowing: she had nothing to wish for, nothing to care about; only she could not help shuddering at the thought of braving the morning light, there, in the street – she was frightened at the thought of spending long hours in the cold. Life might mean anguish, might mean despair; but – oh, she must clutch it, though with bleeding fingers; her feet must cling to the firm earth that the sunlight would revisit, not slip into the untried abyss, where she might long even for familiar pains.

Janet trod slowly with her naked feet on the rough pavement, trembling at the fitful gleams of starlight, and supporting herself by the wall, as the gusts of wind drove right against her. The very wind was cruel: it tried to push her back from the door where she wanted to go and knock and ask for pity.

Mrs Pettifer's house did not look into Orchard Street: it stood a little way up a wide passage which opened into the street through an archway. Janet turned up the archway, and saw a faint light coming from Mrs Pettifer's bedroom window. The glimmer of a rushlight from a room where a friend was lying, was like a ray of mercy to Janet, after that long, long time of darkness and loneliness; it would not be so dreadful to awake Mrs Pettifer as she had thought. Yet she lingered some minutes at the door before she gathered courage to knock; she felt as if the sound must betray her to others besides Mrs Pettifer, though there was no other dwelling that opened into the passage – only warehouses and outbuildings. There was no gravel for her to throw up at the window, nothing but heavy pavement; there was no door-bell; she must knock.

Her first rap was very timid – one feeble fall of the knocker; and then she stood still again for many minutes; but presently she rallied her courage and knocked several times together, not loudly, but rapidly, so that Mrs Pettifer, if she only heard the sound, could not mistake it. And she *had* heard it, for by-and-by the casement of her window was opened, and Janet perceived that she was bending out to try and discern who it was at the door.

'It is I, Mrs Pettifer; it is Janet Dempster. Take me in, for pity's sake.'

'Merciful God! what has happened?'

'Robert has turned me out. I have been in the cold a long while.'

Mrs Pettifer said no more, but hurried away from the window, and was soon at the door with a light in her hand.

'Come in, my poor dear, come in,' said the good woman in a tremulous voice, drawing Janet within the door. 'Come into my warm bed, and may God in heaven save and comfort you.'

The pitying eyes, the tender voice, the warm touch, caused a rush of new feeling in Janet. Her heart swelled, and she burst out suddenly, like a child, into loud passionate sobs. Mrs Pettifer could not help crying with her, but she said, 'Come up-stairs, my dear, come. Don't linger in the cold.'

She drew the poor sobbing thing gently up-stairs, and persuaded her to get into the warm bed. But it was long before Janet could lie down. She sat leaning her head on her knees, convulsed by sobs, while the motherly woman covered her with clothes and held her arms round her to comfort her with warmth. At last the hysterical passion had exhausted itself, and she fell back on the pillow; but her throat was still agitated by piteous after-sobs, such as shake a little child even when it has found a refuge from its alarms on its mother's lap.

Now Janet was getting quieter, Mrs Pettifer determined to go down and make a cup of tea, the first thing a kind old woman thinks of as a solace and restorative under all calamities. Happily there was no danger of awaking her servant, a heavy girl of sixteen, who was snoring blissfully in the attic, and might be kept ignorant of the way in which Mrs Dempster had come in. So Mrs Pettifer busied herself with rousing the kitchen fire, which was kept in under a huge 'raker' – a possibility by which the coal of the midland counties atones for all its slowness and white ashes.

When she carried up the tea, Janet was lying quite still; the spasmodic agitation had ceased, and she seemed lost in thought; her eyes were fixed vacantly on the rushlight shade, and all the lines of sorrow were deepened in her face.

'Now, my dear,' said Mrs Pettifer, 'let me persuade you to drink a cup of tea; you'll find it warm you and soothe you very much. Why, dear heart, your feet are like ice still. Now, do drink this tea, and I'll wrap 'em up in flannel, and then they'll get warm.'

Janet turned her dark eyes on her old friend and

stretched out her arms. She was too much oppressed to say anything; her suffering lay like a heavy weight on her power of speech; but she wanted to kiss the good kind woman. Mrs Pettifer, setting down the cup, bent towards the sad beautiful face, and Janet kissed her with earnest sacramental kisses – such kisses as seal a new and closer bond between the helper and the helped.

She drank the tea obediently. 'It *does* warm me,' she said. 'But now you will get into bed. I shall lie still now.'

Mrs Pettifer felt it was the best thing she could do to lie down quietly, and say no more. She hoped Janet might go to sleep. As for herself, with that tendency to wakefulness common to advanced years, she found it impossible to compose herself to sleep again after this agitating surprise. She lay listening to the clock, wondering what had led to this new outrage of Dempster's, praying for the poor thing at her side, and pitying the mother who would have to hear it all tomorrow.

CHAPTER 16

Janet lay still, as she had promised; but the tea, which had warmed her and given her a sense of greater bodily ease, had only heightened the previous excitement of her brain. Her ideas had a new vividness, which made her feel as if she had only seen life through a dim haze before; her thoughts, instead of springing from the action of her own mind, were external existences, that thrust themselves imperiously upon her like haunting visions. The future took shape after shape of misery before her, always ending in her being dragged back again to her old life of terror, and stupor, and fevered despair. Her husband had so long overshadowed her life that her imagination could not keep hold of a condition in which that great dread was absent; and even his absence – what was it? only a dreary vacant flat, where there was nothing to strive after, nothing to long for.

At last, the light of morning quenched the rush-light, and Janet's thoughts became more and more fragmentary and confused. She was every moment slipping off the level on which she lay thinking, down, down into some depth from which she tried to rise again with a start. Slumber was stealing over her weary brain: that uneasy slumber which is only better than wretched waking, because the life we seem to live in it determines no wretched future, because the things we do and suffer in it are but hateful shadows, and leave no impress that petrifies into an irrevocable past.

She had scarcely been asleep an hour when her movements became more violent, her mutterings more frequent and agitated, till at last she started up with a smothered cry, and looked wildly round her, shaking with terror.

'Don't be frightened, dear Mrs Dempster,' said Mrs Pettifer, who was up and dressing, 'you are with me, your old friend, Mrs Pettifer. Nothing will harm you.'

Janet sank back again on her pillow, still trembling. After lying silent a little while, she said, 'It was a horrible dream. Dear Mrs Pettifer, don't let any one know I am here. Keep it a secret. If he finds out, he will come and drag me back again.'

'No, my dear, depend on me. I've just thought, I shall send the servant home on a holiday – I've promised her a good while. I'll send her away as soon as she's had her breakfast, and she'll have no occasion to know you're here. There's no holding servants' tongues, if you let 'em know anything. What they don't know, they won't tell; you may trust 'em so far. But shouldn't you like me to go and fetch your mother?'

'No, not yet, not yet. I can't bear to see her yet.'

'Well, it shall be just as you like. Now try and get to sleep again. I shall leave you for an hour or two, and send off Phœbe, and then bring you some breakfast. I'll lock the door behind me, so as the girl mayn't come in by chance.'

The daylight changes the aspect of misery to us, as of everything else. In the night it presses on our imagination – the forms it takes are false, fitful, exaggerated; in broad day it sickens our sense with the dreary persistence of definite measurable reality. The man who looks with ghastly horror on all his property aflame in the dead of night, has not half the sense of destitution he will have in the morning, when he walks over the ruins lying blackened in the pitiless sunshine. That moment of intensest depression was come to Janet, when the daylight which showed her the walls, and chairs, and tables, and all the commonplace reality that surrounded her, seemed to lay bare the future too, and bring out into oppressive distinctness all the details of a weary life to be lived from day to day, with no hope to strengthen her against that evil habit, which she loathed in retrospect and yet was powerless to resist. Her husband would never consent to her living away from him: she was become necessary to his tyranny; he would never willingly loosen his grasp on her. She had a vague notion of some protection the law might give her, if she could prove her life in danger from him; but she shrank utterly, as she had always done, from any active, public resistance or vengeance: she felt too crushed, too faulty, too liable to reproach, to have the courage, even if she had had the wish, to put herself openly in the position of a wronged woman seeking redress. She had no strength to sustain her in a course of self-defence and independence: there was a darker shadow over her life than the dread of her husband – it was the shadow of self-despair. The easiest thing would be to go away and hide herself from him. But then there was her mother: Robert had all her little property in his hands, and that little was scarcely enough to keep her in comfort without his aid. If Janet went away alone, he would be sure to persecute her mother; and if she *did* go away – what then? She must work to maintain herself; she must exert herself, weary and hopeless as she was, to begin life afresh. How hard that seemed to her! Janet's nature did not belie her grand face and form: there was energy, there was strength in it; but it was the strength of the vine, which must have its broad leaves and rich clusters borne up by a firm stay. And now she had nothing to rest on – no faith, no love. If her mother had been very feeble, aged, or sickly, Janet's deep pity and tenderness might have made a daughter's duties an interest and a solace; but Mrs Raynor had never needed tendance; she had always been giving help to her daughter; she had always been a sort of humble ministering spirit; and it was one of Janet's pangs of memory, that instead of being her mother's comfort, she had been her mother's trial. Everywhere the same sadness! Her life was a sun-dried, barren tract, where there was no shadow, and where all the waters were bitter.

No! She suddenly thought – and the thought was like an electric shock – there was one spot in her memory which seemed to promise her an untried spring, where the waters might be sweet. That short interview with Mr Tryan had come back upon her – his voice, his words, his look, which told her that he knew sorrow. His words had implied that he thought his death was near; yet he had a faith which enabled him to labour – enabled him to give comfort to others. That look of his came back on her with a vividness greater than it had had for her in reality: surely he knew more of the secrets of sorrow than other men; perhaps he had some message of comfort, different from the feeble words she had been used to hear from others. She was tired, she was sick of that barren exhortation – Do right, and keep a clear conscience, and God will reward you, and your troubles will be easier to bear. She wanted *strength* to do right – she wanted something to rely on besides her own resolutions; for was not the path behind her all strewn with *broken* resolutions? How could she trust in new ones? She had often heard Mr Tryan laughed at for being fond of great sinners. She began to see a new meaning in those words; he would perhaps understand her helplessness, her wants. If she could pour out her heart to him! if she could for the first time in her life unlock all the chambers of her soul!

The impulse to confession almost always requires the presence of a fresh ear and a fresh heart; and in our moments of spiritual need, the man to whom we have no tie but our common nature, seems nearer to us than mother, brother, or friend. Our daily familiar life is but a hiding of ourselves from each other behind a screen of trivial words and deeds, and those who sit with us at the same hearth, are often the farthest off from the deep human soul within us, full of unspoken evil and unacted good.

When Mrs Pettifer came back to her, turning the key and opening the door very gently, Janet, instead of being asleep, as her good friend had hoped, was intensely occupied with her new thought. She longed to ask Mrs Pettifer if she could see Mr Tryan; but she was arrested by doubts and timidity. He might not feel for her – he might be shocked at her confession – he might talk to her of doctrines she could not understand or believe. She could not make up her mind yet; but she was too restless under this mental struggle to remain in bed.

'Mrs Pettifer,' she said, 'I can't lie here any longer; I must get up. Will you lend me some clothes?'

Wrapt in such drapery as Mrs Pettifer could find for her tall figure, Janet went down into the little parlour, and tried to take some of the breakfast her friend had prepared for her. But her effort was not a successful one; her cup of tea and bit of toast were only half finished. The leaden weight of discouragement pressed upon her more and more heavily. The wind had fallen, and a drizzling rain had come on; there was no prospect from Mrs Pettifer's parlour but a blank wall; and as Janet looked out at the window, the rain and the smoke-blackened bricks seemed to blend themselves in sickening identity with her desolation of spirit and the headachy weariness of her body.

Mrs Pettifer got through her household work as soon as she could, and sat down with her sewing, hoping that Janet would perhaps be able to talk a little of what had passed, and find some relief by unbosoming herself in that way. But Janet could not speak to her; she was importuned with the longing to see Mr Tryan, and yet hesitating to express it.

Two hours passed in this way. The rain went on drizzling, and Janet sat still, leaning her aching head on her hand, and looking alternately at the fire and out of the window. She felt this could not last – this motionless, vacant misery. She must determine on something, she must take some step; and yet everything was so difficult.

It was one o'clock, and Mrs Pettifer rose from her seat, saying, 'I must go and see about dinner.'

The movement and the sound startled Janet from

her reverie. It seemed as if an opportunity were escaping her, and she said hastily, 'Is Mr Tryan in the town to-day, do you think?'

'No, I should think not, being Saturday, you know,' said Mrs Pettifer, her face lighting up with pleasure; 'but he *would* come, if he was sent for. I can send Jesson's boy with a note to him any time. Should you like to see him?'

'Yes, I think I should.'

'Then I'll send for him this instant.'

CHAPTER 17

When Dempster awoke in the morning, he was at no loss to account to himself for the fact that Janet was not by his side. His hours of drunkenness were not cut off from his other hours by any blank wall of oblivion; he remembered what Janet had done to offend him the evening before, he remembered what he had done to her at midnight, just as he would have remembered if he had been consulted about a right of road.

The remembrance gave him a definite ground for the extra ill-humour which had attended his waking every morning this week, but he would not admit to himself that it cost him any anxiety. 'Pooh,' he said inwardly, 'she would go straight to her mother's. She's as timid as a hare; and she'll never let anybody know about it. She'll be back again before night.'

But it would be as well for the servants not to know anything of the affair; so he collected the clothes she had taken off the night before, and threw them into a fire-proof closet of which he always kept the key in his pocket. When he went down stairs he said to the housemaid, 'Mrs Dempster is gone to her mother's; bring in the breakfast.'

The servants, accustomed to hear domestic broils, and to see their mistress put on her bonnet hastily and go to her mother's, thought it only something a little worse than usual that she should have gone thither in consequence of a violent quarrel, either at midnight, or in the early morning before they were up. The housemaid told the cook what she supposed had happened; the cook shook her head and said, 'Eh, dear, dear!' but they both expected to see their mistress back again in an hour or two.

Dempster, on his return home the evening before, had ordered his man, who lived away from the house, to bring up his horse and gig from the stables at ten. After breakfast he said to the housemaid, 'No one need sit up for me to-night; I shall not be at home till to-morrow evening;' and then he walked to the office to give some orders, expecting, as he returned, to see the man waiting with his gig. But though the church clock had struck ten, no gig was there. In Dempster's mood this was more than enough to exasperate him. He went in to take his accustomed glass of brandy before setting out, promising himself the satisfaction of presently thundering at Dawes for being a few minutes behind his time. An outbreak of temper towards his man was not common with him; for Dempster, like most tyrannous people, had that dastardly kind of self-restraint which enabled him to control his temper where it suited his own convenience to do so; and feeling the value of Dawes, a steady punctual fellow, he not only gave him high wages, but usually treated him with exceptional civility. This morning, however, ill-humour got the better of prudence, and Dempster was determined to rate him soundly; a resolution for which Dawes gave him much better ground than he expected. Five minutes, ten minutes, a quarter of an hour, had passed, and Dempster was setting off to the stables in a back street to see what was the cause of the delay, when Dawes appeared with the gig.

'What the devil do you keep me here for?' thundered Dempster, 'kicking my heels like a beggarly tailor waiting for a carrier's cart? I ordered you to be here at ten. We might have driven to Whitlow by this time.'

'Why, one o' the traces was welly i' two, an' I had to tek it to Brady's to be mended, an' he didn't get it done i' time.'

'Then why didn't you take it to him last night? Because of your damned laziness, I suppose. Do you think I give you wages for you to choose your own hours, and come dawdling up a quarter of an hour after my time?'

'Come, give me good words, will yer?' said Dawes, sulkily, 'I'm not lazy, nor no man shall call me lazy. I know well anuff what you gi' me wages for; it's for doin' what yer won't find many men as 'ull do.'

'What, you impudent scoundrel,' said Dempster, getting into the gig, 'you think you're necessary to me, do you? As if a beastly bucket-carrying idiot like you wasn't to be got any day. Look out for a new master, then, who'll pay you for not doing as you're bid.'

Dawes's blood was now fairly up. 'I'll look out for a master as has got a better charicter nor a lyin', bletherin' drunkard, an' I shouldn't hev to go fur.'

Dempster, furious, snatched the whip from the socket, and gave Dawes a cut, which he meant to fall across his shoulders, saying, 'Take that, sir, and go to hell with you!'

Dawes was in the act of turning with the reins in his hand when the lash fell, and the cut went across his face. With white lips, he said, 'I'll hev the law on yer for that, lawyer as yer are,' and threw the reins on the horse's back.

Dempster leaned forward, seized the reins, and drove off.

'Why, there's your friend Dempster driving out without his man again,' said Mr Luke Byles, who was chatting with Mr Budd in the Bridge Way. 'What a fool he is to drive that two-wheeled thing! he'll get pitched on his head one of these days.'

'Not he,' said Mr Budd, nodding to Dempster as he passed; 'he's got nine lives, Dempster has.'

CHAPTER 18

It was dusk, and the candles were lighted before Mr Tryan knocked at Mrs Pettifer's door. Her messenger had brought back word, that he was not at home, and all afternoon Janet had been agitated by the fear that he would not come; but as soon as that anxiety was removed by the knock at the door, she felt a sudden rush of doubt and timidity: she trembled and turned cold.

Mrs Pettifer went to open the door, and told Mr Tryan, in as few words as possible, what had happened in the night. As he laid down his hat and prepared to enter the parlour, she said, 'I won't go in with you, for I think perhaps she would rather see you go in alone.'

Janet, wrapped up in a large white shawl which threw her dark face into startling relief, was seated with her eyes turned anxiously towards the door when Mr Tryan entered. He had not seen her since their interview at Sally Martin's long months ago; and he felt a strong movement of compassion at the sight of the pain-stricken face which seemed to bear written on it the signs of all Janet's intervening misery. Her heart gave a great leap, as

521

her eyes met his once more. No! she had not deceived herself: there was all the sincerity, all the sadness, all the deep pity in them her memory had told her of; more than it had told her, for in proportion as his face had become thinner and more worn, his eyes appeared to have gathered intensity.

He came forward, and, putting out his hand, said, 'I am so glad you sent for me – I am so thankful you thought I could be any comfort to you.' Janet took his hand in silence. She was unable to utter any words of mere politeness, or even of gratitude; her heart was too full of other words that had welled up the moment she met his pitying glance, and felt her doubts fall away.

They sat down opposite each other, and she said in a low voice, while slow difficult tears gathered in her aching eyes:—

'I want to tell you how unhappy I am – how weak and wicked. I feel no strength to live or die. I thought you could tell me something that would help me.' She paused.

'Perhaps I can,' Mr Tryan said, 'for in speaking to me you are speaking to a fellow-sinner who has needed just the comfort and help you are needing.'

'And you did find it?'

'Yes; and I trust you will find it.'

'O, I should like to be good and to do right,' Janet burst forth, 'but indeed, indeed, my lot has been a very hard one. I loved my husband very dearly when we were married, and I meant to make him happy – I wanted nothing else. But he began to be angry with me for little things and . . . I don't want to accuse him. . . . but he drank and got more and more unkind to me, and then very cruel, and he beat me. And that cut me to the heart. It made me almost mad sometimes to think all our love had come to that. . . . I couldn't bear up against it. I had never been used to drink anything but water. I hated wine and spirits because Robert drank them so; but one day when I was very wretched, and the wine was standing on the table, I suddenly. . . . I can hardly remember how I came to do it. . . . I poured some wine into a large glass and drank it. It blunted my feelings, and made me more indifferent. After that, the temptation was always coming, and it got stronger and stronger. I was ashamed, and I hated what I did; but almost while the thought was passing through my mind that I would never do it again, I did it. It seemed as if there was a demon in me always making me rush to do what I longed not to do. And I thought all the more that God was cruel; for if He had not sent me that dreadful trial, so much worse than other women have to bear, I should not have done wrong in that way. I suppose it is wicked to think so. . . . I feel as if there must be goodness and right above us, but I can't see it, I can't trust in it. And I have gone on in that way for years and years. At one time it used to be better now and then, but everything has got worse lately: I felt sure it must soon end somehow. And last night he turned me out of doors. . . . I don't know what to do. I will never go back to that life again if I can help it; and yet everything else seems so miserable. I feel sure that demon will be always urging me to satisfy the craving that comes upon me, and the days will go on as they have done through all those miserable years. I shall always be doing wrong, and hating myself after – sinking lower and lower, and knowing that I am sinking. O can you tell me any way of getting strength? Have you ever known any one like me that got peace of mind and power to do right? Can you give me any comfort – any hope?'

While Janet was speaking, she had forgotten everything but her misery and her yearning for comfort. Her voice had risen from the low tone of timid distress to an intense pitch of imploring anguish. She clasped her hands tightly, and looked at Mr Tryan with eager questioning eyes, with parted, trembling lips, with the deep horizontal lines of overmastering pain on her brow. In this artificial life of ours, it is not often we see a human face with all a heart's agony in it, uncontrolled by self-consciousness; when we do see it, it startles us as if we had suddenly waked into the real world of which this everyday one is but a puppet-show copy. For some moments Mr Tryan was too deeply moved to speak.

'Yes, dear Mrs Dempster,' he said at last, 'there *is* comfort, there *is* hope for you. Believe me there is, for I speak from my own deep and hard experience.' He paused, as if he had not made up his mind to utter the words that were urging themselves to his lips. Presently he continued, 'Ten years ago, I felt as wretched as you do. I think my wretchedness was even worse than yours, for I had a heavier sin on my conscience. I had suffered no wrong from others as you have, and I had injured another irreparably in body and soul. The image of the wrong I had done pursued me everywhere, and I seemed on the brink of madness. I hated my life, for I thought, just as you do, that I should go on falling into temptation and doing more harm in the world; and I dreaded death, for with that sense of guilt on my soul, I felt that whatever state I entered on must be one of misery. But a dear friend to whom I opened my mind showed me it was just such as I – the helpless who feel themselves helpless – that God specially invites to come to Him, and offers all the riches of His salvation: not forgiveness only; forgiveness would be worth little if it left us under the powers of our evil passions; but strength – that strength which enables us to conquer sin.'

'But,' said Janet, 'I can feel no trust in God. He seems always to have left me to myself. I have sometimes prayed to Him to help me, and yet everything has been just the same as before. If you felt like me, how did you come to have hope and trust?'

'Do not believe that God has left you to yourself.

525

How can you tell but that the hardest trials you have known have been only the road by which He was leading you to that complete sense of your own sin and helplessness, without which you would never have renounced all other hopes, and trusted in His love alone? I know, dear Mrs Dempster, I know it is hard to bear. I would not speak lightly of your sorrows. I feel that the mystery of our life is great, and at one time it seemed as dark to me as it does to you.' Mr Tryan hesitated again. He saw that the first thing Janet needed was to be assured of sympathy. She must be made to feel that her anguish was not strange to him; that he entered into the only half-expressed secrets of her spiritual weakness, before any other message of consolation could find its way to her heart. The tale of the Divine Pity was never yet believed from lips that were not felt to be moved by human pity. And Janet's anguish was not strange to Mr Tryan. He had never been in the presence of a sorrow and a self-despair that had sent so strong a thrill through all the recesses of his saddest experience; and it is because sympathy is but a living again through our own past in a new form, that confession often prompts a response of confession. Mr Tryan felt this prompting, and his judgment too told him that in obeying it he would be taking the best means of administering comfort to Janet. Yet he hesitated; as we tremble to let in the daylight on a chamber of relics which we have never visited except in curtained silence. But the first impulse triumphed, and he went on. 'I had lived all my life at a distance from God. My youth was spent in thoughtless self-indulgence, and all my hopes were of a vain worldly kind. I had no thought of entering the Church; I looked forward to a political career, for my father was private secretary to a man high in the Whig Ministry, and had been promised strong interest in my behalf. At college I lived in intimacy with the gayest men, even adopting follies and vices for which I had no taste, out of mere pliancy and the love of standing well with my companions. You see, I was more guilty even then than you have been, for I threw away all the rich blessings of untroubled youth and health; I had no excuse in my outward lot. But while I was at college that event in my life occurred, which in the end brought on the state of mind I have mentioned to you – the state of self-reproach and despair, which enables me to understand to the full what you are suffering; and I tell you the facts, because I want you to be assured that I am not uttering mere vague words when I say that I have been raised from as low a depth of sin and sorrow as that in which you feel yourself to be. At college I had an attachment to a lovely girl of seventeen: she was very much below my own station in life, and I never contemplated marrying her; but I induced her to leave her father's house. I did not mean to forsake her when I left college, and I quieted all scruples of conscience by promising myself that I would always take care

527

of poor Lucy. But on my return from a vacation spent in travelling, I found that Lucy was gone – gone away with a gentleman, her neighbours said. I was a good deal distressed, but I tried to persuade myself that no harm would come to her. Soon afterwards I had an illness which left my health delicate, and made all dissipation distasteful to me. Life seemed very wearisome and empty, and I looked with envy on every one who had some great and absorbing object – even on my cousin who was preparing to go out as a missionary, and whom I had been used to think a dismal, tedious person, because he was constantly urging religious subjects upon me. We were living in London then; it was three years since I had lost sight of Lucy; and one summer evening about nine o'clock, as I was walking along Gower Street, I saw a knot of people on the causeway before me. As I came up to them, I heard one woman say, "I tell you, she's dead." This awakened my interest, and I pushed my way within the circle. The body of a woman, dressed in fine clothes, was lying against a door-step. Her head was bent on one side, and the long curls had fallen over her cheek. A tremor seized me when I saw the hair: it was light chestnut – the colour of Lucy's. I knelt down and turned aside the hair; it was Lucy – dead – with paint on her cheeks. I found out afterwards that she had taken poison – that she was in the power of a wicked woman – that the very clothes on her back were not her own. It was then that my past life burst upon me in all its hideousness. I wished I had never been born. I couldn't look into the future. Lucy's dead painted face would follow me there, as it did when I looked back into the past – as it did when I sat down to table with my friends, when I lay down in my bed, and when I rose up. There was only one thing that could make life tolerable to me; that was, to spend all the rest of it in trying to save others from the ruin I had brought on one. But how was that possible for me? I had no comfort, no strength, no wisdom in my own soul; how could I give them to others? My mind was dark, rebellious, at war with itself and with God.'

Mr Tryan had been looking away from Janet. His face was towards the fire, and he was absorbed in the images his memory was recalling. But now he turned his eyes on her, and they met hers, fixed on him with the look of rapt expectation with which one clinging to a slippery summit of rock, while the waves are rising higher and higher, watches the boat that has put from shore to his rescue.

'You see, Mrs Dempster, how deep my need was. I went on in this way for months. I was convinced that if I ever got help and comfort, it must be from religion. I went to hear celebrated preachers, and I read religious books. But I found nothing that fitted my own need. The faith which puts the sinner in possession of salvation seemed, as I understood it, to be quite out of my reach. I had no faith; I only felt utterly wretched, under the power of habits and dispositions which had wrought hideous evil. At last, as I told you, I found a friend to whom I opened all my feelings – to whom I confessed everything. He was a man who had gone through very deep experience, and could understand the different wants of different minds. He made it clear to me that the only preparation for coming to Christ and partaking of His salvation, was that very sense of guilt and helplessness which was weighing me down. He said, You are weary and heavy laden; well, it is you Christ invites to come to Him and find rest. He asks you to cling to Him, to lean on Him; He does not command you to walk alone without stumbling. He does not tell you, as your fellow-men do, that you must first merit His love; He neither condemns nor reproaches you for the past, He only bids you come to Him that you may have life: He bids you stretch out your hands, and take of the fullness of His love. You have only to rest on Him as a child rests on its mother's arms, and you will be upborne by His divine strength. That is what is meant by faith. Your evil habits, you feel, are too strong for you; you are unable to wrestle with them; you know beforehand you shall fall. But when once we feel our helplessness in that way, and go to Christ, desiring to be freed from the power as well as the punishment of sin, we are no longer left to our own strength. As long as we live in rebellion against God, desiring to have our own will, seeking happiness in the things of this world, it is as if we shut ourselves up in a crowded stifling room, where we breathe only poisoned air; but we have only to walk out under the infinite heavens, and we breathe the pure free air that gives us health, and strength, and gladness. It is just so with God's spirit: as soon as we submit ourselves to His will, as soon as we desire to be united to Him, and made pure and holy, it is as if the walls had fallen down that shut us out from God, and we are fed with His spirit, which gives us new strength.'

'That is what I want,' said Janet; 'I have left off minding about pleasure. I think I could be contented in the midst of hardship, if I felt that God cared for me, and would give me strength to lead a pure life. But tell me, did you soon find peace and strength?'

'Not perfect peace for a long while, but hope and trust, which is strength. No sense of pardon for myself could do away with the pain I had in thinking what I had helped to bring on another. My friend used to urge upon me that my sin against God was greater than my sin against her; but – it may be from want of deeper spiritual feeling – that has remained to this hour the sin which causes me the bitterest pang. I could never rescue Lucy; but by God's blessing I might rescue other weak and falling souls; and that was why I entered the Church. I asked for nothing through the rest of my life but that I might be devoted to

531

God's work, without swerving in search of pleasure either to the right hand or to the left. It has been often a hard struggle – but God has been with me – and perhaps it may not last much longer.'

Mr Tryan paused. For a moment he had forgotten Janet, and for a moment she had forgotten her own sorrows. When she recurred to herself, it was with a new feeling.

'Ah, what a difference between our lives! you have been choosing pain, and working, and denying yourself; and I have been thinking only of myself. I was only angry and discontented because I had pain to bear. You never had that wicked feeling that I have had so often, did you? that God was cruel to send me trials and temptations worse than others have.'

'Yes, I had; I had very blasphemous thoughts, and I know that spirit of rebellion must have made the worst part of your lot. You did not feel how impossible it is for us to judge rightly of God's dealings, and you opposed yourself to His will. But what do we know? We cannot foretell the working of the smallest event in our own lot: how can we presume to judge of things that are so much too high for us? There is nothing that becomes us but entire submission, perfect resignation. As long as we set up our own will and our own wisdom against God's, we make that wall between us and His love which I have spoken of just now. But as soon as we lay ourselves entirely at His feet, we have enough light given us to guide our own steps; as the foot-soldier who hears nothing of the councils that determine the course of the great battle he is in, hears plainly enough the word of command which he must himself obey. I know, dear Mrs Dempster, I know it is hard – the hardest thing of all, perhaps – to flesh and blood. But carry that difficulty to Christ along with all your other sins and weaknesses, and ask Him to pour into you a spirit of submission. He enters into your struggles; He has drunk the cup of our suffering to the dregs; He knows the hard wrestling it costs us to say, "Not my will, but Thine be done."'

'Pray with me,' said Janet – 'pray now that I may have light and strength.'

CHAPTER 19

Before leaving Janet, Mr Tryan urged her strongly to send for her mother.

'Do not wound her,' he said, 'by shutting her out any longer from your troubles. It is right that you should be with her.'

'Yes, I will send for her,' said Janet. 'But I would rather not go to my mother's yet, because my husband is sure to think I am there, and he might come and fetch me. I can't go back to him . . . at least, not yet. Ought I to go back to him?'

'No, certainly not, at present. Something should be done to secure you from violence. Your mother, I think, should consult some confidential friend, some man of character and experience, who might mediate between you and your husband.'

'Yes, I will send for my mother directly. But I will stay here, with Mrs Pettifer, till something has been done. I want no one to know where I am, except you. You will come again, will you not? you will not leave me to myself?'

'You will not be left to yourself. God is with you. If I have been able to give you any comfort, it is because His power and love have been present with us. But I am very thankful that He has chosen to work through me. I shall see you again to-morrow – not before evening, for it will be Sunday, you know; but after the evening lecture I shall be at liberty. You will be in my prayers till then. In the mean time, dear Mrs Dempster, open your heart as much as you can to your mother and Mrs Pettifer. Cast away from you the pride that makes us shrink from acknowledging our weakness to our friends. Ask them to help you in guarding yourself from the least approach of the sin you most dread. Deprive yourself as far as possible of the very means and opportunity of committing it. Every effort of that kind made in humility and dependence is a prayer. Promise me you will do this.'

'Yes, I promise you. I know I have always been too proud; I could never bear to speak to any one about myself. I have been proud towards my mother, even; it has always made me angry when she has seemed to take notice of my faults.'

'Ah, dear Mrs Dempster, you will never say again that life is blank, and that there is nothing to live for, will you? See what work there is to be done in life, both in our own souls and for others. Surely it matters little whether we have more or less of this world's comfort in these short years, when God is training us for the eternal enjoyment of His love. Keep that great end of life before you, and your troubles here will seem only the small hardships of a journey. Now I must go.'

Mr Tryan rose and held out his hand. Janet took it and said, 'God has been very good to me in sending you to me. I will trust in Him. I will try to do everything you tell me.'

Blessed influence of one true loving human soul on another! Not calculable by algebra, not deducible by logic, but mysterious, effectual, mighty as the hidden process by which the tiny seed is quickened, and bursts forth into tall stem and broad leaf, and glowing tasselled flower. Ideas are often poor ghosts; our sun-filled eyes cannot discern them; they pass athwart us in thin vapour, and cannot make themselves felt. But sometimes they are made flesh; they breathe upon us with warm breath, they touch us with soft responsive hands, they look at us with sad sincere eyes, and speak to us in appealing tones; they are clothed in a living human soul, with all its conflicts, its faith, and its love. Then their presence is a power, then they shake us like a passion, and we are drawn after them with gentle compulsion, as flame is drawn to flame.

Janet's dark grand face, still fatigued, had become quite calm, and looked up, as she sat, with a humble childlike expression at the thin blond face and slightly sunken grey eyes which now shone with hectic brightness. She might have been taken for an image of passionate strength beaten and worn with conflict; and he for an image of the self-renouncing faith which has soothed that conflict into rest. As he looked at the sweet submissive face, he remembered its look of despairing anguish, and his heart was very full as he turned away from her. 'Let me only live to see this work confirmed, and then . . .'

It was nearly ten o'clock when Mr Tryan left, but Janet was bent on sending for her mother; so Mrs Pettifer, as the readiest plan, put on her bonnet and went herself to fetch Mrs Raynor. The mother had been too long used to expect that every fresh week would be more painful than the last, for Mrs Pettifer's news to come upon her with the shock of a surprise. Quietly, without any show of distress, she made up a bundle of clothes, and, telling her little maid that she should not return home that night, accompanied Mrs Pettifer back in silence.

When they entered the parlour, Janet, wearied out, had sunk to sleep in the large chair, which stood with its back to the door. The noise of the opening door disturbed her, and she was looking round wonderingly, when Mrs Raynor came up to her chair, and said, 'It's your mother, Janet.'

'Mother, dear mother!' Janet cried, clasping her closely. 'I have not been a good tender child to you, but I *will* be – I will not grieve you any more.'

The calmness which had withstood a new sorrow was overcome by a new joy, and the mother burst into tears.

CHAPTER 20

On Sunday morning the rain had ceased, and Janet, looking out of the bedroom window, saw, above the house-tops, a shining mass of white cloud rolling under the far-away blue sky. It was going to be a lovely April day. The fresh sky, left clear and calm after the long vexation of wind and rain, mingled its mild influence with Janet's new thoughts and prospects. She felt a buoyant courage that surprised herself, after the cold crushing weight of despondency which had oppressed her the day before: she could think even of her husband's rage without the old overpowering dread. For a delicious hope – the hope of purification and inward peace – had entered into Janet's soul, and made it spring-time there as well as in the outer world.

While her mother was brushing and coiling up her thick black hair – a favourite task, because it seemed to renew the days of her daughter's girlhood – Janet told how she came to send for Mr Tryan, how she had remembered their meeting at Sally Martin's in the autumn, and had felt an irresistible desire to see him, and tell him her sins and her troubles.

'I see God's goodness now, mother, in ordering it so that we should meet in that way, to overcome my prejudice against him, and make me feel that he was good, and then bringing it back to my mind in the depth of my trouble. You know what foolish things I used to say about him, knowing nothing of him all the while. And yet he was the man who was to give me comfort and help when everything else failed me. It is wonderful how I feel able to speak to him as I never have done to any one before; and how every word he says to me enters my heart, and has a new meaning for me. I think it must be because he has felt life more deeply than others, and has a deeper faith. I believe everything he says at once. His words come to me like rain on the parched ground. It has always seemed to me before as if I could see behind people's words, as one sees behind a screen; but in Mr Tryan it is his very soul that speaks.'

'Well, my dear child, I love and bless him for your sake, if he has given you any comfort. I never believed the harm people said of him, though I had no desire to go and hear him, for I am contented with old-fashioned ways. I find more good teaching than I can practise in reading my Bible at home, and hearing Mr Crewe at church. But your wants are different, my dear, and we are not all led by the same road. That was certainly good advice of Mr Tryan's you told me of last night – that we should consult some one that may interfere for you with your husband; and I've been turning it over in my mind while I've been lying awake in the night. I think nobody will do so well as Mr Benjamin Landor, for we must have a man that knows the law, and that Robert is rather afraid of. And perhaps he could bring about an agreement for you to live apart. Your husband's bound to maintain you, you know; and, if you liked, we could move away from Milby and live somewhere else.'

'O, mother, we must do nothing yet; I must think about it a little longer. I have a different feeling this morning from what I had yesterday. Something seems to tell me that I must go back to Robert some time – after a little while. I loved him once better than all the world, and I have never had any children to love. There were things in me that were wrong, and I should like to make up for them if I can.'

'Well, my dear, I won't persuade you. Think of it a little longer. But something must be done soon.'

'How I wish I had my bonnet, and shawl, and black gown here!' said Janet, after a few minutes' silence. 'I should like to go to Paddiford church and hear Mr Tryan. There would be no fear of my meeting Robert, for he never goes out on a Sunday morning.'

'I'm afraid it would not do for me to go to the house and fetch your clothes,' said Mrs Raynor.

'O no, no! I must stay quietly here while you two go to church. I will be Mrs Pettifer's maid, and get the dinner ready for her by the time she comes back. Dear good woman! She was so tender to me when she took me in, in the night, mother, and all the next day, when I couldn't speak a word to her to thank her.'

CHAPTER 21

The servants at Dempster's felt some surprise when the morning, noon, and evening of Saturday had passed, and still their mistress did not reappear.

'It's very odd,' said Kitty, the housemaid, as she trimmed her next week's cap, while Betty, the middle-aged cook, looked on with folded arms. 'Do you think as Mrs Raynor was ill, and sent for the missis afore we was up?'

'O,' said Betty, 'if it had been that, she'd ha' been back'ards an' for'ards three or four times afore now; leastways, she'd ha' sent little Ann to let us know.'

'There's summat up more nor usal between her an' the master, that you may depend on,' said Kitty. 'I know those clothes as was lying i' the drawing-room yisterday, when the company was come, meant summat. I shouldn't wonder if that was what they've had a fresh row about. She's p'raps gone away, an's made up her mind not to come back again.'

'An' i' the right on't, too,' said Betty. 'I'd ha' overrun him long afore now, if it had been me. I wouldn't stan' bein' mauled as she is by no husband, not if he was the biggest lord i' the land. It's poor work bein' a wife at that price: I'd sooner be a cook wi'out perkises, an' hev roast, an' boil, an' fry, an' bake all to mind at once. She may well do as she does. I know I'm glad enough of a drop o' summat myself when I'm plagued. I feel very low, like, to-night; I think I shall put my beer i' the saucepan an' warm it.'

'What a one you are for warmin' your beer, Betty! I couldn't abide it – nasty bitter stuff!'

'It's fine talkin'; if you was a cook you'd know what belongs to bein' a cook. It's none so nice to hev a sinkin' at your stomach, I can tell you. You wouldn't think so much o' fine ribbins i' your cap then.'

'Well, well, Betty, don't be grumpy. Liza Thomson, as is at Phipps's, said to me last Sunday, 'I wonder you'll stay at Dempster's,' she says, 'such goins on as there is.' But I says, 'There's things to put up wi' in ivery place, an' you may change, an' change, an' not better yourself when all's said an' done.' Lors! why, Liza told me herself as Mrs Phipps was as skinny as skinny i' the kitchen, for all they keep so much company; and as for follyers, she's as cross as a turkey-cock if she finds 'em out. There's nothin' o' that sort i' the missis. How pretty she come an' spoke to Job last Sunday! There isn't a good-natur'der woman i' the world, that's my belief – an' hansome too. I al'ys think there's nobody looks half so well as the missis when she's got her 'air done nice. Lors! I wish I'd got long 'air like her – my 'air's a-comin' off dreadful.'

'There'll be fine work to-morrow, I expect,' said Betty, 'when the master comes home, an' Dawes a-swearin' as he'll niver do a stroke o' work for him again. It'll be good fun if he sets the justice on him for cuttin' him wi' the whip; the master 'll p'raps get his comb cut for once in his life!'

'Why, he was in a temper like a fi-end this morning,' said Kitty. 'I dare say it was along o' what had happened wi' the missis. We shall hev a pretty house wi' him if she doesn't come back – he'll want to be leatherin' *us*, I shouldn't wonder. He must hev somethin' t' ill-use when he's in a passion.'

'I'd tek care he didn't leather me – no, not if he was my husban' ten times o'er; I'd pour hot drippin' on him sooner. But the missis hesn't a sperrit like me. He'll mek her come back, you'll see; he'll come round her somehow. There's no likelihood of her coming back to-night, though; so I should think we might fasten the doors and go to bed when we like.'

On Sunday morning, however, Kitty's mind became disturbed by more definite and alarming conjectures about her mistress. While Betty, encouraged by the prospect of unwonted leisure, was sitting down to continue a letter which had long lain unfinished between the leaves of her Bible, Kitty came running into the kitchen and said,

'Lor! Betty, I'm all of a tremble; you might knock me down wi' a feather. I've just looked into the missis's wardrobe, an' there's both her bonnets. She must ha' gone wi'out her bonnet. An' then I remember as her night-clothes wasn't on the bed yesterday mornin'; I thought she'd put 'em away to be washed; but she hedn't, for I've been lookin'. It's my belief he's murdered her, and shut her up i' that closet as he keeps locked al'ys. He's capible on't.'

'Lors-ha'-massy, why you'd better run to Mrs Raynor's an' see if she's there arter all. It was p'raps all a lie.'

Mrs Raynor had returned home to give directions to her little maiden, when Kitty, with the elaborate manifestation of alarm which servants delight in, rushed in without knocking, and holding her hands on her heart as if the consequences to that organ were likely to be very serious, said,—

'If you please 'm, is the missis here?'

'No, Kitty; why are you come to ask?'

'Because 'm, she's niver been at home since yesterday mornin', since afore we was up; an' we thought somethin' must ha' happened to her.'

'No, don't be frightened, Kitty. Your mistress is quite safe; I know where she is. Is your master at home?'

'No 'm; he went out yesterday mornin', an' said he shouldn't be back afore to-night.'

'Well, Kitty, there's nothing the matter with your mistress. You needn't say anything to any one about

545

her being away from home. I shall call presently and fetch her gown and bonnet. She wants them to put on.'

Kitty, perceiving there was a mystery she was not to inquire into, returned to Orchard Street, really glad to know that her mistress was safe, but disappointed nevertheless at being told that she was not to be frightened. She was soon followed by Mrs Raynor in quest of the gown and bonnet. The good mother, on learning that Dempster was not at home, had at once thought that she could gratify Janet's wish to go to Paddiford church.

'See, my dear,' she said, as she entered Mrs Pettifer's parlour; 'I've brought you your black clothes. Robert's not at home, and is not coming till this evening. I couldn't find your best black gown, but this will do. I wouldn't bring anything else, you know; but there can't be any objection to my fetching clothes to cover you. You can go to Paddiford church now, if you like; and I will go with you.'

'That's a dear mother! Then we'll all three go together. Come and help me to get ready. Good little Mrs Crewe! It will vex her sadly that I should go to hear Mr Tryan. But I must kiss her, and make it up with her.'

Many eyes were turned on Janet with a look of surprise as she walked up the aisle of Paddiford church. She felt a little tremor at the notice she knew she was exciting, but it was a strong satisfaction to her that she had been able at once to take a step that would let her neighbours know her change of feeling towards Mr Tryan: she had left herself now no room for proud reluctance or weak hesitation. The walk through the sweet spring air had stimulated all her fresh hopes, all her yearning desires after purity, strength, and peace. She thought she should find a new meaning in the prayers this morning; her full heart, like an overflowing river, wanted those ready-made channels to pour itself into; and then she should hear Mr Tryan again, and his words would fall on her like precious balm, as they had done last night. There was a liquid brightness in her eyes as they rested on the mere walls, the pews, the weavers and colliers in their Sunday clothes. The commonest things seemed to touch the spring of love within her, just as, when we are suddenly released from an acute absorbing bodily pain, our heart and senses leap out in new freedom; we think even the noise of streets harmonious, and are ready to hug the tradesman who is wrapping up our change. A door had been opened in Janet's cold dark prison of self-despair, and the golden light of morning was pouring in its slanting beams through the blessed opening. There was sunlight in the world; there was a divine love caring for her; it had given her an earnest of good things; it had been preparing comfort for her in the very moment when she had thought herself most forsaken.

Mr Tryan might well rejoice when his eye rested on her as he entered his desk; but he rejoiced with trembling. He could not look at the sweet hopeful face without remembering its yesterday's look of agony; and there was the possibility that that look might return.

Janet's appearance at church was greeted not only by wondering eyes, but by kind hearts, and after the service several of Mr Tryan's hearers with whom she had been on cold terms of late, contrived to come up to her and take her by the hand.

'Mother,' said Miss Linnet, 'do let us go and speak to Mrs Dempster. I'm sure there's a great change in her mind towards Mr Tryan. I noticed how eagerly she listened to the sermon, and she's come with Mrs Pettifer, you see. We ought to go and give her a welcome among us.'

'Why, my dear, we've never spoke friendly these five year. You know she's been as haughty as anything since I quarrelled with her husband. However, let bygones be bygones: I've no grudge again' the poor thing, more particular as she must ha' flew in her husband's face to come an' hear Mr Tryan. Yis, let us go an' speak to her.'

The friendly words and looks touched Janet a little too keenly, and Mrs Pettifer wisely hurried her home by the least-frequented road. When they reached home, a violent fit of weeping, followed by continuous lassitude, showed that the emotions of the morning had overstrained her nerves. She was suffering, too, from the absence of the long-accustomed stimulant which she had promised Mr Tryan not to touch again. The poor thing was conscious of this, and dreaded her own weakness, as the victim of intermittent insanity dreads the on-coming of the old illusion.

'Mother,' she whispered, when Mrs Raynor urged her to lie down and rest all the afternoon, that she might be the better prepared to see Mr Tryan in the evening –'mother, don't let me have anything if I ask for it.'

In the mother's mind there was the same anxiety, and in her it was mingled with another fear – the fear lest Janet, in her present excited state of mind, should take some premature step in relation to her husband, which might lead back to all the former troubles. The hint she had thrown out in the morning of her wish to return to him after a time, showed a new eagerness for difficult duties, that only made the long-saddened sober mother tremble.

But as evening approached, Janet's morning heroism all forsook her: her imagination, influenced by physical depression as well as by mental habits, was haunted by the vision of her husband's return home, and she began to shudder with the yesterday's dread. She heard him calling her, she saw him going to her mother's to look for her, she felt sure he would find her out, and burst in upon her.

'Pray, pray, don't leave me, don't go to church,' she said to Mrs Pettifer. 'You and mother both stay with me till Mr Tryan comes.'

At twenty minutes past six the church bells were

ringing for the evening service, and soon the congregation was streaming along Orchard Street in the mellow sunset. The street opened toward the west. The red half-sunken sun shed a solemn splendour on the everyday houses, and crimsoned the windows of Dempster's projecting upper story.

Suddenly a loud murmur arose and spread along the stream of church-goers, and one group after another paused and looked backward. At the far end of the street, men, accompanied by a miscellaneous group of onlookers, are slowly carrying something – a body stretched on a door. Slowly they pass along the middle of the street, lined all the way with awe-struck faces, till they turn aside and pause in the red sunlight before Dempster's door.

It is Dempster's body. No one knows whether he is alive or dead.

CHAPTER 22

It was probably a hard saying to the Pharisees, that 'there is more joy in heaven over one sinner that repenteth, than over ninety and nine just persons that need no repentance.' And certain ingenious philosophers of our own day must surely take offence at a joy so entirely out of correspondence with arithmetical proportion. But a heart that has been taught by its own sore struggles to bleed for the woes of another – that has 'learned pity through suffering' – is likely to find very imperfect satisfaction in the 'balance of happiness,' 'doctrine of compensations,' and other short and easy methods of obtaining thorough complacency in the presence of pain; and for such a heart that saying will not be altogether dark. The emotions, I have observed, are but slightly influenced by arithmetical considerations: the mother, when her sweet lisping little ones have all been taken from her one after another, and she is hanging over her last dead babe, finds small consolation in the fact that the tiny dimpled corpse is but one of a necessary average, and that a thousand other babes brought into the world at the same time are doing well, and are likely to live; and if you stood beside that mother – if you knew her pang and shared it – it is probable you would be equally unable to see a ground of complacency in statistics.

Doubtless a complacency resting on that basis is highly rational; but emotion, I fear, is obstinately irrational: it insists on caring for individuals; it absolutely refuses to adopt the quantitative view of human anguish, and to admit that thirteen happy lives are a set-off against twelve miserable lives, which leaves a clear balance on the side of satisfaction. This is the inherent imbecility of feeling, and one must be a great philosopher to have got quite clear of all that, and to have emerged into the serene air of pure intellect, in which it is evident that individuals really exist for no other purpose than that abstractions may be drawn from them – abstractions that may rise from heaps of ruined lives like the sweet savour of a sacrifice in the nostrils of philosophers, and of a philosophic Deity. And so it comes to pass that for the man who knows sympathy because he has known sorrow, that old, old saying about the joy of angels over the repentant sinner outweighing their joy over the ninety-nine just, has a meaning which does not jar with the language of his own heart. It only tells him, that for angels too there is a transcendent value in human pain, which refuses to be settled by equations; that the eyes of angels too are turned away from the serene happiness of the righteous to bend with yearning pity on the poor erring soul wandering in the desert where no water is; that for angels too the misery of one casts so tremendous a shadow as to eclipse the bliss of ninety-nine.

Mr Tryan had gone through the initiation of suffering: it is no wonder, then, that Janet's restoration was the work that lay nearest his heart; and that, weary as he was in body when he entered the vestry after the evening service, he was impatient to fulfil the promise of seeing her. His experience enabled him to divine – what was the fact – that the hopefulness of the morning would be followed by a return of depression and discouragement, and his sense of the inward and outward difficulties in the way of her restoration was so keen, that he could only find relief from the foreboding it excited by lifting up his heart in prayer. There are unseen elements which often frustrate our wisest calculations – which raise up the sufferer from the edge of the grave, contradicting the prophecies of the clear-sighted physician, and fulfilling the blind clinging hopes of affection; such unseen elements Mr Tryan called the Divine Will, and filled up the margin of ignorance which surrounds all our knowledge with the feelings of trust and resignation. Perhaps the profoundest philosophy could hardly fill it up better.

His mind was occupied in this way as he was absently taking off his gown, when Mr Landor startled him by entering the vestry and asking abruptly,

'Have you heard the news about Dempster?'

'No,' said Mr Tryan, anxiously; 'what is it?'

'He has been thrown out of his gig in the Bridge Way, and he was taken up for dead. They were carrying him home as we were coming to church, and I stayed behind to see what I could do. I went in to speak to Mrs Dempster, and prepare her a little, but she was not at home. Dempster is not dead, however; he was stunned with the fall. Pilgrim came in a few minutes, and he says the right leg is broken in two places. It's likely to be a terrible case, with his state of body. It seems he was more drunk than usual, and they say he came along the Bridge Way flogging his horse like a madman, till at last it gave a sudden wheel, and he was pitched out. The servants said they didn't know where Mrs Dempster was: she had been away from home since yesterday morning; but Mrs Raynor knew.'

'I know where she is,' said Mr Tryan; 'but I think it will be better for her not to be told of this just yet.'

'Ah, that was what Pilgrim said, and so I didn't go round to Mrs Raynor's. He said it would be all the better if Mrs Dempster could be kept out of the house for the present. Do you know if anything new has happened between Dempster and his wife lately? I was surprised to hear of her being at Paddiford church this morning.'

'Yes, something has happened; but I believe she is anxious that the particulars of his behaviour

towards her should not be known. She is at Mrs
Pettifer's – there is no reason for concealing that,
since what has happened to her husband; and
yesterday, when she was in very deep trouble, she
sent for me. I was very thankful she did so: I
believe a great change of feeling has begun in her.
But she is at present in that excitable state of mind
– she has been shaken by so many painful emotions
during the last two days, that I think it would be
better, for this evening at least, to guard her from
a new shock, if possible. But I am going now to
call upon her, and I shall see how she is.'

'Mr Tryan,' said Mr Jerome, who had entered
during the dialogue, and had been standing by
listening with a distressed face, 'I shall tek it as a
favour if you'll let me know if iver there's anything
I can do for Mrs Dempster. Eh, dear, what a world
this is! I think I see 'em fifteen 'ear ago – as happy
a young couple as iver was; and now, what it's all
come to! I was in a hurry, like, to punish Dempster
for pessecutin', but there was a stronger hand at
work nor mine.'

'Yes, Mr Jerome; but don't let us rejoice in
punishment, even when the hand of God alone
inflicts it. The best of us are but poor wretches
just saved from shipwreck: can we feel anything
but awe and pity when we see a fellow-passenger
swallowed by the waves?'

'Right, right, Mr Tryan. I'm over hot an' hasty, that
I am. But I beg on you to tell Mrs Dempster – I
mean, in course, when you've an opportunity – tell

her she's a friend at the White House as she may send for any hour o' the day.'

'Yes; I shall have an opportunity, I dare say, and I will remember your wish. I think,' continued Mr Tryan, turning to Mr Landor, 'I had better see Mr Pilgrim on my way, and learn what is exactly the state of things by this time. What do you think?'

'By all means: if Mrs Dempster is to know, there's no one can break the news to her so well as you. I'll walk with you to Dempster's door. I dare say Pilgrim is there still. Come, Mr Jerome, you've got to go our way too, to fetch your horse.'

Mr Pilgrim was in the passage giving some directions to his assistant, when, to his surprise, he saw Mr Tryan enter. They shook hands; for Mr Pilgrim, never having joined the party of the Anti-Tryanites, had no ground for resisting the growing conviction, that the Evangelical curate was really a good fellow, though he was a fool for not taking better care of himself.

'Why, I didn't expect to see you in your old enemy's quarters,' he said to Mr Tryan. 'However, it will be a good while before poor Dempster shows any fight again.'

'I came on Mrs Dempster's account,' said Mr Tryan. 'She is staying at Mrs Pettifer's; she has had a great shock from some severe domestic trouble lately, and I think it will be wise to defer telling her of this dreadful event for a short time.'

'Why, what has been up, eh?' said Mr Pilgrim,

whose curiosity was at once awakened 'She used to be no friend of yours. Has there been some split between them? It's a new thing for her to turn round on him.'

'O, merely an exaggeration of scenes that must often have happened before. But the question now is, whether you think there is any immediate danger of her husband's death; for in that case I think, from what I have observed of her feelings, she would be pained afterwards to have been kept in ignorance.'

'Well, there's no telling in these cases, you know. I don't apprehend speedy death, and it is not absolutely impossible that we may bring him round again. At present he's in a state of apoplectic stupor; but if that subsides, delirium is almost sure to supervene, and we shall have some painful scenes. It's one of those complicated cases in which the delirium is likely to be of the worst kind – meningitis and delirium tremens together – and we may have a good deal of trouble with him. If Mrs Dempster were told, I should say it would be desirable to persuade her to remain out of the house at present. She could do no good, you know. I've got nurses.'

'Thank you,' said Mr Tryan. 'That is what I wanted to know. Good-bye.'

When Mrs Pettifer opened the door for Mr Tryan, he told her in few words what had happened, and begged her to take an opportunity of letting Mrs Raynor know, that they might, if possible, concur in preventing a premature or sudden disclosure of the event to Janet.

'Poor thing!' said Mrs Pettifer. 'She's not fit to hear any bad news; she's very low this evening – worn out with feeling; and she's not had anything to keep her up, as she's been used to. She seems frightened at the thought of being tempted to take it.'

'Thank God for it; that fear is her greatest security.'

When Mr Tryan entered the parlour this time, Janet was again awaiting him eagerly, and her pale sad face was lighted up with a smile as she rose to meet him. But the next moment she said, with a look of anxiety,

'How very ill and tired you look! You have been working so hard all day, and yet you are come to talk to me. O, you are wearing yourself out. I must go and ask Mrs Pettifer to come and make you have some supper. But this is my mother; you have not seen her before, I think.'

While Mr Tryan was speaking to Mrs Raynor, Janet hurried out, and he, seeing that this good-natured thoughtfulness on his behalf would help to counteract her depression, was not inclined to oppose her wish, but accepted the supper Mrs Pettifer offered him, quietly talking the while about a clothing club he was going to establish in Paddiford, and the want of provident habits among the poor.

Presently, however, Mrs Raynor said she must

go home for an hour, to see how her little maiden was going on, and Mrs Pettifer left the room with her to take the opportunity of telling her what had happened to Dempster. When Janet was left alone with Mr Tryan, she said,

'I feel so uncertain what to do about my husband. I am so weak – my feelings change so from hour to hour. This morning, when I felt so hopeful and happy, I thought I should like to go back to him, and try to make up for what has been wrong in me. I thought, now God would help me, and I should have you to teach and advise me, and I could bear the troubles that would come. But since then – all this afternoon and evening – I have had the same feelings I used to have, the same dread of his anger and cruelty, and it seems to me as if I should never be able to bear it without falling into the same sins, and doing just what I did before. Yet, if it were settled that I should live apart from him, I know it would always be a load on my mind that I had shut myself out from going back to him. It seems a dreadful thing in life, when any one has been so near to one as a husband for fifteen years, to part and be nothing to each other any more. Surely that is a very strong tie, and I feel as if my duty can never lie quite away from it. It is very difficult to know what to do: what ought I to do?'

'I think it will be well not to take any decisive step yet. Wait until your mind is calmer. You might remain with your mother for a little while; I think you have no real ground for fearing any annoyance from your husband at present; he has put himself too much in the wrong; he will very likely leave you unmolested for some time. Dismiss this difficult question from your mind just now, if you can. Every new day may bring you new grounds for decision, and what is most needful for your health of mind is repose from that haunting anxiety about the future which has been preying on you. Cast yourself on God, and trust that He will direct you; He will make your duty clear to you, if you wait submissively on Him.'

'Yes; I will wait a little, as you tell me. I will go to my mother's tomorrow, and pray to be guided rightly. You will pray for me, too.'

CHAPTER 23

The next morning Janet was so much calmer, and at breakfast spoke so decidedly of going to her mother's, that Mrs Pettifer and Mrs Raynor agreed it would be wise to let her know by degrees what had befallen her husband, since as soon as she went out there would be danger of her meeting some one who would betray the fact. But Mrs Raynor thought it would be well first to call at Dempster's, and ascertain how he was: so she said to Janet,

'My dear, I'll go home first, and see to things, and get your room ready. You needn't come yet, you know. I shall be back again in an hour or so, and we can go together.'

'O no,' said Mrs Pettifer. 'Stay with me till evening. I shall be lost without you. You needn't go till quite evening.'

Janet had dipped into the *Life of Henry Martyn*, which Mrs Pettifer had from the Paddiford Lending Library, and her interest was so arrested by that pathetic missionary story, that she readily acquiesced in both propositions, and Mrs Raynor set out.

She had been gone more than an hour, and it was nearly twelve o'clock, when Janet put down her book; and after sitting meditatively for some minutes with her eyes unconsciously fixed on the opposite wall, she rose, went to her bedroom, and, hastily putting on her bonnet and shawl, came down to Mrs Pettifer, who was busy in the kitchen.

'Mrs Pettifer,' she said, 'tell mother, when she comes back, I'm gone to see what is become of those poor Lakins in Butcher Lane. I know they're half starving, and I've neglected them so, lately. And then, I think, I'll go on to Mrs Crewe. I want to see the dear little woman, and tell her myself about my going to hear Mr Tryan. She won't feel it half so much if I tell her myself.'

'Won't you wait till your mother comes, or put it off till to-morrow?' said Mrs Pettifer, alarmed. 'You'll hardly be back in time for dinner, if you get talking to Mrs Crewe. And you'll have to pass by your husband's, you know; and yesterday, you were so afraid of seeing him.'

'O, Robert will be shut up at the office now, if he's not gone out of the town. I must go – I feel I must be doing something for some one – not be a mere useless log any longer. I've been reading about that wonderful Henry Martyn; he's just like Mr Tryan – wearing himself out for other people, and I sit thinking of nothing but myself. I *must* go. Good-bye; I shall be back soon.'

She ran off before Mrs Pettifer could utter another word of dissuasion, leaving the good woman in considerable anxiety lest this new impulse of Janet's should frustrate all precautions to save her from a sudden shock.

Janet, having paid her visit in Butcher Lane, turned again into Orchard Street on her way to Mrs Crewe's, and was thinking, rather sadly, that her mother's economical housekeeping would leave no abundant surplus to be sent to the hungry Lakins, when she saw Mr Pilgrim in advance of her on the other side of the street. He was walking at a rapid pace, and when he reached Dempster's door he turned and entered without knocking.

Janet was startled. Mr Pilgrim would never enter in that way unless there were some one very ill in the house. It was her husband; she felt certain of it at once. Something had happened to him. Without a moment's pause, she ran across the street, opened the door and entered. There was no one in the passage. The dining-room door was wide open – no one was there. Mr Pilgrim, then, was already up-stairs. She rushed up at once to Dempster's room – her own room. The door was open, and she paused in pale horror at the sight before her, which seemed to stand out only with the more appalling distinctness because the noonday light was darkened to twilight in the chamber.

Two strong nurses were using their utmost force to hold Dempster in bed, while the medical assistant was applying a sponge to his head, and Mr Pilgrim was busy adjusting some apparatus in the background. Dempster's face was purple and swollen, his eyes dilated, and fixed with a look of dire terror on something he seemed to see approaching him from the iron closet. He trembled violently, and struggled as if to jump out of bed.

'Let me go, let me go,' he said in a loud, hoarse whisper; 'she's coming. . . . she's cold. . . . she's dead. . . . she'll strangle me with her black hair. Ah!' he shrieked aloud, 'her hair is all serpents. . . . they're black serpents. . . . they hiss. . . . they hiss. . . . let me go. . . . let me go. . . . she wants to drag me with her cold arms. . . . her arms are serpents. . . . they are great white serpents. . . . they'll twine round me. . . . she wants to drag me into the cold water. . . . her bosom is cold. . . . it is black. . . . it is all serpents. . . .'

'No, Robert,' Janet cried, in tones of yearning pity, rushing to the side of the bed, and stretching out her arms towards him, 'no, here is Janet. She is not dead – she forgives you.'

Dempster's maddened senses seemed to receive some new impression from her appearance. The terror gave way to rage.

'Ha! you sneaking hypocrite!' he burst out in a grating voice, 'you threaten me. . . . you mean to have your revenge on me, do you? Do your worst! I've got the law on my side. . . . I know the law. . . . I'll hunt you down like a hare. . . . prove it. . . . prove that I was tampered with. . . . prove that I took the money. . . . prove it. . . . you can prove nothing. . . . you damned psalm-singing maggots!

I'll make a fire under you, and smoke off the whole pack of you. . . . I'll sweep you up. . . . I'll grind you to powder. . . . small powder. . . . (here his voice dropped to a low tone of shuddering disgust). . . . powder on the bed-clothes. . . . running about. . . . black lice. . . . they are coming in swarms. . . . Janet! come and take them away. . . . curse you! why don't you come? Janet!'

Poor Janet was kneeling by the bed with her face buried in her hands. She almost wished her worst moment back again rather than this. It seemed as if her husband was already imprisoned in misery, and she could not reach him – his ear deaf for ever to the sounds of love and forgiveness. His sins had made a hard crust round his soul; her pitying voice could not pierce it.

'Not there, isn't she?' he went on in a defiant tone. 'Why do you ask me where she is? I'll have every drop of yellow blood out of your veins if you come questioning me. Your blood is yellow. . . . in your purse. . . . running out of your purse. . . . What! you're changing it into toads, are you? They're crawling. . . . they're flying. . . . they're flying about my head. . . . the toads are flying about. Ostler! ostler! bring out my gig. . . . bring it out, you lazy beast. . . . ha! you'll follow me, will you?. . . . you'll fly about my head. . . . you've got fiery tongues. . . . Ostler! curse you! why don't you come? Janet! come and take the toads away. . . . Janet!'

This last time he uttered her name with such a

shriek of terror, that Janet involuntarily started up from her knees, and stood as if petrified by the horrible vibration. Dempster stared wildly in silence for some moments; then he spoke again in a hoarse whisper:—

'Dead. . . . is she dead? *She* did it, then. She buried herself in the iron chest. . . . she left her clothes out, though. . . . she isn't dead. . . . why do you pretend she's dead?. . . . she's coming. . . . she's coming out of the iron closet. . . . there are the black serpents. . . . stop her. . . . let me go. . . . stop her. . . . she wants to drag me away into the cold black water. . . . her bosom is black. . . . it is all serpents. . . . they are getting longer. . . . the great white serpents are getting longer. . . .'

Here Mr Pilgrim came forward with the apparatus to bind him, but Dempster's struggles became more and more violent. 'Ostler! ostler!' he shouted, 'bring out the gig . . . give me the whip!' – and bursting loose from the strong hands that held him, he began to flog the bed-clothes furiously with his right arm.

'Get along, you lame brute! – sc – sc –! that's it! there you go! They think they've outwitted me, do they? The sneaking idiots! I'll be up with them by-and-by. I'll make them say the Lord's Prayer backwards. . . . I'll pepper them so that the devil shall eat them raw. . . . sc – sc – sc – we shall see who'll be the winner yet. . . . get along, you damned limping beast. . . . I'll lay your back open. . . . I'll. . . .'

He raised himself with a stronger effort than ever to flog the bed-clothes, and fell back in convulsions. Janet gave a scream, and sank on her knees again. She thought he was dead.

As soon as Mr Pilgrim was able to give her a moment's attention, he came to her, and, taking her by the arm, attempted to draw her gently out of the room.

'Now, my dear Mrs Dempster, let me persuade you not to remain in the room at present. We shall soon relieve these symptoms, I hope; it is nothing but the delirium that ordinarily attends such cases.'

'O, what is the matter? what brought it on?'

'He fell out of the gig; the right leg is broken. It is a terrible accident, and I don't disguise that there is considerable danger attending it, owing to the state of the brain. But Mr Dempster has a strong constitution, you know: in a few days these symptoms may be allayed, and he may do well. Let me beg of you to keep out of the room at present: you can do no good until Mr Dempster is better, and able to know you. But you ought not to be alone; let me advise you to have Mrs Raynor with you.'

'Yes, I will send for mother. But you must not object to my being in the room. I shall be very quiet now, only just at first the shock was so great; I knew nothing about it. I can help the nurses a great deal; I can put the cold things to his head. He may be sensible for a moment, and know me.

Pray do not say any more against it: my heart is set on being with him.'

Mr Pilgrim gave way, and Janet, having sent for her mother and put off her bonnet and shawl, returned to take her place by the side of her husband's bed.

CHAPTER 24

Day after day, with only short intervals of rest, Janet kept her place in that sad chamber. No wonder the sick-room and the lazarettohave so often been a refuge from the tossings of intellectual doubt – a place of repose for the worn and wounded spirit. Here is a duty about which all creeds and all philosophies are at one: here, at least, the conscience will not be dogged by doubt, the benign impulse will not be checked by adverse theory; here you may begin to act without settling one preliminary question. To moisten the sufferer's parched lips through the long night-watches, to bear up the drooping head, to lift the helpless limbs, to divine the want that can find no utterance beyond the feeble motion of the hand or beseeching glance of the eye – these are offices that demand no self-questionings, no casuistry, no assent to propositions, no weighing of consequences. Within the four walls where the stir and glare of the world are shut out, and every voice is subdued – where a human being lies prostrate, thrown on the tender mercies of his fellow, the moral relation of man to man is reduced to its utmost clearness and simplicity: bigotry cannot confuse it, theory cannot pervert it, passion, awed into quiescence, can neither pollute nor perturb it. As we bend over the sick-bed, all the forces of our nature rush towards the channels of pity, of patience, and of love, and sweep down the miserable choking drift of our quarrels, our debates, our would-be wisdom, and our clamorous selfish desires. This blessing of serene freedom from the importunities of opinion lies in all simple direct acts of mercy, and is one source of that sweet calm which is often felt by the watcher in the sick-room, even when the duties there are of a hard and terrible kind.

Something of that benign result was felt by Janet during her tendance in her husband's chamber. When the first heart-piercing hours were over – when her horror at his delirium was no longer fresh, she began to be conscious of her relief from the burden of decision as to her future course. The question that agitated her, about returning to her husband, had been solved in a moment; and this illness, after all, might be the herald of another blessing, just as that dreadful midnight when she stood an outcast in cold and darkness, had been followed by the dawn of a new hope. Robert would get better; this illness might alter him; he would be a long time feeble, needing help, walking with a crutch, perhaps. She would wait on him with such tenderness, such all-forgiving love, that the old harshness and cruelty must melt away for ever under the heart-sunshine she would pour around him. Her bosom heaved at the thought, and delicious tears fell. Janet's was a nature in which hatred and revenge could find no place; the long bitter years drew half their bitterness from her ever-living remembrance of the too short years of love that went before; and the thought that her husband would ever put her hand to his lips again, and recall the days when they sat on the grass together, and he laid scarlet poppies on her black hair, and called her his gypsy queen, seemed to send a tide of loving oblivion over all the harsh and stony space they had traversed since. The Divine Love that had already shone upon her would be with her; she would lift up her soul continually for help; Mr Tryan, she knew, would pray for her. If she felt herself failing, she would confess it to him at once; if her feet began to slip, there was that stay for her to cling to. O she could never be drawn back into that cold damp vault of sin and despair again; she had felt the morning sun, she had tasted the sweet pure air of trust and penitence and submission.

These were the thoughts passing through Janet's mind as she hovered about her husband's bed, and these were the hopes she poured out to Mr Tryan when he called to see her. It was so evident that they were strengthening her in her new struggle – they shed such a glow of calm enthusiasm over her face as she spoke of them, that Mr Tryan could not bear to throw on them the chill of premonitory doubts, though a previous conversation he had had with Mr Pilgrim had convinced him that there was not the faintest probability of Dempster's recovery. Poor Janet did not know the significance of the changing symptoms, and when, after the lapse of a week, the delirium began to lose some of its violence, and to be interrupted by longer and longer intervals of stupor, she tried to think that these might be steps on the way to recovery, and she shrank from questioning Mr Pilgrim, lest he should confirm the fears that began to get predominance in her mind. But before many days were past, he thought it right not to allow her to blind herself any longer. One day – it was just about noon, when bad news always seems most sickening – he led her from her husband's chamber into the opposite drawing-room, where Mrs Raynor was sitting, and said to her, in that low tone of sympathetic feeling which sometimes gave a sudden air of gentleness to this rough man,—

'My dear Mrs Dempster, it is right in these cases, you know, to be prepared for the worst. I think I shall be saving you pain by preventing you from entertaining any false hopes, and Mr Dempster's state is now such that I fear we must consider recovery impossible. The affection of the brain might not have been hopeless, but, you see, there is a terrible complication; and I am grieved to say, the broken limb is mortifying.'

Janet listened with a sinking heart. That future

of love and forgiveness would never come, then: he was going out of her sight for ever, where her pity could never reach him. She turned cold, and trembled.

'But do you think he will die,' she said, 'without ever coming to himself? without ever knowing me?'

'One cannot say that with certainty. It is not impossible that the cerebral oppression may subside, and that he may become conscious. If there is anything you would wish to be said or done in that case, it would be well to be prepared. I should think,' Mr Pilgrim continued, turning to Mrs Raynor, 'Mr Dempster's affairs are likely to be in order – his will is. . . .'

'O, I wouldn't have him troubled about those things,' interrupted Janet; 'he has no relations but quite distant ones – no one but me. I wouldn't take up the time with that. I only want to . . . .'

She was unable to finish; she felt her sobs rising, and left the room.

'O God!' she said inwardly, 'is not Thy love greater than mine? Have mercy on him! have mercy on him!'

This happened on Wednesday, ten days after the fatal accident. By the following Sunday, Dempster was in a state of rapidly increasing prostration; and when Mr Pilgrim, who, in turn with his assistant, had slept in the house from the beginning, came in, about half-past ten, as usual, he scarcely

573

believed that the feebly struggling life would last out till morning. For the last few days he had been administering stimulants to relieve the exhaustion which had succeeded the alternations of delirium and stupor. This slight office was all that now remained to be done for the patient; so at eleven o'clock Mr Pilgrim went to bed, having given directions to the nurse, and desired her to call him if any change took place, or if Mrs Dempster desired his presence.

Janet could not be persuaded to leave the room. She was yearning and watching for a moment in which her husband's eyes would rest consciously upon her, and he would know that she had forgiven him.

How changed he was since that terrible Monday, nearly a fortnight ago! He lay motionless, but for the irregular breathing that stirred his broad chest and thick muscular neck. His features were no longer purple and swollen; they were pale, sunken, and haggard. A cold perspiration stood in beads on the protuberant forehead, and on the wasted hands stretched motionless on the bed-clothes. It was better to see the hands so, than convulsively picking the air, as they had been a week ago.

Janet sat on the edge of the bed through the long hours of candle-light, watching the unconscious half-closed eyes, wiping the perspiration from the brow and cheeks, and keeping her left hand on the cold unanswering right hand that lay beside her on the bed-clothes. She was almost as pale as her dying husband, and there were dark lines under her eyes, for this was the third night since she had taken off her clothes; but the eager straining gaze of her dark eyes, and the acute sensibility that lay in every line about her mouth, made a strange contrast with the blank unconsciousness and emaciated animalism of the face she was watching.

There was profound stillness in the house. She heard no sound but her husband's breathing and the ticking of the watch on the mantelpiece. The candle, placed high up, shed a soft light down on the one object she cared to see. There was a smell of brandy in the room; it was given to her husband from time to time; but this smell, which at first had produced in her a faint shuddering sensation, was now become indifferent to her; she did not even perceive it; she was too unconscious of herself to feel either temptations or accusations. She only felt that the husband of her youth was dying; far, far out of her reach, as if she were standing helpless on the shore, while he was sinking in the black storm-waves; she only yearned for one moment in which she might satisfy the deep forgiving pity of her soul by one look of love, one word of tenderness.

Her sensations and thoughts were so persistent that she could not measure the hours, and it was a surprise to her when the nurse put out the candle, and let in the faint morning light. Mrs

Raynor, anxious about Janet, was already up, and now brought in some fresh coffee for her; and Mr Pilgrim, having awaked, had hurried on his clothes, and was come in to see how Dempster was.

This change from candle-light to morning, this recommencement of the same round of things that had happened yesterday, was a discouragement rather than a relief to Janet. She was more conscious of her chill weariness; the new light thrown on her husband's face seemed to reveal the still work that death had been doing through the night; she felt her last lingering hope that he would ever know her again forsake her.

But now Mr Pilgrim, having felt the pulse, was putting some brandy in a tea-spoon between Dempster's lips; the brandy went down, and his breathing became freer. Janet noticed the change, and her heart beat faster as she leaned forward to watch him. Suddenly a slight movement, like the passing away of a shadow, was visible in his face, and he opened his eyes full on Janet.

It was almost like meeting him again on the resurrection morning, after the night of the grave.

'Robert, do you know me?'

He kept his eyes fixed on her, and there was a faintly perceptible motion of the lips, as if he wanted to speak.

But the moment of speech was for ever gone

– the moment for asking pardon of her, if he wanted to ask it. Could he read the full forgiveness that was written in her eyes? She never knew; for, as she was bending to kiss him, the thick veil of death fell between them, and her lips touched a corpse.

CHAPTER 25

The faces looked very hard and unmoved that surrounded Dempster's grave, while old Mr Crewe read the burial-service in his low, broken voice. The pall-bearers were such men as Mr Pittman, Mr Lowme, and Mr Budd – men whom Dempster had called his friends while he was in life; and worldly faces never look so worldly as at a funeral. They have the same effect of grating incongruity as the sound of a coarse voice breaking the solemn silence of night.

The one face that had sorrow in it was covered by a thick crape-veil, and the sorrow was suppressed and silent. No one knew how deep it was; for the thought in most of her neighbours' minds was, that Mrs Dempster could hardly have had better fortune than to lose a bad husband who had left her the compensation of a good income. They found it difficult to conceive that her husband's death could be felt by her otherwise than as a deliverance. The person who was most thoroughly convinced that Janet's grief was deep and real, was Mr Pilgrim, who in general was not at all weakly given to a belief in disinterested feeling.

'That woman has a tender heart,' he was frequently heard to observe in his morning rounds about this time. 'I used to think there was a great deal of palaver in her, but you may depend upon it there's no pretence about her. If he'd been the kindest husband in the world she couldn't have felt more. There's a great deal of good in Mrs Dempster – a great deal of good.'

'*I* always said so,' was Mrs Lowme's reply, when he made the observation to her; 'she was always so very full of pretty attentions to me when I was ill. But they tell me now she's turned Tryanite; if that's it we shan't agree again. It's very inconsistent in her, I think, turning round in that way, after being the foremost to laugh at the Tryanite cant, and especially in a woman of her habits; she should cure herself of *them* before she pretends to be over-religious.'

'Well, I think she means to cure herself, do you know,' said Mr Pilgrim, whose goodwill towards Janet was just now quite above that temperate point at which he could indulge his feminine patients with a little judicious detraction. 'I feel sure she has not taken any stimulants all through her husband's illness; and, she has been constantly in the way of them. I can see she sometimes suffers a good deal of depression for want of them – it shows all the more resolution in her. Those cures are rare; but I've known them happen sometimes with people of strong will.'

Mrs Lowme took an opportunity of retailing

Mr Pilgrim's conversation to Mrs Phipps, who, as a victim of Pratt and plethora, could rarely enjoy that pleasure at first-hand. Mrs Phipps was a woman of decided opinions, though of wheezy utterance.

'For my part,' she remarked, 'I'm glad to hear there's any likelihood of improvement in Mrs Dempster, but I think the way things have turned out seems to show that she was more to blame than people thought she was; else, why should she feel so much about her husband? And Dempster, I understand, has left his wife pretty nearly all his property to do as she likes with; *that* isn't behaving like such a very bad husband. I don't believe Mrs Dempster can have had so much provocation as they pretended. I've known husbands who've laid plans for tormenting their wives when they're underground – tying up their money and hindering them from marrying again. Not that *I* should ever wish to marry again; I think one husband in one's life is enough in all conscience;' – here she threw a fierce glance at the amiable Mr Phipps, who was innocently delighting himself with the *facetiæ* in the *Rotherby Guardian*, and thinking the editor must be a droll fellow – 'but it's aggravating to be tied up in that way. Why, they say Mrs Dempster will have as good as six-hundred a-year at least. A fine thing for her, that was a poor girl without a farthing to her fortune. It's well if she doesn't make ducks and drakes of it somehow.'

Mrs Phipps's view of Janet, however, was far

from being the prevalent one in Milby. Even neighbours who had no strong personal interest in her, could hardly see the noble-looking woman in her widow's dress, with a sad sweet gravity in her face, and not be touched with fresh admiration for her – and not feel, at least vaguely, that she had entered on a new life in which it was a sort of desecration to allude to the painful past. And the old friends who had a real regard for her, but whose cordiality had been repelled or chilled of late years, now came round her with hearty demonstrations of affection. Mr Jerome felt that his happiness had a substantial addition now he could once more call on that 'nice little woman Mrs Dempster,' and think of her with rejoicing instead of sorrow. The Pratts lost no time in returning to the footing of old-established friendship with Janet and her mother; and Miss Pratt felt it incumbent on her, on all suitable occasions, to deliver a very emphatic approval of the remarkable strength of mind she understood Mrs Dempster to be exhibiting. The Miss Linnets were eager to meet Mr Tryan's wishes by greeting Janet as one who was likely to be a sister in religious feeling and good works; and Mrs Linnet was so agreeably surprised by the fact that Dempster had left his wife the money 'in that handsome way, to do what she liked with it,' that she even included Dempster himself, and his villainous discovery of the flaw in her title to Pye's Croft, in her magnanimous oblivion of past offences. She and Mrs Jerome agreed over a friendly cup of tea that there were 'a maeny husbands as was very fine spoken an' all that, an' yit all the while kep' a will locked up from you, as tied you up as tight as aenything. I assure *you*,' Mrs Jerome continued, dropping her voice in a confidential manner, 'I know no more to this day about Mr Jerome's will, nor the child as is unborn. I've no fears about a income – I'm well awear Mr Jerome 'ud niver leave me stret for that; but I should like t' hev a thousand or two at my own disposial; it meks a widder a deal more looked on.'

Perhaps this ground of respect to widows might not be entirely without its influence on the Milby mind, and might do something towards conciliating those more aristocratic acquaintances of Janet's, who would otherwise have been inclined to take the severest view of her apostasy towards Evangelicalism. Errors look so very ugly in persons of small means – one feels they are taking quite a liberty in going astray; whereas people of fortune may naturally indulge in a few delinquencies. 'They've got the money for it,' as the girl said of her mistress who had made herself ill with pickled salmon. However it may have been, there was not an acquaintance of Janet's, in Milby, that did not offer her civilities in the early days of her widowhood. Even the severe Mrs Phipps was not an exception; for heaven knows what would become of our sociality if we never visited people we speak ill of: we should live, like Egyptian hermits, in crowded solitude.

Perhaps the attentions most grateful to Janet

were those of her old friend Mrs Crewe, whose attachment to her favourite proved quite too strong for any resentment she might be supposed to feel on the score of Mr Tryan. The little deaf old lady couldn't do without her accustomed visitor, whom she had seen grow up from child to woman, always so willing to chat with her and tell her all the news, though she *was* deaf; while other people thought it tiresome to shout in her ear, and irritated her by recommending ear-trumpets of various construction.

All this friendliness was very precious to Janet. She was conscious of the aid it gave her in the self-conquest which was the blessing she prayed for with every fresh morning. The chief strength of her nature lay in her affection, which coloured all the rest of her mind: it gave a personal sisterly tenderness to her acts of benevolence; it made her cling with tenacity to every object that had once stirred her kindly emotions. Alas! it was unsatisfied, wounded affection that had made her trouble greater than she could bear. And now there was no check to the full flow of that plenteous current in her nature – no gnawing secret anguish – no overhanging terror – no inward shame. Friendly faces beamed on her; she felt that friendly hearts were approving her, and wishing her well, and that mild sunshine of goodwill fell beneficently on her new hopes and efforts, as the clear shining after rain falls on the tender leaf-buds of spring, and wins them from promise to fulfilment.

And she needed these secondary helps, for her wrestling with her past self was not always easy. The strong emotions from which the life of a human being receives a new bias, win their victory as the sea wins his: though their advance may be sure, they will often, after a mightier wave than usual, seem to roll back so far as to lose all the ground they had made. Janet showed the strong bent of her will by taking every outward precaution against the occurrence of a temptation. Her mother was now her constant companion, having shut up her little dwelling and come to reside in Orchard Street; and Janet gave all dangerous keys into her keeping, entreating her to lock them away in some secret place. Whenever the too well-known depression and craving threatened her, she would seek a refuge in what had always been her purest enjoyment – in visiting one of her poor neighbours, in carrying some food or comfort to a sick-bed, in cheering with her smile some of the familiar dwellings up the dingy back-lanes. But the great source of courage, the great help to perseverance, was the sense that she had a friend and teacher in Mr Tryan: she could confess her difficulties to him; she knew he prayed for her; she had always before her the prospect of soon seeing him, and hearing words of admonition and comfort, that came to her charged with a divine power such as she had never found in human words before.

So the time passed, till it was far on in May, nearly a month after her husband's death, when, as she and her mother were seated peacefully at breakfast in the dining-room, looking through the open window at the old-fashioned garden, where the grass-plot was now whitened with apple-blossoms, a letter was brought in for Mrs Raynor.

'Why, there's the Thurston post-mark on it,' she said. 'It must be about your Aunt Anna. Ah, so it is, poor thing; she's been taken worse this last day or two, and has asked them to send for me. That dropsy is carrying her off at last, I dare say. Poor thing! it will be a happy release. I must go, my dear – she's your father's last sister – though I'm sorry to leave you. However, perhaps I shall not have to stay more than a night or two.'

Janet looked distressed as she said, 'Yes, you must go, mother. But I don't know what I shall do without you. I think I shall run in to Mrs Pettifer, and ask her to come and stay with me while you're away. I'm sure she will.'

At twelve o'clock, Janet, having seen her mother in the coach that was to carry her to Thurston, called, on her way back, at Mrs Pettifer's, but found, to her great disappointment, that her old friend was gone out for the day. So she wrote on a leaf of her pocket-book an urgent request that Mrs Pettifer would come and stay with her while her mother was away; and, desiring the servant-girl to give it to her mistress as soon as she came home, walked on to the Vicarage to sit with Mrs Crewe, thinking to relieve in this way the feeling of desolateness and undefined fear that was taking possession of her on being left alone for the first time since that great crisis in her life. And Mrs Crewe, too, was not at home!

Janet, with a sense of discouragement for which she rebuked herself as childish, walked sadly home again; and when she entered the vacant dining-room, she could not help bursting into tears. It is such vague undefinable states of susceptibility as this – states of excitement or depression, half mental, half physical – that determine many a tragedy in women's lives. Janet could scarcely eat anything at her solitary dinner; she tried to fix her attention on a book in vain; she walked about the garden, and felt the very sunshine melancholy.

Between four and five o'clock, old Mr Pittman called, and joined her in the garden, where she had been sitting for some time under one of the great apple-trees, thinking how Robert, in his best moods, used to take little Mamsey to look at the cucumbers, or to see the Alderney cow with its calf in the paddock. The tears and sobs had come again at these thoughts; and when Mr Pittman approached her, she was feeling languid and exhausted. But the old gentleman's sight and sensibility were obtuse, and, to Janet's satisfaction, he showed no consciousness that she was in grief.

'I have a task to impose upon you, Mrs Dempster,' he said, with a certain toothless pomposity habitual to him: 'I want you to look over those letters again in Dempster's bureau, and see if you can find one from Poole about the mortgage on those houses at Dingley. It will be worth twenty pounds, if you can find it; and I don't know where it can be, if it isn't among those letters in the bureau. I've looked everywhere at the office for it. I'm going home now, but I'll call again to-morrow, if you'll be good enough to look in the mean time.'

Janet said she would look directly, and turned with Mr Pittman into the house. But the search would take her some time, so he bade her good-bye, and she went at once to a bureau which stood in a small back room, where Dempster used some-times to write letters and receive people who came on business out of office hours. She had looked through the contents of the bureau more than once; but to-day, on removing the last bundle of letters from one of the compartments, she saw what she had never seen before, a small nick in the wood, made in the shape of a thumb-nail, evidently intended as a means of pushing aside the movable back of the compartment. In her examination hitherto she had not found such a letter as Mr Pittman had described – perhaps there might be more letters behind this slide. She pushed it back at once, and saw – no letters, but a small spirit decanter, half full of pale brandy, Dempster's habitual drink.

An impetuous desire shook Janet through all her members; it seemed to master her with the inevi-table force of strong fumes that flood our senses before we are aware. Her hand was on the decanter; pale and excited she was lifting it out of its niche, when, with a start and a shudder, she dashed it to the ground, and the room was filled with the odour of the spirit. Without staying to shut up the bureau, she rushed out of the room, snatched up her bonnet and mantle which lay in the dining-room, and hurried out of the house.

Where should she go? In what place would this demon that had re-entered her be scared back again? She walks rapidly along the street in the direction of the church. She is soon at the gate of the churchyard; she passes through it, and makes her way across the graves to a spot she knows – a spot where the turf was stirred not long ago, where a tomb is to be erected soon. It is very near the church wall, on the side which now lies in deep shadow, quite shut out from the rays of the west-ering sun by a projecting buttress.

Janet sat down on the ground. It was a sombre spot. A thick hedge, surmounted by elm trees, was in front of her; a projecting buttress on each side. But she wanted to shut out even these objects. Her thick crape veil was down; but she closed her eyes behind it, and pressed her hands upon them. She wanted to summon up the vision of the past; she wanted to lash the demon out of her soul with the stinging memories of the bygone misery; she wanted to renew the old horror and the old anguish, that she might throw herself with the more desperate clinging energy at the foot of the cross, where the Divine Sufferer would impart divine strength. She tried to recall those first bitter moments of shame, which were like the shuddering discovery of the leper that the dire taint is upon him; the deeper and deeper lapse; the on-coming of settled despair; the awful moments by the bedside of her self-maddened husband. And then she tried to live through, with a remembrance made more vivid by that contrast, the blessed hours of hope, and joy, and peace that had come to her of late, since her whole soul had been bent towards the attainment of purity and holiness.

But now, when the paroxysm of temptation was past, dread and despondency began to thrust themselves, like cold heavy mists, between her and the heaven to which she wanted to look for light and guidance. The temptation would come again – that rush of desire might overmaster her the next time – she would slip back again into that deep slimy pit from which she had been once rescued, and there might be no delieverance for her more. Her prayers did not help her, for fear predominated over trust; she had no confidence that the aid she sought would be given; the idea of her future fall had grasped her mind too strongly. Alone, in this way, she was powerless. If she could see Mr Tryan, if she could confess all to him, she might gather hope again. She *must* see him; she must go to him.

Janet rose from the ground, and walked away with a quick resolved step. She had been seated there a long while, and the sun had already sunk. It was late for her to walk to Paddiford and go to

Mr Tryan's, where she had never called before; but there was no other way of seeing him that evening, and she could not hesitate about it. She walked towards a footpath through the fields, which would take her to Paddiford without obliging her to go through the town. The way was rather long, but she preferred it, because it left less probability of her meeting acquaintances, and she shrank from having to speak to any one.

The evening red had nearly faded by the time Janet knocked at Mrs Wagstaff's door. The good woman looked surprised to see her at that hour; but Janet's mourning weeds and the painful agitation of her face quickly brought the second thought, that some urgent trouble had sent her there.

'Mr Tryan's just come in,' she said. 'If you'll step into the parlour, I'll go up and tell him you're here. He seemed very tired and poorly.'

At another time Janet would have felt distress at the idea that she was disturbing Mr Tryan when he required rest; but now her need was too great for that: she could feel nothing but a sense of coming relief, when she heard his step on the stair and saw him enter the room.

He went towards her with a look of anxiety, and said, 'I fear something is the matter. I fear you are in trouble.'

Then poor Janet poured forth her sad tale of temptation and despondency; and even while she was confessing she felt half her burden removed.

The act of confiding in human sympathy, the consciousness that a fellow-being was listening to her with patient pity, prepared her soul for that stronger leap by which faith grasps the idea of the divine sympathy. When Mr Tryan spoke words of consolation and encouragement, she could now believe the message of mercy; the water-floods that had threatened to overwhelm her rolled back again, and life once more spread its heaven-covered space before her. She had been unable to pray alone; but now his prayer bore her own soul along with it, as the broad tongue of flame carries upwards in its vigorous leap the little flickering fire that could hardly keep alight by itself.

But Mr Tryan was anxious that Janet should not linger out at this late hour. When he saw that she was calmed, he said, 'I will walk home with you now; we can talk on the way.' But Janet's mind was now sufficiently at liberty for her to notice the signs of feverish weariness in his appearance, and she would not hear of causing him any further fatigue.

'No, no,' she said earnestly, 'you will pain me very much – indeed you will, by going out again to-night on my account. There is no real reason why I should not go alone.' And when he persisted, fearing that for her to be seen out so late alone might excite remark, she said imploringly, with a half sob in her voice, 'What should I – what would others like me do, if you went from us? *Why* will you not think more of that, and take care of yourself?'

He had often had that appeal made to him before, but to-night – from Janet's lips – it seemed to have a new force for him, and he gave way. At first, indeed, he only did so on condition that she would let Mrs Wagstaff go with her; but Janet had determined to walk home alone. She preferred solitude; she wished not to have her present feelings distracted by any conversation.

So she went out into the dewy starlight; and as Mr Tryan turned away from her, he felt a stronger wish than ever that his fragile life might last out for him to see Janet's restoration thoroughly established – to see her no longer fleeing, struggling, clinging up the steep sides of a precipice whence she might be any moment hurled back into the depths of despair, but walking firmly on the level ground of habit. He inwardly resolved that nothing but a peremptory duty should ever take him from Milby – that he would not cease to watch over her until life forsook him.

Janet walked on quickly till she turned into the fields; then she slackened her pace a little, enjoying the sense of solitude which a few hours before had been intolerable to her. The Divine Presence did not now seem far off, where she had not wings to reach it; prayer itself seemed superfluous in those moments of calm trust. The temptation which had so lately made her shudder before the possibilities of the future, was now a source of confidence; for had she not been delivered from it? Had not rescue come in the extremity of danger? Yes; Infinite Love was caring for her. She felt like a little child whose hand is firmly grasped by its father, as its frail limbs make their way over the rough ground; if it should stumble, the father will not let it go.

That walk in the dewy starlight remained for ever in Janet's memory as one of those baptismal epochs, when the soul, dipped in the sacred waters of joy and peace, rises from them with new energies, with more unalterable longings.

When she reached home she found Mrs Pettifer there, anxious for her return. After thanking her for coming, Janet only said, 'I have been to Mr Tryan's; I wanted to speak to him;' and then remembering how she had left the bureau and papers, she went into the back-room, where, apparently, no one had been since she quitted it; for there lay the fragments of glass, and the room was still full of the hateful odour. How feeble and miserable the temptation seemed to her at this moment! She rang for Kitty to come and pick up the fragments and rub the floor, while she herself replaced the papers and locked up the bureau.

The next morning, when seated at breakfast with Mrs Pettifer, Janet said,

'What a dreary, unhealthy-looking place that is where Mr Tryan lives! I'm sure it must be very bad for him to live there. Do you know, all this morning, since I've been awake, I've been turning over a little plan in my mind. I think it a charming one – all the more, because *you* are concerned in it.'

'Why, what can that be?'

'You know that house on the Redhill road they call Holly Mount; it is shut up now. That is Robert's house; at least, it is mine now, and it stands on one of the healthiest spots about here. Now, I've been settling in my own mind, that if a dear good woman of my acquaintance, who knows how to make a home as comfortable and cozy as a bird's nest, were to take up her abode there, and have Mr Tryan as a lodger, she would be doing one of the most useful deeds in all her useful life.'

'You've such a way of wrapping up things in pretty words. You must speak plainer.'

'In plain words, then, I should like to settle you at Holly Mount. You would not have to pay any more rent than where you are, and it would be twenty times pleasanter for you than living up that passage where you see nothing but a brick wall. And then, as it is not far from Paddiford, I think Mr Tryan might be persuaded to lodge with you, instead of in that musty house, among dead cabbages and smoky cottages. I know you would like to have him live with you, and you would be such a mother to him.'

'To be sure I should like it; it would be the finest thing in the world for me. But there'll be furniture wanted. My little bit of furniture won't fill that house.'

'O, I can put some in out of this house; it is too full; and we can buy the rest. They tell me I'm to have more money than I shall know what to do with.'

'I'm almost afraid,' said Mrs Pettifer, doubtfully, 'Mr Tryan will hardly be persuaded. He's been talked to so much about leaving that place; and he always said he must stay there – he must be among the people, and there was no other place for him in Paddiford. It cuts me to the heart to see him getting thinner and thinner, and I've noticed him quite short o' breath sometimes. Mrs Linnet will have it, Mrs Wagstaff half poisons him with bad cooking. I don't know about that, but he can't have many comforts. I expect he'll break down all of a sudden some day, and never be able to preach any more.'

'Well, I shall try my skill with him by-and-by. I shall be very cunning, and say nothing to him till all is ready. You and I and mother, when she comes home, will set to work directly and get the house in order, and then we'll get you snugly settled in it. I shall see Mr Pittman to-day, and I will tell him what I mean to do. I shall say I wish to have you for a tenant. Everybody knows I'm very fond of that naughty person, Mrs Pettifer; so it will seem the most natural thing in the world. And then I shall by-and-by point out to Mr Tryan that he will be doing you a service as well as himself by taking up his abode with you. I think I can prevail upon him; for last night, when he was quite bent on coming out into the night air, I persuaded him to give it up.'

'Well, I only hope you may, my dear. I don't desire anything better than to do something towards prolonging Mr Tryan's life, for I've sad fears about him.'

'Don't speak of them – I can't bear to think of them. We will only think about getting the house ready. We shall be as busy as bees. How we shall want mother's clever fingers! I know the room up-stairs that will just do for Mr Tryan's study. There shall be no seats in it except a very easy chair and a very easy sofa, so that he shall be obliged to rest himself when he comes home.'

CHAPTER 26

That was the last terrible crisis of temptation Janet had to pass through. The goodwill of her neighbours, the helpful sympathy of the friends who shared her religious feelings, the occupations suggested to her by Mr Tryan, concurred, with her strong spontaneous impulses towards works of love and mercy, to fill up her days with quiet social intercourse and charitable exertion. Besides, her constitution, naturally healthy and strong, was every week tending, with the gathering force of habit, to recover its equipoise and set her free from those physical solicitations which the smallest habitual vice always leaves behind it. The prisoner feels where the iron has galled him, long after his fetters have been loosed.

There were always neighbourly visits to be paid and received; and as the months wore on, increasing familiarity with Janet's present self began to efface, even from minds as rigid as Mrs Phipps's, the unpleasant impressions that had been left by recent years. Janet was recovering the popularity which her beauty and sweetness of nature had won for her when she was a girl; and popularity, as every one knows, is the most complex and self-multiplying of echoes. Even anti-Tryanite prejudice could not resist the fact that Janet Dempster was a changed woman – changed as the dusty, bruised, and sun-withered plant is changed when the soft rains of heaven have fallen on it – and that this change was due to Mr Tryan's influence. The last lingering sneers against the Evangelical curate began to the out; and though much of the feeling that had prompted them remained behind, there was an intimidating consciousness that the expression of such feeling would not be effective – jokes of that sort had ceased to tickle the Milby mind. Even Mr Budd and Mr Tomlinson, when they saw Mr Tryan passing pale and worn along the street, had a secret sense that this man was somehow not that very natural and comprehensible thing, a humbug; that, in fact, it was impossible to explain him from the stomach and pocket point of view. Twist and stretch their theory as they might, it would not fit Mr Tryan; and so, with that remarkable resemblance as to mental processes which may frequently be observed to exist between plain men and philosophers, they concluded that the less they said about him the better.

Among all Janet's neighbourly pleasures, there was nothing she liked better than to take an early tea at the White House, and to stroll with Mr Jerome round the old-fashioned garden and orchard. There was endless matter for talk between her and the good old man, for Janet had that genuine delight in human fellowship which gives an interest to all personal details that come warm from truthful lips; and, besides, they had a common interest in good-natured plans for helping their poorer neighbours. One great object of Mr Jerome's charities was, as he often said, 'to keep industrious men an' women off the parish. I'd rether give ten shillin' an' help a man to stan' on his own legs, nor pay half-a-crown to buy him a parish crutch; it's the ruination on him if he once goes to the parish. I've see'd many a time, if you help a man wi' a present in a neeborly way, it sweetens his blood – he thinks it kind on you; but the parish shillins turn it sour – he niver thinks 'em enough.' In illustration of this opinion Mr Jerome had a large store of details about such persons as Jim Hardy, the coal-carrier, 'as lost his hoss,' and Sally Butts, 'as hed to sell her mangle, though she was as decent a woman as need to be;' to the hearing of which details Janet seriously inclined, and you would hardly desire to see a prettier picture than the kind-faced white-haired old man telling these fragments of his simple experience as he walked, with shoulders slightly bent, among the moss-roses and espalier apple-trees, while Janet in her widow's cap, her dark eyes bright with interest, went listening by his side, and little Lizzie, with her nankin bonnet hanging down her back, toddled on before them. Mrs Jerome usually declined these

599

lingering strolls, and often observed, 'I niver see the like to Mr Jerome when he's got Mrs Dempster to talk to; it sinnifies nothin' to him whether we've tea at four or at five o'clock; he'd goo on till six, if you'd let him alone – he's like off his head.' However, Mrs Jerome herself could not deny that Janet was a very pretty-spoken woman: 'She al'ys says, she niver gets sich pikelets as mine nowhere; I know that very well – other folks buy 'em at shops – thick, unwholesome things, you mut as well ate a sponge.'

The sight of little Lizzie often stirred in Janet's mind a sense of the childlessness which had made a fatal blank in her life. She had fleeting thoughts that perhaps among her husband's distant relatives there might be some children whom she could help to bring up, some little girl whom she might adopt; and she promised herself one day or other to hunt out a second cousin of his – a married woman of whom he had lost sight for many years.

But at present her hands and heart were too full for her to carry out that scheme. To her great disappointment, her project of settling Mrs Pettifer at Holly Mount had been delayed by the discovery that some repairs were necessary in order to make the house habitable, and it was not till September had set in that she had the satisfaction of seeing her old friend comfortably installed, and the rooms destined for Mr Tryan looking pretty and cozy to her heart's content. She had taken several of his chief friends into her confidence, and they were warmly wishing success to her plan for inducing him to quit poor Mrs Wagstaff's dingy house and dubious cookery. That he should consent to some such change was becoming more and more a matter of anxiety to his hearers; for though no more decided symptoms were yet observable in him than increasing emaciation, a dry hacking cough, and an occasional shortness of breath, it was felt that the fulfilment of Mr Pratt's prediction could not long be deferred, and that this obstinate persistence in labour and self-disregard must soon be peremptorily cut short by a total failure of strength. Any hopes that the influence of Mr Tryan's father and sister would prevail on him to change his mode of life – that they would perhaps come to live with him, or that his sister at least might come to see him, and that the arguments which had failed from other lips might be more persuasive from hers – were now quite dissipated. His father had lately had an attack of paralysis, and could not spare his only daughter's tendance. On Mr Tryan's return from a visit to his father, Miss Linnet was very anxious to know whether his sister had not urged him to try change of air. From his answers she gathered that Miss Tryan wished him to give up his curacy and travel, or at least go to the south Devonshire coast.

'And why will you not do so?' Miss Linnet said; 'you might come back to us well and strong, and have many years of usefulness before you.'

'No,' he answered quietly, 'I think people attach more importance to such measures than is warranted. I don't see any good end that is to be served by going to die at Nice, instead of dying amongst one's friends and one's work. I cannot leave Milby – at least I will not leave it voluntarily.'

But though he remained immovable on this point, he had been compelled to give up his afternoon service on the Sunday, and to accept Mr Parry's offer of aid in the evening service, as well as to curtail his weekday labours; and he had even written to Mr Prendergast to request that he would appoint another curate to the Paddiford district, on the understanding that the new curate should receive the salary, but that Mr Tryan should co-operate with him as long as he was able. The hopefulness which is an almost constant attendant on consumption, had not the effect of deceiving him as to the nature of his malady, or of making him look forward to ultimate recovery. He believed himself to be consumptive, and he had not yet felt any desire to escape the early death which he had for some time contemplated as probable. Even diseased hopes will take their direction from the strong habitual bias of the mind, and to Mr Tryan death had for years seemed nothing else than the laying down of a burden, under which he sometimes felt himself fainting. He was only sanguine about his powers of work: he flattered himself that what he was unable to do one week he should be equal to the next, and he would not admit that in desisting from any part of his labour he was renouncing it permanently. He had lately delighted Mr Jerome by accepting his long-proffered loan of the 'little chacenut hoss;' and he found so much benefit from substituting constant riding exercise for walking, that he began to think he should soon be able to resume some of the work he had dropped.

That was a happy afternoon for Janet, when, after exerting herself busily for a week with her mother and Mrs Pettifer, she saw Holly Mount looking orderly and comfortable from attic to cellar. It was an old red-brick house, with two gables in front, and two clipped holly-trees flanking the garden gate; a simple, homely-looking place, that quiet people might easily get fond of; and now it was scoured and polished and carpeted and furnished so as to look really snug within. When there was nothing more to be done, Janet delighted herself with contemplating Mr Tryan's study, first sitting down in the easy-chair, and then lying for a moment on the sofa, that she might have a keener sense of the repose he would get from those well-stuffed articles of furniture, which she had gone to Rotherby on purpose to choose.

'Now, mother,' she said, when she had finished her survey, 'you have done your work as well as any fairy mother or god-mother that ever turned a pumpkin into a coach and horses. You stay and have tea cozily with Mrs Pettifer while I go to Mrs Linnet's. I want to tell Mary and Rebecca the good news, that I've got the exciseman to promise that he will take Mrs Wagstaff's lodgings when Mr Tryan leaves. They'll be so pleased to hear it, because they thought he would make her poverty an objection to his leaving her.'

'But, my dear child,' said Mrs Raynor, whose face, always calm, was now a happy one, 'have a cup of tea with us first. You'll perhaps miss Mrs Linnet's tea-time.'

'No, I feel too excited to take tea yet. I'm like a child with a new baby-house. Walking in the air will do me good.'

So she set out. Holly Mount was about a mile from that outskirt of Paddiford Common where Mrs Linnet's house stood nestled among its laburnums, lilacs, and syringas. Janet's way thither lay for a little while along the high-road, and then led her into a deep-rutted lane, which wound through a flat tract of meadow and pasture, while in front lay smoky Paddiford, and away to the left the mother-town of Milby. There was no line of silvery willows marking the course of a stream – no group of Scotch firs with their trunks reddening in the level sunbeams – nothing to break the flowerless monotony of grass and hedgerow but an occasional oak or elm, and a few cows sprinkled here and there. A very commonplace scene, indeed. But what scene was ever commonplace in the descending sunlight, when colour has awakened from its noonday sleep, and the long shadows awe us like a disclosed presence? Above all, what scene is commonplace to the eye that is filled with serene gladness, and brightens all things with its own joy?

And Janet just now was very happy. As she walked along the rough lane with a buoyant step, a half smile of innocent, kindly triumph played about her mouth. She was delighting beforehand in the anticipated success of her persuasive power, and for the time her painful anxiety about Mr Tryan's health was thrown into abeyance. But she had not gone far along the lane before she heard the sound of a horse advancing at a walking pace behind her. Without looking back, she turned aside to make way for it between the ruts, and did not notice that for a moment it had stopped and had then come on with a slightly quickened pace. In less than a minute she heard a well-known voice say, 'Mrs Dempster;' and, turning, saw Mr Tryan close to her, holding his horse by the bridle. It seemed very natural to her that he should be there. Her mind was so full of his presence at that moment, that the actual sight of him was only like a more vivid thought, and she behaved, as we are apt to do when feeling obliges us to be genuine, with a total forgetfulness of polite forms. She only looked at him with a slight deepening of the smile that was already on her face. He said gently, 'Take my arm;' and they walked on a little way in silence.

It was he who broke it. 'You are going to Paddiford, I suppose?'

The question recalled Janet to the consciousness that this was an unexpected opportunity for beginning her work of persuasion, and that she was stupidly neglecting it.

'Yes,' she said, 'I was going to Mrs Linnet's. I knew Miss Linnet would like to hear that our friend Mrs Pettifer is quite settled now in her new house. She is as fond of Mrs Pettifer as I am – almost; I won't admit that any one loves her *quite* as well, for no one else has such good reason as I have. But now the dear woman wants a lodger, for you know she can't afford to live in so large a house by herself. But I knew when I persuaded her to go there that she would be sure to get one – she's such a comfortable creature to live with; and I didn't like her to spend all the rest of her days up that dull passage, being at every one's beck and call who wanted to make use of her.'

'Yes,' said Mr Tryan, 'I quite understand your feeling; I don't wonder at your strong regard for her.'

'Well, but now I want her other friends to second me. There she is, with three rooms to let, ready furnished, everything in order; and I know some one, who thinks as well of her as I do, and who would be doing good all round – to every one that knows him, as well as to Mrs Pettifer, if he would go to live with her. He would leave some uncomfortable lodgings which another person is already coveting and would take immediately; and he would go to breathe pure air at Holly Mount, and gladden Mrs Pettifer's heart by letting her wait on him; and comfort all his friends, who are quite miserable about him.'

Mr Tryan saw it all in a moment – he saw that it had all been done for his sake. He could not be sorry; he could not say no; he could not resist the sense that life had a new sweetness for him, and that he should like it to be prolonged a little – only a little, for the sake of feeling a stronger security about Janet. When she had finished speaking, she looked at him with a doubtful, inquiring glance. He was not looking at her; his eyes were cast downwards; but the expression of his face encouraged her, and she said, in a half-playful tone of entreaty,—

'You *will* go and live with her? I know you will. You will come back with me now and see the house.'

He looked at her then, and smiled. There is an unspeakable blending of sadness and sweetness in the smile of a face sharpened and paled by slow consumption. That smile of Mr Tryan's pierced poor Janet's heart: she felt in it at once the assurance of grateful affection and the prophecy of coming death. Her tears rose; they turned round without speaking, and went back again along the lane.

607

CHAPTER 27

In less than a week Mr Tryan was settled at Holly Mount, and there was not one of his many attached hearers who did not sincerely rejoice at the event.

The autumn that year was bright and warm, and at the beginning of October Mr Walsh, the new curate, came. The mild weather, the relaxation from excessive work, and perhaps another benignant influence, had for a few weeks a visibly favourable effect on Mr Tryan. At least he began to feel new hopes, which sometimes took the guise of new strength. He thought of the cases in which consumptive patients remain nearly stationary for years, without suffering so as to make their life burdensome to themselves or to others; and he began to struggle with a longing that it might be so with him. He struggled with it, because he felt it to be an indication that earthly affection was beginning to have too strong a hold on him, and he prayed earnestly for more perfect submission, and for a more absorbing delight in the Divine Presence as the chief good. He was conscious that he did not wish for prolonged life solely that he might do God's work in reclaiming the wanderers and sustaining the feeble: he was conscious of a new yearning for those pure human joys which he had voluntarily and determinedly banished from his life – for a draught of that deep affection from which he had been cut off by a dark chasm of remorse. For now, that affection was within his reach; he saw it there, like a palm-shadowed well in the desert; he *could* not desire to die in sight of it.

And so the autumn rolled gently by in its 'calm decay.' Until November, Mr Tryan continued to preach occasionally, to ride about visiting his flock, and to look in at his schools; but his growing satisfaction in Mr Walsh as his successor saved him from too eager exertion and from worrying anxieties. Janet was with him a great deal now, for she saw that he liked her to read to him in the lengthening evenings, and it became the rule for her and her mother to have tea at Holly Mount, where, with Mrs Pettifer and sometimes another friend or two, they brought Mr Tryan the unaccustomed enjoyment of companionship by his own fireside.

Janet did not share his new hopes, for she was not only in the habit of hearing Mr Pratt's opinion that Mr Tryan could hardly stand out through the winter, but she also knew that it was shared by Dr Madely of Rotherby, whom, at her request, he had consented to call in. It was not necessary or desirable to tell Mr Tryan what was revealed by the stethoscope, but Janet knew the worst.

She felt no rebellion under this prospect of bereavement, but rather a quiet submissive sorrow. Gratitude that his influence and guidance had been given her, even if only for a little while – gratitude that she was permitted to be with him, to take a deeper and deeper impress from daily communion with him, to be something to him in these last months of his life, was so strong in her that it almost silenced regret. Janet had lived through the great tragedy of woman's life. Her keenest personal emotions had been poured forth in her early love – her wounded affection with its years of anguish – her agony of unavailing pity over that death-bed seven months ago. The thought of Mr Tryan was associated for her with repose from that conflict of emotion, with trust in the unchangeable, with the influx of a power to subdue self. To have been assured of his sympathy, his teaching, his help, all through her life, would have been to her like a heaven already begun – a deliverance from fear and danger; but the time was not yet come for her to be conscious that the hold he had on her heart was any other than that of the heaven-sent friend who had come to her like the angel in the prison, and loosed her bonds, and led her by the hand till she could look back on the dreadful doors that had once closed her in.

Before November was over Mr Tryan had ceased to go out. A new crisis had come on: the

610

cough had changed its character, and the worst symptoms developed themselves so rapidly that Mr Pratt began to think the end would arrive sooner than he had expected. Janet became a constant attendant on him now, and no one could feel that she was performing anything but a sacred office. She made Holly Mount her home, and, with her mother and Mrs Pettifer to help her, she filled the painful days and nights with every soothing influence that care and tenderness could devise. There were many visitors to the sick-room, led thither by venerating affection; and there could hardly be one who did not retain in after years a vivid remembrance of the scene there – of the pale wasted form in the easy-chair (for he sat up to the last), of the grey eyes so full even yet of inquiring kindness, as the thin, almost transparent hand was held out to give the pressure of welcome; and of the sweet woman, too, whose dark watchful eyes detected every want, and who supplied the want with a ready hand.

There were others who would have had the heart and the skill to fill this place by Mr Tryan's side, and who would have accepted it as an honour; but they could not help feeling that God had given it to Janet by a train of events which were too impressive not to shame all jealousies into silence.

That sad history, which most of us know too well, lasted more than three months. He was too feeble and suffering for the last few weeks to see any visitors, but he still sat up through the day.

The strange hallucinations of the disease which had seemed to take a more decided hold on him just at the fatal crisis, and had made him think he was perhaps getting better at the very time when death had begun to hurry on with more rapid movement, had now given way, and left him calmly conscious of the reality. One afternoon, near the end of February, Janet was moving gently about the room, in the fire-lit dusk, arranging some things that would be wanted in the night. There was no one else in the room, and his eyes followed her as she moved with the firm grace natural to her, while the bright fire every now and then lit up her face, and gave an unusual glow to its dark beauty. Even to follow her in this way with his eyes was an exertion that gave a painful tension to his face; while *she* looked like an image of life and strength.

'Janet,' he said presently, in his faint voice – he always called her Janet now. In a moment she was close to him, bending over him. He opened his hand as he looked up at her, and she placed hers within it.

'Janet,' he said again, 'you will have a long while to live after I am gone.'

A sudden pang of fear shot through her. She thought he felt himself dying, and she sank on her knees at his feet, holding his hand, while she looked up at him, almost breathless.

'But you will not feel the need of me as you have done . . . You have a sure trust in God . . . I shall not look for you in vain at the last.'

'No . . . no . . . I shall be there . . . God will not forsake me.'

She could hardly utter the words, though she was not weeping. She was waiting with trembling eagerness for anything else he might have to say.

'Let us kiss each other before we part.'

She lifted up her face to his, and the full life-breathing lips met the wasted dying ones in a sacred kiss of promise.

CHAPTER 28

It soon came – the blessed day of deliverance, the sad day of bereavement; and in the second week of March they carried him to the grave. He was buried as he had desired: there was no hearse, no mourning-coach; his coffin was borne by twelve of his humbler hearers, who relieved each other by turns. But he was followed by a long procession of mourning friends, women as well as men.

Slowly, amid deep silence, the dark stream passed along Orchard Street, where eighteen months before the Evangelical curate had been saluted with hooting and hisses. Mr Jerome and Mr Landor were the eldest pall-bearers; and behind the coffin, led by Mr Tryan's cousin, walked Janet, in quiet submissive sorrow. She could not feel that he was quite gone from her; the unseen world lay so very near her – it held all that had ever stirred the depths of anguish and joy within her.

It was a cloudy morning, and had been raining when they left Holly Mount; but as they walked, the sun broke out, and the clouds were rolling off in large masses when they entered the churchyard, and Mr Walsh's voice was heard saying, 'I am the Resurrection and the Life.' The faces were not hard at this funeral; the burial-service was not a hollow form. Every heart there was filled with the memory of a man who, through a self-sacrificing life, and in a painful death, had been sustained by the faith which fills that form with breath and substance.

When Janet left the grave, she did not return to Holly Mount; she went to her home in Orchard Street, where her mother was waiting to receive her. She said quite calmly, 'Let us walk round the garden, mother.' And they walked round in silence, with their hands clasped together, looking at the golden crocuses bright in the spring sunshine. Janet felt a deep stillness within. She thirsted for no pleasure; she craved no worldly good. She saw the years to come stretch before her like an autumn afternoon, filled with resigned memory. Life to her could never more have any eagerness; it was a solemn service of gratitude and patient effort. She walked in the presence of unseen witnesses – of the Divine love that had rescued her, of the human love that waited for its eternal repose until it had seen her endure to the end.

Janet is living still. Her black hair is grey, and her step is no longer buoyant; but the sweetness of her smile remains, the love is not gone from her eyes; and strangers sometimes ask, Who is that noble-looking elderly woman, that walks about holding a little boy by the hand? The little boy is the son of Janet's adopted daughter, and Janet in her old age has children about her knees, and loving young arms round her neck.

There is a simple gravestone in Milby church-yard, telling that in this spot lie the remains of Edgar Tryan, for two years officiating curate at the Paddiford Chapel-of-Ease, in this parish. It is a meagre memorial, and tells you simply that the man who lies there took upon him, faithfully or unfaithfully, the office of guide and instructor to his fellow-men.

But there is another memorial of Edgar Tryan, which bears a fuller record: it is Janet Dempster, rescued from self-despair, strengthened with divine hopes, and now looking back on years of purity and helpful labour. The man who has left such a memorial behind him, must have been one whose heart beat with true compassion, and whose lips were moved by fervent faith.